PRAISE FOR UNRAVELLED

"M. K. Tod's skilful debut novel spanning two world wars deftly illuminates the subtle stirrings of the human heart as movingly as it depicts the horrors of battle. Poignant and generous, Unravelled gives us Edward, scarred by war, and Ann, alive with longing, two people bound by the heartbreaking bonds of a marriage forged in the crucible of secrets and war."
- Barbara Kyle, author of *Blood Between Queens.*

"A compulsive and convincing read: a story of webs that were innocently woven - and lives that subsequently become unravelled."
- Helen Hollick, author of historical fiction and historical adventure.

"An engrossing historical saga. With narrative insight, compassion, and a strong sense of time and place, M.K. Tod observes the inner workings of a marriage as it's affected by the uncertainty and tumult of both world wars."
- Sarah Johnson, Historical Novel Society Book Review Editor.

"Wartime relationships have always been compelling reading, and M.K. Tod's Unravelled beautifully evokes an era of heightened tension, in which her characters' decisions become all the more heart-rending. A well researched and very enjoyable book."
- Anne Easter Smith, author of *A Rose for the Crown, Queen By Right* and *Royal Mistress*

"A beautiful rendering of the healing journey of two war torn hearts."
- Elisabeth Storrs, author of *The Golden Dice* and *The Wedding Shroud*

UNRAVELLED

A NOVEL

M. K. TOD

Tod Publishing
TORONTO, CANADA

Tod Publishing may be contacted at Todpublishing@gmail.com

The author M. K. Tod may be contacted at mktod@bell.net. For more information visit www.awriterofhistory.com

Author's Note: This is a work of fiction. Names, characters, places, and incidents are a product of the author's imagination. Locales and public names are sometimes used for atmospheric purposes. Any resemblance to actual people, living or dead, or to businesses, companies, events, institutions, or locales is completely coincidental.

Permission granted by the Canadian Broadcasting Corporation to quote from the radio broadcast by Robert Bowman: *1942: Carnage on the beaches of Dieppe.*

Cover design by Jenny Toney Quinlan, Historical Editorial
Interior Design based on a template from BookDesignTemplates.com

Unravelled / M. K. Tod. -- 1st ed.
ISBN 978-0-9919670-1-8

For my mother, Edythe, who shared so many of her stories.

And in memory of my grandparents, Leslie and Marjorie James,
whose lives inspired Unravelled.

1 OCTOBER 1935

Edward Jamieson tapped the thick, cream-colored envelope against his left palm. He turned away from his wife and glanced out the window where scattered leaves caught fading threads of light. When the letter arrived that afternoon, a hint of disquiet had spread through his body. The opening words— *To Those Who Served*—had punched hard. Phrases had leapt from the page like sudden bursts of gunfire: *Glorious dead . . . great monument . . . lie beneath French soil . . . Vimy Ridge.*

"Do you want to go?" Ann said, eyebrows raised in a way he had come to know as concern edged with caution.

"It'll stir up something I've tried to forget. Not sure if that's a good thing."

"Maybe seeing some old friends would help." She touched his cheek.

Old friends, he thought. *They're all dead. Except for Eric.*

Instead of replying, he opened the envelope and passed her a sheet of paper embossed with a government seal. He watched her scan the page with a small smile, then furrowed brow, and finally, lips pursed thin and tight.

"Sixty thousand Canadian dead. Was it really that many?"

He nodded and shuddered at the thought.

"'This monument on Vimy Ridge will proclaim to the world of the future that you and your countrymen fought gloriously when the need arose. We ask that you consider attending the dedication to be recognized for your valiant service and to honour your fellow soldiers.' That's what the prime minister wrote." He felt the warmth of her hand on his. "You should go. We should both go."

"Well . . . anyway, I'm not sure we can afford it. And what would we do with Emily and Alex?"

"We have until July to sort that out. My parents would be happy to look after them. Mother said just the other day that she misses having them stay overnight, now that we're back in the city. And we have some money set aside   you know we do."

Ann was only being logical, an approach Edward normally took. He loosened his tie and shrugged off his suit jacket, draping it on the back of a kitchen chair.

"I'll think about it."

He formed a small smile to take the sting out of his dismissal. Ann did not deserve his anger and he knew he should explain himself. He would do so, only not now when he could barely control his thoughts. How could anyone use the word "glorious" in reference to war? As far as he was concerned, nothing about his experience deserved to be remembered, let alone celebrated.

After dinner and a lengthy telephone call with his father, Edward sat in the living room with only the ticking hallway clock and clunking of cooling radiators to keep him company. A chunk of wood fell through the grate. Shards of blue quivered amidst the orange glow of embers.

Ann had gone upstairs over an hour earlier and he wondered whether to stoke the fire or follow her to bed. He knew he would not sleep. Memories would claw, grab, suck and twist, swallowing him once more into that world of death.

* * *

A burst of light in the distance. Edward checked his watch. At five fifteen, a still-hidden sun smudged the black of night and after hours of random machine-gun fire, the Germans were quiet. Through stinging sleet, shapes in no man's land were barely visible. A cart, lopsided in the mud, the carcass of a horse, a lightweight howitzer damaged beyond repair, remnants of a large wooden barrel. The massive ridge loomed four hundred yards away.

Five twenty-five. Edward scanned his unit.

"Tell Robertson to keep alert," he whispered to the soldier on his left.

The reminder was unnecessary but he could not restrain himself. Time ticked away as hordes of men held their collective breath.

At five thirty, the ripple of light was strangely beautiful, spreading like an endless wave in that instant of calm before the fury of one thousand guns erupted. Though Lieutenant Burke had described the battle plan in detail, no words could have prepared them for such brutal vibration. Shockwaves compressed Edward's chest, his ears distinguished nothing but pain, his legs braced to remain upright while he fought for breath. Death crooked its finger.

In the distance, flames erupted over German trenches followed by a continuous line of red, white and green SOS signals. Edward's platoon sprang into action as messages poured in.

Night receded inch by inch, revealing the field of battle. German artillery stuttered, then replied with more conviction, deadly shells flashing against the clouds. Reaching for his earphones, Edward saw a red light mushroom beyond enemy lines, followed by a boom that scattered bits of clay across his makeshift table.

"Christ, that felt close," Eric Andrews said.

"Ammunition dump?"

"Probably. But theirs, not ours."

Edward grunted at the friend who had been with him since the beginning, then cocked his head as another message came through. He hunched forward, a gas mask around his neck, rifle propped against a wall of sandbags. His job was to keep information flowing, whatever the cost.

By six a.m., sleet had turned to drizzle while thirty thousand infantry advanced in three waves of attack.

"Snowy," Edward used Eric's nickname, "get a runner for this message."

"Binny is ready. Just back from the sap."

"He'll do." Edward tore the message from his pad as the telephone rang. "Wait a minute till I see what this is." He scribbled a few words. "Yes. Yes. Got it." He held out the second message. "Tell Binny to take this one too."

Another member of Edward's team staggered in covered in mud. "It's hell out there but we're advancing on schedule."

Edward twisted around to look at his linesman. "What about casualties?"

"Hard to say. Germans are getting the worst of it. Their shelling is weak compared to ours."

"That's good news, Arty. I need you to head back out. The line from here to Duffield crater is down. Take Simmons and Tiger with you and get it repaired." The telephone rang again. Edward turned back to his work without waiting for a reply.

Hours passed like minutes. Duties swept Edward and his men from forward trenches to command posts stationed up to five miles behind the lines. Twice he was blown off his feet by the concussion of exploding shells. His mind quivered with the unceasing flash and rumble of guns. Falling shrapnel screamed overhead.

As they worked to install new lines and roll out signal cable behind advancing troops, shells roared liked angry beasts and confused men stumbled to find their way. Silent prisoners filed by. Edward heard bagpipes and sudden shouts and the anguished moans of wounded men. All the while, British planes buzzed overhead, swooping low to assess the damage.

In the comfort of his Toronto home, the chaotic intensity of battle was with him again. At the time he had felt nothing, thinking only of his next task, his mind focused like a microscope on the minute details of execution. He had known that if he survived, there would be more than enough time for reflection.

Staring into the neglected fire now giving off mere dribbles of heat, he questioned what they had achieved. Taking the ridge had been followed by failure to exploit success. All those lives, he thought, all that sorrow which my country will commemorate next July.

Edward wondered if he could bear the pain of being there again.

2 NOVEMBER 1935

Edward glanced up as Ann came down the stairs, blue dress cinched at the waist. At thirty-three, her slim figure, full breasts and wide, almost sensuous lips seemed even more attractive than when they had first met. He supposed that motherhood had something to do with the change, rounding the sharp bones of her hips and adding a certain softness to her face, and perhaps time had done the rest, like an artist daubing extra brush strokes on a work only he sees as incomplete. Thinking of the feel of her ripened body against his, he smiled.

"We need to talk," she said.

His smile slipped away. Ann's grey eyes seemed deliberately cool and he wondered what direction their conversation would take. He knew what the topic would be.

"Of course," he said, and then waited for her opening thrust.

The first week after he brought the invitation home, she had mentioned the trip several times but he had deflected or ignored each comment. Lately, when she seemed on the verge of speaking, she would purse her lips instead or take a deep breath and look away. Once he had seen her put the invitation back into its envelope and slip it beneath the pile of accumulated mail. Preferring to avoid questions where he had no clear answer, he had not pursued the matter. Eventually, a decision would emerge.

Each day, when neither business nor family held his attention, he considered what travelling to France would entail. Some days he thought he might be able to manage, other days he worried about being overwhelmed. Not once did he think the trip would be enjoyable. Perhaps it was time to tell Ann about the war, or at least a sanitized version of events.

She sat on the sofa and crossed her arms. "You've been avoiding my questions about going to France. You need to share with me what you've been thinking."

"You're right, I do."

Ann's eyes warmed. "Ever since that invitation came, you've been distant and tight-lipped. You haven't asked my opinion. You've just closed yourself off like you usually do. I can imagine how difficult this is, but if I knew more, perhaps I could help."

Edward had the impression that his wife had rehearsed what to say, since she rushed to complete the last sentence before dropping her eyes. Closing down was indeed his usual course of action, one that had caused friction in the past. Each time she confronted him, he promised to do better, but the habit of bottling his feelings was a hard one to break. Ann's frustration was justified.

"You want to know about what happened." She nodded. "It's not pretty." She nodded again. He set aside the newspaper then rubbed a hand across his face, feeling the scrape of that day's stubble.

"A sniper's bullet nearly killed me at Vimy Ridge." Ann's sharply drawn breath sounded like a muted whistle. "We prepared for months," he continued, his voice devoid of emotion.

"My battalion arrived in December and right away we began building a communication system that could support a line of attack more than five, maybe six, miles in length. Eric and I and the others in our group worked in underground tunnels much of the time, installing telephone lines and other devices so that we had a fail-safe network. At times we went out into no man's land to place special equipment designed to intercept German signals. I lost more than one friend doing that nasty work. In three months, we signallers laid more than twenty-one miles of cable and sixty-six miles of telephone wire.

"By late March we were almost ready. Every day we rehearsed the plan. I knew what to do if my sergeant fell, and even if our lieutenant fell. I was in charge of a platoon and we were told to keep messages flowing regardless of cost." A laugh scraped from his throat. "'Regardless of cost' meant that it didn't matter how many of us died. Did you know they dug graves before battle began? I have no idea how many bodies they planned for, but the area set aside was enormous, and every time I walked past it I wondered whether I would be buried there."

Edward noticed a flicker of horror on his wife's face. Her arms were no longer crossed; instead she leaned forward slightly and kept her eyes on his.

"For three weeks prior to zero hour, our guns hammered German positions. Afterwards, we heard that twenty-five hundred tons of shells were used each day. Tons, not pounds, Ann. The sounds and vibrations were staggering, and still we worked and rehearsed day after day, again and again.

"You can't imagine the opening barrage of a battle on that scale. We'd been waiting underground for hours. I kept looking at my watch. My stomach was in such knots that I threw up, and I wasn't the only one who did. Fear also makes you sweat. Imagine thousands of men waiting, crammed together so tight you could barely move.

"Like other assaults, once we began, I felt strangely calm. All morning and most of the afternoon, I was too busy to think about anything except my men and our duties. Vimy wasn't the only battle we endured. I was at Cambrai and Ypres—I'm sure you've heard about the bloodbaths at Ypres. Valenciennes, the Somme. For me they aren't cities, they're places of slaughter.

"And you can't believe how we lived. The filth and smells were so terrible, we were rarely clean. I wore the same socks for weeks. Lice? Everyone suffered from lice. At times I scratched my scalp so hard it bled. And there were rats. Disgusting beasts with their beady little eyes staring at me. The food was terrible and rarely hot.

"I lived through gas attacks. Even breathed in some gas once or twice, but not enough to kill me. Watching someone die in a gas attack is the most horrible experience and there's nothing you can do to help. I killed people, Ann, even though my job was in signals. I killed people." Edward looked and sounded bewildered. He closed his eyes and shook his head back and forth, back and forth. "Sometimes I was close enough to see their faces. A man who's been shot often looks surprised for a moment. The whole thing was horrible. Gruesomely horrible. So you see, that's why it's so difficult for me to decide whether to go."

Edward closed his eyes. He was exhausted. He doubted whether he could even stand. He had not intended to disclose so much, but once he had started, he felt compelled to go on. Ann had been silent the entire time. She had barely moved, her expression slipping from concern to dismay and shock.

"Oh, Edward. What you lived through sounds so horrible. I don't know what to say. No wonder you never spoke about it. The thought that you might have died . . ."

"I don't think I can tell you about that."

"Of course, dear. Only if you feel like telling me. To think I might never have known you."

A tear trailed down one cheek. Ann got up and came to sit on the arm of Edward's chair. She took his hand and held it to her lips. The gentleness of her kiss eased his pain a fraction.

"I didn't mean to be so remote," he said.

"Hush. You did nothing wrong. I should have been more patient."

"If you think we should go . . ."

"Darling, it's your decision, not mine. I love you. Whatever you want to do is fine with me."

"That bloody invitation. Ever since it arrived, I've been remembering things I thought were long buried," he said. "So many things." Edward shook his head slowly from side to side. "So many things."

3 NOVEMBER 1935

For several nights, Edward went to bed exhausted. Though he kissed Ann, he made no effort to draw her close, and he sensed that she understood his desire for distance. Lying on his side, he watched shadows on the wall and wondered at the role fate played in life. A fraction to the left and the sniper's bullet would have pierced his head. A fraction to the right and it could have missed him entirely, in which case he might have delivered the message and died at some other point that day. Or lived.

On Saturday, when he climbed into bed, Ann reached for his hand and pulled it close.

"Will you be all right?" she said.

"Yes. I'm just tired."

"I went to the library. I've been reading about the war and about Vimy Ridge. The stories are so awful, it's no wonder you had nightmares. How did you manage another year and a half after that?"

"Eric and I had a pact. Every day we could, we raised a cup and toasted our survival. He would say 'another day won against the devil'."

"And what did you say?"

"Oh, you don't want to hear what I said."

"Yes, I do. Tell me."

"I said 'Fuck the Germans'. It always made him laugh."

Ann chuckled. "You never swear."

"I used a lot of foul language then. A way to cope, I suppose."

She shifted closer, the rise and fall of her chest nudging against him. "Was I part of your recovery?"

Edward kissed the curve between her neck and shoulder. "You were. You still are."

He traced a fingertip along the line of her cheek and touched her lips, the top and then the bottom. The silk of her nightgown grazed his arm. As he leaned forward to kiss her, he caught the scent of perfume, dusky and sweet. Ann's lips parted and he probed with his tongue at the same time cupping her breasts, first one and then the other. Her nipples hardened. She opened the front of her gown and pulled his mouth down. He sucked on each nipple, flicking his tongue back and forth.

"I love you," he whispered.

Making love had been a source of great pleasure ever since they married. Even the first time, Ann had responded to his touch, welcoming his body despite moments of discomfort. Gradually, he had learned the positions and caresses that would bring her to orgasm, and from time to time, they had even considered themselves daring as they explored different ways to satisfy each other. But eventually, a certain routine had settled in.

Afterwards, holding her so that her head rested beneath his chin, he ran one hand along her figure, enjoying the feel of soft skin. As someone who did not readily express emotion, the tenderness of lovemaking was a way to show Ann how he felt.

He hoped she would know that his sighs signalled contentment and his open eyes commitment to her alone. Ann kissed the tight curl of hairs at the top of his chest.

"Do you want to go?"

He knew she referred to the invitation. "I'm not sure want is the right word. Perhaps I need to go. Will you come with me?"

"Of course."

Once plans were in motion, Edward questioned his decision each time another letter or document arrived, and there were many: train reservations, ship bookings, hotel details, battle-field tours, insurance forms, passport applications. When he received a letter advertising memorial wreaths, he thought of all the men he knew who had died, and a few he knew he had killed, and wondered how many wreaths would be necessary to ease that burden.

4 FEBRUARY 1936

The sharp odours of boiled brisket and cabbage lingered after Sunday lunch. Edward stuffed tobacco into his pipe while hot water gushed into the kitchen sink, clinking glasses against silverware.

"I'm worried about my father," he said, tucking the pipe into his jacket pocket.

Ann slipped on rubber gloves to do the washing up. "I didn't think he looked very well the last time we saw him. Rather gaunt in the face."

At that moment, Alex, their eight-year-old son, entered the kitchen. He held a sheet of paper in one hand waving it in the air.

"Mommy, when are you going to help me?" Alex said as he slumped into a kitchen chair.

"Alex, please stop whining. Daddy doesn't want to listen to that noise. We'll work on your project after I finish the dishes. I won't be long." Ann looked at Edward and rolled her eyes.

"Sorry, dear. What does your mother say?"

"Mother was hinting that he's been to the doctor, and you know how my father hates doing that. He thinks it's a sign of weakness. Bloody English fortitude, if you ask me."

"You go, dear. He loves to see you. You've always been his favourite."

"I really think I should. I won't be too long." He kissed her cheek.

"Give them my love," she said as he left the kitchen. "And drive carefully," she called after him.

Drifting snow clogged the streets, snarling traffic as drivers avoided stalled cars or slithered around corners. More than an hour passed before he parked on a street full of narrow, three-storey houses with wooden porches amply sized for rocking chairs on long summer nights. As he approached his parents' house, Edward recalled the day he had introduced Ann to his family, the way she had memorized the names of his eight brothers and sisters in advance, her attentiveness to his mother and father and the laughter that had ensued during dinner.

Later that evening, Edward had followed his father to the back porch where both men lit their pipes, a ritual that had begun after Edward returned from the war. It had been a starry night, faint wisps of cloud drifting like pale silk across the sky.

"Lovely girl," Ernest Jamieson said.

"I think so."

"What's her family like?"

"Two brothers and a sister. Mr. Winston works in a bank. The Commerce, I think. A bit more formal that we are. I've only been there twice."

His father puffed on his pipe in silence, blowing thin threads of smoke out of the corner of his mouth. Edward waited.

"What do you like about her?"

"She's warm and intelligent. Likes to laugh. Occasionally she seems impulsive. She's been working for three years for an insurance company."

"Does she want to settle down?"

"We haven't talked about that yet."

"Well, you should, before someone else catches her eye."

"I want a bit more money set aside before I make any commitments."

His father chuckled. "You've always been our cautious one, haven't you?"

Ernest Jamieson had set his hand on Edward's shoulder and the two men had retreated into comfortable silence. Their evening smoke often prompted brief exchanges of a serious nature. At times they touched on politics, at times his father expressed concern about one or other of his children, occasionally they deliberated on financial matters. That evening, his father's intuition had been correct. Edward had almost waited too long to ask Ann to marry him. As he knocked the snow off his boots and opened the door, Edward smiled at the memory.

His parents were in the parlour, his mother on a faded sofa adorned with hand-tatted doilies and his father on a tall leather chair next to a circular table covered with family photos. The chair with its carved wooden legs and arms had been in the Jamieson family for several generations and was one of the only pieces of furniture his parents had brought with them when they emigrated from England. Beyond the parlour, the long oak table was already set for dinner. Only his two youngest brothers, Duncan and Jimmy, still lived at home, but the table was set for eight.

"Who's coming for dinner?" he asked after greeting his father with a firm handshake and his mother with a kiss.

"Stan and his family. Are you able to stay?"

His mother always made more than enough food in case someone stopped by. Having cooked for ten people much of her married life, she was accustomed to large quantities. Edward inhaled. Apple pie and cinnamon.

"Smells delicious, but not this time, Mother. Ann is expecting me home. I left her doing a school project with Alex. She'll need my company after that. You know what he's like when it comes to homework. How are you, Dad? You looked tired the other day."

"Nothing to worry about, son. Just a little peaked. Your mother is after me to see the doctor again. But I'm fine. Just fine."

"You would never admit otherwise, would you?" Edward said.

His father's smile was followed by a frown. "Did you see that article about Baron von Neurath having diplomatic meetings in London? I can't believe what those Germans are up to or why Sir Anthony Eden is so willing to negotiate."

While his mother's fingers worked a piece of embroidery, Edward and his father talked at length about Germany, England's conciliatory posture and American indifference.

"Neville Chamberlain will never stand up to Germany."

"I agree, Father. It worries me."

"Maybe the Russians have enough backbone."

"Didn't help in the last war, did it? They made peace with the bloody Hun right after their revolution. Who's to say we can depend on them this time?"

For a moment or two, the only sounds were the clicking of knitting needles and a crackling sound from the kitchen.

"Mother, do you still have those boxes I stored away after the war?"

"Boxes?" Her fingers continued to work a skein of thick wool. Edward had the same long, slim fingers as his mother. Indeed, everything about him was long and slim. "What boxes, dear?"

"There were four or five of them. I put all my old gear and uniforms in them."

"Oh, yes. I think so. Look in the crawl space. Why do you want them after so long? Everything is probably mouldy by now."

Edward cleared his throat. "I suppose it's the trip to France that made me think of them. I want to see what I packed away. Could be a surprise or two in there."

* * *

On Monday he took a small, metal tin to the office and locked it in his credenza. For three days he ignored it, attending to the many demands of his management role at the telephone company. He was considered senior management now, having advanced steadily from installing telephone equipment to section head and then first line manager. Shortly after marrying Ann, the company moved him to Montreal where his role was to bring installation expertise to the design of new telephone equipment. Further promotions followed and now he was responsible for the entire complex of switching systems that kept telephones operating across the city. Hundreds of people worked for him.

On Thursday, with no meetings to keep him occupied, he pulled the tin from his credenza and lifted the lid. A musty odour filled his nostrils. Edward hesitated. At the sharp ring of a telephone, he dropped the lid with a jarring clatter.

He rose and stood by the window. On the street below, a woman in a heavy coat and thick, woven scarf pulled the handle of a wooden sled on which a child sat, bundled in a blue snowsuit. Edward watched as the woman dragged the sled up and over a snow bank and prepared to cross the road. He remembered using such a sled to shop for groceries during cold Montreal winters. When the children were very small, they sat together, Alex resting against Emily's sturdy, little body while Ann walked alongside or held Edward's arm.

"Damn," he muttered.

Edward crossed the room and thrust his head into the corridor.

"No interruptions, Miss Nicholls."

Without waiting for a reply, he shut the door, returned to his desk, and stared at his past. Thirty-nine envelopes, their tattered, brown edges and French stamps faded with age. He extracted one at random and for the first time in seventeen years, saw his name, rank and military address in round, even script. Edward unfolded a brittle sheet of paper.

November 4, 1917
Dearest Edward,
It is Sunday and as you can imagine, Maman, Jean and I have been to church suffering through another of Father Marcel's sermons. Today he spoke of charity and my thoughts soon drifted to you. I'm sure I was blushing, however, Maman did not seem to notice.
Germaine was in church today for the first time since the funeral. She was dressed in black, of course, and I spoke with her after the service. You will be happy to know that I was able to make her smile. She asked me to send you her good wishes and reminds you to be careful. Having lost her dear Jacques, she says she will pray every day for your safety.
Papa is still in Bordeaux, although his last letter suggests that he will soon return to Paris. We had a letter from Guy and know that he is safe. As usual we have no idea where he is located, but Maman is always happy when she hears from him.
With the cold weather, my chores are more difficult, but nothing compared with what you must endure. How many more months of war will there be? I worry about you so much. Now I know how Maman has felt about Guy, although a lover is different from a son, n'est-ce pas?
When will I see you again? You are in my thoughts every moment.
With all my love, Helene

Banished memories spilled like a spring torrent, tumbling, gushing, pulling, swirling. The night they met in Monsieur Garnier's barn, and the shepherd's hut, their private place of refuge high on a hill. He heard her voice, the way she laughed. He felt the weight of her hair, its smooth, silky texture brushing against him in intimate moments, the length of her eyelashes, the way her lips parted when they made love. He felt her soft breath as she lay next to him, and recalled her gentle half smile. She had promised never to spoil their time together with tears, but he knew that smile—lips together, the corners of her mouth turned up—betrayed sadness and fear just below the surface.

Edward pressed a fist to his mouth and closed his eyes. When he opened them, he reached for another envelope and this time began at the beginning. With each letter memory sharpened and emotion stirred. At times he paced back and forth, at other times he read and reread the same passage over and over. At times he stared at nothing, his inner eye working furiously to recall a moment, a look, a conversation. He never discovered where she went or why she had not waited for him.

* * *

The war had ended in November. After another two months in occupied Germany, Edward's unit had returned to Belgium to await notice of demobilization. Edward knew that if he did not look for Helene now, there might never be another chance. He had discovered that a supply convoy was heading to Arras: he would hitch a ride from there or walk if he had to.

"How will you find her?" Eric asked as Edward stuffed his rucksack full of clothes. "You've written every week for ten months. She hasn't answered even one of them."

"Shut up, Snowy. Don't you think I know that?" He jerked the straps of his rucksack tight and buckled them with the speed of everyday practice. "I'm going to Beaufort. Burke has given me one week. I'm going to ask everyone I find if they know where she is. That's my plan."

"Good luck, Fuzz." Eric squeezed Edward's shoulder. "I'll see you when you get back."

The truck jumped and jittered along rutted tracks as it made its way to a main road heading south. Edward sat in the cargo area amongst empty crates smelling of rotten onions. Every hour he lifted the canvas flap to stare at fields and farms destroyed by war. A barren wasteland. He could still taste the bite of tea brewed in gritty pots and smell decaying bodies mixed with the cordite that lingered long after incoming explosions. Light was fading fast and his feet felt like frozen blocks of ice.

He wondered what he would find. Would Tante Camille's house be abandoned, the shutters closed and furniture draped in protective cloth, enticing aromas of coffee and country food replaced by must and mildew? Because the house was close to the front, he knew it was possible Helene had been caught in some sort of skirmish and forced to flee. He refused to imagine her being wounded in any way, but what if she no longer loved him? Why else had she failed to write?

Around midnight, he noticed a sign to Souchez and banged hard on the panel separating him from the front cabin. *Better to get out here*, he thought, *than travel all the way to Arras and then back track.*

The truck slowly halted. Leaning out the window, the driver shouted at Edward. "This is the middle of bloody nowhere, mate. Haul your ass out on the double, before you hold up the entire convoy." The man threw his cigarette onto a bank of snow piled beside the road.

Rucksack in hand, Edward jumped down and stood with his back pressed hard against a stone fence, while the convoy rattled by. When the last truck had passed, shifting gears to climb the hill leading south, he stepped into the middle of the road and looked around. Nothing but tufts of grass poking through windswept fields. No barns in which to bed down for the night, no farm huts, no distant chimneys trailing smoke— only stars and a sliver of moon. Accompanied by the squeak of his boots on old snow, he turned towards Souchez, setting one foot in front of the other, as he had on countless marches from battle to battle.

At Neuville-Saint-Vaast he turned west and at Mont-Saint-Eloi headed south. Tense with nervous excitement, he followed the familiar road from there to Beaufort, entering that still-sleeping town just before five. Though shuttered and dark, Café Pitou felt like a beacon of hope, a place where he and Helene had had coffee only three days after they met. Passion had stirred so quickly between them, he had fallen in love that day, or at least, halfway in love.

Edward checked the time. If he hurried, in less than thirty minutes, he could reach Tante Camille's and then he would know.

After Monsieur Garnier's farm, poignant landmarks were everywhere—the stone where Helene had waited, picnic basket in hand, the path to the shepherd's hut where they had first made love, the tree where wild lilies had grown, the fence where they had kissed before returning to Tante Camille's—and his entire body pulsed with expectation. Over the next rise, he would be able to see the house. Anticipating the tall oaks marking the entrance, he rushed forward.

The answer was immediately clear. With the drive covered in snow and the gate hanging from only one hinge, he knew no one would be there. Yet he continued forward, determined to see the desolation with his own eyes. No evidence of footsteps, no curtains drawn back from the kitchen window. No wisp of smoke rising from either chimney. No scattering of crumbs for the birds to find. Blank, everything blank. Nevertheless, he banged on the doors and windows, shouting Helene's name again and again.

At the neighbouring farm, Monsieur Doucet said he thought the family had returned to Paris. At Café Pitou, Edward asked the proprietor for news of the Noisette family and was told they had gone to Bordeaux to be with Monsieur Noisette. He found the building where Helene's friend Germaine lived, only to discover the apartment abandoned. Gaston, the family's handyman, had gone to live with his daughter in Lyon. Madame Lalonde, a close friend of Helene's mother, had suffered a stroke that left her incapable of speech.

Five days later, after exhausting every avenue of inquiry, Edward sat in a bar, looking more like a vagrant than a well-trained soldier, his senses registering little of his surroundings.

Patrons had come and gone all evening while he consumed glass after glass of local wine with the intention of becoming very, very drunk. He had no choice, the following day he had to return to Belgium or risk military sanction.

In the quiet of his downtown office, Edward recalled that his head had ached for hours while his stomach had violently rejected every piece of food he had attempted to eat en route back to camp. Rising to his feet, he opened the door to find that Miss Nicholls had gone home. Except for an illuminated exit sign, the fourth floor was dark.

One by one, he returned each letter to its envelope, ordering them by date. After snapping the lid closed, he placed the tin in his credenza. The weight of sadness was excruciating.

5 July 1936

Eight months after the invitation arrived, they were finally leaving for France. Excitement and agitation were palpable. From halfway up the steps of a train bound for Montreal, Edward called Ann's name loud enough to be heard above the boisterous shouts of other passengers and the squeak and clatter of baggage carts.

"Coming," she replied.

He watched his wife hug their children one more time and kiss her mother's cheek. Alex held his grandfather's hand. Though Edward detected a hint of sadness in Emily's smile, his son bounced from one foot to the other. Ann smiled as she climbed the stairs.

"I'm all set. They'll be fine, won't they?"

"They'll be fine," he echoed. "Let me carry your bag."

Holding his wife's overnight bag in one hand and a brief-case full of travel documents in the other, he squeezed past a man whose belly took far more than half the aisle. Blue berets and Vimy pilgrimage pins marked fellow soldiers. Wives sported bright lipstick and jaunty hats. Ann was no exception. She had shopped for days before buying a royal blue hat with a turned-up brim and large, stiff bow, the concoction designed to angle across her face. In addition to the hat, his wife's hair was somehow different reminding him of a time early in their marriage when he had arrived home to discover that she had cut her beautiful long hair into a short bob. Without thinking, he had demanded an explanation, a tactic that had led to a rousing argument and then tempestuous lovemaking. Now, after thirteen years of marriage he was wise enough to keep his opinions about fashion to himself, nonetheless, he could not decide whether he liked her new sultry look.

Once settled in their seats, he and Ann leaned through the window and waved to their children, whose small arms swung back and forth in unison. Steam hissed and a whistle blew and Edward felt the grind of metal against metal as the train jerked forward. Emily's white-gloved hand remained visible until the tracks curved north and the station disappeared from view.

"We won't see them for six weeks." Ann's nose turned pink as tears threatened to fall.

"Your mother and father will look after them and spoil them too, I imagine," he said, squeezing her hand. "Why don't you take the window seat? We'll be at least five hours to Montreal."

Ann dabbed her eyes with a hankie. "Too bad we don't have time to visit Bob and Hannah." She slipped off her jacket and hung it from a metal hook by the window. "We haven't seen them since our move."

"You miss her, don't you?"

Ann nodded. "She's like an older sister. When we moved to Montreal, I never imagined finding such a good friend. She was my saviour after Alex was born."

"That was a difficult time." An image of household chaos and a wife who spent most days in her dressing gown came to mind. Ann had experienced post-partum depression, only diagnosed after Hannah Wilson, his boss's wife, had stepped in to help.

"Two babies barely one year apart. 'Difficult' is an understatement." Ann wiped the corner of each eye. "How did your mother ever manage nine?"

"I have no idea, but it always felt chaotic to me."

"Thank goodness for Hannah." She returned Edward's squeeze and left her hand linked with his.

Before marriage, he and Ann had talked about children. A maximum of four, they had agreed. Edward had had no intention of being poor, of living with frayed shirt cuffs and stew that was mainly vegetables. As the eldest, he had been the one to leave school at fifteen and contribute to the family income. He promised himself that his children would have a better life.

Emily had arrived three years after their marriage and Alex fourteen months later. Two years after that, Ann had miscarried, and ensuing complications had resulted in a hysterectomy. Dr. Fillmore's look of controlled concern as he had explained the need for surgery and the imperative to act before it was too late had been alarming. Although Ann occasionally mentioned the episode with regret, Edward was perfectly content with Emily and Alex.

From Montreal's Windsor Station, they took a taxi to Pier 26 and found the ship that would take them to France. The *Antonia*'s dark blue hull and freshly painted white decks promised comfort; her huge red funnel promised a maximum speed of fifteen knots. After waiting in a long line of Vimy pilgrims, they took their luggage to room 383.

"It's lovely, dear."

"Not very big, though. Where will we put everything?"

Twin beds separated by a night table occupied two-thirds of the room. A small desk and chair stood near the foot of one bed. On the end wall were two narrow cupboards and a glossy wooden door.

Edward opened the door and leaned in. "Barely enough room to turn around in there."

Ann laughed. "At least we don't have to share the bathroom with anyone. Don't worry, we won't spend much time in our cabin."

"Probably right. But it looked larger in the brochure." He tossed his hat on the bed. "Let's watch the ship depart. We can unpack later."

Although the observation deck was already crowded, they found a spot on the starboard side where late day sun angled across their faces.

"We should be on our way any moment," he said, shading his eyes while pointing to men on shore loosening heavy ropes from thick black cleats.

A horn sounded three sharp blasts. Engines that were previously humming began to rumble and shake, water churned on both sides of the ship, sailors moved here and there with purpose. A snub-nosed tug attached to the ship's bow tooted and the ocean liner slipped from its berth. Ann tightened her hold on Edward's arm and together they watched the *Antonia* make a graceful turn into a wide channel marked with green and red buoys.

"Will you tell me about your trip over in 1915?"

The wind tossed Ann's dark curls, reminding him of the day they first met at a church picnic on Hanlon's Point. Edward hesitated. Counting down the weeks to departure, tension had spun tighter and tighter, and he had made a supreme effort not to snap at Ann or allow his anxieties to erupt into disagreement.

Like so many other returning soldiers, he had refused to talk about the war. What happened was far too gruesome. Unspeakable was the term he and Eric used. They were among the lucky ones who had survived. Edward felt that living life was a duty to those who had died and the only way to live his life was to bury the memories in as deep a hole as possible. Over time, Ann had learned not to ask. But now that they were going to France, she had a right to expect some candour.

"I was nineteen years old. We had trained for four months by then and I suppose I thought I knew everything. My family came to see me off. I never even considered whether or not I would return.

"My stomach churned as I watched my parents and brothers and sisters waving good-bye. Mother wept, of course. Even Father wiped a tear or two away. We took the train to Halifax then boarded a ship called *Morovia*. There were three thousand of us jammed together and the crossing was less than smooth. After twelve miserable days, we landed in Southampton."

* * *

England had been the staging ground for troops preparing to reinforce decimated battalions or to be parcelled out in advance of major battles. Edward's group had arrived at Shorncliffe in the early evening after more than a dozen tedious delays. Patience had long since disappeared.

"All right men, form up outside and wait for further instructions," the sergeant said.

"All we seem to do is wait," muttered Bill Simpson, a thin man who was a genius with anything mechanical and the best shot amongst those Edward knew from camp. At twenty-five, Bill was considered old by most of his colleagues.

"Anxious to get at Fritz, are you?" a voice called out.

Known for having a short fuse, Simpson bristled at the taunt. "Can't stand being herded like cattle. That's all."

Upon arrival, they were assigned ten men to a tent, the tents laid out row upon row, like pawns on an endless chessboard. Bugle call woke them at six the following morning and every morning thereafter. Barking loudly at them, their sergeant made sure that by 6:02 everyone was out of bed.

"Breakfast in Fielding Hall, far side of the parade ground. Report back by seven for inspection. Training begins at eight." He shouted rather than spoke and would not take any questions. "Save 'em for later."

Returning from breakfast, they found a training schedule posted outside their tent. Edward and the others crowded around. Each day began with an hour of physical training, but from there no two days were alike: map reading, musketry, infantry drill with arms, gas drill, cable drill, cable testing, flag reading, mounted cable drill, cable jointing, bayonet drill, parade drill.

"We won't have a moment to rest," one of the soldiers said.

"No doubt that's the point," said Eric Andrews, stuffing a copy of the schedule into his breast pocket. He was a square-faced redhead who joined Signals the same month as Edward. The two men shared a love for football and were fast becoming friends.

Training was vigorous, perfection the only acceptable outcome. The rigour and intensity worked; they learned more in six weeks than during four months back home and had no time to themselves except just before lights out.

In early September 1915, following a lull in the fighting in northern France, Edward's platoon crossed the channel. Within two weeks they were approaching the front lines, their bodies cold and miserable as a steady drizzle hampered their efforts. This was their first experience in the trenches.

Sergeant Finnegan led them behind an imposing chateau then past a house that once belonged to a local winemaker. The house had suffered little damage; only a few panes of broken glass and bullet holes above the front door marked the shelling that occurred in May. Ten soldiers and the sergeant were laden with sandbags, bearing more weight than was comfortable and that weight increasing with each drop of rain. They adopted an Indian technique called a tumpline—a strap around the forehead to help support the weight on their shoulders—in order to carry loads in excess of two hundred pounds. Finnegan urged them on, setting a brisk pace along a boggy path before reaching a communication trench about forty-five minutes later. At the entrance to the trench Simpson slipped, falling into a ditch.

"Jesus Christ, Simpson. Can't ya do anything right?" Finnegan reached out a hand to haul Simpson, now oozing mud, back on his feet.

No one could see more than a few feet ahead. They proceeded single file past a ragged hedge, then zigzagged for a while. As the trench deepened, Edward heard stray bullets zinging to their left near an old haystack. Once the trench was six to seven feet deep they would be fairly safe from rifle fire, but for now they were in a crouched position. Edward's load slipped as he walked and the muzzle of his rifle caught on the trench wall, clogging up with dirt. He wondered if the rifle still worked.

"Five minute rest," Finnegan whispered.

Edward leaned his load against the trench wall to ease the pain in his shoulders and neck. Bill Simpson wiped the mud from his face. No one spoke.

With a brisk wave, Finnegan motioned them forward and in a few minutes turned right, entering a lightly wooded section. Zing, snap. Bullets cracked in the trees. Edward flinched.

"Keep low," the sergeant said.

Earlier Finnegan had explained that when darkness set in, both sides launched random but continuous fire to prevent attacks and keep patrols out of no man's land.

Night magnified innocent sounds. The cry of an owl. A darting squirrel. A muffled cough. As they passed a support line branching off on the right, the trench began to rise. Only a few hundred yards from the enemy, the sergeant signalled for silence. Bullets hissed overhead.

Having reached their destination, they spent two hours digging out a section of the communication trench that had collapsed under intense shelling and reinforcing the walls with sandbags before returning silently and exhausted to their base.

"Good work, men. A bit of rum before you sleep." Sergeant Finnegan poured the dark liquid with care and tossed his own measure down in one smacking gulp. "You've got three hours.

Don't waste 'em."

* * *

As he relayed this story, Edward kept his eyes on the horizon, not once looking at Ann. Waves splashed against the ship's hull. The mournful cries of seagulls rose and fell. Behind them the city's tall buildings and squat factories belching smoke had faded into the distance.

"Sergeant Finnegan sounds like a bit of a brute," she said.

"He was, but he had our safety in mind. I rather liked him after awhile."

"Did he survive?"

"No."

Ann remained silent as their ship continued along the St. Lawrence flanked by its sister ship, the *Ascania*. Edward pointed to one of two warships manoeuvring into place ahead of them.

"*HMCS Saguenay* will only go as far as the gulf, but the *Champlain* will escort us all the way across."

"Which ships are behind us?"

"*Montcalm* and *Montrose*. The paper said more than six thousand are coming from Canada for the ceremony."

"We're like a little convoy, aren't we?" Ann looked at his face. "Are you okay?" she asked, still holding his arm.

"I'm all right. A bit anxious, I suppose."

"I never thought we'd have a chance to go to Europe. I hope my stomach settles down."

They had a full week before the dedication; a week of touring battle sites and the towns and cities located nearby, a combination of memorial and sightseeing. Arras, Lille, Armentieres, Ypres, Cambrai—names that filled Edward with sorrow.

"I'm sure it will. The last time I sailed, most of the men were seasick, but just for the first day or two. You'll be fine. Why don't you stay outside while I go for the captain's briefing?"

For the remainder of the journey they spent hours strolling

the decks, watching the endless roll of waves and seagulls dipping into the ocean and the occasional freighter on the horizon. During dinner other veterans told stories, but Edward
said little, answering only when asked a direct question and
even then with the briefest of replies.

As Ann leaned towards the mirror to remove her makeup,
the neck of her white nightgown opened, revealing full, pink-
tipped breasts.

"You were very abrupt with Enid Crawford. I hope they
don't think you're rude."

Edward drew back the curtain and peered out their small
porthole. Light from the upper deck illuminated a small patch
of waves, but otherwise all was black.

"She was prying. My feelings are none of her business. The
men understand and that's good enough for me."

Ann gave him a look but did not argue. Instead she turned
down the sheets on their narrow beds.

"Tomorrow we dock first thing," she said.

"Yes. First thing." Edward buttoned his pyjama top.

"Will you set the alarm for six? I don't want to miss the
view coming into Le Havre."

He reached for the travelling clock, which had been a
Christmas gift from his parents, and turned a small dial to
the number six.

"Good night, sweetheart." Ann reached out and touched
his shoulder. "I'll be glad when we can sleep in the same bed
together."

Edward turned on his side and closed his eyes but his
thoughts refused to rest. Long after Ann slept he remained
awake, listening to the soft tick, tick, tick of the clock.

* * *

"Jamieson! Report to Captain Weston immediately."

Sergeant Finnegan never spoke at less than a bellow. Edward drew his wide shoulders back, saluted, turned on his heel
and hurried off towards the captain's quarters. They had left

Arras two days earlier and were now on the move, so little distinguished the captain's tent from others except a triangular flag bearing the Signals crest. Edward knew that the words *Velox, Versutus, Vigilans—Swift, Accurate, Alert*—surrounded the crest, a motto learned on his first day in the army.

Expecting some sort of sanction, he tried to think of what offense he might have committed. A few minutes later, he saluted once again, this time to the adjutant who stood in front of Weston's tent. The soldier poked his head into the tent.

"Jamieson reporting as ordered, Captain," the adjutant said, motioning for Edward to enter.

Captain Weston was in the midst of writing what looked like an official report. He grunted but did not look up. Edward kept his eyes on the back wall of the tent, assuming he should not see what the officer wrote. He listened to the scritch, scritch of the pen and the occasional muttered curse until several minutes later when Weston finally capped his pen and pushed back from the desk.

"I'm told you're smart and your penmanship is excellent."

"Sir?" Edward had no idea what the captain was talking about.

"Right, Jamieson. Let's get down to work. I want you to help me with my daily war diary entries. Bring that chair over to my desk so you can see how it works."

Edward placed the wooden chair opposite Captain Weston, the distance separating them less than twenty-four inches. A leather-bound notebook with ruled columns faced him.

"Place, date and hour." Weston stabbed at each heading with a metal ruler. "No need to fill in the hour unless we're in the midst of battle. And it's not likely you'll be with me then, given your other duties." Edward kept his face clear of emotion. "Summary of events and information is where you'll note the most important items of the day. Place names are to be in capital letters. Always. No exceptions. Names of senior officers should also be capitalized. Not regular officers. Understood?"

"I think so, sir. What about this column?" Edward pointed

to the last column with the heading 'Remarks and references to appendices'.

"Hardly ever use it. I'll dictate the report for the next few nights and then we'll see what you can do. Use that pen. Don't make a mess."

Edward pulled the notebook closer.

"Bailleul. December tenth. Always use numerals for dates and times. Fire in men's billets broke out one-thirty am, got under control by three-thirty am, damage slight, would have been less had there been an adequate water supply. Fire caused through faulty brickwork at the back of a grate adjoining the CQMS stores."

While Weston spoke, Edward wrote using neat, thin letters with minimal flourishes, blocking out everything except the captain's voice.

"Read it back to me." Edward complied. "Good. What else would you include from today's work?"

"Umm. Not sure, sir." He tapped the pen against his lower lip. "Perhaps Corporal Wells's transfer to CCHQ and our work on the Bailleul-Nieppe route?"

"Right. Don't forget all caps for place names."

When Edward finished, Weston motioned for the notebook, read the entry and affixed his signature.

"Dismissed, Jamieson. Report back tomorrow and every night at five p.m. Let my adjutant know if you're detained."

"Yes, sir."

From that day forward, Edward wrote the captain's official war diary entries. At all other times, he carried out his signals duties—repairing lines, transmitting messages, burying cable, setting up telephone equipment, digging communication trenches. But each evening at five, he worked with Captain Weston, writing entries into the official war diary, compiling reports, drawing diagrams of communications installations, and tabulating statistics.

Day after day, Edward recorded their efforts: maintenance of lines, laying new lines, burying cable, enemy actions, straightening routes, cutting poles, soldiers coming and going, supply problems, casualties, incidents, commendations. For a while he recorded what Captain Weston dictated, but over time he wrote the reports based on his own knowledge and reviewed them briefly with the captain, who then affixed his signature.

Gradually Edward became used to the panic of battle and the boredom in between, fatigue, bad food, lice and never-ending damp. Working with Captain Weston offered a brief reprieve from the grinding hours of duty and the opportunity to learn the business of war.

* * *

Edward glanced once more at his alarm clock. *Christ*, he thought, *one fifteen.* He turned onto his other side and tried to mimic Ann's soft, regular breathing. Instead his mind filled with endless rounds of trench duty and shorter and shorter rest periods as the German stranglehold continued.

6 July 1936

The wide sweep of the Seine as they came round the headland looked the same, but twenty-one years ago the basin had been full of battleships and cruisers, their grey hulks signalling the brooding presence of war. A line of hospital ships had been anchored close to shore, each ship marked by a red cross in case German aircraft swooped low intent on destruction. Grey-clad nurses, their heads topped by white winged caps, could be seen on deck helping wounded soldiers hobble a few strength-building steps. The quays had been crowded with khaki, and along the boardwalk, French flags had snapped with each gust of wind.

A surge of memory pulled Edward back: soldiers crowded on deck bearing full packs and anxious faces, officers calling orders, their voices sharp with intensity, the splash of dropping anchors and cries of scavenging seagulls. Not far from their berth, a long line of artillery guns had descended the ramp of a merchant vessel. His muscles had tensed. The spit in his mouth had run dry.

Throughout this trip across the Atlantic with Ann, past and present had collided with increasing frequency such that he seemed to exist in parallel times, his self divided between then and now, war memories slithering like a nest of snakes. Edward was fearful that at any moment he might lose control. From late 1919 onward, he had reconstructed a man of character and strength, one who took on responsibility and found accomplishment in career, family, friends and public contributions. Looking at the harbour of Le Havre, he wondered if those years were about to unravel.

The ship turned to nestle against the pier. Four sharp blasts emanated from the bridge where the captain supervised his crew to a perfect docking. Sailors flung ropes to waiting hands and readied gangways for lowering, while passengers—the men solemn, the women white-gloved and smiling—waited for a signal to disembark. Edward knew from conversations each night at dinner that this was a trip few had expected to make, and while some prepared for a jolly holiday, most feared old wounds would fester, oozing once more with the pus of war.

"Are you ready, dear?" Ann stood by his side, looking fresh in a polka-dot dress and navy jacket.

"As ready as I'll ever be," he said.

After the jumble of disembarking passengers, they boarded a bus for their journey from Le Havre to Arras, suitcases stowed in great cavities beneath the bus, a light lunch packed in brown paper bags and tucked onto a shelf above their heads. They sat up front to keep Ann's motion sickness at bay and nodded as fellow veterans took their seats amidst much bantering and bits of grumbling. Maurice Benoit, their guide for the next seven days, gave instructions as the driver set off.

Through the window, Edward saw a fleet of fishing boats bobbing blue, red, green and white, while on shore men repaired nets or sorted the early morning catch. Pungent smells of fish mixed with oil and bilge water. Out the opposite window, narrow, slate-roofed houses lined the street and the morning market bustled as men and women haggled and laughed in equal measure.

"This part of France was settled first by the Vikings." Maurice said, "and for years the French and English battled over these lands. Who knows the name of the famous English king who came from Normandy?" Maurice waited for an answer. "*Oui.* Yes. That is correct. William the Conqueror."

Edward ignored their guide's prattling and returned to his musing, contemplating how strange life was, unfolding in expected and unexpected ways, punctuated by random happenings that forever changed one's future. Why did he live while others died? Why did Helene leave him? Had his life turned in the best direction? What would this trip bring?

Having left the port behind, the bus travelled along winding roads, cutting through verdant fields, passing wood-framed houses and grazing cattle. Villages marked the miles, their French names both familiar and strange. Their first stop was Rouen, where Claude Monet had endlessly painted the Cathedrale de Notre-Dame, beautiful for its lacy stonework and towering spires. After seeing the cathedral, they went to the old marketplace where Joan of Arc was burned alive, and to the Great Clock whose bells, according to Maurice, still tolled a curfew every night. At Ann's request, Edward took pictures to record each site.

After lunch the bus continued, passing Neufchatel-en-Bray. Poix-de-Picardie, Amiens, Doullens, places that heaved memory from hidden recesses, often the terrain's uneven profile hinted at battles lost or won, of hideous conditions, of explosions and low-flying planes, of green poison seeping along the ground. Edward's head ached from the effort to control his emotions. He wiped his brow with a handkerchief.

Ann turned in his direction. "You haven't spoken for ages."

"A little headache," he said with a limp smile.

"We should be in Arras soon. Maurice said we'd go straight to the hotel and have dinner there."

"Sounds fine." He attempted to make his voice livelier. "I'm looking forward to French food. Their breads are delicious, Ann. And the cheese."

"When did you get to sample them? I thought army food was atrocious."

"When I was on leave, which wasn't very often. I remember staying outside Paris with Eric. Every day we went into the city to enjoy the shops and cafes full of normal people. Paris was beautiful, despite the war."

They talked until the bus halted in front of a five-storey stone building with ground-level arches creating a wide walkway. Situated just off the Grande Place, the hotel was busy with so many people on pilgrimage. While they waited for the porter to deliver their bags, Ann wrote a letter to her parents and Edward dozed in their small but comfortable room.

* * *

That evening, Edward and Ann ate at a small restaurant located on the ground floor of what was once a large, private residence. Brick walls and arched alcoves created an air of intimacy. They sat at a round table for two located just beyond two floor-to-ceiling shelves full of wine bottles. When Ann had opened the door to determine the restaurant's suitability, flickering candlelight and rich aromas had drawn them in.

"I don't have much appetite," Edward said, placing his fork and knife together on a plate still full of food.

Ann readied another bite of fish. "I'm not surprised," she sad. "Each day you've looked more and more distracted. I can only imagine what being in these places feels like for you. I'm sorry, sweetheart. Is there anything I can do to help?" He shook his head and took a large gulp of wine. "When were you in Arras?"

"Many times. Parts of it were damaged but much remained intact. Often we came here for supplies or after training."

"Did you have time off here?"

He nodded. "Arras was very near the front; in a way it's more Belgian than French. I was often in this vicinity, especially during the lead up to Vimy. Old tunnels run beneath the city and we used them, extending them so that we were right below the Germans." He closed his eyes and shook his head as if the memory was impossible to believe. "The last time I saw the Grande Place was in 1919 when it was full of rubble and scaffolding as the French began to rebuild."

"The city looks charming now. Maurice said they used photos and drawings to recreate damaged buildings."

"I think they've done that in a lot of towns affected by the war. Must have been a staggering cost."

Back in their hotel room, he looked out the window, imagining the square as it had been so long ago, hearing the echo of boots drumming on cobblestones, seeing the belfry framed against a weary sky.

* * *

Their unit had been on trench rotation. While others slept, Eric and Edward had manned the signals equipment from a cave-like dugout. A tangle of wires connected three boxes laid out on top of a wooden table.

"Fuck." Eric threw his earphones down.

Edward turned his head to look at his friend but said nothing.

"Gotta get a breath of air." Eric pushed away from their shared table and jammed on his helmet. "This place smells worse than a pigsty."

Edward nodded. He did not need to remind Eric to keep his head down; night was a favourite time for snipers. A flashing light demanded his attention. Edward plugged in his headphones and scribbled furiously. Less than a minute later, Eric returned yelling, "Gas attack!" and reaching for a gas mask hanging on a nail beside their water canteens.

"Edward! Stop what you're doing. Now!"

Eric grabbed his bayonet and banged an empty shell case hanging near the periscope to sound the alarm. Edward said nothing as he continued to work on a message from 2nd Division. Gongs rang up and down the trenches and men scrambled to don their respirators. A putrid yellow cloud crept towards them, hugging the ground then spiralling upward towards their trench, sniffing the edges. A cloud carrying death.

"Man the fire step," an officer shouted, words muffled, face unrecognizable.

Crews mounted machine guns on the parapet. Men readied their bayonets, metal slapping metal.

"Enemy coming!" shouted Purdy, a serious man who seemed better suited to academia than soldiering.

Edward could not hold his breath any longer. Fumbling to remove his headset, he grabbed his own mask. A jab of toxic fumes. Heavy pressure on his lungs. Final strap in place. Mouth tube in. He gasped.

"You okay?" Eric asked in a muffled voice.

Edward nodded. In his mask, he looked part man and part gargoyle. Rifles at hand, he and Eric peered over the top and watched the chlorine creep through low-lying areas, disappearing into shell holes and craters like a spreading amoeba. Ghostly forms rose from enemy trenches followed by the squelch of boots in thick mud and the clink of swinging rifles.

"Stand to!" They heard the officer once again and clutched their rifles; Eric stuffed two grenades into his pocket. They were going to counter-attack.

"Over the top, men."

Two hundred men climbed up and over. The soldier next to Edward carried a Lewis machine gun, which was light enough to be fired from the shoulder. He let off a five-second burst, firing more than forty rounds against the enemy. Heavy artillery blasted no man's land in an attempt to disperse the gas. German soldiers jerked and twisted then disappeared like slumping wraiths.

Luck turned their way. The wind shifted eastwards carrying gas back towards German lines. Edward, Eric and the gunner took cover in a large shell hole as confused Germans began to retreat, coughing and choking on their own gas. The gunner's weapon jammed. Edward fired and saw a soldier spin around, his mouth wide open as he cried out before falling face down in the mud.

* * *

"What are you thinking about?" Ann said.

Edward stared once more at the belfry, each tier of its impressive length glowing against the night sky. He turned away from the window. "This and that."

She did not press for more. "Time to come to bed, dear. We have a busy day tomorrow."

Yes, he thought, *a busy day.*

7   July 1936

The next morning Ann and Edward boarded the bus before eight-thirty, and while they toured the city, Maurice provided commentary, touching on history, art, French customs and the war.

"In September 1914, it was here that the French managed to halt the German advance and dig in. Then as trench warfare took over, Arras became an important base for the Allies. I'm sure many of you men will have been to Arras during your war service." Several men nodded in agreement. "Because it was so close to the front, the town became known as *la ville martyre*—martyr's town. The town hall was destroyed in 1917 but has been completely rebuilt in the same style. Below the town hall are underground chambers that were used as a British field hospital. We will stop for a visit to the town hall and then pass by an important memorial to the British flying corps." Maurice stopped and took his seat for the short drive to the town hall.

After Arras the bus took them north en route to Lille. Edward gazed out the window at the slow, steady climb of land.

"What are you looking at?" Ann asked.

"That's the ridge in the distance."

"Vimy Ridge?" He nodded. "This is difficult for you, isn't it?" He nodded again. She squeezed his hand but said nothing more until the bus turned east, following a sign for Lille.

"Were you in Lille?" she asked.

"No. Lille was occupied by the Germans during the war. The French thought the flat terrain surrounding the city would be too difficult to defend, which meant that the Germans had control of the coalfields around Lille and Lens. We could've used some of that coal. The damp made each winter so cold. When Fritz retreated, they destroyed the city, all the bridges, many, many buildings and every means of communication."

"It must have looked like a wasteland."

"I'm sure it did," he said. "I was stationed near Cambrai towards the end. When we advanced into German-held territory near there, we found the same devastation."

Ann pulled out their itinerary. "We have two nights in Lille. The schedule says Armentieres, Ypres and the Somme. Then we'll go to Cambrai. I'm worried about you, sweetheart. Your face is becoming more and more drawn. And your eyes . . . you look like you haven't been sleeping at all."

"I'm not sleeping very well. But I'm sure I'll be fine."

"I won't pester you with questions. You tell me when you feel like talking."

Unlike others on tour, Edward was oblivious to the commentary Maurice provided. At every site war spewed forth like a lanced boil and, like several other men, he often wandered away from the group until he could control his emotions.

* * *

Lieutenant Burke told them the Canadian Corps were to take Vimy Ridge from the Germans. During the months preceding battle, he reminded them frequently that previous at-

tacks by the French and British had failed, resulting in more
than one hundred thousand soldiers wounded or lost. Could
they succeed when so many had failed? Edward and others
debated this question every day as they prepared.

"The enemy has built deep defensive positions consisting of
bunkers, narrow passages and artillery-proof trenches. These
are heavily protected by concrete machine gun emplacements
and connected with a network of natural caves. And thick
barbed wire, with sixteen barbs to the foot, surrounds their
fortifications." He paused to let these facts sink in. "Our advance work has to be perfect, otherwise we too will fail. Communication is vital for success."

Burke never minced his words. He wanted every soldier fully briefed and seemed to take satisfaction in their discomfort
as he outlined the challenges. He did not believe in what he
called "molly coddling".

Preparations for Vimy were massive in scale—in addition
to cable and telephone wires, sappers were digging eleven underground tunnels to aid in the movement and protection of
troops. These underground roads, fanning out in three nest-
ed arcs, would be equipped with electricity, medical stations,
supplies and rest areas. The Engineer Corps were building
portable bridges to move artillery pieces over difficult terrain.
All had to be done in absolute secrecy within close proximity
to German positions. In the biting cold they worked amidst
the debris of body parts, barbed wire, unexploded shells, slush
and garbage to construct a six-mile long network of trenches
and tunnels running back from the Allied front lines. Difficult,
demanding, exacting work.

After more than seventeen months of war, Edward had
strategies to control his thoughts while on duty, but when he
slept, he often woke with a start, sweating at some unknown
horror. Ghosts crowded his brain, dead men clamouring for
attention. On the rare occasions when he considered the future, he had trouble imagining that he would survive to have
a future. Yet he could still light a cigarette with a steady hand

and mask his fear most of the time.

By late January, Edward was in a constant state of exhaustion from the demands of preparation.

"Lance Corporal Jamieson!" Edward jerked out of a half doze to full attention as Burke shouted at him. "Have we finished laying cable in tunnel C32?"

"Yes, sir." Edward saluted. While Canadian troops were not expected to salute on every occasion, he preferred not to give Burke any reason to find fault.

"Are all tests complete?" Burke offered no pleasantries. A sharp chin and hooded eyes gave him a fierce look that caused others to stay out of his way as much as possible.

"Not yet, sir."

"Then what are you standing around for?"

There was no point in answering. Burke found fault whether the job was done to perfection or not. Edward had learned the hard way that his lieutenant enjoyed wielding power, bullying juniors at the least provocation. Yes, sir, was the only response.

They had been at it for weeks. Plans called for over twenty-one miles of signal cable and sixty-six miles of telephone wire to be buried on the battlefront to enable communications before and during the upcoming offensive. Exhausting, back-breaking work, crouched or kneeling underground for hours, carrying great rolls of cable along with heavy equipment, keeping track of every connection and testing, testing, testing.

Working with a team of signallers and engineers, Edward was responsible for quadrant three. He carried a mental map of the entire communication grid for this quadrant in his head. The days he actually got some sleep, dreams of breakdowns often woke him.

"Finish testing before four p.m. and report back to me." Burke's eyes narrowed in annoyance.

The lieutenant offered no hint as to why Edward should report back, but asking would only risk further reprimand.

Edward brought his right arm into a crisp salute then hurried off to find Andrews and Kilpatrick, two members of his team. They were the most reliable, and with Eric he could vent his frustrations in confidence.

Two hours later, Edward reported to Lieutenant Burke, who was in the command area in tunnel C01. Within ten minutes, more than thirty men had assembled, jammed together in a space designed for ten as they listened to Major Somers describe their task. Smells of sweat mingled with dirty, damp wool.

"Before battle we have to map enemy positions accurately. We'll have aircraft and balloons spotting where possible and we'll gather information from trench raids and captured German soldiers." Somers voice deepened as he made deliberate eye contact with those in the room. "The Corps has designed a new approach involving microphones to triangulate enemy positions. Your job is to position the microphones in no man's land." An audible, collective intake of breath followed his words as each man imagined what that would entail. "I've asked Lieutenant Burke to coordinate."

Burke unveiled a map of the area and took over the briefing. Jabbing at the map with a riding crop, he pointed to proposed microphone placements as he rattled off names of those responsible and outlined the timetable they would follow. He waved his hand at a pile of briefing books and told them to return at the same time the following day.

"Study these. Sleep with them. Eat with them. I don't care how you do it. Make sure you know every detail." They filed out without a word.

A week later, in the pitch black of a half-snowing night, Edward and eleven others made their way from the tunnels via support and reserve trenches to the forward lines. Taking each step with care, they trudged through narrow, zigzagging paths, passing men snatching sleep, cooking, playing cards, cleaning equipment—the tasks of soldiers at rest.

As they turned a sharp corner, an explosion shook the section of trench not far behind them. The blast rattled Edward's eardrums; screams of pain indicated the injuries suffered by men he had passed only minutes earlier. Whistles blew, summoning stretcher-bearers to carry what was left of the wounded away for treatment, and others to restore the trench. Edward knew the medics would waste little time on those who were beyond saving, just the barest of comfort, if that.

Battle savvy after months at the front, Edward steeled himself not to turn around, and instead put one foot in front of the other as he moved himself and over fifty pounds of equipment forward. He thought back to another night, sitting at a small wireless station, receiver in hand as an explosion ripped a section of the trench no more than thirty feet away. The blast crushed a nearby soldier as support beams, earth and sandbags caved in. Numb to such destruction, he had continued his transmission without interruption. Edward shut the memory away and focused on the present. Distraction could be fatal.

Within thirty minutes the twelve men, equally divided between signallers and engineers, reached their destination, where a support team with ladders and extra gear was waiting. Without speaking, the sergeant motioned them to unload and check their packs then blacken their faces. The plan was to head out in teams of two with one set of equipment each, return and head out again, placing twenty-four microphones and connecting cable in their designated section of no man's land. A quick chop of the sergeant's hand and six ladders were hoisted like coordinated ballet movements against the parapet. Another chop followed by two fingers pointing forward and the men climbed silently up the ladders.

They fanned out, crouching low, creeping through the mud from shell hole to shell hole, replicating what they had practiced, counting paces, checking positions. Triangulating sound required accurate placement of the microphones.

When a star shell burst, lighting up the sky, Edward froze. The slightest movement could betray their location to the

Germans and attract enemy fire. Random shots rang out as the flash receded and darkness descended again.

Reaching their destination, Edward and his teammate John Hobbs unhooked their packs and began to set out microphones, wires, connectors and other items. They dug the microphones into position, secured them and attached the loose end of a large spool of connecting wire to the microphones. Edward motioned to John: time to return. Painstakingly, they made their way back, unrolling the spool of wire and covering each section as they went. Another flash. They froze again. Night reflected in a thousand eyes.

When it was safe, they continued with their task until they found the ladders and descended into the trench. Breathing heavily, heart thudding, Edward picked up his next pack, ready for the second trip. The sergeant repeated his signals and they climbed up and out, heading for a different location. Secure microphones, attach wires, begin unrolling. Edward and John worked flawlessly.

Without warning, a rifle sounded. John grunted and pitched forward. Edward did not move. When satisfied that the sniper had turned his attention elsewhere, he dropped his equipment, picked John up and slung him over his shoulder. Staggering under the weight, he crossed the remaining distance and handed John to those below. Now he had to make another journey in order to complete both his and John's tasks.

Stealth was crucial. He retraced his route and found one spool. After unrolling it, he returned again but could not find the other spool of wire. Patting the ground around him, he touched something hard, not the right shape. Precious seconds ticked by. *Where is it? Think Edward, think*, he told himself. *Panic is the enemy. It must have rolled when John fell.*

He began a methodical search in ever widening arcs moving closer to where the microphones had been positioned, deeper into no man's land. *Found it. Thank God. Now slowly, slowly, do it right. Burke will only send me back if it doesn't work.* Finally, he returned to the ladder and temporary safety.

"John?" he whispered to one of the other signallers.

"Not good."

"Shit. We were almost done."

Edward made his way to a dugout where John lay, his face grey, breath shallow. John groaned in pain as a medic rolled him onto a stretcher.

"Hold on, John," Edward said, though he could see blood seeping through the temporary dressing. He looked at the medic who shook his head. Edward cursed beneath his breath.

Tension built as zero hour approached like a rogue wave silently gathering speed and force. No one knew whom the wave would take and who would survive. No one knew the cost of survival.

* * *

As Edward walked the fields where battles had raged almost twenty years earlier, passed by cemeteries filled with simple white crosses, memorials both large and small and toured rebuilt churches, he saw not the present but the past: Bill Simpson chomping on his pipe long after he ran out of tobacco, Dave Purdy making tea, Eric racing after Tigger, a small dog they adopted, Sergeant Finnegan barking at them during training, Captain Weston hunched over his maps late at night.

Though now lush and green, to him the landscape was filled with trees devoid of life, their trunks marking platoons caught in heavy shelling, barbed wire stretching to infinity, fields thick with muck, villages smouldering in the distance.

8 JULY 26, 1936

On the day of the dedication ceremony, Edward and Ann stood atop the ridge gazing at the view. Behind a thin line of trees were the small villages of Vimy and Givenchy en Gohelle and lush green farmland dotted with cows. In the far distance, the town of Lens spread in a north to south line, a few buildings glinting in the sun.

"What are those large black mounds?" Ann said.

"Coal tailings. I remember seeing them during the war. The tailings are what's left behind when the good quality coal is extracted."

"They really take away from the peaceful setting, don't they?"

Edward nodded. "The Germans held this ridge which meant that they controlled everything you see in this direction as well as the coal mines. Our troops had to fight their way to the top where we're standing." He turned around and pointed towards a distant ruin atop a far off hill. "That's the abbey of Mont St. Eloi. We started the assault from underground tunnels located near that hill. The slope from there to here might look gentle but when you're under attack . . ." He stopped speaking.

Ann squeezed his hand and drew a bit closer. "You don't have to tell me if it's too painful."

"Perhaps I'll feel like telling you more about it later." Edward returned Ann's squeeze. "Let's walk over there towards the monument."

Framed against a vivid blue sky, the memorial was breathtaking. Approaching from the front, Edward was struck by its central figure: a woman, hooded and cloaked, facing east towards the new day. The woman's eyes were downcast, her chin resting on her left hand, right hand grasping an olive branch. Below her was a tomb, draped in laurel and a single soldier's helmet.

According to the official program, the figure represented Canada, a young nation mourning her fallen sons. Behind the woman, two massive spires thrust upward, stark and uncompromising. Even more moving was the sight of over eleven thousand names, individually carved to honour each Canadian soldier who died in France with no known grave. Edward's emotions were so fraught he felt nauseous.

The memorial was not some abstract idea of recognizing the fallen and those who succeeded in taking the ridge. To him it represented the whole war, millions of lives obliterated, friends dying in agony, lost innocence, a part of him that had never healed, and never would. He could not bear to look at the names in case he recognized even one.

An army of ghosts marched at his side, keeping time with his memories. Since the war, he found it impossible to describe his experiences in a way that those who were not there could understand. He found it equally impossible to reminisce with those who had been there. His own private hell would remain exactly that, private.

In the crush of attendees, Edward wondered if they would

reach their designated area before the ceremony began. The mood was both sombre and jovial, befitting a day celebrating victory and loss. Thousands of middle-aged men, loved ones at their side, waited for the ceremony to begin. Broad chests sported medals of various sizes and shapes, hung on colourful ribbons one next to another—medals for heroism, for length of service or distinguished service, victory medals, the Victoria Cross. A great hubbub of conversation swirled as men exchanged greetings, exclaimed in amazement at what they had endured, and talked about post-war circumstances. Just like conversations on board ship, Edward heard many wonder why they were the lucky ones who survived.

Near the memorial, royal purple ropes encircled a stage where dignitaries would soon appear, including King Edward VIII, the presidents of France and Belgium, and the Canadian prime minister. French soldiers flanked each section where attendees assembled by division and battalion. The day was sunny and hot with just a little breeze to ease the humidity and billow the flags from around the world positioned left and right of the stage. Eventually Ann and Edward found their place with others from the Signal Corps.

To begin the dedication, a lone bugler played *Last Post*, its haunting sound echoing across the ridge. Tears ran freely: tears for fallen comrades, tears for lost youth, tears for what was and what might have been. When the last note faded, a formation of Amiot 143s, French twin-engine bombers, roared across the horizon. For Edward, time slid backwards.

* * *

Pushing through a knot of soldiers, Edward was breathing hard as he approached Lieutenant Burke.

"Jamieson. Why aren't you at your post?" Burke lifted his head from the communications grid-map and shouted to be heard over the machine gun firing to his left.

"Vital communication from HQ, sir." Unable to find a runner to take the message to Burke, Edward had abandoned his

post to take it himself. He would experience serious consequences if Burke disagreed with that decision. "There was no
one else to bring this to you."

Burke scanned the message. "Bloody hell. How'll we alert
them in time?"

"I've tried wireless and airlines. Can't reach them."

"Someone will have to go on foot." The Lieutenant gripped
his forehead as if that would help him focus. "I'll find Andrews. He's back."

Edward checked his watch. "There isn't time, sir. You take
over my post while I run the message forward." Burke nodded;
after all, a lance corporal was the more dispensable man.

The message announced a delay to Z-hour. The Eighty-Seventh Battalion, along with two other battalions, were to take
the highest point of the ridge called Hill 145, which was critical to destroying Germany's stranglehold in the northeast. By
now, the Eighty-Fifth would also be in position and all would
be waiting for Z-hour before commencing action. If the battalions advanced at the old Z-hour without artillery cover they
would be destroyed by enemy fire. Edward had less than thirty
minutes to reach them.

Wasting no time saluting, he put on a red armband, tucked
the message in his tunic pocket and immediately headed east,
his destination five hundred yards away but more than three
times that distance using the trenches. Going above ground
would be suicide.

Unlike their own trenches, which he could navigate in his
sleep, Edward knew only the general layout of newly won German trenches; information gleaned from training diagrams and
captured soldiers. He would have to work his way through
fighting trenches, communication trenches and finally the resistance trenches. Once he got there, he could follow the resistance trench to find the Eighty-Seventh.

To avoid snipers, Edward moved in a crouched position as
he scrambled over a ledge of fallen sandbags where a recent
barrage had weakened the retaining wall and destroyed the fire

step. He passed by a Maxim gun still on its sledge mount, an unused roll of ammunition hanging out one end. On his right, several stocks of stick grenades remained intact on a dirt shelf. A dead German soldier lay only a few feet away, his helmet off, the left side of his face missing.

Despite the cold, Edward sweated in his greatcoat. Mud oozed with each step, slowing his pace. His foot slipped. He grabbed at a section of chicken wire attached to the retaining wall to steady himself. A few yards ahead, a pool of water lay in front of a tunnel entrance. While slogging through the water, an explosion ripped the sky, spraying earth and shrapnel. Large clods of dirt struck his helmet.

Just inside the tunnel the ground wobbled beneath his feet. Struggling to keep his balance, he realized he was standing on two dead soldiers. He shuddered but kept going, barely able to see in the tunnel's gloom. Panting, he slowed his pace to avoid falling; not one second could be wasted. Outside, the bursting curtain of steel continued its deadly assault.

He emerged from the tunnel and hurried along an empty trench as snow swirled in a sudden flurry, biting his face and limiting his sight. A low-flying aircraft swooped overhead looking for flag wavers reporting on objectives achieved. Edward heard the blaring of its klaxon. His legs pounded up and down, pleading for rest.

He lifted his eyes from the footpath, searching for a communication trench to take him forward. There it was. He could see the junction ahead. He turned left to follow its zigzag pattern. After a few minutes he found another fighting trench, then fifty feet later a second communication trench. Glancing up, he cursed, ducking quickly to avoid a roll of barbed wire. The second communication trench would be longer than the first as it bridged the gap between fighting trenches and resistance trenches. In the distance he heard the sound of howitzers launching another offensive.

Scrambling over piles of rubble and fallen support beams, Edward thought he could see another T-junction ahead. If

that were the case, he would be at the first resistance trench.
When he reached the junction, he cursed again and stopped.
his path completely blocked. He retraced his steps to a scaling
ladder and climbed out of the trench to proceed above ground
beyond the blockage. The sudden buzz of a whizbang warned
him of danger and he threw himself to the ground as a shell
exploded no more than twenty feet away. He got to his feet
and ran forward a short distance before jumping back into the
communication trench beyond the blocked area. The sharp
tang of cordite hung in the air.

Stark flashes of red lit the clouds as he rounded another
corner and saw stretcher-bearers coming towards him followed
by a stumbling line of German prisoners, one of them dressed
in pyjamas. On the stretcher lay a grey-faced soldier bleeding
from wounds in the arm and leg. Edward squeezed past the
smells of blood and fear.

A few steps later he entered the first of three resistance
trenches. He had to reach the third, most forward trench.
Edward looked at his watch; unless he went above ground.
he wouldn't make it. Around the next bend he found another
ladder, slung his rifle off his shoulder and scrambled out.

As he emerged from the trench, sunshine broke the gloom.
flaming against a distant spire. Wreckage surrounded him:
barbed wire, torn sandbags, abandoned artillery. stinking shell
holes. Wounded men littered the field, begging for help. Dusk
would soon close in; he stopped for no one.

Machine-gun fire crackled on his far right as German gun-
ners emerged from a dugout desperate to inflict pain and
damage on those who would soon force them out. Edward
dodged to the left. He was almost there. Keeping low to the
ground, he hurried on with only one purpose reaching the
Eighty-Seventh.

When the sniper's bullet hit him, all thought of the message tucked in his pocket disappeared. He crumpled to the
ground like a rag doll.

* * *

Nineteen years later Edward could still feel the heart-pumping anxiety of that afternoon, the way he had been both hot with sweat and cold with fear, the way his legs had screamed for him to stop and his throat had clogged with smoke. With noise pounding from every direction, he had not heard the sniper's bullet nor had he been aware of medics taking him by stretcher to a clearing station behind the lines.

The French president took the podium, but Edward did not bother to listen; instead, he looked at each group of people, searching for a face, the one face he had come to find. With so many in attendance, this task was like finding a single buttercup in a field of daisies. Would she be there? He had no idea and yet he continued to scan the crowd as methodically as possible.

He had not expected so many women. The hats they wore obscured their faces and hair, making the search more difficult. Ignoring the Canadian sections, Edward instead concentrated on clusters of attendees looking French or Belgian. A flash of auburn hair caught his eye, but the chin was not right. A slim silhouette in the distance held his attention, but again the woman was not Helene. *I'm being foolish*, he thought, but nonetheless continued to look up and down each row. On the far left, he glimpsed a profile. His heart raced.

He extracted his arm from Ann's. "Sweetheart, I need to step away for a few minutes."

"Oh, dear. You look very pale. Do you want me to come along?" She laid a hand on his shoulder.

"No. I'll be fine. I just need to get away from the crowd."

Ann nodded. "Will you be able to find me again?"

"I'm sure I will." He waved in the opposite direction of the way he planned to go. "I'll walk to an open spot and get some air."

Edward turned and walked away from the group gathered near the French delegation, imagining Ann following him with her eyes. He could almost feel the heat of her gaze. The King was speaking about sacrifice, dedication, defending liberty and democracy, about eternal friendship between two great countries. Edward knew he should remain with Ann; it was out of character for him to leave during such a moving part of the ceremony. Each step pulled him away from her, from all that was certain in his life, thrusting him into the unknown.

Turn around you fool, he thought. *Don't unleash the past any more than you already have.*

Invisible threads drew him on and now that Ann was no longer in view, he turned towards the face he had seen in the distance. For a moment the crowd blocked his passage and he feared she might disappear before he reached her. He circled around and found the face again. The woman lifted her head to watch the King and his certainty grew. He pushed closer. She tucked a strand of hair beneath her hat. Closer still. When he was less than ten yards away, she looked in his direction, her face changing from puzzlement to wide-eyed surprise and then a smile that radiated like the sun emerging from clouds.

"You came," she said as he reached her side.

"So did you."

"I had to know if you survived." She touched his arm with the tips of two fingers.

"But you didn't wait for me."

"I did, Edward. I did. I'm at Tante Camille's. Will you come to see me? Then I can tell you what happened."

"I don't . . ." Helene's question caught him off guard. The possibility of finding her at the ceremony had been so remote, he had not considered what to do if he found her. His only quest had been to discover why she had not waited for him. Nothing else. "My wife . . ." She withdrew her fingers. "I might be able to get away . . . for a few days?"

"A few days." Helene closed her eyes. When she opened them she dug into her purse, extracted a pencil and scribbled on a small piece of paper. "A telephone number. I'm in Beaufort. Do you remember?"

"Yes. Almost every day." He searched her face. "I have to

get back."

"Call me, Edouard." She spoke his name with the French pronunciation, the way she had when they first met.

From the stage, trumpets sounded, soaring and hauntingly beautiful after the King's speech. Edward turned to go then glanced at Helene once again but did not smile. Winding his way back to Ann, he felt disconnected, like some third person watching from a great distance. His steps slowed.

For a moment the battle for Vimy Ridge was upon him again. Men torn apart by machine-gun bullets, drowning in the mud, hanging from barbed wire. He heard the ear-splitting scream of shellfire, the panicked cry of a fallen horse, the buzz of airplanes overhead, the scuffle of rats running along the trenches. He could smell it all—blood, mud, gunpowder, urine, smoke and the ominous whiff of chlorine. Every sense assaulted until overwhelmed.

Helene had helped him survive. He remembered her as she used to be: young, vibrant, cascading auburn hair, enticing curves, an occasional pout on her lips, warm embraces, silent longing.

When he reappeared at Ann's side, Mackenzie King, the Canadian prime minister, was moving to the podium.

"Where did you go?"

"I walked around the perimeter for a bit." Edward shifted from one foot to the other.

Ann tucked her arm into his. "Okay now?" He nodded.

As the formal speeches continued, he replayed the scene over and over: searching the French delegation person by person, a glimpse of shoulder, a flash of a familiar profile, the slow walk away from Ann, towards what might be Helene, more purposeful steps as he neared her, the turn of her head and smile of recognition. Despite layers of clothing, her brief touch had aroused him. He fingered the small piece of paper in his pocket.

9 JULY 26, 1936

Following the dedication, the reception was in the Hotel de Ville, where flags from France, Britain, Belgium and Canada flew with pride and wrought iron gates stood wide open to admit the crowds. Leaded windows, accented by stone fleurs-de-lis and evenly spaced across each level of the building, suggested a builder bound by rigid notions of symmetry. Gargoyles, their grotesque faces guarding against evil, protruded at regular intervals just beneath the roofline. At one end, a steeple housed an enormous brass bell, while at the other, a clock tower sounded every hour.

The interior was full of spacious salons with elaborate mouldings, floor-to-ceiling tapestries in muted colours depicting myths of old, paintings of kings and local aristocrats gazing down with a hint of pompous disdain. The rooms were bare of furniture except for the occasional narrow table set with a profusion of flowers. Waiters circulated with trays of canapés and glasses of wine.

"That was such a moving ceremony," Ann said. "I was in tears several times. You seemed very affected by it."

"I was. I'm sorry I stepped away."

"That's all right, sweetheart. I can understand you needing a moment by yourself. The King's speech was so touching. Did you listen to him?"

"Not really. A few bits here and there. I . . . wasn't feeling well."

In a large room containing a wide stone fireplace flanked by pictures of breast-plated soldiers on horseback, Edward found a few men he knew. As he spoke with those who shared the Vimy experience, his thoughts darted here and there like airplanes evading enemy fire. The feeling reminded him of the heat of battle.

Released from one conversation, he and Ann continued through the crowds. Uniforms sparkled with medals, polished buttons and ceremonials swords. Snatches of conversation penetrated his distraction.

"Did you know that France has given the land surrounding the memorial to Canada as an expression of gratitude?"

"The memorial is stunning. Such a tribute to those who died and those who fought."

"I heard it took eleven years to build and cost over four times what Ottawa budgeted."

"Those stories brought tears to my eyes. Such sacrifice."

"I can't believe we lived in those tunnels and trenches for such a long time. I'd forgotten how incredibly claustrophobic they were."

"How about the filth we had to endure? They didn't talk about that."

He knew he should look for relatives of friends who had died: Stewart and McKnight at the Somme, Johnson and Danny Boy at Valenciennes, Wicky, Duff and Red at Vimy, Thompson at Cambrai. His thoughts turned to Bill Simpson, who had been killed by one of their own unexploded shells as they cleared out a German post one night. *How fucking stupid was that?* he thought. Perhaps he could find Bill's wife. but what could he say to ease her pain? And if he found the right words, could he say them and maintain his composure?

A small, balding man tapped Edward's shoulder. "Edward. you're looking pretty good for an old fellow. How are you?"

"Not too bad and yourself, Lenny."

Lenny Johnson was a fellow signalman who had been under Burke's command at Vimy just like Edward. He had been one of those jocular types Edward never quite trusted. for he always wondered what was behind such forced heartiness.

"Fine, fine. Is this your wife? You always did attract the beautiful ones," Lenny chuckled. "Must be your quiet. reserved air."

Edward stiffened. "Stretching the truth as usual. Lenny? You'll have her thinking I had a hundred women over here. And I told her that I was too shy for the ladies." Edward put his arm around Ann. "Ann, this is Lenny Johnson. who was part of Signals."

As he introduced Ann, Edward worried. Lenny had been on guard duty and had caught Edward returning from a visit with Helene after curfew. Had Lenny reported him. Edward would have been sanctioned, perhaps losing his lance corporal stripes. Two packs of cigarettes and a story about an unnamed lover had secured Lenny's silence.

After they exchanged a few pleasantries. Lenny began to reminisce about Vimy. Edward nodded but said little and extracted them from the conversation as soon as politeness allowed. He escorted Ann to the next room, which opened onto an interior courtyard containing two small gardens edged with closely clipped boxwood. Doorways at either end were capped with coats of arms representing local aristocratic families. They stepped into the courtyard.

"I'm sorry for dragging you away. Lenny was never one of my favourite people."

"That's fine. It's good to get a breath of air." Ann looked around at the ivy-covered walls and cascading purple bougainvillea, stunning in its intensity. "The crowd is stifling, isn't it?"

Edward nodded then turned as someone else tapped his shoulder. "Walt Ingram. I wondered if you would be here. It's been a very long time."

"I've been looking for you all afternoon." He put his arm around Edward's shoulders.

"Ann, this is Walt Ingram. We fought together at the Somme." Though heavyset, Walt's face was handsome, except for a vivid scar on his left cheek.

"Edward is responsible for saving my life."

"Now, Walt. You don't need to go into that."

"My husband is far too modest, Mr. Ingram. I'd like to hear."

"Please call me Walt. Or you could call me Wingy. That's the nickname everyone used back then." He glanced at Edward. "I'll tell you the short version."

Walt began to describe the time at the Somme when they were laying cable to keep communications going between forward units and Division. Edward could almost smell the dank, fetid trenches and hear the rumble of action.

"It was exhausting work," said Walt, "but we had to get past our forward stations and re-establish the command centre. Three days later, I was manning the signal post when retreat sirens sounded. During retreat, signallers were often the last to go because we reported as each unit left their posts. As the last regiment passed headquarters, the brigadier sent his final message and we closed the signal office. Our last job was to cut the wires in all directions."

"Why did you do that?" Ann asked.

"To make sure the Germans couldn't use them. Then Edward and I hurried after the brigadier's staff. And that's when I was hit," Walt said. "Got this scar and a few others for my troubles, but Edward carried me back to safety."

Edward protested. "We didn't have too far to go."

"Doesn't matter. I wouldn't have made it without you."

* * *

Following the reception, Edward and Ann walked back to the hotel along narrow, winding streets crowded with bicycles, potted plants, stone steps, protruding balconies and lamps hanging overhead. The houses and buildings along the route they took were charming and typically French, many displaying wide windows on the ground floor and shutters in a myriad of colours on the second and third floors. If he had not been lost in thought, he would have seen French and Canadian flags held at right angles beneath almost every wrought iron balcony.

"Walt seemed nice. I liked hearing the story of what you did."

"He and I were together until the end. Even in Germany."

"You didn't keep up with him."

"No. I didn't keep up with anyone except Eric."

"I wish they could have come. Linda would have loved these charming towns."

Edward did not respond.

They passed a small square with a fountain marking its centre and two restaurants still busy with patrons sitting outside around impossibly small tables drinking wine and espresso in equal measure. Laughter rose and fell. Further on, they passed the Banque de France with its imposing oak doors closed and locked for the night, then a bridge, which led across the river.

Edward paid little attention to Ann's attempts at conversation, a melange of images clamouring for his attention. Clear, logical thinking eluded him as he wavered between two worlds. A dilemma that began with the invitation to Vimy had grown worse once they decided to come, and now he knew that a single act, a single choice, could risk everything.

10 JULY 27, 1936

With great care, Edward closed the door. Carrying his shoes in one hand, he tiptoed along the darkened hall until reaching a corner with two soft-cushioned chairs where he paused to put on his shoes before continuing downstairs. In the lobby he nodded brusquely at a man polishing brass door handles and went outside. He checked his watch. Five twenty-five. Time enough to contact Helene before Ann woke. All he needed was a public telephone.

Except for a battered, black taxi, the street was deserted. He turned right and walked briskly towards the Hotel de Ville. In a large square no more than ten minutes away, he found a phone booth next to the post office. Edward shoved his hands in the pockets of his trousers and leaned against a lamppost.

It had rained overnight and the air smelled of damp earth. A dachshund approached, legs prancing, stomach almost grazing the grass. The little dog sniffed Edward's shoes then tilted his head and wandered off. Church bells sounded the quarter hour just as a black-cassocked priest hurried by. At one end of the square, a door opened and a round-bellied woman wearing a white apron emerged to shake first one and then another cloth rug. A horse-drawn wagon clattered across the cobbles. Each sound and sight evoked the past.

Edward checked his watch again. He crossed the street and entered the phone booth. Taking Helene's slip of paper from his pocket, he lifted the receiver, inserted four coins one by one and dialled.

She answered after the first ring. "It's you, *enfin*," she said, husky and anxious.

With those few words, his tightness eased, his senses sharpened. North became south, adulthood became youth. His groin stirred with memories of passion.

"When can I see you?"

"I'm staying at Tante Camille's for a week."

He remembered her great-aunt's house near the small town of Beaufort, a dinner with Helene's mother and younger brother when Madame Noisette had insisted on meeting him, and two stolen days with Helene when her mother had gone to Paris.

"My wife . . . my wife is with me." The risk of what he was about to do slammed into him and he shivered despite the warm summer air. "I'll have to figure out how to get away."

"I have until Saturday." Helene's voice steadied. "Edward, are you sure?"

For a brief moment he wondered if he had lost his mind. "I'll call you once more to tell you when I'll arrive."

"*Bon. Adieu, mon chéri.*"

He did not answer, but cradled the phone, his head full of images, his heart thudding. He found a bench in the main square and sat for a while as the town came to life with vendors opening stalls and delivery trucks rumbling by. The aroma of fresh bread circled the air. The sun began to spread its warmth.

With a deep sigh, Edward rose.

* * *

Opening the door to their hotel room, he found Ann fully dressed, a mixture of bewilderment and anger on her face, freckles dark against pale skin.

"Where have you been? I've been worried."

"I'm sorry. I had to go out . . . memories were crowding me so much I couldn't breathe." He fingered the carved bedpost. "I kept seeing men blown out of the trenches, hearing the boom of guns and echoes of cannon blasts. I'm sorry, I should've woken you."

Edward paused. He had just lied to his wife. Not a tiny fib but an outright lie. *Can I do this?* he wondered. *Can I really do this to her?* The distance between them was no more than ten feet and yet he made no move towards Ann, no move to comfort her, to acknowledge the togetherness of their marriage, to draw comfort in return.

Ann moved towards him. She touched his cheek. "Sweetheart, I can help. I know I can help. If you'll just let me."

Hands in his pockets, he did not acknowledge her gesture or her words. The seconds ticked by. For a moment he wavered, but like a man hanging too long by his fingertips, his grip let go and he plummeted. Words emerged, one staccato pop at a time. "I . . . need . . . some . . . time. By . . . myself. To deal with things . . . things I thought I had dealt with before. Can you understand?" He caught her eyes for a brief instant.

"I don't know what to understand, what things you're dealing with. Talk to me, Edward." Ann reached out to touch him again then drew back. "You've been tense and preoccupied ever since deciding to come here. We've always handled problems together. Tell me so I can help."

"Don't you see? I can't!"

The words exploded from his mouth. Thudding silence followed. Ann stepped back.

"What's wrong with you? This isn't the way we are with one another. I love you. You're my husband. You can tell me anything. I know this trip has been hard for you, but if we talk about it, you'll feel better. I know you will."

He said nothing. Silence was easier than argument. At no time in his marriage had he imagined treating Ann this way. and for a moment, he thought of changing his mind. She did not deserve what he was about to do, but how else could he end the madness?

"Say something, Edward. Anything." Her eyes pleaded for him to come to his senses.

He made his voice hard and cold. "I have to be alone. I just told you that. What don't you understand?"

"Why? You have to tell me."

"How can I tell you why when I don't know the answer?" Edward shouted.

Ann's cheeks flushed with anger. "I don't even know who you are anymore."

"Neither do I."

"You're expecting far too much from me, Edward. Far too much. This isn't how a man treats his wife. This isn't you. But you've given me no choice. I'll go to London and wait for you until our ship sails. You'd better have an explanation by then."

"Thank you, Ann. I . . ." Her mouth trembled. She tilted her head in expectation, but he said nothing more.

Edward watched her pack. Nothing would ever be the same again, but the sequence he had set in motion was like a roller coaster cresting its highest peak. He could no longer turn back.

Ann moved like a robot, walking back and forth between dresser and suitcase, cupboard and suitcase, focused on the minutiae of folding each garment into its assigned place. She avoided looking at him or touching any of his clothes, as if the sting of his proximity were too much to bear. When she finished, she snapped the locks shut one after the other.

"Let me . . ." Edward moved to lift her case from the bed but retreated when he saw the set of her features.

She clutched her suitcase and opened the door, turned for one backward glance and walked out.

11 July 27, 1936

En route to the train station, the streets of Arras passed in a blur of leafy boulevards and canals busy with early morning skiffs. At a stoplight Ann saw a young boy unfurling a striped awning while a woman brought buckets of fresh flowers outside. When the light changed, the taxi jerked forward and turned the corner heading east. She wondered how the sun could still rise when every familiar certainty had vanished.

When she had awakened to find him gone, Ann had been worried but certain he would have a logical explanation. But when he had returned, his hands clenched and his body so tightly wound, her certainty had disappeared. When he told her he needed time alone, she wondered if her world was about to fall apart. Her body had turned icy cold. When he shouted, something inside her had snapped.

In shock, she had pushed aside thoughts of persuading her husband to be reasonable, of talking calmly and soothingly until he came to his senses, and instead had concentrated on the minutiae of packing. Folding and lifting article after article into her suitcase, closing the lid because that was what one did after packing, snapping the locks, grabbing the handle. Rote actions designed to barricade speculation into some future space and time.

She could not imagine why he refused to explain nor could she understand how Edward had become so unhinged. Was he crazy? Impossible. She knew no one as logical and pragmatic as her husband. To be sure, being in France was difficult and she could tell that many were affected by it. Edward was not alone in that. The few experiences he had described were awful, but he was a strong man, successful, one to whom others turned in a crisis. What clues had she missed? Why had he refused to let her help him?

At that hour of the morning the station was quiet, and after buying a ticket for Dunkirk, she took a seat where she could see a large clock and the board showing arrivals and departures. A porter pushed his wagon through the door, one wheel squeaking, and a woman wearing a straw bonnet swept the floor. The grim grey of the waiting room felt like a prison cell.

Trains came and went, disgorging passengers from Amiens and Lille and Valenciennes. From Albert and Ypres and Cambrai. Their names reminded her that only a few days ago she had been sightseeing, anticipating the ceremony and a chance for Edward to talk more about the war.

Numbness wrapped her body as the minutes passed. Boarding the train, concern, fear and bewilderment stirred together like a boiling stew. On the top step, she hesitated before hunching her shoulders into acceptance. She had to go. Edward had given her no choice. In London she would wait and hope that whatever craziness gripped her husband would release him back to her. Tears slipped down her cheeks as the train pulled away from the station.

In Dunkirk, a wide sweep of ocean signalled the unknown,

disintegrating threads of taut control like an anchor's rope unravelling in a storm. Mindless of choice, she took a small boat
carrying mail between France and England and endured hours
of wind and rolling swells. By the time the boat landed, she
was limp from the effort to control nausea and emotion and
dozed in fitful bursts on the train to London.

The city streets bustled, but Ann hardly noticed as a taxi
took her to Regency Manor, a small four-storey hotel on New
Cavendish Street. When planning the trip, they had decided
to include a week in London at the very end. Edward had
selected Regency Manor because it was modestly priced and
close enough to walk to Soho, the British Museum and several
other sites carefully listed in his pocket-sized notebook. Ann
stepped out of the taxi then watched it disappear down the
tree-lined street. She wiped a tear from her cheek and for one
wild moment, considered walking away.

Inside the hotel, a stout woman wearing a cream-colored
blouse pinned at the neck with a large cameo waited behind
the reception counter. When she noticed Ann, she pinched
her face into a slight frown, which made her upper lip almost
disappear.

Ann explained she was arriving a day earlier than expected. "Would you have a room available?"

"I will have to charge you an additional two pounds."

Ann nodded her agreement.

"I'm Miss Hoppington. Mr. Jamieson contacted me about
the hotel. When will he be arriving?"

"He's been detained in France," she said, wondering whether the woman could tell she had no idea when Edward would
arrive.

"You're in the Sheridan suite." With the barest of smiles,
the woman led the way. "There's a nice view of the park from
your windows," she said.

The room was more spacious than Ann expected. She
walked past a large double bed, its headboard framed by
heavy brocade cascading from high on the wall like the train

of a coronation robe, and gazed out the window.

"Yes. Thank you, Miss Hoppington. I think I'll go straight to bed."

The woman sniffed. "We'll see you at breakfast then. From eight until ten."

After Miss Hoppington left, Ann remained at the window. In the growing darkness all she could see of the park were magnificent stone gates and a stand of tall oaks. She thought of her children. Although evening in London, it would be mid-afternoon at home. Emily would be at camp by now, likely be at the waterfront. Her daughter loved to swim, taking pleasure in smooth, even strokes; the rhythm of moving through water gave her a sense of accomplishment and relieved the awkwardness she felt at being the tallest amongst her friends. Perhaps she'd be wearing the red swimsuit with the blue and white sailboats they had chosen together one afternoon in June.

Next she thought of Alex at the lake, making a mental tour of the cottage her parents rented most summers. The screen door that banged unless closed with care, the smooth rocks defining the fire pit near the picnic table, the sitting room full of overstuffed furniture, bunk beds covered in blue and yellow bedspreads, faded from years of use. She could almost hear the whoosh of pine needles brushing in the wind.

Her father might be organizing the fishing gear so he and Alex could go out at dusk. Last summer, Alex had learned to put his own worms on the hook and had loved to thrust them in her face and hear her squeal.

She gathered these images close, imagining the feel of Alex's plump cheeks and Emily's silken hair as if the very thought of them could protect her from all that she feared.

12 JULY 27, 1936

The door closed with a thud. For a moment Edward wanted to shake off the madness possessing him and run after her. He took a step then stopped and buried his head in his hands. *What have I done? I love Ann and Emily and Alex. I'm a husband and a father.* He slumped on the bed and stared at the ceiling. Like a leaf caught in an eddy, his mind spun round and round.

Edward had no idea how much time had passed when the sound of knocking roused him. He lifted his head. A second knock was accompanied by a few words of French.

"*Non, merci,*" he shouted.

A pause was followed by muttering and then footsteps that slowly retreated down the corridor. Edward's head ached. He wet a small towel and wiped his face, the cool moisture offering a moment of relief. Light streamed through the windows and he became aware of the sounds of traffic mixed with the repeated clang of a bell from the streets below. He had to go. Nothing could prevent him from seeing her. He had to know why she had not waited and who she had become. At the ceremony it had taken all his willpower to resist embracing her. Passion had surfaced so suddenly he had barely been able to stand.

Reaching for his suitcase, he began to pack, his hands fumbling to fold and place his clothes inside.

The distance between Arras and Beaufort was less than ten miles, but the time stretched so that every minute felt like five. Gradually, distress eased into anticipation. Dressed in gray flannels and navy blazer and with his bag on the seat beside him, he waited to see a familiar landmark. As the driver took a series of narrow back roads, sleepy, nondescript villages passed by, but when Edward saw a sign for Neuville-Saint-Vaast, he knew they were close, and not long after, the familiar rise in the road made his heart beat faster.

"*A gauche, ici,*" he said, less than a mile farther on.

"*Oui, monsieur.*" The driver slowed before turning onto the winding gravel path of Tante Camille's.

Edward leaned forward. Beyond a line of tall oak trees, he saw the sprawling house of faded limestone, the nearby pond, and gardens bursting with white hydrangeas, deep purple dahlias and clusters of yellow lilies. Never had he imagined seeing it again.

Exiting the taxi, he shaded his eyes against the bright sun, every nerve buzzing. He noticed a pot of geraniums on the front step and a brass knocker shaped like a lion's head. Edward put down his suitcase and cleared his throat. Before he could raise his hand to knock, Helene opened the door.

Uncertainty slipped away. She was there, close enough to touch, her figure fuller, clothes elegant yet simple, hair swept off her face instead of loose. Tiny wrinkles marked the corner of each eye. But these changes made no difference. They embraced, swaying back and forth, clinging to one another, forgotten contours remembered. She lifted her mouth to his and he drowned himself in her taste.

"Come," she said, clasping his hand in tapered fingers that had once roamed every inch of his body.

"Helene, I—"

She placed a finger against his lips and pulled him inside.

The house was the same and yet different, windows spilling light into all corners of the salon, well-worn furniture mixed with new. Flowers added bursts of colour, their scent evoking the languor of sleepy afternoons and forbidden pastimes. Beyond the entrance hall, tall ceilings and chairs decked with stuffed pillows created a feeling of spacious warmth. Two painted armoires flanked the fireplace. Piles of books and framed photos occupied almost every available surface.

Edward recalled that the kitchen was at the back of the house and the dining room through a door on the left. As he followed Helene he caught a glimpse of a rectangular table and tall-backed chairs, a window that overlooked the garden. She watched him as he remembered.

"Maman and Papa come here each summer," she said.

"And you?"

She shook her head. "I stopped coming long ago." Her lips twitched in a brief smile. "Maman has kept most of it the same."

He reached for her again and held her close. When his hand ran down her back to the curve of her hips, Helene's breath caught in the back of her throat. She pulled away and led him up the stairs to a room of white, where filmy curtains billowed in morning breezes. Without another word, she loosened his tie and unbuttoned his shirt then ran her hands over his chest.

"Dear, God," he said, crushing her to him. "I can't believe I found you."

At that moment, time slowed. Every sense quickened. His skin smouldered with desire. Her scent roused him. Threading his fingers into her silky hair, he kissed her, gentle at first and then urgent and fierce, as she opened her mouth to him.

"I want you," he said.

"And I want you."

Without taking her eyes off him, Helene removed her blouse and skirt, and let them fall to the floor. She unhooked her brassiere and pulled him onto the bed. Their bodies touched, just as they always had, with intensity and pleasure. His clothing tossed aside, he encircled her, lifting her close as she opened herself to him. He lay still, savouring the first moment of penetration.

Time disappeared. They lingered to nibble and caress, to whisper and taste, allowing desire to build until they both cried out, shuddering in release.

* * *

A tapping woodpecker stirred them from the hush that followed.

"Why didn't you wait?" he asked, drawing back to see her face.

"I did wait. For months and months, but your letters never came. At first I was not worried because Papa took us back to Paris and I thought it would take time for you to get my letter with our new address. But then, weeks went by without hearing from you. I became more and more distressed. I lost weight. I would not leave the house. Finally, Maman sent me to the doctor and he said I was on the verge of collapse and prescribed rest, so I went to the seaside to recover."

Edward remembered Madame Noisette, a vibrant, dark-haired woman who questioned him closely on the one occasion he was asked to dinner. He had liked her and Helene's brother, Jean, who was always eager for stories about the war. Edward had expected to get to know them better, along with Helene's other brother, Guy, and her father, after the war ended.

"But I wrote to you every week. Sometimes twice. Your letters just stopped."

Helene traced the line of his lips. "Last month," she paused before continuing, "I found out what happened. My father intercepted our letters. All of them." She began to cry.

"Oh, my God." Edward gripped her arm. "Our letters?

What kind of man would do that?"

"I can't believe it myself. Maman told me. She gave them to me."

"And how long did she know about them?"

Helene replied in a sad, flat tone. "A few years. If I hadn't decided to come to Vimy, I'm not sure she ever would have told me."

"It sounds medieval, from a time when daughters were considered chattel."

"They're old-fashioned—"

"I don't call that old-fashioned; I call it deceitful. I thought you no longer wanted me. Losing you was like losing myself. It took years before I could wake up in the morning and not think of you." He felt hot with anger and gripped her arm again. "Did you know that? Years."

She pressed her forehead against his.

"Why? Why did he do that?"

"I don't know. He called it a wartime romance."

"He had no right." Edward clenched his fist, imagining what he might do if he met Helene's father.

"I don't think I can ever forgive him." A tear trickled down her cheek and he wiped it away.

"We could have been together. All this time."

Helene sobbed and turned towards him. He drew her close and tried to still his anger, wondering if losing her had been some sort of punishment for surviving.

* * *

In mid-afternoon they went outside, Edward's arm around Helene's waist so he could feel her with every step. Blue haze marked the day. Sparrows chirped and crickets hummed with summer warmth. After circling the pond and smiling at the efforts of a swan to herd her seven little ones into the water, they walked down to the road and turned east towards Monsieur Garnier's farm, the place where they first met. The road was quiet, as were the fields beyond, giving the impression of a world lost in time. Helene stopped to pick a purple wildflower then touched his cheek with its feathery blossom, making him think of stolen summer hours when the war seemed far away.

The farm looked almost the same. Sheltering plane trees framed the drive leading to a traditional two-storey farmhouse. Thick vines hugged one wall of the house and wrought iron balconies embraced each second storey window. Beside the front door a wooden bench invited moments of relaxation and a bed of white hydrangeas with large, drooping blossoms anchored the far corner.

"Shall we look at the barn?"

"Do you think they'd mind?"

Helene shook her head. "I'll tell them we met here during the war. They'll think it's romantic. We French love romance."

She lifted the latch on the gate and they walked along the drive, past the house, towards the barn where soldiers danced on a long ago night in May.

"It seems smaller," he said, "as if whittled away by time."

"Do you remember?"

"I remember wondering how to get you to notice me."

"I didn't notice you. You cut in when I was dancing with your friend."

He chuckled. "Eric Andrews. He wasn't your type."

"And you knew you were?"

"Having dodged a bullet, I suppose I was cocky in those days."

Today he felt the very same pull and could no more resist it than he could stop breathing. He kissed the back of her hand.

"Let's go back," he said.

Sunlight danced across the bed. He slipped his hand beneath her blouse to caress first one breast and then the other. Helene's lips parted as she watched him through half-closed eyes. He undid her skirt and let it fall to the floor, a froth of soft pink, then unbuttoned her blouse and unfastened her brassiere. She nodded to his unspoken question and he stripped off his clothes and lay beside her on the bed. Unlike earlier, they did not rush, exploring one another as though they had all the time in the world. Desire built and when he could wait no longer, he pushed into her soft centre.

"*Doucement*," she said, lifting her hips in slow pirouette. "*Doucement, cheri.*"

Afterwards, he traced the strawberry mark on her hip and the faint lines where another man's children had stretched her skin.

"Tell me about your children."

She tensed a moment then relaxed against his body. "I have three: Claire, Juliette and Daniel, seventeen, sixteen and fourteen. When they were little, life was frantic." She drew his arm around her. "Claire is my quiet one. She's tall and slender and good at mathematics." Helene chuckled. "She certainly doesn't get that from me. We play tennis together most weeks. Daniel's my dreamer. He looks exactly like his father but has none of his practical nature. And Juliette is full of mischief. I think that's because she's the middle child. We live in the seventh arrondissement. It's on the Left Bank. Do you remember much about Paris?"

"Only a little."

"The area includes the Eiffel Tower and the Hotel des Invalides. When I was a girl, Maman preferred I stay away from the Left Bank, but Marie and I—do you remember me talking about my best friend, Marie?" He nodded. "Marie and I often walked the streets and parks in the seventh after school. We never told Maman, of course."

"How is your Maman?"

"*Tres bien.* A little arthritis but she says it is nothing."

Edward remembered an awkward conversation with Helene's mother after she had discovered that her daughter was seeing a soldier and had insisted he come for dinner so she could assess his suitability. Madame Noisette had taken Edward out to the garden, her long, grey skirt swishing as she walked, until they reached a bench beneath a pergola draped in wild roses. Lise Noisette had been sharp at first, her questions about the war and his family probing for insight.

He had described his duties in the signal corps, his schooling and his siblings, and when he felt more at ease, talked about playing hockey and fishing with his father. After almost an hour, Madame Noisette had finally smiled and invited him into the house, where the table was set with white linen and deep blue china and Helene's younger brother had asked questions about being a soldier.

"And your husband?" Edward said.

"Francois. He is Marie's older brother. He took a wound at Amiens. Our life is a good one. A pleasant marriage. I think you would like him."

"Does he know you're here?" He felt her nod.

"He knows I have come for the ceremony. And to remember. I told him about you before we married. I don't think he approves."

He pulled her close again, as though the nearness of her could relieve some of his loss. Helene sighed. As the sun's rays slipped beyond the bed to bathe the walls in fading light, her body relaxed into sleep. *This could have been my life*, he thought, though he could not quell the whispering inside his head that reminded him of Emily and Alex. And Ann.

"Did I sleep?" Helene stretched one arm above her head.

"You did."

"Et toi?"

"Not really."

She turned over so they faced one another. "You did not tell me about your children."

He pressed his lips together. "I have two—Emily and Alex."

Edward stopped. Saying their names felt like betrayal, as though speaking of them so briefly denied the essence of their being, the fact that they emerged from his seed and his love for Ann. *And I sent her away. I sent the mother of my children away.*

"It is all right. You do not need to tell me about them." Her face was so close he could see specks of grey in her otherwise blue eyes and tiny creases on the bridge of her nose.

"Yes, I do. They're part of me." He traced a finger beneath her eye where the skin was as soft as that of a newborn. "Emily is ten and Alex is eight, though he'll soon be nine. Emily is probably like your Claire, taller than her friends, quiet, very musical. She's at summer camp right now. I think she takes after me." He smiled. "We waited three years before she was born. I remember she had little wisps of brown hair and looked at me with solemn eyes, even when she was only a few days old. Alex is different. He's funny and boisterous. He has more energy than anyone I know, which makes it hard for him to concentrate on schoolwork. Sometimes I lose patience with him."

"Each child is different. This is what makes them so wonderful. I love how Daniel used to make me see Francois as a little boy and how Juliette reminds me of Jean."

"And your eldest?"

"Claire? Claire is my favourite. I know I should not have a favourite, but her personality blends so well with mine. Soon she will have many young men calling on her."

"Emily is much too young for that."

Her lips curved into a knowing smile. "Where do you work?"

"I work at the telephone company. It's been a good job. I was there even before the war. Do you remember?"

She nodded. "And your wife?"

"Her name is Ann. We were happy until this came along."

"The memorial?"

"Not just the memorial. Ever since October, when the invitation came, I've been thinking about you."

13 July 27, 1936

Over a simple dinner of fish steamed in white wine, Helene asked what happened after he left the area near Beaufort.

"We went south. The first place was Demuin, where I looked after wireless activities from the basement of a ruined chateau. The situation was frantic; I hardly had time to sleep. German desertions became an everyday affair because they knew if they surrendered, they would at least have something to eat. Then we were on the move, constantly setting up and tearing down exchanges. Once the Germans began to retreat, I went to Cambrai."

Helene poured another glass of wine. "And then?"

"Tough fighting there. Then the assault on the Hindenburg Line."

"I remember. That was when Papa told us the war was almost over. With his work in the War Ministry, he knew more than most. It was just before I went to Honfleur." A quiver marked her mouth. She set her glass down and wiped a tear at the corner of her eye.

"Are you all right?"

"I'm just thinking of how sad I was then."

He reached for her hand and brought it to his lips. A dove cooed from a nearby perch as a musky scent drifted in on the night breeze. "Would you prefer me to stop?" Helene shook her head. "I remember Burke explaining the situation to us in an abandoned bakery near Achicourt. With so many deaths, he'd been promoted to captain, which for some reason made him less demanding rather than more." He gazed into the distance. "We were far from the innocents who left home in 1915 with thoughts of a speedy end to the war. By then only Eric was left."

* * *

Burke had ordered the meeting for six p.m.

Before the meeting Edward had recorded the day's events in the battalion's war diaries. The words he wrote were always factual, detailing the work done by their sections but giving little indication of the hardship and danger they faced as battle raged. At times he had thought that his role as recording secretary was the only thing separating him from the slow insanity of war. Writing allowed him to deliberately consider each day's death and destruction, to look evil in the eye and spit on it with tight, precise sentences.

"There's to be a general offensive on the entire front," said Captain Burke once everyone had assembled. "From the Meuse to the English Channel, with four major thrusts delivered at crucial points in the line. The British will attack near Cambrai and Saint-Quentin, the French will push the enemy beyond Aisne, American troops will focus at Saint-Mihiel and the Belgians will move towards Ghent and Bruges. The idea is to deliver a series of crippling punches that will crowd Fritz towards defeat."

"Where will the Canadian Corps be, sir?" asked Lieutenant Routley, a serious man who joined the battalion in

1916. Wounded at Vimy, Routley walked with a stiff right leg, an injury that would have resulted in discharge two or three years earlier.

"Our forces will take Burlon Wood then provide a defensive flank for operations farther south, extending from the outskirts of Cambrai to Aubencheul-au-Bac on the Sensee Canal. We have much preparation to do."

Burke rummaged through a stack of papers spread out on a long marble counter once used to knead dough and prepare pastries.

"Lieutenant Franklin and I will look over proposed airline routes from Le Brulle to Queant. Lieutenant Routley, I want you and your men to lay lines in the vicinity of Le Brulle. We'll also need a team to install test boxes and one to fix routes near Hendecourt. Attack is set for the twenty-fifth, which means we have no time to waste. Specific orders will be ready for you in the morning."

From August twenty-sixth to October eleventh, they fought forward twenty-three miles with over thirty thousand men reported killed, wounded and missing. Then they attacked again, all four divisions across the whole front, with a heavy, creeping barrage across a distance of two miles. That day the Canadian Corps fired seven thousand tons of ammunition and captured over six thousand prisoners. The numbers were staggering.

As the Germans withdrew, they demolished bridges, cratered roads and railways, and took as many cattle, sheep, pigs and poultry as possible, making it increasingly difficult for the Allies to maintain supply lines to feed not only their troops but also hungry civilians and captured German soldiers. French citizens, thin and ragged, greeted them as they advanced, waving flags hidden since the beginning of the war, cheering them on and shouting *"Vive la France!"*

Captain Burke briefed them again, his gruff toughness and unreasonable demands easing as the end neared. In itself, that gave Edward hope; if Burke could afford to relax with his men, then Germany's days were numbered.

"One last battle, men, and it will all be over except the mopping up."

One last battle. The words echoed in Edward's mind. As soon as it was over, he would go to Beaufort and look for Helene. Though he wrote two or three times a week, he had not heard from her since early May. Five painful months. He had no idea what had happened, but he intended to find out.

They rested for more than a week; a rest much needed after being on the move with long forced marches, hours of lost sleep, supply problems, extensive repairs of roads, bridges, and communications lines. Valenciennes would be the last stand.

After Valenciennes, Germany was ready to surrender. On November eleventh, unaware of any official communiqué, Edward and his comrades instead became conscious of the absence of gunfire, a quiet filled with birdsong, the rustle of leaves and the creak of an unhinged shutter. Bells began to chime. Wild shouts filled the air as voice after voice swept the news along.

Clustered in front of their homes, in the fields and along the roadside, the French people seemed stunned at first. But soon Edward's unit heard the sound of drums and the unmistakable rhythm of the Marseillaise. Responding to the call of their homeland, families began singing. Then a procession formed as a man with only one arm held the French flag high in the air, leading whoever would follow into town. Cafes and restaurants filled to capacity, windows and doors opened wide, the smell of food wafted into the streets as though the town itself brimmed with joy.

Gathering in the town square to hear Lieutenant Colonel Gill's briefing, every soldier dreamed of home. The sun shone brilliantly. Gill's voice rang out.

"Men, today marks the beginning of the future. You have fought tirelessly to secure freedom for family and friends, for our country and the Commonwealth. It is a momentous victory, which we have achieved together. You have given of yourselves unstintingly and courageously. You have seen your comrades suffer, seen death close at hand and yet, you have endured. It is a testament to your valour and commitment that Canada has contributed so magnificently to the outcome of this war. The war is over. Peace has been won. We have made the world safe for democracy and soon we'll all go home to our families."

Edward heard a rustle in the back of the ranks and then the applause and cheers began. On and on it went. Elated warriors filled the square with their shouts and four years of pent-up emotions released like floodgates opening on a narrow gorge.

Gill raised his hand and held it there for some time until the square was quiet again.

"Signals officers will be reviewing the needs of the army during occupation. We will assess each and every soldier and proceed in stages to return you all to Canada as soon as possible." He stopped to look around the square as though he wanted to make eye contact with every soldier, one by one. "I am proud, so very proud, to have been your commanding officer for the past three years."

Emotion thickened Gill's gruff voice. He saluted his troops, holding his arm rigid for much longer than usual, then stepped down from the stage. Only a very few who were close enough saw the tears glimmering in his eyes.

The dead had lived on in Edward's nightmares. He remembered feeling like an old man, withered and worn, wise in ways he wished he were not, aware of all that sucks humanity from the marrow of men.

"What did you do after it was over?" Helene asked, bringing Edward back to the present. Candles flickered as summer breezes wafted through the window. Their plates were empty and only a little wine remained. She still held his hand.

"I went to Germany to help with the Armistice. After six weeks we were reassigned to Belgium and Burke gave me a week's leave, so I tried to find you. But you were gone and no one seemed to know where you were. I looked for Germaine, but her family had moved to Amiens." Edward traced a finger along her cheek. "Did you keep in touch with her?"

"I wrote a few times, but after the war everything changed. Do you remember she lost her fiancé?" He nodded. "Maman told me she married someone else and has several children. I have not come to Beaufort in years and this time I had no wish to see anyone from those days. Except you." Her voice trailed off.

"Before I left for England, I looked for you again. Two more weeks of frustration and dead ends. Eventually, there was no place to go except home." He clamped his lips together.

"I am so sorry, *chéri*. After Papa took us to Paris, I waited to hear from you and wondered why you did not write. I wrote letter after letter. Once I wrote to Eric, but I am certain my father concealed that letter too. I read your letters after Maman gave them to me. They made me cry. Each one sounded more desperate than the last."

"I was desperate. You were what kept me going. Even when you didn't write, I thought about our future together. Probably kept me alive. When I first went home I wondered why I survived." He kissed the tips of her fingers. "I saved your letters."

"You did?"

Edward nodded. "I read them again before I came. All of them."

Tears ran down her cheeks. He got up and put his arms around her. What had happened could not be undone. He was with her now and that too could not be undone.

14 JULY 28, 1936

After sleeping in fits and starts, Ann woke very early the next morning and wrote to her parents, describing the Vimy memorial, the King's stirring message, the French countryside and the battlefields they visited. She wrote nothing about her feelings and Edward's desire for solitude. Though they might not receive her letter until she was almost home, the mere act of writing and imagining her parents reading her letter in the garden, surrounded by honeysuckle and roses, gave her comfort.

During the weeks leading up to her own wedding, thoughts of a sedate marriage like her parents' had filled Ann with concern. As far as she could tell, they were happy, life bobbing along like a small boat on placid waters, one day much the same as the next: a peck on the cheek when her father arrived home, a few cryptic comments over the morning newspaper, her mother nagging about forgotten errands or an untidy tool shed, monthly games of bridge, roast beef every Sunday. At the time she had asked herself whether this was the kind of arrangement she had to look forward to with Edward.

Ann's emotions had seesawed back and forth between excitement and trepidation. Everyone had told her that these were the normal jitters of a bride, and Linda, who had known Ann since they were in second grade and who was to be Ann's maid of honour, had regaled her with a story about Eric being so concerned that Linda would call off their marriage, he had suggested that they elope.

"I almost said yes," Linda declared, watching Ann try on a floral print dress of pink and purple.

Ann turned her back to Linda. "Can you zip me up properly?" After the zipper was pulled to the top, Ann cinched the belt snug. "What do you think?" She twirled for effect, enjoying the way the skirt flared. "I can't believe you almost eloped. Edward never told me that story."

"Well, he wouldn't have, would he? Edward is always the soul of discretion. And look at how happy we are. You will be too. You and Edward are perfect together."

And we were, Ann thought. *For many years we've been happy. Now, I would give anything for the kind of stable contentment my parents have.*

She tapped the pen against her lip, wondering how to get through the day. Being busy had always been her way to keep demons at arm's length, so she took another sheet of paper and began a letter to Emily. Afterwards, she would write one to Alex.

*   *   *

"Good morning, Mrs. Jamieson. Did you sleep well?"

"Very well, Miss Hoppington." Ann was not about to admit otherwise.

When she arrived, the breakfast room had been busy, with only two tables unoccupied. She had taken the one nearest the window, which afforded an opportunity to watch fellow guests come and go. Miss Hoppington had bustled through a swinging door a few minutes later.

"Coffee or tea?"

"Coffee, please," Ann said.

Miss Hoppington's efficient service was accompanied by a disapproving frown, causing Ann to think that tea was the approved morning beverage.

"We serve a full English breakfast. Rashers, tomato, scrambled eggs and toast. Black pudding if you like."

"Just toast, please."

Miss Hoppington frowned again. "Will Mr. Jamieson arrive today?"

Ann tilted her head and said nothing.

After cold toast and two cups of coffee, she went outdoors and walked the few blocks to Regent's Park, oblivious to the elegant white stucco houses lining the outer circle road. Once inside the park, she found brief moments of solace in quiet pathways and colourful flowers, noticing children playing and dogs romping in the grass. Near the fishpond Ann sat on an empty bench, calmed by shades of green and tall protective trees, while birds darted and summer insects chattered.

She tried to think of nothing. Whenever her mind spun down a forbidden path, she pulled back into the immediate present, forcing herself to innocuous tasks like studying the veins on a particular leaf or counting the stones outlining the fishpond. At some point she must have dozed because she became aware of her neck jerking down and then up as she opened her eyes. *Goodness, I must look foolish,* she thought, glancing at a woman seated on the far side of the pond.

Ann leaned back, catching the sun on her face. Her watch indicated twelve o'clock, but she felt not the least bit hungry. With no purpose other than to pass the time, she got up to explore. Putting one foot in front of the other, deciding which turn to take as the path meandered and the occasional "good afternoon" were all she could manage. Finally, it was late enough to return to the hotel without arousing further curiosity.

As she lay in bed that night, tight threads of control snapped, releasing serpentine messages of doubt and wild speculation. She imagined Edward was sick with a dreadful disease and would die within months. She recalled the months of nightmares in their first year of marriage and wondered if these had returned and were driving Edward to the brink of despair. Though she continued to rack her mind for something she had said or done to cause him distress. Ann could think of nothing significant beyond the tension that had arisen after Edward decided they would come to France. Her deepest anguish was the possibility that he no longer loved her.

15 JULY 28, 1936

In the morning clouds marched across the sky, forming up then dispersing like troops on parade, the humidity less intense than the day before. Edward carried a picnic basket in one hand and held Helene's hand in the other.

"There's enough food in here to feed an army," he said.

She smiled. "We have places to visit."

"Lead on then. You're in charge."

He soon knew they were going to the shepherd's hut, the sanctuary they used whenever he had been able to come to Beaufort. The path looked overgrown to him, but Helene picked her way across a little stream full of tumbled rocks, over a stile and through a field of grazing cows, past a derelict house that looked vaguely familiar, and finally to a steady climb up the hill.

"The church is abandoned," she said, pointing to a small building with no roof. "I used to stop there each time you left and say a prayer for your safety."

He squeezed her hand. "Your prayers worked."

"Not all of them. I prayed you would return to me. God did not answer that prayer."

They continued to climb until the hut was in view. From the distance it looked the same, but as they drew near, he saw a roof full of holes and the door left ajar.

"Looks like no one uses it anymore. We can sit outside like we used to," Edward said.

"If I recall, we used to do more than sit."

He chuckled. "I remember how peaceful it felt to come here. Like an oasis."

"But as the war went on, you looked more and more tense when you came to visit. I tried to tell stories that would make you laugh. Do you want something to eat?"

He shook his head and spread their blanket in the sun, facing west with a view of rolling fields intersected by red roofs and church spires.

"I was angry with you for a while." Edward spoke as if picking up a thread of conversation. "I thought your promise meant nothing, that you had lied to me."

"I would never lie to you."

Edward noticed a brief frown wrinkle her brow but then she smiled again. He picked a clump of grass and let the blades trickle through his fingers. "I tried to tell myself that, but over time it became more difficult."

"But you kept writing."

"Mm hmm. I didn't know what else to do."

"And when you went back to Canada?"

"I went to England first. Thousands of troops were still waiting to go home." He shifted onto his side and looked up at her. "Not good having so many men pent up in a holding camp waiting to go home."

"What did you do while you waited?"

"In the mornings we drilled and in the afternoon there were sports and opportunities to learn. I studied accounting and read a lot. Nights were bad. Most of us drank too much. Do you know, before I left, I received a letter from the King and seventy-five dollars of war service gratuity?"

Helene lay on her side, her eyes on his. "Seventy-five dollars. After you risked everything. How could they?"

He shrugged. "It's so long ago. I'd forgotten really, until telling you the story. At the time I didn't care."

"Your parents must have been happy to have you home."

An image of his family waiting at the train station surfaced: his mother in tears, his father standing on a step to look over the crowd and be the first to catch a glimpse of his son. Simon and Stan and Cyril, who thumped his shoulders and grinned. Duncan and Jimmy darting amongst the soldiers. Mary and Dorothy all grown up and shy with a man who used to be their brother, Eddy.

"They were. But I wasn't very friendly when I first came home. I remember shouting at Mary once when she came up to my room. Poor Mary, she's the most timid of my siblings and I shouted at her." Edward lay on his back and looked at the clouds. A hawk circled, wings spread wide to catch the wind carrying the scent of wild roses and grasses baked in sunshine. "Now tell me what you did after I left."

"Marie and I spent hours together after I returned. Papa worked day and night and Maman was busy restoring our home, so Marie and I walked and talked most days. Even with sandbags, Paris was beautiful that spring. Part of me was happy to be back. While Marie was nursing, I saw friends and family."

"I didn't know she was a nurse."

Helene's smile faded. "She trained after her family moved back from London. I don't know how she did it. When I used to write letters for wounded soldiers in Beaufort, some of the sights and sounds were horrible. But I don't need to tell you that, do I?"

She laid her head against his shoulder and he drew her close. After the battle at Vimy Ridge, Edward had been in the Beaufort hospital for more than two weeks. He knew about soldiers screaming, the dull eyes of a man about to die, lingering odours of sulphur and vinegar and decaying flesh. Doctors and nurses had hurried by, sparing little time for anyone except those they could save. Occasionally a nurse had tossed a friendly look his way.

Sporadic summer sounds filled the silence. The skitter of a forest animal. Dead leaves rustling like rough sandpaper. A dragonfly with bright red wings edged in black flew past, its chatter reminding him of corn popping in his mother's cast iron pot. Edward watched the rise and fall of Helene's chest and heard her sigh.

"When I didn't hear from you I became worried. More and more worried as the weeks went on. I spent hours in my room reading your letters, remembering each time we were together, staring at your picture. Marie tried to keep my spirits up but eventually I would not even see her. I ate so little and grew so thin that Maman insisted I go to the doctor.

"When the doctor said I needed a quiet place to rest, Maman sent me to Honfleur where my father's sister lived. Chantal was wonderful. She knew when to be quiet and when to talk and when to ask questions. I told her all about you. Every day we walked on the beach and watched the waves roll in and children play. I suppose it gave me perspective. A time to understand that life goes on."

Edward considered his next question with care. Could he ask why she did not come looking for him? Did he want to know the answer? He pulled a stem of purple-tipped clover from the ground. "Why didn't you go back to Beaufort and wait for me?"

Helene's body tensed. "I could not go. I was in Honfleur and still very ill. You must remember how much *agitation*—I do not remember the word in English—there was. Escaped prisoners, soldiers returning home, convoys moving all over France. And Edward," she propped herself up on one elbow so she could look at him, "I had not heard from you since April. What was I to think?" She sank back onto his shoulder. "I'm sorry, *chéri*. I wish I could do it over again."

What does it matter now? Edward thought. *We can't undo the past. We can only accept it and go on.*

He said nothing for a while and Helene seemed to sense his need for silence. He stroked her arm then wound a strand of her hair around his finger. The sun had disappeared behind a bank of clouds and now the wind sprang up and he heard the quiet rustling of leaves.

"When did you meet your husband?"

Helene told him about seeing Marie's brother at a family party. "It was almost a year later. Francois's wounds were bad. His leg was damaged and he had many shrapnel scars. In the early months, the doctors thought they might have to amputate. But he was lucky. Do you remember he used to write to me?" Edward nodded. "I did not know he was fond of me. Since I no longer had any hope of finding you, when he proposed, I accepted."

"When did you marry?"

"In . . . in November of 1919." She looked away and he wondered what she was remembering.

Helene said nothing more and Edward chose not to probe. "I didn't marry until 1923. When I met Ann, for one crazy moment I thought it was you. I suppose that's why I asked her out at first. But she wasn't you, and gradually I liked her for herself. And loved her. And my children."

"Children make life worthwhile, don't they?"

"They do. I always wanted children." He did not mention the times he and Helene had talked about children.

"Francois is angry with me. As soon as I read the notice about Vimy, I knew I had to come. He does not understand. The war is a topic we avoid."

Edward leaned on one elbow. "Why are we here, Helene?"

"This was our special place. I wanted us . . ."

"I don't mean here at the hut; I mean why did you ask me to Beaufort?"

Helene picked a buttercup from the grass beside the blanket and began to remove the petals. "When I saw the notice, I thought the ceremony might offer a chance to close a chapter of my life. I imagined seeing the memorial and feeling close to you again and that in some way this would set me free of all my memories. I needed to know whether you had died." She whispered the last word.

"But when Maman gave me your letters, all that changed. Suddenly there was a chance, a real chance that you had lived. I could not stay away. I could not. The thought of you coming to France was such a wild fantasy and every day I told myself not to be ridiculous. And then I saw you. You, Edward. The happiness I felt was unimaginable. I had no choice but to ask you to see me. No choice at all."

She touched his cheek and kissed him, a soft kiss that changed in intensity as she reached to pull him closer.

16 JULY 29, 1936

Before visiting the park the following day, Ann found a news-stand a few blocks from the hotel and purchased *The Times*. With only two days until the opening ceremonies, the paper's headlines focused on Hitler's handling of the Olympics and speculation about other countries' participation. *Hitler Allows Only Aryans to Compete* screamed one headline while another said *100,000-Seat Stadium Bigger than Los Angeles Games*.

She found her way to the fishpond then sat on a wooden bench and began to read an article summarizing events since the Olympic Committee awarded the games to Berlin. For a while the paper distracted her, but after realizing she had read the same paragraph three times, she put it aside and instead watched the comings and goings of those in the park. At noon a young priest appeared, stopping to watch the lazy meander-ings of the pond's plump goldfish and a turtle attempting to climb upon a small rock. Ann studied his features trying to decide whom he resembled.

"Good afternoon." The priest bowed slightly.

"Hello." Wondering if the priest had become aware of her scrutiny, she blushed.

"Lovely day. Do you come here often?"

"No. I'm just . . . visiting."

The man's smile made him look even younger. "I always come at noon. A much needed break from grumbling old men and needy parishioners. Oh, dear. I can see I've shocked you. You're probably thinking that a priest should be more charitable but some days test the patience of Job. This was definitely one of them. Good. I've got you smiling. You looked so forlorn, I had to stop for a chat."

"Are you always so bold?"

"I am. Miss Simons always told me it would be my undoing. And if the priesthood is an undoing then she was right. Bless her soul." He made the sign of the cross.

"Who was Miss Simons?"

"My English teacher. I had her for both lower-sixth and upper-sixth. That woman ruined English literature for me." He looked at his watch. "Goodness. Look at the time. I'll have to be going. Bridget will have lunch ready and there's Mass to say at one."

Ann laughed. "Good-bye."

"Perhaps I'll see you tomorrow."

She watched the young man saunter down a shaded path. Just before he disappeared around a bend, he turned and gave a jaunty wave. Her mood a bit lighter, Ann opened her book.

Early afternoon brought out the prams pushed by a mix of nannies and mothers. Like dutiful soldiers on parade, the nannies marched along with eyes forward, while the mothers ambled, talking to their babies as though they could understand. A young woman pushing a wicker carriage while chatting with an older woman made Ann think of long walks with her own mother after Emily was born.

After two years of marriage, Ann had wondered if they would ever have children and she had kept herself busy with volunteer work at the Red Cross. She had known at the time that Edward would never accept her taking on a proper job so working three days a week for no pay had been a compromise. Within four months, Ann was pregnant. Despite Edward's concerns, she had continued at the Red Cross until Emily was born.

Emily's arrival had been swift. At Ann's insistence, the birth was at home with a midwife in attendance and a doctor on call just in case. Life changed after that and Ann found contentment at last in the tasks of motherhood and looking after their little home. When Emily was nine months old, they moved to Montreal and Alex's arrival a few months later had triggered post-partum depression.

I wonder why that happened, she thought now. *What would I have done without Hannah?*

Ann resumed reading. By mid-afternoon park traffic eased and quiet settled in. Ann closed her book and thought about Edward. When she remembered how he had shouted, anger surged and she clenched her fists to keep them still. Then she remembered his growing anxiety as they toured battlefields and nearby towns and his retreat into silence and too many glasses of wine, his eyes clouded with what she imagined to be terrible memories and his body somehow shrunken. Ann frowned. She knew he was distressed, profoundly distressed, but could not fathom why he would send her away.

What else could I have done to help him? she wondered.

Two boys ran past chasing a ball and laughing. A mass of clouds billowed on the horizon. Ann's head ached. She grabbed her book and newspaper and with her handbag over one arm made her way towards the south gate to find a few shops to browse and pass the time until dinner.

Short blocks full of large red mansions and curtained windows lined Marylebone High Street. At ground level were elegant shops offering tasteful eveningwear and the occasional café or hair salon. Ann stopped before each window display, pausing to examine the colour of a gown or an intricate piece of beadwork or a shawl of delicate silk. Absorbed in thought, she was startled by a crack of thunder and looked up to see the sky had turned dark. After a threatening flash of lightning, she turned back in the direction of the hotel, but within seconds small drops of rain found their way through the canopy of trees. She hurried, choosing a left turn at a familiar intersection, and a few minutes later was relieved to see Regency Manor in the distance. Larger drops splashed down, seeping into her lightweight summer clothes. By the time she entered the lobby she was drenched from head to toe.

"Damn," she muttered.

Miss Hoppington looked down her nose in disapproval. "Good afternoon, Mrs. Jamieson. Perhaps you should take an umbrella next time. This is London, you know."

"Perhaps," Ann said, attempting to hold her head high despite the squishing sounds coming from her wet shoes.

"Will Mr. Jamieson arrive today?"

Ann pretended not to hear.

17 July 29, 1936

The following morning, Helene moved about the kitchen at Tante Camille's with practiced ease, clearing away their simple breakfast then making second cups of espresso. Since Edward was unaccustomed to the pungent, gritty brew, she added boiling water to his cup but drank her own in one quick gulp.

"How do you do that?" he asked.

She grinned. "I have years of experience. When I was little, Maman mixed mine with warm milk, but in Beaufort, Grandmere made our coffee every morning and only espresso was acceptable. I'm sorry you didn't meet my grandmother. You would have liked her. She was determined but kind and taught me a lot about life. I remember her telling me that she and my grandfather married without being in love. I was only fifteen and the notion of being intimate with someone I did not love was shocking. Very wise, my grandmother."

"Would she have approved of me?"

Helene paused to consider his question. "She would have

liked you but I don't think she would have approved of this."
She waved her index finger back and forth then turned away
to wipe the counters.

"What are we going to do today?"

"Do you remember the hill where Jean and I watched
preparations for Vimy Ridge?"

"I do."

"I thought we would walk up there."

He stirred his coffee round and round, the spoon clanking
against the mug, then blew on the surface before taking a
sip. When they first climbed the hill in 1917. Edward had no
idea where Helene was taking him and had been shocked to
look down at the battlefield less than two months after Vimy
Ridge. So shocked with the raw reality of what lay below. he
had almost fainted.

"Very hot," he said, gesturing at the coffee.

"We don't have to go."

"My doctor would have said going there is part of the healing process." Every session with Billings had been part of the
healing process, and gradually Edward had improved.

"You're not sick, are you?"

"I used to have nightmares. Doctor Billings specialised in
men with shell shock. That's the term he used."

After the war, he had been embarrassed at what he considered unmanly behaviour, his sheets drenched with sweat
and the whimpering that woke his mother at night. Later his
nightmares also woke Ann, who urged him to seek help. Eric
gave him Billings' name.

"We should go to the hill," he said. "Definitely. we should
go." He took another gulp of coffee, stood up and reached for
her hand. "I'm fine."

Though Helene looked uncertain, she gathered some fruit
from a large bowl and wrapped a few slices of cheese and bread
in a small cloth. When they left the house she took them west
along a worn path behind the old chicken coop. then north to
a fence and beyond into a rocky field bordered on one side by

open forest. Helene talked of other matters until he was ready
to tell her more.

"My nightmares were about the war. I would dream of
tunnels. Usually I was running. I had to get somewhere but
every turn I took was wrong or a dead end. Dogs leapt at me,
their fangs bared, saliva hanging in long threads. I stepped
into puddles oozing mud. I stepped on bodies. Sometimes a
hand reached out to grab me but I always twisted away in
time. Dead men leered and laughed. When I tried to touch
them they fell to pieces.

"The noise was deafening. Gunshots, explosions, sirens.
Airplanes overhead. I held my ears but the sounds never went
away. I never reached my destination. Just when I thought I
was there, I saw a man pointing his rifle at me. He pulled the
trigger and I woke up."

"What did the doctor say?"

"He didn't ever say much. He just asked questions until I
found the answers. It was an exhausting process."

"Do you still have them?"

"No. Once I spoke about them, they went away." Edward
did not disclose how long that process took. "They're about
Vimy Ridge and the sniper's bullet that almost killed me. I
suppose I always knew. But for some reason, I couldn't admit it. Sometimes I would hear my friends calling to me in
strange-sounding voices or the shriek of a dying horse." Edward stopped at the edge of a creek that trickled over tumbled
boulders. "I remember when Bill Simpson was killed. We were
together that day repairing some lines the Germans cut as
they retreated. October fifteenth. Less than a month before
it was over. One moment he was talking to me and the next
moment blood was gushing from a hole in his throat. For an
instant he looked surprised. And then . . ."

When he said nothing further, Helene put her hand on his
arm.

". . . then he just fell on to me." Edward's body sagged as
though reliving the weight of his friend's collapse. "Bill and

Eric were the only ones left. After that there was only Eric. And me."

"Do you and Eric talk about it?"

"Not much. He tries sometimes but I shut him down. I can't bear it."

"There is no shame in dreaming about the war."

"I know that now. But not then." He was surprised how much he had disclosed. "I'd forgotten how I could talk to you."

Helene's smile at his compliment quickly faded. "We may have war again," she said. "My husband has two large orders from the French military. Something to do with airplane motors. He's worried."

"I'm worried too. Hitler's become a tyrant. Everything I read spells trouble."

"Papa says . . . damn, I promised I would not mention him." Her mouth flattened into a thin line.

"I'm going to join the reserves. I have to do something," he said, stopping to help her over a muddy section. "Someone has already approached me. They won't send me over here because one of my lungs is damaged." Helene frowned. "Don't worry. It's been that way for years."

"How did it happen?"

"Gas. A surprise attack one night." He did not tell her that in order to finish sending a message, he had neglected his gas mask until it was almost too late.

While talking, they kept a slow, steady pace to the summit, the sun ebbing and flowing as they passed through forest shade and open hill.

"Jean first brought me up here. I forced him to after he told me where he was going every night. He had been watching for weeks by then. I told him I would tell Maman if he did not show me. After that first time, I could not stay away. The work you soldiers did was terrifying but fascinating. I knew right away there would be a battle."

She had told him these details long ago, but Edward did not interrupt. Sometimes the telling had to be repeated.

"Unless it was snowing or too cold, we came up here, leaving the house after Maman was asleep."

"How much could you see at night? We were always so careful to avoid any lights in case the Germans sent planes overhead."

"Some nights were better than others. If the moon was more than half full we could make out the shapes of men and machinery. And we could hear. Jean and I had arguments about what was going on, but soon we knew it would be big."

"Were you worried?"

"Very worried. Tante Camille's was so close to the front, I wondered if we would be safe. Jean made me promise not to tell Maman, but every day I wondered. And when the hospital tents went up, I knew it would be soon."

"I'm sure you and your mother worried throughout the war."

"We did. Almost every day Maman or I went into Beaufort for news. We could hear the artillery from twenty miles away and sometimes it sounded very close. Here we are." Helene pointed at a cluster of rocks near a thicket of bushes. "I have not been here in years."

She held out her hand and together they stepped close to the edge and peered down. He saw a peaceful valley, wide and green, crisscrossed with stone fences, the ridge marking its eastern flank, and the memorial, stark and white, standing guard. No ghosts called out to disturb the happiness of being with the woman he loved.

"It's beautiful now, isn't it?"

"Yes," he said and put his arm around her waist.

18 July 29, 1936

That night while Helene slept, Edward listened to the wind groaning through the trees and the creaking of Tante Camille's house. Pale light glanced through the bedroom window, casting vague shadows on the closet door. Sleep grabbed the edges of his mind then retreated into wakefulness. He had no idea what to do.

Images of Ann packing her suitcase whirled like a merry-go-round. Never would he have imagined adultery, a word he associated with dishonour and cruelty and unmanly behaviour. Yet here he was, lying beside Helene after a lovemaking so tender, he had almost wept.

How could he still be so in love with her?

No future made sense. A future with Ann meant leaving Helene once again. Just the thought made his soul feel empty. A future with Helene meant denying his children, his marriage and his love for Ann. She would hate him. His family would never understand. No one would understand.

Ending a marriage would be like death: denial followed by anger then grief and likely, depression. How could Ann possibly cope with divorce? And his parents would be shocked. His mother might eventually come around but his father would never accept such a decision. Where would they live? Helene would never leave her children and without his job, he would have to begin again. And what about the possibility of war?

He slipped out of bed and stood naked by the window, lanky limbs and tight shoulders casting a blurry shadow on the wall. The breeze shifted as raindrops began and he heard a far-off rumble.

* * *

In the morning when Helene came down, Edward was in the living room reading. She wore a sweater and pants, her cheeks pink from yesterday's sun. The wind hurled raindrops against the house, the sky almost as dark as night.

"I didn't hear you leave the bed."

"That's because I tried not to disturb you." He set his book aside.

"A true gentleman. What do you want for breakfast?"

"Hmm. Just toast, I think."

"Well, I'm hungry. Making love uses lots of energy." She stood behind him and rubbed his shoulders. "What are you reading?"

"A book I bought on one of the tours. *Memoirs of an Infantry Officer*. It's by Siegfried Sassoon. He's also a famous poet. Apparently the story is based on his war experiences. Rather heavy stuff." He gestured at the bookshelves. "Almost everything here is French."

"Of course they are in French." She laughed. "Where did you tour?"

"Lille, Ypres, Cambrai, Amiens. For six days we toured the towns and battlefields and memorials. Row upon row of crosses."

"How did you feel?"

"Honestly?" She nodded. "Depressed. And numb. Sad. Sometimes I think I shouldn't have come. But then we wouldn't have this."

He kissed the palm of her hand and pulled her onto his lap. Helene ruffled his hair then touched the curve of his ear.

"Why don't you come to the kitchen with me. If I stay here, we will get very hungry."

All day it rained. Thunder came and went, reminding him of the sounds of war. Lightning lit the sky in jagged streaks. From time to time they spoke, but for the most part they allowed the quiet to sit amongst gentle glances and the occasional soft caress, as if they had all the time in the world.

When the rain stopped after dinner, Helene turned on the radio and he held her close, one hand on the small of her back, while they danced on the porch and trees shed the day's rain in a pitter-patter of sound. Slow, sultry music spun images of Paris cafes, the clink of glasses and low chatter of lovers bent over narrow tables.

Damp earth released nature's aromas, stripping away gentility. She bit his lip and he responded, pulling her closer so she could feel his thickening erection. They swayed to the music. He kissed her neck and then her eyes. She tilted back so he could see her face and while he held their hips together, she unbuttoned her blouse and then his shirt and brushed her breasts against him. He kissed her again and felt the pulse gather inside his body.

"I want us to be together," he said after they made love.

All day, as he attempted to read, as they talked, as he lifted a glass of burgundy to toast her with his eyes, he had weighed this decision. All day his thoughts had churned, seeking the right path. But there was no right path, only the certainty that he could not exist without her.

She cupped his cheek and held his gaze, then dropped her eyes. "I don't . . . it is not possible. Not anymore. This is all I have thought about, but I cannot see anything except pain for those we love. I don't think I can do that to my family." She raised her eyes. "How could we live with ourselves?"

"Over time they would—"

"And what would their pain do to us?" She grabbed his hand. "I think it would destroy what we have. Maybe not immediately, but gradually. Regrets would become resentment. We cannot secure our happiness at the expense of others. *C'est impossible.*"

"Why should we always put others' needs ahead of ours? Duty. Responsibility. Haven't I done enough?"

"They depend on you, Edward. They need you. Your wife, your children, your parents. I know you cannot abandon them. I cannot ask you to do that."

"But what about us?" His voice was hoarse. "You promised you would wait. You can't leave me again. I don't think I'll survive a second time."

"Darling, I wish . . ."

His body stiffened. "Why did you ask me here if you knew we couldn't be together?"

"I did not know. You have to believe me."

"You said you love me."

"I do, but we can't . . ."

Anger surged and he rolled away from her, grabbing his pants from a wicker chair and pulling them on. Though Helene called his name, he rushed through the bedroom door, slamming it behind him before thumping down the stairs. Barefoot, he went outside and ran towards the road, mindless of the sharp gravel drive. At the bend, he leaned against a tree, pounding the bark with his fists until they bled.

Helene was sobbing when she found him there and wrapped her arms around him, her tears distilling his anger into tiny drops that seeped away as he returned her embrace.

19 AUGUST 1, 1936

On the fifth morning, a misty drizzle blanketed London, the clouds so low Ann could barely see across the street. Dressing for breakfast, she neither fixed her hair nor applied a touch of lipstick, and even Miss Hoppington left her alone as Ann drank a cup of black coffee and tore a slice of toast into pieces. To pass the time, she wrote letters and read the newspaper then struggled with a crossword. No matter how long she considered the clues, a seven-letter word for happiness eluded her.

Finally, a glimpse of sun signalled escape.

A night of rain had left wide puddles along the street. Ann returned to the park and found an unexplored path where trees hung dark and heavy, like a canvas pregnant with gloom. She had no desire to sightsee, no desire to do anything except plod along, pondering Edward's continued silence. Eventually, she found her way to the fishpond and sat with shoulders hunched and eyes drawn inward.

Five days of not knowing why Edward had sent her away.

Five days of not knowing where he was. Nothing felt certain anymore. Their ship would leave in a few days and she had no idea if Edward would be on it.

Two black shoes appeared in her peripheral vision.

"Can I help in any way? I'm Father David. We spoke the other day."

Ann sniffed and shook her head. She said nothing, afraid that quiet tears would turn to noisy, uncontrollable sobs.

He sat down. "Sometimes talking helps."

Ann flicked her eyes in his direction then looked away. A spinning leaf settled on the pond and a fish surfaced to investigate, mouth puckered. A burst of laughter rose and fell. The priest's hands rested on his knees.

"It's my husband," she began. "He's . . . he's not here. I don't know where he is or if he'll ever come to get me."

In later days, she could not recall what prompted her to share her worries with a stranger. Perhaps it was his calm demeanour, perhaps his still, blunt fingers or perhaps just the knowledge that he was a priest accustomed to human tragedies.

Disconnected sentences gradually gave way to a flood of words as Ann disclosed her fears that Edward would never return, that her marriage was over, that life would never be the same, that she would not have the strength to go on. When she finally stopped, they sat in silence again for several minutes. A calming, comforting silence.

"Life is never easy and never what we expect," he said. "That's part of the mystery God gives us. But He never asks too much and often points the way forward, if you listen with your heart."

"I don't know what to do." Ann twisted her handkerchief. "I'm afraid Edward won't come back."

"You'll have to find a way to forgive him when he does." Father David's voice had an Irish cadence, with rhythms like a soothing lullaby.

"You sound so certain he'll come back."

He studied her face, his eyes holding hers. "Your stories have told me what kind of man he is. That kind of man won't abandon his wife and children. But he may not be the same man he was. It all depends on the demons he's been fighting." He rose slowly to his feet. "I have to go now to say Mass at St. Mildred's. You are welcome to come with me, if you wish."

Ann considered his suggestion. "I'd like that," she said. "But I'm not a Catholic."

"God doesn't worry about things like that." A dimple creased his cheek.

Words seemed unnecessary given what she had already shared with Father David, and they walked together without speaking. His concern provided a glimmer of hope. As they left the park, they turned right along the sidewalk, crossing several intersections until reaching a squat stone church situated on a corner, the grounds well tended with flowerbeds full of colour.

"I particularly like the roses," he said, stopping to sniff an unfolding blossom of yellow edged with pink. "One of our parishioners has looked after them for years, although she is almost eighty now and I worry that it's becoming too much for her. Come inside. Why don't you find a comfortable spot? The service starts in fifteen minutes." He rested a hand on her shoulder. "It's a soothing place to be."

Ann sat on the left, contemplating a circular stained-glass window bathed in light. She bowed her head and closed her eyes, allowing calm to settle over her like a soft, warm blanket. Candles flickered on a table in the corner. Hints of incense filled the air.

During the short service, she took comfort from the soothing sounds of liturgy, the motions of kneeling, sitting and standing, the priest's chanting and prayers.

"Thank you," she said, shaking hands with Father David on the way out.

"Will you be all right?"

"I don't know. But you've helped me steady myself."

"Don't hesitate to visit again," he said. "God is always here."

20 AUGUST 1, 1936

Edward watched Helene board the train to Paris. He looked away, unable to hold her gaze, and stared into the distance, failing to notice the ancient statue of St. Benedict, his arms raised to bless the multitudes, and distant slopes of gold-tipped grass.

Turning back, he committed to memory her scarlet lips and auburn hair and shapely neck, the curve of her thigh and slender legs. In a dark suit and plain white blouse, she looked austere, the clothes signalling distance and finality. In the warmth of early morning, he felt lost, dangling on a tightrope between what was and what might have been.

"We will have memories of being together." She brushed a tear from her face.

He had nothing left to say. After years apart and a few days of rekindled passion, she was leaving him again. He thought of their last night together, passion embracing them until the stars flickered and disappeared.

Helene waited at the top of the stairs, her eyes never leaving his. As the train whistle blew and the wheels began to turn, she braved a small smile.

Grief gathered within him like surging rapids. Somewhere in the crevices of his conscience, a small voice whispered that she was right; there was no solution that would allow them to live together happily. They had had five days, and now, somehow, he would have to go on with his life.

Edward watched her disappear, his body as rigid as the stone spires of the Vimy memorial where they had found each other. When the train was merely a speck in the distance, he slumped against the wall, and tears ran unchecked down his face.

* * *

After leaving his suitcase at a run-down hotel, all he could do was put one foot in front of the other, wandering the streets of Arras, his mind incapable of coherence. A sudden rain dampened the city and he found a bistro on a narrow, winding street and ordered a glass of Calvados, which he swirled and sniffed and sipped for most of an hour, watching patrons come and go, mainly old men who seemed worn and rumpled and talked in garrulous bursts while waving thin cigarettes with a smell that reminded him of soldiers smoking in crowded trains on the way to the front.

When he imagined going to London, he could not conceive what he would say to Ann. She would be looking for some sign that he was all right, that he loved her. Would she see through his story of dealing with the emotions of war? Should he confess? Could he bear the consequences of losing Ann's love as well as Helene's? He drained his glass and signalled a slouching, black-clad waiter for another.

I never should have come to France, he thought. *A fool's decision.*

But his body and soul had moved of their own volition, hypnotized by the potential of Helene's presence. Like a well-banked fire, their love still burned and he relived each moment, each touch, each look and phrase. Now that she was gone, he felt as though his life had been smashed to pieces—pieces that could never fit back together. He sniffed his drink, the amber liquid hinting of apples and dried apricots and toasted nuts. Edward drained the glass.

The waiter asked if he wanted another, but this time Edward shook his head, and after paying the bill, asked for directions to the telegraph office.

* * *

By the time Ann left the church, the bustle of midday traffic had eased. A double-decker bus drew to a stop, allowing four nuns to exit, and the sight of them crossing the road, chatting and waddling like friendly penguins, made her smile. Ann nodded as the women passed then retraced her steps through the park and on to the hotel. As she entered the lobby, Miss Hoppington rushed forward.

"I've received this telegram for you, Mrs. Jamieson. Perhaps it's from your husband."

"Thank you."

She took the small yellow envelope but said nothing more and turned to mount the stairs. When she reached the privacy of her room, she removed a thin slip of paper.

CONTEMPLATION FINISHED STOP YOUR PATIENCE HAS BEEN WONDERFUL STOP ARRIVING TOMORROW 5PM STOP MY BEHAVIOUR WAS DREADFUL PLEASE FORGIVE STOP

Clutching the telegram, she sank into an easy chair by the window. The message contained no hint of what was wrong, no words of love. *What am I supposed to forgive,* she wondered. *Where has he been for five days?* Immobilized by a sense of foreboding, she stared at passing cars and buses and thought about home.

21 AUGUST 2, 1936

Lost in a blur of wrenching sorrow, Edward remembered little of the trip to London. Images struck like lashing blows, crushing attempts at logical thought. Ann, half-asleep with Emily tugging at her breast, gave way to a memory of walking his wailing son up and down in the middle of the night. He remembered Ann's bewilderment as she turned to leave, suitcase in hand, and Helene's face when they made love for the last time, full of poignant regret.

The train jolted north, occasionally stopping at nondescript towns. Thankfully, he sat alone in a sparsely populated coach. Near the front, two women were dressed in black, their sporadic conversation punctuated by weeping. On the right, a priest, his lined face a testament to the burdens of his calling, alternated between his rosary and his prayer book, occasionally dozing against the window frame. Two seats ahead, a young businessman crossed and uncrossed his legs, impatience increasing with each delay, the man's otherwise handsome face bearing a deep purple birthmark on his left cheek. Beyond the window, rolling fields and small villages sparked memories of war, each striking hard until he felt like a losing boxer, hoping for a final, knockout punch.

Disembarking at Calais, Edward paused at a café to purchase an espresso and baguette then found a boat heading across the channel. Normally he loved being on the water, but today there was no joy in contemplating seagulls soaring overhead and the smell of the wind and gentle swells of a calm summer sea. His thoughts clashed and clanged amidst the whoosh of waves and bright clouds that gathered over the sheared cliffs of England. Blue seas sharpened, leaping wide, rushing towards Dover's coast, pulling him closer to Ann. As they docked, he heard the grating slash of pebbles along the shore.

Arriving at Paddington station, he found a taxi and ignored the driver's attempts at conversation. His brain was sluggish and he was unshaven. His clothes looked as though he had slept in them.

"What will people think?" he muttered, then laughed, a harsh, barking sound.

* * *

Ann sat in the lobby. She had been there more than an hour, lifting her head at the slightest noise. She waited and wondered, attempting to still thoughts leaping alarmingly to ever more dreadful scenarios, a deadly disease, some sort of mental breakdown, an attempt at suicide. She felt like someone about to jump from a very high cliff into the smallest of ponds, where the chances of finding the one spot deep enough to absorb the weight of her fall were next to zero.

Finally, he came through the door, looking left and right with skittish eyes, his clothing rumpled and tie askew. Edward's attempt to smile emerged as a grimace and she took him by the arm to lead him away from the scrutiny of Miss Hoppington and other guests standing near the entrance. *He looks shell-shocked,* she thought, as she struggled to set aside her desire to rage at him, to accuse him of abandoning her, to tell him of her anguish, her own private hell.

Once inside their room, he stood motionless.

"You look terrible. Are you sick?" Edward shook his head and mumbled that he had not slept. "It's more than that," she said, lips pursed. "You'd better rest. Then we can talk."

Edward nodded and lay on the bed without undressing. Within minutes he was asleep, leaving her with unthinkable thoughts until she dozed in a chair pulled close to the bed. At midnight his slight movements woke her and they looked at one another. Edward looked away.

"You have to tell me, Edward. I can't bear it anymore."

After a moment's hesitation, he cleared his throat and took a ragged breath. "During the war, I fell in love. Her name is Helene. I met her right after Vimy Ridge. She came to the ceremony to find me and I suppose I did too." He flicked his eyes at her then covered his face with his hands.

"I found her there, at the memorial. That's why I needed to be by myself. I had to see her. I had to find out why she didn't wait for me after the war."

Ann sat perfectly still, hands clasping the wooden arms of her chair. She could not fathom what he was telling her.

"After Vimy, she was the only thing that kept me sane. I would not have survived without her. Ever since coming to France, I've felt like I was back there . . . in the midst of it all again. When I saw her . . . I've been with her the past five days."

As he continued in long, staggered sentences that ended abruptly and jerked from admission to admission, Ann's knuckles whitened and colour drained from her face. When he finished, he looked half-dead, his cheeks pasty, his eyes like burned-out pits.

"It was a mistake, and now it's over. I hope you can forgive me." He lifted one hand to punctuate this final point then let it fall into his lap.

Ann listened to the ticking of the bedside clock. as though
its regular rhythm could wipe away Edward's words. She
looked at her husband, the man she thought would always
love her, the man who knew her most intimate places. who
understood her worries. The father of her children.

"What are you saying, Edward? Is it over because you
don't love her anymore?"

He responded slowly. "It's over because I love you and our
children."

"Love me? How can you speak of loving me in the same
breath as adultery? Shameful, disgusting adultery. Men who
love their wives," she emphasized the word love. "don't commit adultery. You sent me away so you could screw this woman." Ann had never before used such a vulgar word and she
put all the contempt and vehemence she could muster into it.
The chair fell backward as she shot to her feet. "I think you
should leave, Edward. I can't have you here. I can't even look
at you. I don't know how to cope with what you've told me."
She gripped her shaking hands together.

"Ann, please! Give me a chance to explain."

"I don't think you can explain adultery." For one brief
moment she considered hitting him, as if smacking her hand
against his flesh could somehow erase Edward's words. "I want
you to leave now."

"Please, Ann. I need you. I'll make it up to you. I won't
ever fail you again."

"Just go, Edward. You have to go."

"Don't send me away. What will I do without you? I'm lost.
Ann. Can't you see that I'm lost?"

The irony was not lost on her. Edward had sent her away
and now was pleading for her not to do the same. Except in
this case, he would know why. He would not spend days in
agony wondering what had happened.

Although she wanted to shout, Ann spoke with slow deliberation. "Perhaps you should have thought of that before you
went to see this woman."

Edward picked up his suitcase. He looked defeated. He paused, his eyes pleading, but she turned away to face the window. Finally, he opened the door then closed it with a soft click, and she heard his footsteps fade down the corridor.

* * *

Ann wanted to scream. Her eyes darted left and right. The room spun in and out of focus. The same word clanged over and over: adultery. It made her feel discarded, used and dirty, like a wet rag tossed on a heap of garbage. Adultery, an ugly word spawning notions of provocative clothes and bright lipstick, spawning other words like whore and harlot and thoughts of rundown hotels and hidden alleys and crude sex that some called fucking.

She staggered to the window and leaned her forehead against the frame, seeing nothing but deserted streets and the distorted glow of porch lights in the mist. An ache gathered, spreading from her neck to her head like a tightening winch. Her breath clogged. She reached the bathroom in time to be violently sick, her body retching uncontrollably, leaving her face grey. When Ann stopped heaving, she pressed her head against the cold, porcelain tub and began to weep.

22 AUGUST 1936

Ann did not leave her room except for breakfast in the hotel and tasteless dinners at The Midnight Swan, a low-ceilinged pub merely steps away from Regency Manor. Two nights later, she packed her bag for an early departure and slept in snatches; vivid dreams, in which she was either falling from a great height or screaming, left her ragged with exhaustion.

She had no idea where Edward had stayed during the past two days. But he would be at the train station the following morning for the trip to Southampton and then they would have to share a cabin just as they had on the trip over to France. Her mind was numb. Her body ached with bruising emotion. She had no choice; there was no other way to return home.

At eight-fifteen the following morning, Ann was at Victoria Station amidst a crowd of travellers who laughed or grumbled, wrestling bulging suitcases and bags full of souvenirs. One part of her ached to see Edward while the rest shrank from the possibility. He was waiting on the platform.

"Can I carry your suitcase?" He offered a hand to help her climb on board.

"No, I don't want your help. I want nothing from you." She maintained a sharp silence as he led the way to their seats then dealt with their luggage. For the entire journey, Ann looked out the window and said nothing.

Along with hundreds who had made the Vimy pilgrimage, Ann walked from Southampton station to the docks where their ship lay in her berth, flags flying, portholes sparkling, rigging taut with expectation of long days at sea. With hands encased in thick gloves, dockworkers hauled baggage and bundles, their heavy boots clumping along wooden gangways. The air was pungent with the smells of sea and smog. Noise and confusion offered momentary distraction.

Ann put away her clothes, then without a word, left the room. She stood by the railing of the uppermost deck, waiting for the ship to pull away from shore. Almost everyone on board had been to the dedication ceremony and she wondered how she would listen, night after night, to fellow passengers sharing memories of France. She wondered what she would say when they asked the inevitable questions about her own journey. The truth would be unacceptable.

Ann saw Edward arrive on the deck below and look around at the crowd gathered by the railings. She wondered if he was looking for her. Eventually he leaned against a metal pole and watched as England's shore receded, barely moving until the last edge of coastline flickered and was gone. He lit one cigarette after another, flicking each butt into the frothy sea. Finally he went below.

Brisk sea winds made her shiver, but Ann remained long after most passengers left the deck, the ebb and flow of misery beating dully against her heart. Eyes red from weeping, she held every part of her body taut to maintain a thread of control. Time and again, she asked how Edward, a conscientious family man, could have committed such as act. Anger burned like hot coals. Why had a long ago love captivated him? Betrayal hung like a stone around her neck.

* * *

Each day as their ship steamed across the ocean, Ann wrote brief entries in the travel diary she had purchased for their trip to France. The mere act of writing seemed to help, if only momentarily.

August 6
Everywhere I go on this boat full of people, I am alone. Even when I am talking, I feel alone. I have no one to confide in. The burden of being unloved taunts me every morning. The shame of Edward's deception crowds my thoughts. It's unbearable to contemplate divorce, but how can I live with him? Let alone forgive him.

Today I watched a boat pass us in the distance. It was visible for quite some time and then faded to nothingness. Still, I watched and watched, thinking that if I could see it only one more time then that would mean that Edward still loves me. I never saw it again.

August 7
We sat with the McCormicks at dinner. They wanted to reminisce about Vimy and I left the talking to Edward. I hate the word Vimy. It will forever mean betrayal. Thank goodness Vivienne is such a chatterbox. I barely needed to say anything before she was off again on another topic. Mary and Stuart Dodge stopped at our table and asked what we did after the ceremony. Edward lied. He told them we had a good time in London. I can now add liar to his new list of skills.

August 8
I stayed in our cabin most of the day. Just lay on the bed, my head aching so terribly I felt sick to my stomach. I can't seem to cry. Each time Edward looked in, I pretended to be

asleep. Eventually he gave up. I'm sure he lied about why I wasn't at lunch. The only bright spot is the thought of seeing Emily and Alex.

The boat is shuddering up and down so much; I will have to go up on deck soon, otherwise I really will be sick.

August 9

Grief is my lover, waking me at daybreak, embracing me at night. The sea was rough again today, so I walked up and down C deck and tried to avoid conversation. My mind is such a jumble, I can hardly think straight. What will I do when we get home? People are sure to know something is wrong. I can't imagine finding enough strength to pretend day after day, to wash his clothes and make his food and sleep in the same bed. I can't imagine being naked in front of him again. He's like a stranger. Or worse.

August 10

Only two more days at sea. I can hardly stand being confined to the ship. I'm so restless, all I can think of is being home with the children. I don't want Edward near me, which is impossible in our tiny cabin. Neither one of us is sleeping. We are barely polite. Dinners are dreadful. I'm sure everyone knows something is wrong. I see them talking but they always stop when I pass by.

We haven't spoken about it. Each time Edward tries, I cut him off. I don't care what he thinks. He deserves only anger and contempt.

* * *

Edward woke every day to fleeting memories of what could only be thought of as madness, now that the consequences lay at his feet. The numbness of leaving Helene receded bit by bit, replaced by confusion and pain, his logical brain unable to make sense of the past few weeks. The day before they docked in Montreal, he toured the upper deck again and again, paying little attention to fields laid out in narrow strips along the St. Lawrence, houses with bright red roofs sloped to ensure the slide of winter snow, tall poplar and maple trees waving in the wind as if beckoning him to visit, and the occasional collection of discarded farm machinery rusted by years of snow and rain. Children paused in their play to wave at the big ship. As the land passed by, he wondered whether Ann would be able to forgive him and could not fathom how to explain his actions.

On his sixth turn around the deck, he found her in an alcove formed by two lifeboats.

"We have to talk," he said, "if only to agree on what we say to the children."

Ann wrapped her arms tight across her chest. "I won't allow you to destroy their happiness. We'll have to find a way to go on." Her voice a dull monotone, she shivered as the wind found their sheltered space. "We'll be living a lie, but that's what you've done to us."

"I know." She looked at him with such despair that he had to turn away to maintain his composure. "I'll sleep in the spare room for now." She nodded. He cleared his throat. "We board the train straightaway and I'm sure one of my brothers will meet us at Union Station. I doubt the children will be there."

"All right. I'll pack my things after dinner."

Edward stretched his hand out to touch her arm. It was a familiar gesture practiced over the years, intended to reassure them both, but there had been no physical contact between them since she had led him up to their hotel room in London.

"Don't touch me," she said.

* * *

With so many returning from Vimy, each coach car was completely full, and they sat in a double seat, four rows from the front on the left-hand side. Ann placed her purse between them and hunched against the window.

Leaving Windsor station, he felt the power of the locomotive and saw a trail of black cinders chasing one another like swarming insects. The train rumbling and shaking as it accelerated made him think of a huge beast awakening from sleep. Ann shifted further away from him and closed her eyes.

On and on they rolled. Trees, fields, lakes, flowers, farms and animals passed by. Cornwall, Brockville, Kingston and Belleville marked the hours. Edward got up to walk through their coach and three others until he reached the dining car, where he purchased a cup of coffee from a surly porter. Hair rumpled and eyes bleary, he paused on the way back between two cars, sipping coffee and watching Lake Ontario spread its blue ripples, blending in the distance with the sky. When the train began to slow, he returned to his seat.

"I'll get our bags. Will you wait here for me?"

"I'll wait on the platform." Ann placed a book in her handbag then turned away from him.

"All right. I'll find you."

With hundreds returning from Europe, confusion engulfed the platform as children, parents, friends and family jostled for space. Harried conductors shouted directions, attempting to create order. Ann stood to one side waiting for Edward, who appeared ten minutes later, struggling with their bags.

"I can manage my own bag," Ann said. "You can't carry both of them through this."

He nodded and handed over one bag then moved ahead, clearing a space for her to follow. They made slow progress amidst the hiss of steam, the din of voices, the scrape of trunks and the slow click, click, click of a luggage wagon a few feet in front of them. Taller than most, Edward saw the wiry curls of his brother Simon's head several yards away and called his name. When Simon turned, Edward saw the black armband and his chest tightened with dread.

"Who?" he asked in a low voice, as soon as they reached him.

Simon's eyes were swollen and his lips barely moved. Normally, he would have given his older brother a friendly clasp around the shoulder and made a joke, perhaps a comment about thinning hair or thickening waist or too much luggage. Normally, his eyes sparkled and he would canvas the scene with interest, pointing out someone with an unusual feature or launching into a story about one of their siblings.

"Father. Just a few days ago."

"Oh, my God."

For a moment, Edward could think of nothing else to say. He shook his head, as if the motion might erase the news. As second eldest, Simon would have carried the burden of looking after their mother and coping with death's myriad demands. Edward embraced his brother, feeling him shake with suppressed grief.

Edward loved his father. Being firstborn had created a special bond between them. They were more than parent and son; they were friends. His father's advice was always welcome; in fact, they advised one another, and unlike his other brothers, he and his father had quiet personalities and could enjoy one another in both silence and conversation. One of their favourite pastimes was fishing, allowing the boat to drift through shallow waters, taking pleasure in the arc of a well-cast rod, taking pleasure in one another's company regardless of how many fish they caught. How could he possibly cope with the loss of his father?

"Was it his heart?" Edward asked.

Simon nodded, mopping his eyes with a wrinkled handkerchief.

"Mother said it had been acting up. But I thought he was looking better before we left for France."

Ann hugged Simon tight. "How awful," she said. "I wish we'd been here. How's Mother Jessie coping?"

"The family is looking after her. Someone is there day and night. Mother is so anxious to see you. Let me take your bag, Ann. I have a taxi waiting for us on Front Street. I'll tell you more when we're on our way."

23 AUGUST 1936

Beyond the station entrance, taxis honked to secure a fare, while people mingled about, burdened by too many bags and too many family members. A chestnut vendor stood nearby doing brisk business, occasionally blowing his whistle to alert potential customers. The pungent smell of nuts and smoke filled the air. A streetcar rattled along heading west. Despite the news of her father-in-law's death, the sights and sounds of Toronto offered Ann a sliver of comfort.

Simon spoke as soon as the taxi started moving. "He was in the garden when the heart attack happened. Mother was with him. She called for an ambulance right away. Jim Carter came. Do you remember him, Edward? He was in the ambulance corps during the war. Anyway, they took him to the General. Mother said he was in a lot of pain. A nurse called me at work and I called the others. When Stan and I got there, the doctors thought he might not last the night. But he rallied."

Simon's voice faltered and when Ann turned to look, he

had his handkerchief out again and was wiping his eyes. Edward's face had no colour and he licked his lips several times, which she knew was a sign of distress.

"After the attack, the doctors kept him in intensive care. He was in no shape to come home. Mother slept at the hospital every night with the rest of us taking turns. We read to him, told stories, held his hand. Father knew what was happening. I think he wanted to hold on until you returned, but every day he got weaker. On Friday he just slipped away. We were all there. One moment he was breathing and the next he wasn't."

"I can't believe he's gone." Edward's voice was thin and wispy, full of regret.

"Neither can I. It's been horrible. Mother's so anxious to see you. She's been very strong. Amazing really. I don't think she's broken down once, at least not in front of us. We're going straight to the house. The funeral's tomorrow. She wanted to wait until you returned. Ann's parents will bring the children over tonight."

"Why didn't you try to reach me?"

"What could you have done? You were halfway across the Atlantic when he died."

And when the heart attack occurred, thought Ann, *you were with another woman*. She closed her eyes and let the sadness gather.

* * *

A few cars were parked outside the house and Dorothy and Mary were on the porch talking to a woman who waved a pink handkerchief as she spoke. Edward paused to hug his sisters.

"Go right inside," said Dorothy. "Mother's been waiting for almost an hour. Mrs. Lewis has just brought over a casserole."

"Where are the boys?"

"They'll be here soon. We've made a cold supper, which wasn't difficult given how many people have stopped by with food."

Though Dorothy spoke, Mary nodded along with each

sentence, which had been their practice ever since they were young. Dorothy, plump and voluble; Mary, slim and silent. Edward opened the door, leaving Ann to greet his sisters. Inside, the curtains were drawn and the house was still, every room tidy, every surface clean, as though evidence of living had been banned while death was honoured. He found his mother in the parlour, thin and stooped, wearing black from head to toe.

"I'm so sorry I wasn't here." He put his arms around her.

"He spoke of you the day he died," she replied, a tear trickling down one cheek. "He was so pleased you decided to go to Vimy, and so proud of the man you've become. I read him the letter you sent from Arras."

Well, he wouldn't be proud of me now, Edward thought, glancing at the console table cluttered with family pictures. Three pictures of him were on the table: one from a fishing trip when he was nine, one as he went off to war and one with Ann on their wedding day.

"I remember when Father took the one of me in uniform. He said I looked full of piss and vinegar. I was ready to ship out. Thought I knew everything." He picked up the picture. "The cockiness of youth, I suppose."

"You were his confidant, not just his son. Especially after the war."

"I'll miss him terribly."

He remembered the comfort of his father's hand on his shoulder and the quiet contemplation of smoking together at the end of an evening, and his bits of wisdom, doled out without authority or the sense of parent teaching child. Knowing he had violated his father's strict code of ethics in a way he would never have understood, Edward hesitated to put the picture back in its place of honour.

"Mother Jamieson, I am so dreadfully sorry." Ann put an arm around her mother-in-law's shoulder. "What do you need us to do for tomorrow?"

By six the house was full with Edward's brothers and sisters, their wives and husbands and fourteen of his parents'

grandchildren. Conversation tumbled around the room, while
people bustled in and out of the kitchen until every inch of
the table was covered with plates and bowls of food, and his
mother smiled for the first time since he and Ann arrived.

"Edward, will you ask the blessing?"

Saying grace had always been his father's role and his
mother's request brought reality close once more. The family
waited while Edward swallowed the lump in his throat. As he
opened his mouth, the doorbell rang, then the door opened
and he heard his father-in-law's voice followed by the sound of
shoes running through the hall.

"Mommy!" Emily threw her arms around Ann.

"Daddy!" Alex did the same with Edward.

He glanced at Ann but her face was buried in their daughter's slim body.

* * *

With so many children and grandchildren, there was barely room for the whole family to cluster around the grave.
Surrounded by solemn faces and black garb, Ann held her
children's hands. Edward shovelled the first earth on top of
his father's casket, the sputtering sound of falling dirt evoking
death with more finality than any earlier action.

"Unto Almighty God we commend the soul of our brother
departed, and we commit his body to the ground: earth to
earth, ashes to ashes, dust to dust; in sure and certain hope
of the resurrection unto eternal life, though our Lord Jesus
Christ," the minister chanted.

Edward's five brothers came forward one by one to add
another shovel full of dirt. Ann cringed with each thud.

"Blessed are the dead who die in the Lord."

She glanced at her mother-in-law, flanked by Dorothy and
Mary. All three had tears trickling down their cheeks. Ann
loosened her grip on Emily's hand and wiped her own tears
away. She had come to love Edward's father, his gentle soul
and warm embrace of family. He had always been so kind to

her. She knew of her father-in-law's pride, but also knew that Edward had left school at fifteen to help support them all. Over the years, son and father had become equals, and from time to time, Edward had acted the parent.

Once when they were on vacation and driving through Vermont's rolling countryside, Edward had asked if she ever wanted to run away from her responsibilities. Ann had known he was relaxing because he had told stories about his childhood: placing pennies on railway tracks and waiting until a train passed to find the penny squished flat; delivering newspapers in the summer to earn money for an occasional candy bar; swinging on an old tire before jumping in the river; making bows and arrows with a group of friends; helping his mother make lemonade on a hot summer day. She had been delighted with these stories, enjoying the way Edward's voice lightened as he told them. His question had startled her.

"Why did you say that?" she had asked.

He had replied that he worried that work and family responsibilities were preventing him from spending enough time with her. She remembered telling him they could be strong together if he would let her help. As the years passed, she understood how he had been shaped by the dynamic of his parents and siblings, by being the eldest and the one who went to war, wearing that awful burden as a badge of distinction to those who didn't understand.

That long ago summer, they had driven on in comfortable silence, passing cow-spotted hills and small towns clustered along river valleys, and had stopped in a sprawling meadow, spreading a soft wool blanket for their picnic. Wind had stirred the springing grass while cicadas whirred and swallows skimmed lightly overhead, and here and there, scarlet poppies waved their lips. They had made love, secure in one another and bathed in summer warmth, the pastoral scene creating an intimacy that eluded them in their day-to-day city life.

As the minister led the final prayers, Edward came to stand beside her. Ann glanced at his profile, his straight nose and full lips and cheeks that sagged with grief, his dark hair with bits of grey here and there. She gazed at a distant tree swaying with the breeze then watched a cloud float by, its shape stretching until pieces broke off and drifted away. Though noonday heat seeped through her clothes, she shivered.

24   SEPTEMBER 1936

Death provided a smokescreen for their emotions, a reason to be sad and an excuse for the occasional tear. Avoiding each other, they sought comfort from their children and from friends who came to offer sympathy.

September 3, 1936

It seems fitting to write about my feelings on our anniversary. Edward came home early tonight. Perhaps he thought that would make me happy.

The past weeks have been hell as we've tried to cope with Edward's father's death and to coexist in the house while keeping our feelings from the children. It's easier for Edward since he can bury himself in work, while I cope with getting them back to school and keeping them busy. Mercifully, they don't seem to notice anything is wrong and are preoccupied with the prospect of new teachers and being with their friends.

For the most part, I feel empty and detached, but I have

periods of intense anger when I want to throw something.
Sometimes, when I'm in the same room as Edward, I feel an
almost uncontrollable urge to hit him.

I know he is also in pain, but I can't summon any feelings
for him or offer any hope. That may come, I don't know.

* * *

Edward allowed the shell of everyday life to encase him, its
exterior hard and protective, its interior hollow. As autumn
unfolded with school events and family gatherings, the children became a buffer. Ann joined the Red Cross and spent
long hours volunteering there and with a women's group at
their church. She was often out when Edward was home. The
tide of unnourished love sucked them further and further
apart.

"We need to talk," Edward said one Saturday in late September when Emily and Alex were playing with friends in
huge piles of leaves raked earlier that day. Six romping children took long runs across the lawn before leaping into one
pile or another. He watched Alex toss fistfuls of red and gold
into the air and laugh as he flopped backward, while Emily
grabbed a rake and tidied the piles for another jump.

"Why?"

"We can't go on like this."

"Really? It's your fault we're in this mess."

"Ann, please. Can't we at least try? I know I was wrong.
You have every right to be furious. But, please, talk to me."

"No."

"No. Just no. That's all you can say. Doesn't our marriage
deserve something more?"

"Don't you dare talk to me about what our marriages deserves." A flush of red marked her cheeks. "Don't you dare."

She threw her knitting in the wicker basket beside the sofa
and stood up. Edward reached out to catch her hand, but she
shrugged him away, and without another word, left the room.

He tried again the following weekend after arranging for

Alex and Emily to spend Saturday with Simon's three children. Ann was making pea soup from a leftover ham bone. She turned away when he entered the kitchen and busied herself with the dishes.

"Please listen, Ann. I know I deserve your anger, even your contempt, but I wasn't myself. Not my real self. Every place in France was so full of memories, such awful memories, I could barely think straight. And then to see Helene at the memorial—"

"Do not speak that name. Do not. Did you even give me a moment's thought? When you came back to the hotel and I was so upset, did you hesitate for more than a second? No, you did not. You didn't even give me the courtesy of talking to me. Did you?

"And look what you've done to us. We were happy with our little family and now that's gone. How do you think your betrayal feels to me? You've destroyed my contentment and security, my hopes for the future. I can barely get through most days. So, the answer is no. I don't want to talk to you about it. Maybe I never will."

Her voice, which had been fierce to the point of shrill, dwindled into a whisper while her eyes burned with anguish.

Though he made several more attempts, his efforts always ended in the same fashion, and eventually he retreated, although every day he wondered how to persuade Ann to forgive him. Ironically, he was now the one who wanted to talk while Ann was the one who would not share her thoughts and emotions.

The day he had met Ann, she had been leaning against a gnarly old chestnut tree with her best friend Linda Haig, a wicker basket open beside them. It was the annual church picnic. Edward had liked the way Ann smiled and the way she pulled her dark hair to one side exposing her long neck. He had nudged Eric Andrews' shoulder and suggested they introduce themselves.

Edward's mother had been urging him to find someone, had

even declared one day that it was time for him to get on with
life. "You can't dwell in the past forever, son." she had said.
He had moved on with some aspects of life: working hard for
the telephone company, seeing a few surviving friends, singing in the church choir where his deep baritone had been a
welcome addition. Eric had convinced him to join a football
league and the lively bantering of teammates had reminded
him of the camaraderie of soldiering.

After a few moments of awkwardness, Linda had invited
the two men to join them on the red and black tartan blanket
spread beneath the tree and the rest of that warm summer
day had been full of laughter for Eric was a great storyteller.
Within a few months, two couples had formed.

One day, not long after Eric had asked Linda to marry him,
Edward had taken Ann out for dinner. Afterwards, he had suggested a walk. The moon had cast pale shadows while leaves
had scrunched underfoot in the chill October air. Edward had
had his arm around Ann to keep her warm and eventually he
had stopped in front of a narrow Victorian house.

"This is Roy's place. He has the top floor but he's out of
town this weekend. I have a key. He's always told me to use it
whenever I want."

Ann looked up at him with a small frown. "Don't worry,"
he said as he opened the door and stepped aside.

The sitting room was furnished with a faded green sofa
situated under the bay window, a rectangular coffee table in
front of the sofa and a large armchair in off-white brocade. Although there were a few stains on the coffee table, it was decorated with a heavy glass ashtray and a silver cigarette box.
A picture of a sailboat crashing through the waves dominated
one wall. Edward helped Ann take off her coat and laid it on
the back of the armchair.

"Shall I make us some tea?" she asked.

Edward reached for her hand. "Can I kiss you first?"

They had kissed before but this one lingered and he
wrapped his arms tight around her slenderness, feeling the

curve of her breasts pressed against him. All he wanted at that moment was to make love with her but he knew that would have to wait.

"Will you sit with me on the sofa?"

Ann nodded.

Edward had rehearsed what he wanted to say. With Ann beside him, her hand in his, he began slowly, speaking first of his family and his responsibilities to them then about his job, how much he earned and his hopes for future advancement. He talked about their early days together and how he had been attracted to her as soon as he had seen her at Hanlon's Point. His voice thickened as he told her that he loved to dance with her and hold her in his arms, he loved kissing and touching her, he admired her outlook on life and the fact that she truly enjoyed her job. Spreading his dreams at her feet, he spoke of his desire for children and family life, his hopes for peace and contentment.

"You make me see the world differently. My feelings for you aren't just based on physical attraction. I think that you could be my dearest friend as well as my lover. I love you, Ann."

She blinked away tears threatening to spill. "I don't know what to say."

He moved closer. "Say you'll marry me."

It had been as simple as that. Declaring his love had erased all uncertainties and they had married six months later. And now, in the harsh glare of his wife's scorn, Edward cursed himself for failing to honour his vows. He deserved her contempt. Her anger. But he had to find a way to bring her back. The thought of living without her love made him feel like the homeless souls of the Depression, shrunken beyond humanity into nothingness.

How would he survive without her?

25   OCTOBER 1936

In October, Edward joined the reserves as a major in A Corps Signals.

"Because it's a reserve unit, I can maintain my full-time job," he told Ann after Sunday lunch. Uncertain whether she was listening, he nevertheless continued. "I've been given the rank of major, which means they need my expertise. Apparently, the rank is highly unusual since I wasn't an officer in the war." He scooped a spoonful of sugar into his coffee and stirred. "In the event of war, I can't go into active service though." Edward noticed a flick of eyebrows and thought he had Ann's momentary attention. "Apparently I have a damaged lung." At this news, Ann's nostrils twitched. "It's becoming clear that Hitler's a maniac who will do anything to restore German supremacy. I told Eric he should enlist too. Dave Jenkins is very supportive and I'm anxious to do something that might make a difference."

"Dave Jenkins will work you as hard as he always does."

Ann folded the newspaper in half and continued reading.

Because it gave the illusion of normal conversation, Edward continued talking. "I know others think there won't be war, but I can feel it in my gut. Nothing will stop Hitler, neither concessions nor threats. He's eliminated all opposition. The industrialists and the military are in his pocket. He's violated the treaty of Versailles by introducing conscription. He's put political prisoners in work camps, made all sorts of rules against Jews, and burned books containing what he calls 'un-German sentiments'. Some believe what Hitler really wants is to purify the German race. And the world is just standing by, watching."

* * *

Early Saturday morning he laid his new uniform on the bed and stood back to survey the snug-fitting jacket with shiny brass buttons and a major's crown prominent on each shoulder. Beside the jacket were a wide leather belt and narrow cross strap, a beige shirt and brown tie, brown woollen trousers and a stiff-peaked cap with the Signals crest. Fingers that had donned garments like these in minutes during the war fumbled as he dressed.

The last time he had worn a uniform was in 1919 when he returned from overseas. He had spent most of his first week home leaning on a pillow propped against the headboard of his unmade bed, a blanket heaped on the floor like a decaying carcass. His desk had been littered with army gear, discharge papers, his last paybook, a postcard from the ship that brought him home, his ceremonial sword and a German helmet, items he had dumped out of a duffel bag on the first day. Stale odours of sweat and tobacco had permeated the room.

One day, just as Edward had been lighting another cigarette, someone had knocked. Three quick taps. Without waiting for permission, his father had opened the door.

Ernest Jamieson had been a smaller version of his son: reserved, slim, thinning dark hair and calm brown eyes. Deep ridges had marked each side of his mouth and his knuckles had been thick with arthritis. Always dressed in jacket and tie, his collars and cuffs had been snowy white and crisply starched.

"Son, you have to come out. If not for your sake, then for your mother's."

Edward made no reply.

"You've been home for days. We all thought this would be a happy time." As Ernest looked at his eldest, his eyes softened. "Your mother is very worried." He pulled the chair away from the window and sat facing the bed.

"I'm sorry." Edward tilted his head and regarded his father.

"Can you tell me what's wrong?"

"I don't think so, Father."

"I'm sure it was dreadful."

"Yes."

When silence became uncomfortable, his father made another attempt. "Perhaps we could get away fishing. Relax a bit."

"Perhaps."

Fishing, Edward thought. The contrast between sleepy hours on a gentle river and the hell he had endured was almost laughable. Almost.

"Make an effort for your mother, will you?"

"I'll try."

"Good. I'll tell her you'll be down for dinner." He squeezed Edward's shoulder and left the room, closing the door behind him with hardly a sound.

Despite resenting his father's intrusion, dinner with his family brought a hint of relief. He even smiled—once when his youngest brother stuck a pea up his nose and the second time when his mother offered a slice of his favourite lemon meringue pie.

A few days later, he rolled up his sleeves with precision and surveyed the bedroom with disgust. Bed sheets were askew and clothes still littered the floor. Two pairs of scuffed shoes and his army boots lay under the desk. A dirty towel hung from the doorknob. Every surface was littered with faded newspapers, stained coffee cups, crusts of toast, shrivelled apple cores, and assorted papers. On the window ledge stood a flowerpot full of cigarette butts.

He imagined Lieutenant Burke barking orders. "Jamieson, get a grip. Clean up this pigsty. Report back to me on the double." Burke was one of his least favourite officers, and for some reason, it amused Edward to think of him.

When the room was neat enough for Burke's high standards, he paused and stared at the closet, the only place left to clean. Edward had not looked inside the closet since the first day home. He sniffed hard and turned the bevelled glass handle. After pulling the door open, he reached in and grabbed his dress uniform, the rough wool and brass buttons as familiar as his own skin.

By early afternoon, three neatly labelled boxes were stacked in the hallway, a fourth box remained open. Edward reached once more into the closet and extracted the small metal container full of Helene's letters. He leaned back and wiped the dust off the lid then placed the container on top of his military papers. With a long sigh, he sealed the final box.

With time Edward had realized that boxing his things up had been the first tiny step to recovery. Dealing with his nightmares had taken much longer. Loving Ann had closed the gaping hole in his heart. As Edward wound one end of his tie around and under the other, and then stuffed it though to complete the knot, he stared at his reflection. Sallow cheeks flanked sombre eyes. *If I had thrown those boxes out, I might not be in this mess.*

With Ann's continued remoteness and refusal to bend in any way, work and the reserves became his companions, though he made more time for Emily and Alex, as they too were part of his guilt. Whenever he imagined life without them, he shuddered in the deepest part of his soul.

As autumn released all vestiges of warmth, he buried his memories deep just as he had before, only this time they offered less resistance and nightmares did not flare. While he still thought of the days spent with Helene, he began to consider that perhaps he had succumbed to some form of temporary insanity.

* * *

Every Thursday night and Saturday afternoon. A Corps met in the armoury, a large, drafty building on Queen Street where close to one hundred men learned the craft of signals. Though new to senior command, Edward found parallels to his management role at the telephone company. discovering that clear directions, constant reinforcement, praise when warranted and disciplined follow-up earned respect and results.

He had been pleased when Eric joined the Corps. Their friendship and shared war experience meant he could rely on him in ways he had no need to define, and often Eric anticipated what was required before Edward even thought to ask. After one Saturday session instructing recruits in wireless radio repair, the two men walked together to catch the streetcar. moving briskly along Queen Street and then south in order to cut across St. James park where roses bore valiant blooms and crisp leaves swirled in untidy heaps along the path.

"You never told me much about your trip to France." Eric said.

"It was fine." He watched a ratty brown squirrel halt. stand on its hind legs, turn its head back and forth. then dart up a nearby tree.

"Fine. That's all you have to say? What did you see?"

"In addition to the memorial?" Eric nodded. "Arras. Lille. Valenciennes, Amiens. A few other places. Lots of cemeteries."

"How did it feel to be back?"

"Do we have to talk about this?"

"Damn it, Edward. What's wrong with you? Tell me about it. You haven't looked like yourself since you returned." Eric threw up his hands. "I'm allowed to be concerned about an old friend, aren't I?"

"You're right. Sorry."

They waited in silence for a traffic light to turn. Edward knew he could not talk about Helene and he debated how much to disclose of the sadness that had overwhelmed him. He settled on partial truth.

"The whole trip was dreadful. As soon as we docked, I knew I shouldn't have gone. Every place we visited brought back memories. I don't know what was worse, the cemeteries or the displays of war materials."

"Like what?"

"Gas masks and artillery guns and chunks of exploded shells. That kind of thing." Eric glanced at him but said nothing. "One place we went had an entire soldier's kit on display. Made me remember it all. All the shit we endured."

"Did you see anyone you knew?"

"Do you remember Lenny Johnson?"

"He was a bit of a weasel."

"Mm hmm. Seems the same. Didn't spend much time with him. Walt Ingram was there too. He lives in the US now. Minnesota, I think. Stuart Dodge and Andy McCormick were on the same ship coming back. A few others. Mostly it made me remember all the friends who didn't make it."

"We were lucky, weren't we? I think about them too. And about what we went through. Mostly I try to forget."

"And what did we accomplish?" Edward continued as if Eric had not spoken. "We're likely to do it all again. The same fucking shit."

"I still hope that won't be the case. What did Ann think?"

"About the trip?"

Eric nodded.

Edward did not know how to respond. He had been so caught up in his own feelings, he had not asked his wife how she felt about the places they visited and things they saw. All he knew was how angry and upset she was about Helene.

"I think it made her sad."

"Linda would've been in tears half the time. What about the Vimy memorial?"

"There was a huge crowd. Lots of pomp and ceremony. I found I couldn't really listen to the speeches. Can't abide it when people glorify war."

"Was Helene there?"

Edward's mouth tightened. "Why would you ask that?"

"Dunno. Idle question really. I remember how—"

"She wasn't there and that's not a topic for discussion."

Eric went quiet. "Sorry, Fuzz."

At the streetcar stop, their good-byes had none of the usual joking camaraderie, just a brusque "see you next week" as Edward took the Yonge line north and Eric headed west. Jammed in with Saturday shoppers and a giggling bunch of young girls, Edward considered his conversation with Eric. His friend had a right to ask questions, he supposed. Four years of looking out for one another entitled him to that much. But the topic of Helene was taboo, especially now.

Until he had seen her in the crowd, he could not have imagined being unfaithful. He loved Ann. From the beginning he had found her kindness, sense of humour and zest for life enchanting. Her personality had been, and still was, a wonderful complement to his more reserved nature. After two years of dating and courtship, he had been certain that theirs would be an enduring marriage.

Estrangement from Ann had taught him that she was his touchstone, the person who kept him joyful and purposeful. Her ability to celebrate life's surprises, to trust him, to look for the good in everything, these were what he loved, what completed him. Without her he was sinking.

All couples had arguments but theirs had never been serious, never more than an hour or two of being at odds. Emily, and then Alex, had brought joy to their lives and, even through the Depression, difficult thought it had been, they had managed to create small pleasures for one another and hold their family together. Why then had he strayed?

Everything he had been brought up to believe would condemn him for such behaviour, but being with Helene had felt like finding an oasis when he was about to collapse from thirst. Now, looking back, his actions felt like those of a stranger. He felt like his life had unravelled, his careful plans and hard work and dedication lost in a moment of memory.

26 OCTOBER 1936

Every Saturday the officer's mess provided a buffet lunch, hearty food for men who had already put in a half day at the office and now faced a full afternoon of drills and instruction. Only a few blocks from the armoury, the mess was a spartan place, with long wooden tables and military plaques spread along the walls, a vaulted ceiling hung with wrought-iron chandeliers and plain windows on three of four sides. On the windowless wall were crisscrossed ceremonial swords, mounted above a raised platform.

Entering the mess, Edward wrinkled his nose at the smell of liver and onions. He hated liver. When he was little, he used to try to hide it beneath a pile of mashed potatoes, although his mother always knew what he was doing. "Mothers have eyes in the back of their heads," his father used to say with a chuckle. As a senior officer it would be inappropriate to complain about food in the officers mess, but he wished they had liver less frequently. He put a small piece on his plate along with large helpings of potatoes and green beans that looked as though the life had been boiled out of them.

"Why don't you join us, Edward?"

He looked up to see Lieutenant Colonel Grant motioning to him and went to sit with a group of Signals officers. After listening for a while, it soon became clear they were discussing developments in Europe.

"Germany continues to expand its army and navy. Their infantry is almost twice the size it was in thirty-four, and they've created twenty-one divisions of Hitler's Landwehr."

"He's ignoring postwar treaties with compulsory military service."

"Thumbing his nose at us, if you ask me."

"What about the treaty with Japan?" Edward asked. "They're pretending it's part of an anti-communist foreign policy, but Japan is rearming too."

"Neither country can be trusted, as far as I'm concerned. And Italy is getting more belligerent. Do you think they'll join the treaty?" Harvey Wilson, who commanded another reserve corps, spoke for the first time.

For more than an hour, the men debated the situation, and later, on the way home, Edward weighed the arguments in his head. *At least*, he thought, turning up the path to their house, *I'm worrying about something other than my marriage.*

* * *

Eric and Linda Andrews lived in Toronto's west end in a rented bungalow. Linda had made the living and dining rooms look warm and inviting, using plump pillows and simple décor and a pastel palette of peach and cream. Since they were saving for a home of their own, she had scoured secondhand shops and church bazaars for suitable items. Ann wished she had half her friend's talent for decorating.

After setting a plate of lemon tarts and banana loaf on the coffee table, Linda poured two cups of tea.

"Something's worrying me," she said, brushing a stray curl

of blond hair away from her face.

Ann sprinkled half a spoonful of sugar into her cup then stirred until the crystals dissolved. "What's that?"

"You and Edward seem to be at odds."

"We do?"

"Yes, you do." Linda nibbled a piece of banana loaf. "Don't think you can fool me, Ann Jamieson. I've known you far too long."

When they were younger, Linda had always been the one to raise uncomfortable topics and push until she got a satisfactory answer. Ann needed to tread carefully: she wasn't prepared to confide in anyone, and certainly not to Linda, who was married to Edward's best friend.

"I suppose I can tell you. You'll just badger me until I do." Ann kept her voice light. "We saw a lot of places. Fields where battles had occurred and cemeteries with row after row of white crosses. Thousands of them, Linda. It made me want to weep. There was a museum in Ypres full of pictures and mementos of the war. They even had a movie reel showing men marching off to battle and artillery firing bombs on the Germans. It was gruesome."

"That must have been difficult. When we decided we couldn't afford to go, Eric told me that he was relieved in a way, because he felt the memories would be so hard."

"It was a very emotional experience. I think it affected Edward more than he anticipated."

"How so?"

"He seemed to go back in time to the war itself. You know he's so very private and stoic. He wouldn't talk to me about it. I got frustrated with him and lost my temper. He hasn't been easy to live with since we came back. Just a little rough patch."

"Oh, dear. I should have guessed. Sorry to be so nosy."

"That's all right. Good friends are allowed to be nosy when they're concerned. I should have told you. I'm sure it will blow over."

"Let's talk about something else." Linda offered the plate

of sweets and Ann took a lemon tart she really didn't want.

More than an hour later, Ann helped clear away their cups and plates from afternoon tea. "Edward's worried about Germany."

"They all are. Eric talks about it constantly."

Linda filled the sink with hot sudsy water and began to wash and rinse the dishes. There was no need for ceremony between the two of them, chatting while clearing up was a customary routine.

"Eric says the war industry is fuelling growth. I don't understand exactly what the connection is, but he was talking with my father about it after dinner last Sunday."

"That makes it sound like it's a good thing. How can preparations for war be anything other than dreadful?" Ann folded the tea towel and placed it on the rack to dry. "The papers are full of articles about Hitler and what's happening in Germany."

"He's an evil man," Linda said. "Eric says that he's become an absolute dictator. I can't bear the thought of another war. What if it happens when our sons are old enough to enlist?"

The two women looked at one another in horror.

* * *

Edward lay on the bed with his knees bent, his head propped against two pillows, and Emily and Alex snuggled on either side. Rain pelted the window. A sudden flash of lightning made his son jump.

"It's okay, Alex. We're safe inside."

"I know, Daddy. But that was a big flash."

Thunder cracked a few seconds later. "It should soon pass by. When the time between lightning and thunder is short, that means the storm is overhead."

"How do you know so much?" Emily's brown eyes seemed larger than usual.

"I guess I read a lot. Just like you."

His daughter always had her nose in a book, curled up

either on the couch or in her bedroom. From time to time, he saw the dim glow beneath her closed door and knew she had turned on the light after being tucked into bed. He never objected, though. Reading was like a sacred trust, one that he believed would improve his children's chances in life.

"Can you read another chapter? Please."

"Only if each of you reads a paragraph. Let's see. Who will read first?" He tickled his son until Alex wriggled off the bed. "We'll start with Alex."

Later, after getting his son into bed, Edward returned to Emily's room. Pink frills and stuffed animals contrasted sharply with Alex's plain colours and dark furniture.

"Will Mommy be home soon?"

"I'm not sure, sweetheart. She's at one of her volunteer meetings."

He had no idea how late Ann would be. She rarely told him any details and sometimes all he found when he got home was a brief note and a cold supper and one of the teenagers from down the street playing with his children on the living room rug. She was avoiding him, that much was obvious, but he had no idea what she was thinking. *We'll never solve our problems if she won't talk to me.* A thought struck him with sharp force. *What if she's planning to leave me?*

Though he watched his wife closely, seeing evidence of pain in her drawn lips and thinning face, she had perfected the art of masking each day with busyness, taking household chores to new heights of care, while maintaining more than the usual contact with family, both his and hers. Beyond those activities, she filled all other hours either with the children or her volunteer work. He stared out the window at bare-branched trees, their stark frames both majestic and forlorn.

"Daddy?"

Lost in worry, Edward had forgotten his daughter. "Mm hmm."

"Did you and Mommy have a big wedding?"

"That's a funny question to ask at bedtime."

"Betsy's sister is getting married and she's going to be a junior bridesmaid. I wish I could have been a bridesmaid at your wedding."

"But you weren't even born then."

"I know. I'm just saying. Did Mommy look beautiful?"

"She did. Very beautiful. She made me feel like the luckiest man alive."

"Tell me the story, Daddy."

"You should be going to sleep now, Em."

"But Mommy's not here to say goodnight." Emily's pout normally stiffened his resolve. Tonight it merely added weight to his sadness.

"All right. Just a bit of the story then." He sat on the edge of the bed.

"We were married in September. The sky was the bluest blue and the sun was shining as though it was happy for us. Uncle Roy was my best man and he made sure I got to the church on time."

Edward remembered the day perfectly. St. Mathew's had sparkled as afternoon sun bathed the stone walls of the century-old church. The splendour of fall colours had greeted each wedding guest: plump red sumac flaming against a cedar hedge, butterfly bush dangling pink and white blossoms, and purple-tipped hawthorn edging the pathway. Next to the gated cemetery had been a cluster of Russian olive trees, their silver leaves dancing in the soft breeze, and like sentinels flanking the church, the protective arms of maples, birch and oak had burned with golden promise.

Inside, crisp white linen had draped the altar. Candles set on tall silver candelabra had conveyed a sense of occasion. Behind the chancel, a circular stained glass window, the pride of many parishioners, had shone with a scene of Christ surrounded by children and little lambs. Organ pipes had filled the west wall above carved wooden choir stalls and banners, one blue and one green, that proclaimed the word of God. A memorial had hung on the east wall with the names of fifteen

men and one woman engraved in gold. Edward remembered it
as a setting of tradition and sacrament, a place to honour both
living and dead, a place of solace and confession, of celebration
and renewal.

The crowd had rustled as people greeted one another, knelt
in prayer, extracted a handkerchief, adjusted a skirt, a jacket,
a wide-brimmed hat. A happy gathering had awaited the marriage of Edward Jamieson and Ann Winston.

From a door on the right side of the chancel, Edward and
his groomsmen had appeared and taken their places beside
the minister. As best man, Roy Doney had been on Edward's
right. Tall and lanky with sandy hair, a neatly trimmed moustache and narrow face, he had been Edward's friend since they
were eight. Next to Roy had been Eric Andrews. After being
gassed at the Somme, he and Edward had sworn that if they
came back alive they would be at each other's weddings.

Edward had turned briefly to acknowledge his mother, father and seven siblings sitting in the first two pews on the
groom's side. His father had seemed a bit uncomfortable in
the dark blue suit Edward's mother had brushed and pressed
that morning, and Edward had suspected that his father felt
inferior to the social and financial standing of Ann's family.
In contrast, his mother's erect posture and carefully folded
hands, lace collar and feathered hat had indicated that she
was totally at ease. Edward had exchanged smiles with her.

At ten past four the organist's meandering stream had
swept seamlessly to a crescendo of trumpets. Edward's mother's friend, Mrs. Purdy, had straightened her posture, Emma
White had shushed her children, and everywhere lips had
parted in bright smiles of expectation.

The organ had pealed for the second time, directing attention to the wide arched doorway at the back of the nave. The
tableau had hushed.

Nancy Winston, sister of the bride, began the procession,
her studied expression suggesting she was conscious of maintaining a slow, even pace. The crinoline beneath her pink dress

swished with each step. Linda Andrews, Ann's maid-of-honour, waited until Nancy was halfway down the aisle. Blond hair fell in soft curls across the shoulders of her rose-coloured gown and her wide smile indicated the pleasure she felt that Ann and Edward were soon to be husband and wife. Linda brushed a stray hair behind her ear and followed Nancy down the aisle.

The guests stirred as father and daughter emerged from behind the archway, Ann's wedding dress glimmering in the soft light, scalloped edges swirling gently with each step. Rich brown hair and flushed cheeks heightened her beauty. She carried roses and dahlias in a profusion of colours handpicked by her father that morning. From the front Edward held her gaze as she walked towards him, his love for her absolute, the memory of Helene faded to a faint shadow. For those few moments, no one else existed except he and Ann, the glow of her happiness opening him to a life of possibilities.

As Ann and her father approached the red-carpeted steps leading to the chancel, Edward noticed John Winston giving his daughter's hand a brief squeeze. Then, like a knight performing an ancient ritual, he solemnly offered Ann's hand to Edward with a look that said "she's precious to me, take good care of her". Edward acknowledged the commitment with a brief nod of his head. Holding hands, Ann and Edward turned to face the minister, and the ceremony began.

"The grace of our Lord Jesus Christ, the love of God, and the fellowship of the Holy Spirit be with you all," Father Thomas intoned.

"And also with you."

At times during the war, the call to worship had sunk into Edward's soul like the swirling flow of water in a deep, dark eddy; those ancient words pulling him down inside himself, protecting him from the horror of daily existence. At other times those same words ricocheted inside his mind so that breath seemed out of reach and he had wondered whether God had abandoned the world to destruction and death. That day, the words were benignly soothing. Edward held himself erect and controlled.

"In the presence of God, Father, Son and Holy Spirit, we have come together to witness the marriage of Edward Leslie Jamieson and Ann Marjorie Winston, to pray for God's blessing on them, to share their joy and to celebrate their love. The gift of marriage brings husband and wife together in the delight and tenderness of intimacy and joyful commitment to the end of their lives. It is given as the foundation of family life." Father Thomas looked from Edward's face to Ann's as he spoke.

"The marriage vow is an oath," Father Thomas continued. "that presupposes the absolute sovereignty of God. Marriage is a gift designed to fill God's purpose for us, involving solemn promises, to one another, to the children that may ensue and to the broader community. God helps hold us together, but both husband and wife must dedicate themselves to keeping the marriage intact."

Sitting on his daughter's bed, with the minister's words echoing in his memory, Edward paused. *And I didn't keep that vow, he thought. Nor did I dedicate myself to keeping our marriage intact. This whole mess is my fault. Totally my fault.*

"Daddy, why did you stop? I know there was dinner and dancing."

"That's enough for now, Em. If I tell you the whole story we'll be up much too late."

"Okay. But, I have a question." Imagining that his daughter's question had something to do with the wedding, Edward nodded. "Why aren't you sleeping in the same bed as Mommy?"

Edward frowned. He had no idea his children paid attention to where their parents slept, although he had been careful to make the bed each morning before tiptoeing across to Ann's bedroom and dressing for work.

"I've been snoring a lot lately, so I'm sleeping in there to give your mother a chance to get more rest. That way she doesn't wake up when I make loud noises like this."

He snorted a few times like a snuffling pig and soon Emily was giggling.

27 NOVEMBER 1936

Edward placed his hat on the top shelf of the front hall closet.
His fingers were numb and the buttons on his coat felt large
and stiff. When he had left that morning, gusts of wind pulled
him this way and that and he had held onto his hat so it would
not fly away. By midday, the sky was black and for almost an
hour torrents of rain splattered his office windows.

Mrs. Sternway bustled out of the kitchen, wiping her hands
on a faded tea towel.

"Where's Mrs. Jamieson?" Edward said.

Mottled eyebrows drew together, deepening the woman's
dour look. "She said you knew she'd be away for a few days."

He opened his mouth then closed it, then opened it again.
"Oh. Oh, yes. I forgot it was today she was leaving." Mrs.
Sternway's eyebrows relaxed.

When Edward and Ann first returned to Toronto from
Montreal, friends had recommended Mrs. Sternway as a reliable woman to help with heavy housework. She was gruff but

kind and kept their house spotless. Once, when he had business in New York and Ann had joined him for the weekend, Mrs. Sternway had looked after the children.

While Edward turned his back to hang his coat, he asked a neutral question. "Are Emily and Alex upstairs?"

"Yes. They've been in Emily's room since coming home from school. Dinner will be ready at six."

As Mrs. Sternway returned to the kitchen, he removed his toe rubbers and placed them in the cupboard. Edward had no idea where Ann had gone.

He tried to recall the morning's events. Waking at six followed by the usual awkward dance to dress without getting in Ann's way. He still slept in the guest room and their routine had evolved such that his wife was usually wrapped in her housecoat with her hair freshly brushed by the time he crossed the corridor and opened the door. Porridge and toast for breakfast and a quick cup of coffee while he read the headlines. Emily had argued with Ann about why she could not go to her friend's after school. Alex wanted to take one of his toys for show and tell. Nothing had seemed out of place.

He could not imagine why she would go somewhere without telling him but having Mrs. Sternway at the house rather than his mother-in-law meant that Ann had a secret, for Jean Winston made it her business to know what was happening in her children's lives. Not that she was a busybody, but she did expect to know.

Normally, Edward felt in control of his life, but during the past four months all sense of control had slipped. Ann's unexplained absence made him feel like he was in a skidding car, praying for a safe landing.

Deflecting the children's questions with a brusque reply about an old school friend their mother was visiting, Edward endured a supper of overcooked pork chops smothered with applesauce containing too much cinnamon.

"I like Mommy's applesauce better," said Alex, swinging one leg back and forth.

"Finish your dinner."

"If Mommy was here, she wouldn't make me eat it."

"Alex, what did I say?"

His son put another bite into his mouth and chewed while a tear rolled down his cheek. He wiped his nose with his sleeve then sniffed loudly.

"One more bite and you can leave the table." With a snap, Edward turned to the newspaper.

Emily had left the kitchen half an hour earlier. During dinner she had chattered away about a friend who fell off a bicycle and broke her leg, a circumstance that seemed to make his daughter envious. Emily had no trouble with Mrs. Sternway's applesauce.

Normally Ann remained at the table if one of the children was being difficult, allowing Edward to escape into peace and quiet. In the past, after the dishes were done and Alex and Emily were otherwise occupied, he and Ann would have shared the day's events over coffee. But nothing was normal. Nothing at all.

Seeking distraction from the pounding question of his wife's disappearance, Edward continued to glance at headlines, pausing briefly over an article about Switzerland and Hitler's stated guarantee that whatever happened, Germany would respect the neutrality of that country. *Another promise Hitler won't keep*, he thought.

"I'm finished, Daddy."

"So I see. Why don't you run upstairs and see what your sister is doing." Alex looked longingly at a plate of ginger cookies. "You can have one. Just one."

After Alex left the kitchen, Edward sighed. He put down the paper and began to clear the table. A few minutes later he rolled up his sleeves and turned on the hot water tap. If he rinsed the dishes, Mrs. Sternway would have an easier time washing them the following morning.

Where did she go? Edward's bewilderment reflected in the window above the sink. *How could she leave without telling me?* He had checked their bedroom and the study but found nothing to indicate her whereabouts, only the absence of her silver-handled brush and the nightgown she kept tucked beneath her pillow.

Ann's continued distance and refusal to talk about their marriage had been more than frustrating. In the beginning, he had wondered whether her anger would result in separation, but as the months had unfolded he had allowed himself to hope they would find a way to put his affair behind them. Her disappearance slammed him with doubt.

With the water still running, he considered possibilities. Clearly his mother-in-law had no knowledge otherwise she would be looking after Alex and Emily, and Ann was unlikely to have told any of her siblings, since her sister was quite a bit younger and the other two were brothers. He rinsed the knives and forks and a spatula he had used to serve the meat.

Perhaps Linda Andrews would know. Eric had called the other day and Edward had deflected his friend's invitation to the theatre by saying they had other plans. A lie, but lies were easier than the truth. No, Ann would worry that Linda might tell Eric.

Hannah Wilson was a possibility. Bob Wilson had been Edward's boss during the years when he and Ann lived in Montreal. Struggling with two infants in a strange city, Ann had been grateful for Hannah's friendship. Together the women had been involved in fundraising events at the city's museum and had coordinated volunteer services at a downtown women's shelter during the Depression. Hannah was like Ann's older sister.

After rinsing the last plate and drying his hands, he checked his watch. Seven thirty. He could call Bob under the pretence of catching up. If Ann were there, Bob was likely to give some sort of hint. Edward soon had his answer; neither Bob nor Hannah had any knowledge of Ann's disappearance.

He prowled about the house like a restless cat, every room intimately familiar yet oddly strange, as though he had been

away for a very long time. From the kitchen the radio bab-
bled, Jim Parker's low voice followed by Fred Simpson's nasal
tones. He thought about turning the radio off, but instead
stared out the front window as lights bounced and a car drove
past, tires scrunching against the gravel. He pulled a dead
violet from one of the pots sitting on the drop-leaf table and
crushed the dry petals between his fingers.

In his study he picked up a book, *Goodbye Mr. Chips*, which
had been a birthday present from Ann's parents. Although his
birthday was in April, he had yet to read it. Edward went to
the kitchen and poured a large measure of scotch. Returning
to the study, he looked at the story summary on the jacket
cover and flipped to chapter one.

*"When you are getting on in years (but not ill, of course),
you get very sleepy at times, and the hours seem to pass like
lazy cattle moving across a landscape. It was like that for
Chips as the autumn term progressed and the days shortened
till it was actually dark enough to light the gas before call-
over."*

He read the rest of the page, took another sip of scotch and
put the book down; a story about an aging schoolmaster looking back at his life would never hold his attention. Edward
got up and roamed the room touching various items on his
desk and the shelves next to the window. Scotch in hand, he
continued to roam through the kitchen, which led to the hall
and then the living and dining room. Around and around he
went trying to puzzle out where Ann had gone.

Finally, he went to bed, choosing the master bedroom
rather than the guest room across the hall. Sleep occurred in
brief snatches and he woke to an aching head and a throat
scratchy from too much alcohol.

28 November 1936

One hundred miles east of the city, at a sprawling farmhouse overlooking the lake, Ann sat in a wicker rocking chair with a Siamese cat on her lap. Though she disliked cats, this one, with the appropriate name of Duchess, had ignored the many times Ann shooed her away. The cat stretched each leg one by one like a ballet dancer doing warm-up exercises, circled around then curled once more into a purring bundle.

For weeks she had debated what to do. Autumn had been like a wasteland, her life devoid of contentment, her insides shrivelled from lack of love. She felt like a prisoner whose view was restricted to a small barred window as September and October passed, each day unrelenting. And now it was November.

Other than Duchess, Ann was alone. In daylight, the view from the parlour window was of sloping white, punctuated by fences and the spidery arc of apple trees dressed in winter nudity. At four a.m. she saw nothing but black.

A kitchen lamp illuminated the doorway to her far right but otherwise she was in the dark, exhausted by seven months of accumulated anger and two weeks of lying. She had lied to everyone: her children, her family and friends, and those who relied on her volunteer efforts. The only person she had not lied to was Edward, and that was because she had not spoken to him at all.

Yesterday, as the train rattled through windswept countryside, she had tried to think, had even taken out her diary and pen as if the act of writing might add coherence to her actions, but the page remained blank. At Huntington, Aunt Bea's welcoming smile had disappeared into a thin-lipped frown.

"Good Lord, what on earth is the matter? I've never seen you looking so thin. Let's get out of this frightful weather. Your Uncle Morris is waiting in the DeSoto, keeping it warm." Bea gestured at a black car with a snub-nosed grill surrounded by four prominent lights.

After long deliberation, Ann had decided to call Aunt Bea, her father's younger sister, and ask to visit. Although Jean Winston referred to her sister-in-law as a scatterbrain, Ann was very fond of this particular aunt who was only thirteen years older and behaved like a friend. Bea had never scolded but instead chuckled at the antics of her nieces and nephews as though she would have preferred to indulge alongside them rather than be confined to adult pursuits. Ann suspected that her mother's criticism resulted in part from the wealth of Bea's husband, Morris.

All afternoon and evening, Bea had been solicitous, offering tea and scones and the comfort of chicken stew with dumplings and warm apple pie topped with a slice of sharp cheddar cheese. She had asked no questions, although Ann could tell by the glances going back and forth between her aunt and uncle, and by the way Bea drummed her fingers against the mahogany table, that she was more than curious.

Ann bit the ragged edge of one fingernail. Leaving Alex and Emily in Violet Sternway's care made her feel like a captain abandoning ship before his passengers. She thought of them now, sleeping in their beds, Alex with his covers flung off, Emily with hers pulled tight to her chin. Yesterday morning, on the verge of changing her mind, Ann had heard Edward whistling in the bathroom, and for some reason that inconsequential act had hardened her resolve. She had to get away and find a place to think. But now that she was at the farm, nothing made sense.

Duchess continued to purr. Ann rocked her chair back and forth.

"Here you are," Bea said. "I peeked into your room and you weren't there. The bed hardly seemed rumpled at all. Didn't you sleep?"

"I'm not sleeping very well these days. Duchess is keeping me company."

"I can see that." Bea did not clarify which of Ann's statements she meant. "We're up early because Morris has meetings at the university and it takes almost two hours to get there. What would you like for breakfast?"

"Do you have any scones left?"

"I'll warm them up in the oven." Bea waved one hand as she left the room. "Don't get up. You just sit and relax."

With the background clatter of kitchen drawers and cupboards opening and closing and the sound of her aunt's humming, Ann continued to stroke the cat's purring warmth.

* * *

"I'm trying to decide whether to leave Edward."

Bea sputtered then started to cough. After a moment, she wiped her mouth with a napkin and cleared her throat. "You should warn me before you say something like that, so I can swallow my coffee properly."

"I'm sorry, Bea. I've been trying to decide what to tell you and it just came out that way."

"Leave Edward? How can you possibly leave Edward?" Eyes wide, Bea straightened her neck like a groundhog sensing danger. "And why?"

"It turns out he married the wrong woman."

"The wrong woman according to whom? You or Edward?"

In dull tones, Ann recounted the events of the past summer. As the story unfolded, she stroked Duchess again and again, from the cat's bony head all the way to the tip of her tail.

"He keeps trying to talk to me but I won't discuss it. I can hardly be in the same room with him."

"Ann, how dreadful. Now I know why you look so thin."

"You can't tell anyone, Bea. Promise me."

Bea held up her right hand. "Of course not. I promise. But I'm glad you've told me. No one should bear that kind of heartbreak alone." She pursed her lips. "Are you sure leaving is the right answer?"

"No," Ann whispered. "But it's one answer."

"Have you thought about how you would earn a living? I'm certain Edward would provide for the children, but you would need to look after yourself. Or perhaps 'want' is the right word."

Ann was grateful to her aunt. Others would have told her that leaving Edward was out of the question, their children would forever be stained by scandal, Ann shunned by society, friendships lost, family ties strained. She had already considered such arguments. She had a choice, stay and make the best of it or leave and find a different life.

"Do you remember that I used to work at Hart Insurance?" Her aunt nodded. "I still know some people there, so that's a possibility. And I've accumulated skills through my volunteer work. Public speaking. Event organization. Accounting. Dealing with difficult people." Ann itemized these talents finger by finger.

"Dealing with difficult people. Now that's a skill that should be in high demand." Bea's comment prompted a flash of upturned lips.

"Where would you live? Your current house would be too

expensive if Edward had to finance two homes, and even if you secured a job, your salary would be modest. Women never earn as much as men. Could you live with your mother and father?"

Ann shook her head.

"I know. You could bring the children here and live with us. A farm is a wonderful place for children. We have lots of bedrooms. Morris and I have always wanted a family." Bea's voice trailed off.

"Thank you, Bea. You're very generous, but I couldn't take them away from everything that's familiar."

"You're right, of course. I just got carried away." Bea stood up. "I think we should go for a walk. I do my best thinking when I'm walking." She crossed to the window. "The sun is trying to break through. There's a path through the orchard we can take. Bundle up. Do you need a hat?"

"Maybe I'll just stay here."

"Nonsense. Mother always said moping around doesn't solve anything and in this case, I agree with her. I'll get you a hat and one of my warm scarves."

Blustery winds made walking difficult, and until they were beyond the gate and closer to the orchard, Bea led the way and Ann followed. Separated by several feet, talking was difficult. At first the sun offered merely a promise of warmth, but by the time they reached the first row of apple trees, Ann was hot and out of breath.

"Do you always walk this fast?"

"Stirs up the blood, doesn't it? Look at that view." Bea spread her arms like a conductor signalling a crescendo.

In rippling shades of brown and green, the land stretched from east to west, curving to a narrow spit at one end where evergreens punctuated the shore. Beyond the land, light bounced from wave to wave, blues shifting from bright to dark while seagulls raced along the water's surface before soaring high.

"Do you ever get tired of looking at it?"

"No. It changes every day. Can you see the freighter in the

distance? Just over there. Follow my finger."

Ann allowed herself not to think. Instead she felt the wind
and the prickle of cold cheeks and the tight warmth of Aunt
Bea's hat. She turned to look back at the farmhouse appreciating its flowing lines and the symmetry of matching dormer
windows across the second floor. In summer, the front porch
was a gathering spot for visitors, but now it looked forlorn, as
if the house was resting between scenes. Except for her breathing, Ann heard only the quiet of a winter day.

Bea linked her arm with Ann's.

"Let's walk this way. Beyond the orchard there's a creek. I
want to see if it has overflowed with all this rain."

"All right. You lead the way."

They walked between squat trunks planted in parallel lines,
the lowest branches spreading wide, higher branches curving
like an archer's bow ready to launch. Bea squeezed Ann's arm.

"I've been thinking. Sometimes I find it useful to plot my
decisions like branches of a tree. In your situation you would
start with two branches, leave or stay. If we explore the second branch, I can see another branch, fix your marriage or
accept that it's permanently broken. Each has consequences
and more branches.

"I remember when I learned that Morris and I couldn't
have children. The doctor told us something was wrong with
Morris, not me. I had to decide whether my desire for children
was more important than my marriage. I must have filled five
or six pages creating the branches for that decision. I worked
on it for days. I know it sounds almost mathematical, but the
real value was how thoroughly it made me think."

"But this is emotional, not rational."

"You could think of it that way. I prefer to think of it as the
rational behind the emotional. When I make decisions based
on emotion, I often regret them. My approach might not work
for you but you could give it a try. I still have those pages. I'll
show them to you when we get back to the house."

"You said fix my marriage or accept that it's permanently

broken. I can't fix my marriage by myself."

"No. You need Edward's help for that. And you said he wants to talk about it. That could be a good start."

"I don't want to talk to him. Yell at him, maybe. Or throw something at him. I know that makes me sound childish but that's how I feel."

"Maybe you should yell at him. And when you're finished yelling, you can talk. Talking doesn't mean deciding, you know."

29 NOVEMBER 1936

A heart-wrenching decision was bound up in Bea's notes and a diagram connecting the many factors she had considered. "I find another husband" placed alongside "I do not find another husband". "Morris understands" set against "Morris hates me". "I find solace in my nieces and nephews" set against "other people's children make me feel unhappy". Smudges and pale spots that might have been tears marked the pages. Ann stayed awake until well past two a.m. deciphering her aunt's logic.

By Wednesday evening she had sketched her own set of branches and described them to Bea, who asked questions to probe the thoroughness of her niece's thinking.

"That's an excellent beginning, Ann. I can see it taking shape from what you've already written down. What do you think?"

"I wish I could stay another day or two and finish it. Your thoughts are so helpful."

"You're welcome to stay longer if you want, but I think you'll be fine."

"What I don't understand is how to turn this into a decision."

"You will. Trust me. Do the work and you'll find your decision."

Ann pulled her pages together and slipped them inside a manila folder. "Bea?" Her aunt looked up. "I'm glad you stayed with Uncle Morris."

"So am I, dear. So am I."

* * *

When Ann appeared Thursday afternoon, Mrs. Sternway acknowledged her with a brisk nod. The woman had little to say except to explain where she had stored some of Ann's clothes and what she was planning for dinner.

"The children have been good," Violet said, settling a red hat on her head. "A bit fussy about their food, but we've gotten along fine."

"Thank you, Violet. You've been a big help."

"Mr. Jamieson's been rather testy." Violet buttoned her coat and extracted a glove from each pocket.

"I suppose he prefers his routine. He's certainly not accustomed to looking after things at the house."

"Just like most men." Violet Sternway stretched her lips into a smile.

With another word of thanks, Ann ushered the woman out the front door and waved as Violet turned the corner.

Emily and Alex flung their arms around her when they came home from school to find her waiting with a fresh batch of cookies cooling on a wire rack. Ann told them she had gone away to visit someone and they seemed satisfied with her simple explanation. Questions and stories filled the balance of the afternoon while Ann prepared dinner, occasionally stopping to reach out and stroke the hair or touch the cheek of one or the other of her children.

At six fifteen, the front door opened.

"Sorry I'm late, Mrs. Sternway. The streetcar . . ." Edward did not move. "You're back."

Ann nodded.

"Where the hell—"

She placed a finger over her lips. "Later. When the children are asleep."

After dinner she sat on the cold tile floor while Alex played in the bath, then read three chapters of a storybook before tucking them in and turning out their lights one by one. At the top of the stairs, Ann took a deep breath.

"Where have you been?" Edward paced back and forth across the rug.

"I needed to get away."

"And your solution was to disappear for four days without telling anyone? Do you have any idea how worried I've been?"

"If you must know, I was at Aunt Bea's house. I took the train Monday morning."

"If I must know? I have a right to know where my wife is. Common courtesy, if nothing else, would dictate that. Why did you need to get away?" Edward stressed the word need.

"When I'm ready, I'll tell you more. But not until then."

Edward held a hand to his forehead. "I don't know what you expect from me. I've tried to talk to you. I've tried to be patient. If I didn't know better, I would say that you've gone crazy. You're being impossible. I don't . . ."

With one sleeve rolled up, his hair askew and eyes bleary, he looked as though he had not slept for days. But Ann said nothing. Although an answer was emerging from following Aunt Bea's process, she wanted to review it again to be certain.

30 DECEMBER 1936

December brought snow and slush, filling the house with a damp chill. Bullet-grey skies brooded low and threatening. For the most part, the snow did not remain but there were a few wisps of white on the front lawn and neighbours had begun to put Christmas decorations on their homes. Ann watched her children set out for school.

Two nights earlier, whipping winds downed a limb from a large elm, missing the house by only a few feet. Edward had rushed outside as soon as they heard the cracking thud and returned soaking wet to report that no damage had occurred. The following evening, Ann had watched him cut the limb into lengths and carry heaping armfuls into the garage for firewood. When he had finished, he had removed his rubber boots on the back porch then walked along the hall to his study without saying a word.

Since returning from Aunt Bea's, Ann had watched Edward watching her. It was clear that her disappearance followed by her unwillingness to discuss the matter made him nervous. The strain of adultery compounded by a wife whose persona had altered shifted the power balance between them. Edward had responded with avoidance and an easily startled edginess.

Her aunt's decision-making tree had been enormously helpful. For weeks and weeks, thoughts of ending her marriage chased images of reconciliation, while thoughts of remaining remote from Edward collided with the possibility of never again feeling his love. As Bea had pointed out, doing the work, painful though it had been, had led to an answer. Now it was time to tip over the edge towards an uncertain outcome.

* * *

Edward wondered when Ann would decide. Since returning from Aunt Bea's, she had changed. He could not describe the difference; he just knew the signs were there, her posture more erect, her tone of voice firm, her outfits less drab, the way she sang in church more alive. Everything had shifted. But like the infinitesimal shrinking of a glacier, he doubted anyone else would have noticed.

The wait was excruciating, at times reminding him of the hours before battle, when every second was marked and fear stretched thin and brittle. Days when he imagined the worst still outnumbered those when Ann's actions seemed positive, although he debated every slim bit of evidence, from the way she ironed his shirts to the smoothness of the sheets on the guest bed where he slept. Edward looked for some sort of sign, anything to signal that Ann was willing to start putting their nightmare aside. Something about the way she had looked that morning left him wondering.

Amidst the gloom of early evening, lights from the living room through the partially drawn curtains made the house look inviting, despite the straggle of snow that edged their sidewalk. When he opened the door, he sensed an air of calm.

"I'm home," he said, as he did every night.

Usually Emily responded, coming into the hall as if, in

her mother's emotional absence, it was her duty to greet him. Silence. Wearily he hung up his coat, placing his hat on the top shelf. After slipping off his rubbers, he glanced over to find Ann waiting at the kitchen door.

"How was your day?" she asked.

Not once in the past four months had she said those words. Like a skittish colt faced with a bridle, he attempted to assign her words to the positive or negative side of the ledger. Optimism struck first. She would not be asking if she did not care. Pessimism followed. Bad news is delivered more easily after a bit of pleasantry. Ann waited.

Though the hallway was less than twenty feet long, walking towards her felt painful, like a weary warrior struggling to get behind the lines. Not until he was five paces away did she manage a tiny smile, and when he reached her, he said nothing. Instead he put his arms around her and laid his cheek on hers. After a moment, he felt the familiar comfort of her body leaning against him.

"We have to talk." Her words were muffled against his chest.

"I know," he replied, "your silence has been unbearable. For months I've felt like the living dead. I will never, ever do such a thing again. You have to believe me."

"I need you to tell me what happened. Maybe then we can begin to heal."

31 DECEMBER 1936

Skirts arranged and knees crossed, they sat apart, in their usual places. Edward sipped his drink. Silence gathered. The hall clock chimed. He looked at Ann and took a deep breath, like a child about to dive from a frightening height.

"I enlisted two weeks before my nineteenth birthday. All my friends were signing up. We didn't understand a thing about war. It was all talk of excitement, doing one's duty, seeing action before it was over. I didn't think for even one minute that I might be affected so profoundly by the horror of it. When war was declared, the crowds went crazy, flinging hats in the air, singing 'Rule Britannia', shouting slogans. Men rushed to the recruiting offices. We could only imagine triumph."

Edward spoke about training camp, the ship that took him to England, more training once they arrived, landing in France, endless days in the trenches, running dispatches, coding messages, stringing wire, battles fought at Ypres and the Somme, confusion and chaos.

"So many died. It's a terrible thing seeing war up close. One day, I watched a soldier tossed in the air by the force of an explosion like Alex might toss one of his stuffed animals. As I delivered messages or crawled between trenches, I found severed arms and legs in the mud. I remember holding the hand of a dying friend in a makeshift field hospital. I carried him there, although I knew he wouldn't make it."

He sat quietly, shoulders slumped, the shadows in their living room emphasizing the deep lines of stress around his mouth and eyes.

"I went to Vimy in January 1917, three months prior to the actual battle. The area around Vimy had been in a stalemate since the early part of the war. No headway had been made on either side and the Germans were entrenched in what we called 'Fortress Vimy'. Men lived and fought and died in an underground world or amidst the mud and craters of no man's land. The generals called it a war of attrition."

He told her about preparing for Vimy, the massive build up as Canadians dug tunnels, built underground railroads, brought in supplies and ammunition. With a faraway look in his eyes, he saw it all again.

"Vimy was a turning point in the war, although we didn't know it then. You saw the ridge. It held a commanding view of the entire plain where Germany controlled the war for over two years. Loss of the ridge exposed their positions to our guns. Vimy was our responsibility. We wanted to make a difference. To prove ourselves. Every day the tension mounted as we worked to make sure there would be no mistakes.

"You can't imagine how terrible the actual battle was. We rehearsed endlessly. Everyone knew their orders and was fully briefed so that if officers were killed, we could continue without them. My job was to coordinate all communications in one of four quadrants."

He told her that during the week preceding the attack over one million shells rained down on German positions, destroying transportation and communication routes, stopping food, ammunition and fresh troops from arriving, creating confusion, and undermining morale.

". . . a deafening sound, day after day, hour after hour. I lived in a world of death."

Once he began, Edward could not stop, purging war from his soul, where it had been locked away for close to twenty years.

"The weather that day was sleet and rain. Our infantry and artillery worked in concert, man and shell advanced together so that we were right on top of the Germans as they emerged from their trenches, expecting to use machine gun fire to take out our infantry. Instead, we mowed them down. We exploded underground mines, fired gas shells on their positions, attacked and attacked again. The battlefield was mired in blood, body parts, unexploded shells, discarded equipment, barbed wire."

Ann's face grew paler with each gruesome detail.

"I had a group of ten men and I roamed up and down the lines, never knowing whether I would make it back. On four occasions shells missed me by only a few feet, the whine as they came in made me crazy not knowing which way to turn. Even as a signaller, I killed several men that day, but only one remains in my memory—he was blond and blue-eyed and could not have been more than fifteen. He looked at me in surprise after I shot him and cried out for his mother when I approached to see if he was dead. His brains spilled out from under his helmet as blood ran from his mouth and he twitched a few times. It was over in seconds. I turned away and continued with my duties, not even pausing to say a prayer or reflect on the life I had ended. I felt like some kind of animal.

"Late that day, I was shot by a sniper's bullet, as I ran with an urgent message to our forward lines. Fortunately, someone pulled me to safety. They told me it was days before they knew I would live. After I recovered, I was numb, feeling nothing, reacting like a robot. I couldn't get the images, or the sounds, or the awful smells out of my mind. They kept replaying like a tire spinning on ice. Eventually, after all the clean up, our unit moved out of Vimy and encamped in an area near the small town of Beaufort."

For the most part he hadn't looked at Ann, but instead stared out the front window, stopping when lights flashed as the occasional vehicle drove by on an otherwise dark street.

"You look exhausted," Ann said. "Do you want to stop now and continue tomorrow?"

"No. I have to finish, so you understand what happened to me and how it continues to haunt me. It never leaves me, Ann. The war, the dying, the suffering. Never lets me forget for very long."

Edward took a long, ragged breath. "It was in Beaufort that I met Helene."

He told her that Helene provided a refuge for him both physically and spiritually. That she helped him to heal as none of his companions, or, for that matter, the medical doctors and pastors who counselled him, had been able to.

"She was engaging and yet serene. She soothed me and loved me; she talked to me and listened to me. She didn't judge me. Without her I would have succumbed to such deep depression I may never have recovered. I loved her with all that my twenty-one-year-old self had to offer. And when I couldn't find her at the end of the war, I felt like my lifeline had been severed and I was at sea, tossed about by threatening storms with only a flimsy raft to carry me to safety. My reservoir of courage had run out. I didn't know how I would survive."

Glancing at Ann's face, Edward paused. "I know these details are hurtful, but I have to tell you. I don't think there's a future without the truth."

Ann closed her eyes for a moment then nodded.

"I never understood why she didn't wait for me. Seeing her again at Vimy brought it all back. I had to be with her. It feels like insanity now, but that day I felt wounded, afraid and abandoned all over again. I wasn't in control—in some way, I think my wartime self took over."

"But how could you do that to me? Why couldn't you talk
with me?"

"Every day I regret that decision. But you weren't part
of that life. You hadn't been there and I wasn't the man you
knew. I had returned to being the young, confused, no longer
innocent man who had been shattered by war. I felt I had lost
myself again and Helene would rescue me."

"That's not what marriage is supposed to be."

He buried his face in his hands. "Marriage doesn't usually
deal with war or inhumanity and devastating loss. It's con-
ceived in hope and expectations of love and happy outcomes."

"But you told me almost nothing about the war. How was
I to know of the ghosts haunting you? You weren't honest
with me. I've borne your children, lived with you through the
Depression, supported you and your career, set aside my own
desires." Ann shook her head back and forth as if trying to
erase what Edward had said. "You hurt me so much."

"I love you, Ann. This has become so clear to me. I don't
know how or why I lost sight of it, why I put us in jeopardy.
Perhaps my unfinished past possessed me, reawakened some
devil sleeping inside me. Helene knew that and I didn't."

Suddenly he realized that his statement was true. Helene
understood he was different, not the young soldier he once
was. She knew they could never go back. Until he had really
examined his feelings for Ann, he could not put his love for
Helene in perspective. Such realization was painful. Over the
years he had become too comfortable with his wife, too familiar. He had stopped trying to figure out who she was and
how she was evolving. He recalled one evening coming to the
humbling awareness that Ann had become the stronger one.

Ann wrapped her arms around her shoulders, as if holding
herself together.

"Is it done now? Can you find yourself in our life together?
Can I trust you again?"

"Yes." Edward was emphatic, his eyes pleading for understanding. "I know now that you and the children are the only important things in my life. I've thought about this for months. You sustain me, Ann—not some ghostly memory from the past. Our children give me such joy and hope. You and our life together have healed the holes inside me. I don't know why I didn't realize it before, but I didn't and for that I am so dreadfully sorry." He paused, "I want us to mend, Ann. Can we find a way to do that?"

Ann glanced away and when she turned back, tears were falling. "Do you still love me?"

"More than I can say. All these months I've thought about my love for you, remembering so many times together. Remembering making love to you and how we cherished one another. You are my love, my soul's desire. Without you and the children, I am nothing."

For hours they had been in separate spaces, as if touching might shatter whatever tenuous bonds remained. Edward rose from his chair and crossed the few feet between them. He sat down beside Ann and held her in his arms. She began to sob, gulping sobs that shook her whole body. The depth of her sorrow frightened him. He shushed her like a tiny child with soft murmuring phrases. He kissed her forehead and brushed the tears from her face. Then he waited for Ann to speak.

32 DECEMBER 1936

All fall Ann had struggled to make sense of her feelings. Like
a gardener, she had worked the earth of her married life, lifting heavy, damp clods of memory to dig deep into their past,
extracting arguments that had spread like weeds to choke the
beauty of once-bright colours and intricate shapes, pruning
and discarding tangled branches brittle with decay. She wondered how to explain so he would understand.

Gradually, the comfort of Edward's arms and soft, soothing
words helped Ann control her emotions. Drawing back so she
could see him, she pulled a handkerchief out of her pocket and
wiped her tears before taking a deep, ragged breath.

"I must look dreadful," she said.

"Not to me. To me, you look beautiful." He ran a finger beneath her bottom lip. "Do you want to wait until tomorrow?"

Ann shook her head. "I just need a minute to gather my
thoughts."

She moved a little distance away so she could see his face.

Before she began, she offered a tentative smile.

"Even before we went to Vimy, I knew something was wrong. It was as though we'd lost the magic we had during our early years of marriage . . . and love had faded as time went by . . . we lived on parallel paths, close but not intersecting. I suppose I thought it was normal for married couples to ease into some other state." Each sentence sputtered like a candle flame in a draft.

"Motherhood was lonely despite the children and having friends in the same circumstance. I felt inadequate. At times I thought Emily and Alex were coming between us, and there were times when their demands were so great, I wished I could get away." Ann closed her eyes and hung her head. "I can't believe I thought that way. They are so precious to me, but as babies they seemed to suck every bit of life out of me. Hannah understood. I'm not sure what I would have done without her.

"Montreal was like exile when we first went there. And you were so busy, so sure of yourself. So successful. I was a failure, or so I thought. Hannah made me see myself differently. Getting involved with her at the museum gave me a place where I could contribute. I could be me, not Emily and Alex's mother. Not just your wife.

"The Depression was hard . . . it frightened me. All the difficulties and tragedy. We didn't talk about it. I would open my mouth to say something then see the look on your face. Eventually, I stopped trying. I occupied myself with more and more volunteer work, as if that would make up for what we no longer shared. I resented the amount of work you did and the feeling that life teetered on the edge every day. I know that's unfair, you shouldered so many burdens, but we didn't shoulder them together. Intimacy vanished, swallowed up in our struggle to hang on.

"Before we married, I worried about being intimate. Not just making love but binding our selves together, giving myself to you in total commitment. I felt you were dominating our relationship and that my acquiescence was required, not mine to give. I remember wondering if it would be my job to please and your job to demand. And I wondered if you would be open to my strength and opinions that differed from yours."

Ann looked at Edward to see if he understood. Her sentiments were harsh and he was unaccustomed to criticism, particularly from his wife. Edward was indeed listening. She could tell by the slightly puzzled look on his face and the way he leaned towards her.

"I knew you loved me, but I didn't know whether you would make room for me. And you did—or we did—for a while. But over time your opinions and preferences took precedence. I've thought about it a lot. It's like the balance of power—I can't think of any other way to express it—is too one-sided.

"When we returned to Toronto our pattern became one of work and family. We forgot about us again. I felt you were coddling me, maybe because you thought I was weak and no longer your equal. I had the sense of being parented by you. You didn't seek my opinion. Sometimes I felt like I was losing myself."

Ann squeezed his arm to take the sting out of her words. She saw Edward wanted to interrupt, though he held himself back. She was grateful; she needed to finish the telling. He needed to hear it all.

"I didn't know how to hold on to you. You kept slipping farther and farther away from me. When we went to France, you became another person. A person I didn't know. I was afraid. Afraid for you, at first. Then you sent me away and I was afraid for us.

"I've been frozen, incapable of functioning since you told me about Helene. So angry and bitter. Sometimes I felt betrayed, at other times inadequate. I hated what you had done to us.

"When I visited Aunt Bea, I told her I was going to leave you." Edward jerked back as though she had slapped him. "I didn't know how else to end the pain. She's so much wiser than I ever imagined. She didn't tell me what to do, merely showed me how to think things through. I don't know what I would have done without her.

"Eventually the one thing I could cling to was the knowledge that I love you. It kept me sane, thinking that if we both loved each other, we could salvage things. But I didn't know whether you loved me anymore. And I had to find out."

Ann's voice ended in a ragged whisper, her body limp from emotion. She kept her head down, afraid of what she might see in Edward's face.

Edward put his arms around her. "I love you," he whispered, holding her so tight she could hardly breathe. "Can we start again? I want to prove to you what our life together means to me. That we have something precious. What can I do to convince you?"

Overwhelming relief flooded through her as he said the words she had longed to hear. She had been so utterly spent with sadness and fear, and here he was, holding her like he would never let her go.

"Just hold me. For now, that will make me happy."

33 FEBRUARY 1937

February 12, 1937

At this time last year we were planning our trip to Vimy. So much has happened since. We are closer now than we were then, perhaps closer than we have ever been. Edward confides in me more often and seems to be able to admit his uncertainties and problems. In turn, I have found my own strength, so that our relationship is more balanced than in the past. I can almost say that I'm happy again, though perhaps content is a better word.

We haven't made love yet—and it's been seven months.

* * *

"Ann, I'm home. Sorry I'm late."

Edward tossed his hat on the shelf and hung up his coat. He put his suit jacket on the newel post then removed his tie. February had been a funny month, mixing weeks of perishing cold with unusual warmth, the temperature going up and down like a seesaw. Forecasters were now predicting a wintry

March. He rolled his cuffs over twice and undid his top button.

"Ann, where are you?"

"I'll be down in a minute. I'm just changing into something nice for dinner."

He leaned over the bannister and called up the stairs. "Where are Emily and Alex?"

"Mother wanted to take them for the weekend. She said they hadn't visited her and Daddy for a long time and I think she has some outings planned. You know how much she likes to spoil them."

Edward listened from the bottom of the stairs before heading into the living room. He was sure she would be down soon. In the meantime, he could unwind. With office pressures and his reserves duties, he had little time for himself and during the past two months, any spare time went to strengthening his relationship with Ann.

They took long walks in the snow, Emily and Alex scampering ahead or lingering far behind, while he and Ann linked arms, the mere feel of her making him hopeful. Late night conversations, with a brandy or small glass of scotch to loosen their tongues, allowed them to explore the past like archaeologists uncovering one layer at a time, occasionally treading on sensitive ground, daring to ask questions that might, just might, expose potential fault lines.

With the logjam unplugged, he spoke more of the war, telling stories about friends and the camaraderie they shared. These memories were painful but more bearable with Ann sitting close, holding his hand when he faltered. Beyond the war, they spoke of Ann's concerns, and he made a real effort to understand that what he had thought of as looking after her, in reality undermined her confidence and enthusiasm, and the very impulsiveness that had attracted him to her.

One night, just before bed, he had touched her, a brief caress along the length of one arm. She flinched then looked at him, her eyes full of regret. The next time he tried, she held his hand and kissed it before moving away. Every night she undressed in the bathroom and slipped into bed, saying "good night, dear" in quiet tones before turning away from him.

He sighed. *Perhaps a weekend without the children will help*, he thought.

Edward opened the newspaper, snapping the sheets in a brisk, practiced motion. He always kept up with the news, even if he only had time for the lead articles. At this point, news from Europe, and more particularly, news of Hitler, was uppermost in his mind. A headline about the Spanish Civil War caught his attention. Absorbed in reading, he did not notice when Ann came downstairs.

"Do you want a drink before dinner?"

Ann's question caused him to look up. She wore a light wool dress with a fitted bodice and deep V-neck, and the fabric clung to her body's contours. As she passed by, he smelled her light, spicy perfume.

"I'll get the drinks." He rose quickly and followed her to the kitchen. "You look wonderful. Have I forgotten an occasion?"

"Oh, no, nothing like that. Do you like my new dress?" She twirled around and waited for his nod. "I have a few last minute touches to make on dinner."

Ann put on an apron and began to make a salad. The kitchen smelled delicious, the aroma of roast chicken blending with some other scent he could not identify. While she grated cabbage and chopped vegetables for coleslaw, Edward measured shots of bourbon and added three ice cubes to each glass.

"The table's already set, so why don't we sit in the living room while the chicken finishes cooking." She hung the apron on the doorknob.

As Ann took a drink from Edward's hand, her fingers brushed against his. She sat on the couch and he joined her instead of sitting in his usual chair. As they chatted, sharing inconsequential stories of the day, his gaze drifted to her neckline from time to time. Her nearness aroused him.

Ann stood up. "I need to finish a few things or we won't

be having dinner at all. Why don't you fix us another drink?"

In the dining room, a vase full of yellow flowers sat on the table in between silver candlesticks and white tapered candles. *We haven't had dinner by candlelight in ages*, he reflected, appreciating the warm glow and soft shadows.

Ann set their plates on the table while Edward made a flourish of holding out her chair. The light-hearted mood continued. After a while Ann lifted her napkin from her lap and placed it on the table, a sure sign she was about to clear the dishes.

"Let's sit here for a bit," he said, "it hasn't been just the two of us for a long while."

Under her steady gaze, he reached over and touched her fingers one by one, then traced a slow path up her arm and down again. She closed her eyes as he took her hand and kissed each finger then took one in his mouth and sucked on it. Ann parted her lips.

Edward got up and stood behind her chair, massaging her shoulders gently. Then he unhooked the back of her dress and eased the zipper down so that one shoulder slipped off. His right hand traced the line of her neck to the soft skin below her collar and then to her breast, cupping it, feeling the weight of it, flicking a finger softly across her nipple. Ann arched her neck to look at him.

"Not here," she said, her voice husky.

They climbed the stairs together, pausing at the landing to press their bodies and mouths together, tongues mingling. His erection stiffened against her body and a small sigh escaped her lips.

Once in the bedroom, Edward unzipped the rest of Ann's dress and it fell to the floor, exposing white lace underpants and a bra that barely covered her nipples. She stepped closer, pulling his shirt out from beneath his belt, and unbuttoning each button, and pressed against him. He released the clasp of her bra, slid it off her shoulders and felt the smooth curve of her breasts. Keeping his eyes on hers, he removed the rest of his clothes and lifted her onto their bed.

He kissed her mouth, then her eyes, earlobes and neck. He lay on his side and traced his fingertips along her body, touching her breasts, her torso, circling around and around.

Ann reached for him. "I want you inside me," she said.

"I've been waiting so long for you to say that."

PART II

34 June 1942

The day began in haste, porridge burbling on the stove, Alex muttering as he searched for his poetry anthology. Sandwiches, wrapped in wax paper, were on the kitchen counter. In the garden, a cardinal dove amongst the bushes, and raindrops from last night's storm lingered on the grass. The sharp, orange glow of early morning had faded. Ann knew the day would be hot.

Edward was in uniform. After three years as a major, he had been promoted in 1940 to the position of Lieutenant Colonel of A Corps Signals. Before preparing breakfast, Ann had packed Edward's suitcase with a mix of civilian and military clothes. She looked at her still-handsome dark-haired husband and wondered why he had asked her to pack his dress uniform, reserved for formal occasions. He had never taken it with him before. She knew not to ask; he would only look at her as if she should know better.

Secrets had invaded their life again. In fact, secrets had become their way of life, or, at least, Edward's way of life. She could almost pinpoint when they started, shortly after a meeting he had with General Hastings in early 1941. Although her husband knew Paul Hastings through business, a meeting with a high-ranking general in the regular army was unusual for someone in the reserves, and Edward had seemed puzzled when he came home, so puzzled he had drifted away from their conversation several times and she had given up in frustration. In the months that followed, she often caught a look of bemusement on his face, although he was not at all amused when she began calling him Sherlock.

More than a year later, she still knew almost nothing of what drew him away from home time and again. The only information Edward had imparted was that he had agreed to support an effort requiring extreme confidentiality—Ann had been surprised at the deliberate way he had repeated those words—and that this effort required his absence from time to time.

Secrets had already caused so much pain; she could not help wondering, even as she attempted to dismiss such thoughts, whether a woman had captured his attention again. When she broached the topic in a light-hearted manner, his mouth had hung open in shocked surprise followed by a denial that was swift and absolute. Still, like waves eroding the shoreline, Edward's secret life nibbled at her stability.

Ann stirred the porridge, which was beginning to stick. Another minute and it might have burned and that would have caused grumbling. Edward preferred something hot to start his day, often saying that porridge was the only food to sustain him until lunch.

I do cater to that man, she thought, her mouth twitching with a mix of amusement and exasperation.

The aroma of percolating coffee filled the kitchen. With windows on two sides, the room was bright, morning sun pouring in as soon as it crested the cedar hedge in their backyard.

Emily arrived just as Ann ladled steaming-hot cereal into four bowls. With little ceremony, except to check that Alex was paying attention, Edward asked for God's blessing. Ann picked up a spoon, glancing one after another at her family: Emily with a finger marking a spot in her textbook, Alex stirring milk into his porridge, Edward absorbed in the news. No one spoke. Though breakfast was often a time of little conversation, today's silence felt vaguely unsettling, and she thought Edward was more distracted than usual.

As always, he was preoccupied with the newspaper, following every war development, checking names of the deceased, pausing for a quick glance at business news, such as it was; the business of business being war. Since September 1939, each day was bookended by dreadful news in the morning paper and dreadful news on the evening radio. Retrieving *The Globe and Mail* from the front doorstep earlier that morning, she had glanced quickly at the headlines screaming of loss.

After two years of German successes, the first six months of 1942 had brought further devastation. U-boats sank more and more Allied naval and supply ships. Hitler had attacked Russia. Rommel had driven across the desert to El Alamein. News from Asia was equally grim: Japan relentlessly destroying everything in its path, invading Singapore, Burma, Hong Kong and the Philippines and sinking dozens of Allied naval vessels. A few weeks ago, US Navy success at the battles of Coral Sea and Midway offered a glimmer of faraway hope. Ann clung to this news like a lost sailor to driftwood.

"Here's something you should consider, Emily. A way to help during the summer months," Edward said.

Emily looked at her father, while Alex, who disliked porridge without sugar, continued to stir the lumpy mass in his bowl. Edward cleared his throat and began to read from the paper.

"A new responsibility has been thrust on the women of Ontario. It will be their job to see that the fruit and vegetable crops of the Province are not wasted . . . casual labour, on which the canneries depended in past years, does not exist. Crops are being harvested by volunteer workers of the Ontario Farm Service Force, and their work will be for nothing if the canneries aren't staffed to handle the fruits and vegetables. What is wanted is that all available food resources be preserved against the uncertainties of war and weather . . . there is no more worthwhile service any woman can do." He raised his eyes from the paper to glance at Emily. "The Minister of Agriculture is appealing for five thousand women. There's a number you can call to volunteer."

Ann knew how strongly Edward felt the call of duty to country and family, and to faith and community. He expected his children to uphold the same values. She saw the look of dismay mingled with rebellion forming on Emily's face and shook her head, ever so slightly, to warn her daughter not to protest. Edward's mood was such that opposition could easily escalate into argument. He would be more malleable another time.

"When will you be back?" she asked, pouring two cups of coffee then adding a small amount of milk. Neither took sugar any longer, every spoonful saved for special occasions.

"I'm not certain, but I think it will be more than a week this time." He looked over the top of the paper with an apologetic smile.

Ann did not ask his destination, but the trip's duration made her wonder. Usually he was away two or three days on these trips she referred to as "Edward's private war".

"I hate it when you're gone so long. And we're supposed to go to that fundraiser Marge is organizing. Remember?" Edward nodded. "I was looking forward to it."

"I'm sorry, sweetheart, but I have no choice in the matter. Why don't you go anyway? It won't be the first time a woman has appeared without her husband." He folded the newspaper back into its original order.

"You know I prefer being with you."

Ann took a sip of coffee. Not a week went by without some

reminder of sacrifice. From the beginning, she had told herself not to be one of those who complained. At least Edward had not gone overseas and Alex was too young to enlist. Life could have been much worse.

"Well, lots of officers will want to dance with a beautiful woman like you. I'd only get in the way," Edward teased.

Ann swatted his shoulder playfully then leaned over to press her cheek against his. "I'll miss you."

"What are you doing today?"

"I'm off to Signals Welfare. It's my first day as President. I'm a little nervous. One or two of the women can be difficult."

"You'll handle them with your usual tact." He put his arm around her and let his hand linger briefly on her hip. "I really should get going, darling. The car is due to arrive shortly."

By eight thirty, Ann was alone. After a second cup of coffee, she put on her hat and gloves, found her purse and meeting notes, and left the house. She walked along their leafy street and across the bridge. The Don River chattered quietly, its innocence a sharp contrast to April when the river surged, swollen with brown silt, and rose every half hour until it crested the banks and flooded many houses in the valley. The men and older boys in the neighbourhood had worked three nights in a row to prevent serious damage. Edward and Alex had taken turns manning the pumps, some in their own house and others at homes along the riverbank. Ann and Emily had been part of the food brigade, producing an endless stream of tuna, egg and cheese sandwiches. The floods had been a time of neighbourhood bonding and a chance to forget, if only for a few days, the awful presence of war.

Turning on to Donino Crescent, she passed several houses set well back from the street and noticed a bin full of discarded shingles on the Campbells' front lawn. With building materials almost exclusively reserved for military purposes, she wondered what strings John Campbell had pulled to secure permission to rebuild their roof. A little further on, she waved at Bill Williams as he stooped to pick up the morning newspaper from his front step.

Ann and Edward's house in Hogg's Hollow was located in a river valley, requiring a steep climb to reach the streetcar stop and nearby shops. Commencing the climb, she slowed her pace, enjoying the feeling of quiet solitude. In the heat of late June, lilac bushes drooped with fading blossoms and she paused to inhale their sweet fragrance. A little further on, a chipmunk scurried across the road. Ann smiled as the small animal scampered up a spreading elm tree. Nearing the top of the hill, she saw the streetcar in the turning loop and quickened her pace.

She climbed on board, deposited her ticket and took a seat on the right-hand side. Within minutes, the driver released the handbrake and rang the bell as he turned left onto Yonge Street and headed south.

Ann sat back, pondering the morning's conversation, worried about Edward's absences. He was working long, hard hours, not sleeping well, his face drawn. Wrinkles that had previously appeared only when he smiled or frowned were now permanently etched on his face, his hair stained grey. It was no longer the face of a young man.

Each trip seemed to be worse than the one before and she wondered what this one was about. "Just another one of my meetings," he always said, but instinct told her he was involved in something else, something unusual.

With so much work and travel, they had less time for one another and often the time they did have involved Edward's duties with the reserves: parades and military ceremonies, fund-raising dances and picnics, and seasonal activities that required his appearance. At these affairs Ann was the dutiful wife, the smiling wife, the helpful wife, the concerned, sympathetic wife. She could not remember the last time they went out as a twosome.

The streetcar trundled on, its wheels occasionally screeching before jerking to a stop to gather more passengers. People, hats, briefcases and parcels competed for space. The air smelled of cramped bodies, shaving cream, wool and worn leather.

Ann's thoughts turned to her responsibilities at Signals Welfare. With more than twenty thousand fatalities and four thousand men missing or in POW camps, helping women cope had become an essential war service. As the incoming president, she would be expected to run today's meeting. Their team of volunteers struggled to keep up, but every month more cases piled in than were satisfied. Ann had hoped to ask Edward for ideas, but he had been too wrapped up in his own concerns.

When the streetcar stopped at the corner of Yonge and Dundas, Ann got off and began the short walk to the group's main office. At the next corner, a cluster of soldiers emerged from a small, run-down hotel, talking energetically, full of life, jostling one another as young men do until suddenly, as though they were one connected body, they snapped to attention, saluting a senior officer passing by.

"Good morning, sir!" they chorused.

With more order than before, the young soldiers proceeded along the sidewalk and turned sharply right to cross the street, the pulse of thumping boots fading as they went. Beyond men and women dressed in uniform, reminders of the war shouted at Ann from every direction. Newsboys called out headlines, posters exhorted sacrifice, shop windows listed ration rules and shortages. Flags at half-mast signalled casualties.

The deaths of her friends' husbands and sons hung like chains around her shoulders, the list growing longer and longer as time passed. Eleanor Sanderson's son had been the first. Telephone calls had spread like wildfire, rallying every woman at the church in less time than one of Father Stephen's sermons. Food and comfort helped for a few weeks, but eventually Eleanor had to face a future without her Jimmy. "Death is a busy time at first," she had said to Ann one afternoon at Dickson's grocery store, "but afterwards the days are endless, every moment filled with missing him."

Ann walked up the few steps leading to a large red brick house with columns flanking the front door.

"Good morning, Ginny," she said after entering the house. "Is our meeting in the Blue Room?"

A ginger-haired woman looked up from her typewriter. "Hello, Ann. Yes, it is. I'm just finishing a report for Angela, so I'll join you in a minute. Some of the ladies are already here. Eileen Hurley, for one." Ginny Marks scrunched her mouth in a way Ann interpreted as empathy.

Eileen was a difficult woman who made her opinions known regardless of sensitivities. On more than one occasion, she had criticised Ann's suggestions, pretending to comment discreetly but always ensuring that Ann was near enough to hear. Eileen Hurley was the only reason Ann had hesitated before accepting the role of president.

"Lovely," Ann said.

"Just ignore her."

"That's easy for you to say."

Signals Welfare operated out of three floors of an old house bequeathed by the estate of Brigadier Lewis, a WWI Signals commander. With pale blue walls and blue velvet curtains, the dining room had been designated the Blue Room and was now the group's main meeting area. Ann ducked into her office, a room full of dark wood and filing cabinets and collected a pad of paper and two pencils before proceeding to her meeting.

* * *

By the time Ann arrived home, Emily had changed out of her school uniform into a grey pleated skirt acquired from one of her cousins and a white blouse patterned with tiny pink roses. Emily's eyebrows traced the same arc as her mother's. Brown hair curled behind her ears. A shapely young woman with smooth skin and high cheekbones had replaced the gangly, awkward girl. Although Emily had inherited her father's quiet reserve and sharp intellect, all of Ann's friends said

Emily looked like her.

With shoes and clothing rationed, Emily rarely had anything new. At seventeen she was mature enough not to complain, but Ann wished she could buy something beautiful for
her daughter instead of accepting hand-me-downs or purchas-
ing used items at rummage sales. A few months ago she had
helped Emily make a blouse out of old curtain material.

Every element of family living was regulated in some way.
Newspapers and radio programs exhorted them to fulfil their
civic duty by making frequent blood donations and recycling
items like aluminum foil, household metals of any sort and
fats. Fat was needed to make explosives.

"There you are, dear." Ann emptied her packages onto the
counter. "I bought a small piece of corned beef. Mr. Dickson
said he was saving it for me."

"Good thing it's Monday," Emily said. "Isn't it funny how
Alex hates Tuesdays? And Daddy does too."

Ann chuckled. "But Meatless Tuesday has turned out to be
a great success. I remember reading that the first one saved
enough meat to stock a battleship for five months. Or something like that. Every bit helps."

After unwrapping the brown paper, Ann tied a string
around the beef and set it to simmer in a pot full of water and
dried spices.

"How was your day?" Emily said, slicing carrots into a
small pot.

In the fall they stored bushels of carrots, potatoes and onions in the root cellar. After so many months, these vegetables
were spotted with age and Emily cut away rotting sections
with practised hands. Their backyard victory garden supplied
them with fresh vegetables, many of which they canned in
the fall, but June was too early for anything more than green
shoots to show above ground. Shortages came and went, often
with little warning. Last month they could not buy eggs, and
the month before tea and coffee were almost impossible to
find. Ann, constantly on the alert for opportunities, guarded

their coupons with care.

Ann sighed. "My meeting was difficult. Do you remember Mrs. Hurley?"

"I do. She's the woman who refused to help clean the group's new premises. Didn't she tell you that it was the sort of work her maid performed? You were furious, weren't you?"

"That's the one. Well, she was very disruptive at our meeting today. Took exception to everything I suggested. I felt she was deliberately undermining me. So unproductive." Ann stabbed a fork into the meat at regular intervals.

"Maybe she's jealous because you're the incoming president."

"Very astute, sweetie. But she doesn't realize how her behaviour looks to everyone else. No one would have voted for her." Ann paused, thinking about how infuriating Eileen Hurley had been. Ginny Marks had commiserated with her over a cup of tea after the meeting.

"Can't you get rid of her?"

"No. That's the problem with volunteers. You get them even if you don't want them. Some people are so petty, it makes my blood boil. We're supposed to be helping others, not worrying about ourselves."

Ann decided to change the topic and asked about school. Emily chatted happily for several minutes before switching to a more serious topic.

"I was annoyed at Dad this morning."

"I could see that. Your father's only thinking of what will help the war effort."

"I know. But I'd rather find my own way to help this summer. When he acts that way, I just become stubborn. Silly, I suppose."

Ann laughed. "Not silly at all, my love. I know exactly how you feel. You must have inherited your stubbornness from me." She put her arm around Emily. "Because he was in the last war, he seems to feel more responsible somehow. I don't understand his logic. Did you know he wanted to serve in the regular army?"

Emily's face turned serious. "But then he might have gone overseas. That would have been terrible."

"We're lucky, you know. Think of all the husbands and sons who have gone. This morning, I watched a group of young recruits and all I could think of was how many of them would die."

"Mom, what a dreadful thought."

"I know. I couldn't help myself. Time to finish dinner," Ann said. She moved away from Emily and lifted a pot from the stove, drained the potatoes and shook them vigorously to release some of the steam. "Is Alex home?"

"He was home, but then he went out again. I think he's down at the Stewarts'."

"Can you call Mrs. Stewart and ask her to send him home?"

After dinner Ann and Emily sat together in the living room listening to their regular news program.

"*. . . thirty-six merchant ships left Iceland two days ago after a refuelling stop. They were delivering supplies to Russian troops fighting on Hitler's second front. According to sources, six destroyers and four corvettes closely escorted the convoy. Reportedly, Rear Admiral Pound, fearing attack by German ships and the loss of significant naval power, instructed the convoy to scatter and withdrew all six British destroyers. The CBC has received information that German aircraft and U-boats have already sunk fifteen of the merchant ships.*" The announcer paused, as if gathering himself to deliver another blow. "*We have no information concerning Canadian casualties but are monitoring this situation closely. And now, turning to other items, President Roosevelt, in an unexpected joint press conference with British Prime Minister Winston Churchill, has once again publicly acknowledged American support for Britain . . .*"

Ann stopped what she was doing, knitting needles poised, wool wrapped around her finger for the next stitch. She imagined men dying in frigid waters or caught in an explosion on board ship, and when the next day dawned, only floating debris and oil slicks would commemorate their sacrifice.

"I can't bear to think about those ships and all the men left defenceless in the middle of the Atlantic," she said.

"When will it end, Mom? Joan's brother left last week. She told me her mother hasn't stopped crying since."

"Your father says it's a long way from being over. Linda is so worried about her David, and Hannah already had to watch Michael go. I can't imagine . . ."

"Maybe it's better not to imagine."

"Maybe you're right. This relentless destruction makes me feel sick. I hate that you and Alex have to grow up amidst war."

"Why did David enlist instead of going to university? He's only eighteen."

"I don't know, dear. I'm sure his mother and father ask that question every day."

"I hope nothing happens to him," Emily said.

"From your lips to God's ears," Ann replied.

The two women fell silent. The radio droned on.

Ann could not decide which was worse, the written or spoken word. Some days she thought the power of the written word to describe the horror of a ship going down, the terror as bombs destroyed street after street, the awful panic of looking for lost children, the weight of waiting to hear whether a son, husband or brother fell in battle—that written words were the worst. On other days it was the sombre, solemn voice of the announcer, his calm accepting tone marked by an occasional quaver as he told the tales of war. Some days she thought she could not bear to learn of one more tragedy and avoided the day's news, *The Globe and Mail* haunting her from its place on the coffee table, the silent radio shaming her for cowardice.

"I've heard enough, Mom. I think I'll go up to my room."

Ann responded with a weak smile. Her children were growing up fast, their childhood sucked away by a world embroiled in conflict.

"Sleep well, sweetheart," she said, needles clicking.

Knitting socks while men were drowning made her feel helpless. All her friends were relentless knitters. With so much practice, Ann could make a pair of socks in one or two evenings and a sweater in less than two weeks. Some of her efforts went to Signals Welfare and others went to the Red Cross, destined for Canadian soldiers overseas.

Members of the Ladies Auxiliary to A Corps Signals made many items and cajoled individual donors and businesses for others. With Edward's prominent role in the Corps, Ann had organized the auxiliary during the early months of war and served as its first chairwoman. On Saturdays, Emily helped, spending hours wrapping goods and packing boxes for overseas, seated with friends at long trestle tables, patiently handling box after box while listening to the older women. In the past three years, the auxiliary had contributed to hundreds of shipments. Demand was endless.

With Edward away so often, Ann was glad to be busy. She got up to stretch for a few minutes and looked outside. Ordinarily she loved June evenings, when dusk crept into darkness well after nine. They reminded her of summer holidays and the beginning of picnic season. But on this particular night, she was too unsettled by the news broadcast to appreciate the light shifting from gold to pink and then purple.

Edward's absence worried her. For a few years after they reconciled, they were as happy as newlyweds, learning new ways to communicate and adjusting the balance between them, nourishing each other in the quiet spaces of their marriage. But as war unfolded and Edward's trips became more frequent, intimacy suffered.

Ann picked up her knitting again. She switched her needles to make the ribbed top of a sock as the radio announcer introduced a concerto by Mozart and soon a soothing blend of piano and violin unfolded.

Her mind itemized family members one by one. Alex seemed moodier than usual and she wondered whether this was just a stage teenage boys went through. She worried when he disappeared after supper, not that there was any evidence of trouble but she wondered where he went and if asked, would complain that he was old enough to look after himself.

Ann's mother was noticeably slowing down, coping with high blood pressure after the scare of a mild heart attack one year ago and arthritis in one knee. Ann's father had retired, but he still gardened extensively and now looked after many chores his wife previously handled. When her brothers enlisted, her father's hair had gone white almost overnight. Ann's older brother Alan was a navigator, flying aboard troop transport planes, while her younger brother Harry was part of a tank brigade. With two sons fighting overseas, her mother and father greeted every day with anxiety and although her mother made much of each letter they received, grasping at every bit of positive news, tears appeared whenever she spoke of their sons. Ann knew they feared the worst just as she did.

She sighed again. Her parents' increasing fragility worried her, but there was nothing she could do to stem the aging process. Ann did not want to imagine a time without them.

As the clock began to chime eleven o'clock, she lifted her head. "I wish I knew where Edward's gone," she muttered.

35 June 1942

At that very moment, Edward was boarding an overnight train bound for Washington, accompanied by Paul Hastings and Colonel Charles Dupuis. There would be much to discuss on the journey, but for now they were occupied in finding their seats.

"We're right behind you, Edward," said Charles, with the barest of French accents.

Based on the numbers above the seat nearest him, Edward figured they were at the far end and he gestured in that direction. Paul Hastings grunted and followed the dark-haired Dupuis, whose long legs and short, thick torso made him stand out in any group of men. Amidst blue- and grey-suited men were a smattering of army and navy uniforms and one woman, her serious face and crisp attire suggesting someone accustomed to authority.

"Let me help with that," Edward said.

"You're very kind."

As he placed her suitcase on the rack and waited for the woman to settle into her seat, he wondered whether she was a nurse or perhaps even a doctor. With so many doctors serving overseas, women now filled many senior positions at hospitals and medical institutions. Edward continued along the aisle. Blackout curtains covered each window and small brass lamps provided shallow arcs of light. Covered in faded brown fabric, the arms and backs of many seats were threadbare. A sour smell added to the feeling of neglect.

When they reached their seats, Edward took one facing backward, opposite Hastings and Dupuis. As the train began to move, a fourth man joined them, a man Edward met in 1941 when he had been summoned to a briefing with Hastings as Hitler's troops rolled across Europe.

They had been at the Military Institute, an imposing, three-storey building housing artefacts from various wars and serving as a club for officers. Though military in bearing, Hastings was always slightly rumpled, as if his clothes had not been properly pressed. His head was bald, except for a band of sandy brown hair around his ears. During WWI, he had caught a piece of shrapnel in his right leg, which left him with a slight limp.

"Do you want to serve beyond the reserves?" Hastings' question had been clipped and gruff as he pushed back the sleeve of his left arm and looked at his watch.

"Yes . . ." The question had startled Edward. "But I was told when I joined A Corps that I wouldn't be able to enlist. One of my lungs doesn't function properly. Ironic that it was damaged in the first war." Being judged inadequate still rankled.

"It's good enough for what I want you for."

"What's that?"

"You have to swear that you won't disclose anything I tell you." Hastings pulled on one earlobe.

"Good heavens, General . . ."

"It's Paul." Hastings interrupted impatiently. "Edward,

we've known each other for years; just because I wear these stripes doesn't mean you need to be so bloody formal."

Edward allowed a small smile to form; Hastings was rarely rattled. "Paul," he emphasized the name, "what on earth are you going to tell me that requires such secrecy?"

Although they were alone, Paul Hastings leaned closer. "Churchill has authorized the formation of a secret service to work outside military channels. Europe's in such a dreadful state after the Nazi blitzkrieg and the failure at Dunkirk. Allied troops are unlikely to land there for at least a year. He wants to organize underground movements in enemy-occupied territory."

"Do you mean espionage?"

Paul nodded.

"Wouldn't that take months to set up? A whole raft of logistics. Staff, electronics, equipment." Edward's brain ticked in logical sequence. "And how would Canada be involved?"

"Our government has agreed to establish a training centre here. We'll recruit and train as many men and women as we can." Edward sat up straight and frowned. "Hear me out," Paul continued. "Those who work for this organization will have to use a range of methods—sabotage, labour agitation, propaganda, boycotts, riots. You can imagine what would be needed. Apparently Churchill believes that a group of this scale and character is not something that can be handled by the normal civil service machinery or even the military. It needs a new organization to work underground with nationals of oppressed countries. It has to be flexible. And creative. Canada was chosen because of our close connection to Britain and our proximity to the US."

Edward snorted. "If you haven't noticed, Paul, the Americans aren't fighting this war."

Like most Canadians, he bitterly resented the US for remaining neutral. In his mind, the first war was proof enough that they should stand with the Allies.

"They will eventually, and in the meantime, Churchill is

counting on their support, even if indirectly. And we have another strength to offer—our diverse population of immigrants. Who better to train than an Italian-born Canadian or a man whose parents were raised in Belgium or the Balkans? We have an Asian population too. And we can't forget Quebec."

"They're against conscription."

"We'll find the ones who want to serve," Paul said. "We'll need absolute secrecy, men and women who are completely reliable, a host of supplies which you and I cannot even fathom."

Edward was beginning to see the potential. "What do you want me to do?" His mind jumped in several directions at once, imagining the possibilities of how he could contribute and the pride he would feel being in active service, even if in secret.

"You're capable and clever. I want your signals experience, your telephone background and your management skills. I know you can help coordinate efforts, particularly communications training. Beyond that, I'm not sure yet, but we need to start with planning. You'll be an asset."

Someone knocked on the door.

"Come in," said Paul, without hesitation.

The man who entered was in his early forties and of medium stature. He had a ruddy complexion and wore gold wire-rimmed glasses.

"Have you told him?" When Paul nodded, he turned to Edward. "Well?"

Edward frowned and looked at Paul.

"Edward Jamieson. William Stephenson." The two men shook hands.

Stephenson plunged right in. "Paul has told me all about you. We need men like you with military experience and communications expertise."

"And your job is?"

"Oh. Sorry. Let me explain." Stephenson took the chair facing Edward. "I'm operating under the authority of Hugh Dalton, the Minister of Economic Warfare. Churchill has appointed him to oversee what we're calling Special Operations Executive. SOE. Hugh has sent me to North America. I'm working with General Hastings to get things set up in Canada. I'm also working with the US. Behind the scenes. All very hush-hush."

Still somewhat confused, Edward nodded. "I see."

Stephenson went on to provide his credentials, a hint of pride creeping into his voice as he recited numerous honours received in WWI.

"After WWI, business interests brought me into contact with people from across Europe. With a little manoeuvring, I was able to provide confidential information to the British about Hitler's military build up prior to thirty-nine. Churchill and Dalton selected me to head British Security Coordination and have charged me with investigating enemy activities and coordinating underground warfare."

Edward shook his head rapidly back and forth, a habit he picked up after World War I when his ears were damaged. He could not believe he was having this conversation. Never would he have imagined that this was what Hastings wanted to talk about. He said yes, of course, not only because he loved his country, but also because the possibilities intrigued him.

After months of planning and complex negotiations with British and US counterparts, they found a site on sloping farmland and called it Camp X. With a diverse topography of shoreline bluffs, sandy beach and rough land, easy access from British Security Coordination headquarters in New York and unique suitability for long distance radio installations, the Glenrath farm was almost perfect.

Upon securing the property, barracks and training facilities were added, as well as an underground shooting range. After months of operation, Edward could have found his way around blindfolded.

As soon as the camp was ready, he worked with a team of officers to develop training courses for intelligence agents bound for Europe. At the beginning, his specialty was wireless operations, though he also dealt with other matters including sabotage of telephone and radio installations. Just like every other instructor, Edward was required to take the full training program that included parachute jumping, explosives, mountain climbing, silent killing techniques, elementary Morse code and the art of blending in with the local population. Camp X was the reason for his frequent absences from home.

SOE called the site Special Training School 103, or STS 103. When Edward first heard that designation, he was shocked to think there were more than one hundred other such facilities. He knew it was also called Project J by the Canadian military. Only insiders called it Camp X.

After the training school was fully operational, Edward's role had expanded and he now liaised with BSC New York and was often called in for broader discussions of strategy. Having sworn an oath to maintain secrecy for twenty-five years, he said almost nothing to Ann of these clandestine responsibilities, but after so many trips she had developed a quizzical look that involved tipping her head slightly and widening her eyes, whenever he asked her to pack a suitcase. To his profound dismay, she had once joked that he must have acquired a mistress, a comment he had swiftly and vehemently denied. Nothing could have been further from the truth, and yet he knew she worried. In turn, he worried about the added burden his absences had on her.

On this occasion, Edward was not going to Camp X. Instead the four men were heading to Washington to attend the second formal war conference between the US and Britain. Churchill and Roosevelt would be the main players, however, discussions between military and intelligence representatives on a wide range of topics would parallel the formal conference.

As the train left the station, Stephenson leaned forward.

"Churchill flew in on the eighteenth to visit Roosevelt in his Hyde Park home. Both leaders will travel to Washington by train and meet with the Combined Chiefs of Staff as well as shipping and military advisors." Though no one sat nearby,

Stephenson kept his voice low.

"Why is the King of Yugoslavia attending?" Hastings asked. "He's on the agenda for Wednesday evening."

"I'm not sure. Their resistance groups have had some success lately against the Nazis. The government-in-exile must have something to offer."

"In exchange for what?"

"Good question. Keep your ears open and let me know if you hear anything. We may need to warn our people in Belgrade." Stephenson rubbed his nose then sniffed.

Paul Hastings flipped through a three-page agenda. "The conference is tightly scripted."

As he leaned back, William Stephenson unbuttoned his jacket. "That's because every Tom, Dick and Harry wants time with Churchill and Roosevelt in the same room. While Paul and I attend the main conference, I want you two focused on joint intelligence gathering and protocols to coordinate efforts. Don't expect to get much sleep, gentlemen."

36 JUNE 1942

After so many years as a wife and mother, Ann was accustomed to putting communal needs before personal preference, sparing little time for herself. With the added burden of war, her life jerked along like a marionette, pulled by obligations to her children, her extended family, endless volunteer work, and by her husband's expectations. Like almost every woman she knew, Ann felt drained at the end of each day.

With only one cryptic telegram from Edward saying that all was well and he would soon let her know his return date, Ann decided Marge and Roy's dinner dance would be just the thing to ease her frustrations. Friday morning she was up early. A blue evening dress hung from the closet doorframe while shoes and accessories lay on the bed. Louise Deacon, a friend who lived two streets away, had offered to help with Ann's hair. Emily had promised to make dinner.

Ann hurried out the door before nine, going straight to

a Ladies Auxiliary meeting held in St. Margaret's church basement. By ten o'clock, eighteen women had arrived and conversation bubbled as competing voices clamoured to be heard.

Like a schoolteacher, Ada MacLean rapped on the table with a long wooden ruler.

"Ladies. Ladies. We should get started. I appreciate your help this morning. Let me tell you what needs to be done."

Barely five feet tall, Ada made up for her lack of size with a sharp, penetrating voice. Ann liked her brisk, no-nonsense approach.

"I know it's only June, but today we're packaging items for Christmas. I'd like one table to work on food, another on men's clothing and the third on children's items. We'll do the surgical compresses if we have time. I've put instructions on each table to illustrate how the Red Cross wants items grouped. If we organize them properly, they'll be easier to handle once they get to England."

Since someone else was in charge, Ann relaxed amongst the easy chatter, and when Ada finished speaking, poured herself a coffee and settled in beside Esther Stevens.

"You're all dressed up today, Esther."

Her friend wore a double strand of pearls, a purple hat positioned at a jaunty angle, and a sparkling brooch on her lapel. In contrast, Ann had on what she referred to as "working clothes", a simple cotton shirtwaist and sensible black pumps, the only item of decoration a white lace hankie, stuffed into her breast pocket just before leaving the house.

"I'm so tired of looking drab just because Mimi Hazelton says we should."

"Why would you pay any attention to her? She's a gossip columnist."

"I know. But her advice seemed sensible at the time. Now I'm fed up with it. Just because there's a war on doesn't mean we have to look frumpy all the time."

Ann laughed. "That's the spirit. Maybe we should send you over to handle Herr Hitler. For that matter, we'll send

you and Ada. I think the combination could prove deadly for
that man."

"If only we could. Why can't someone assassinate that
monster?"

"Oh, dear. I didn't mean to start that kind of conversation.
Let's talk about something else."

"Yes, let's," Joyce Randall said. "I promised myself a day
without war talk. Here's the instruction sheet. They want
each food packet to contain Corn Flakes, Shreddies and Bran
Flakes, Lushus Jelly Desserts in lime, orange and pineapple,
tea, fruitcake and chocolates. Christmas treats for our troops."

For the next hour the women spoke about summer holidays, Sunday picnics, outdoor concerts, and trips to the island
on hot days when tempers frayed and children, overwhelmed
by the exhilaration of swimming and running and tumbling,
became fractious. Laughter and stories made time disappear.

* * *

"What do you think of these for Belinda's wedding gift?"
Ann placed a pair of crystal candlesticks decorated with hum-
mingbirds on the dining room table and stood back to admire
the way they sparkled.

"They're beautiful," Emily said. "But I thought you were
going to get mixing bowls."

"I was and I also looked at towels and sheets, but everything seemed so dull and practical. Others will get gifts like
that. I thought Belinda might appreciate something romantic." Ann wrapped each candlestick in tissue paper and returned them to the gift box. "She's only nineteen, you know.
And her fiancé is due to ship out in August. I see too many
women like that at Signals Welfare. They end up with babies
to cope with on their own or with husbands who die before the
marriage is more than a few months old."

"How do you know that will happen to Belinda? Her fiancé's in the Medical Corps, so he's not on the front lines. I'm
sure he'll be fine."

"Well, some doctors are sent closer to the action than others. But hopefully he'll be one of the lucky ones."

Although she did not voice this thought to Emily, Ann knew that some of these young women experienced loneliness or regret and were susceptible to adultery. She hated handling cases involving adultery, imagining in each story aspects of Edward and Helene, seeing in each woman a feature of his lover. Perhaps she has curving lips like this one or slender fingers like that one, perhaps her earrings dangled just so, her smile this wide, her hair that soft.

"Mom, stop being so gloomy. You're going to a party tonight."

"You're right, dear." Ann shook her head. "And if I don't get started, I won't be ready in time."

Ann soaked in the bath with a few drops of her favourite perfume, Fleur de Nuit. The hot water and pleasing scent allowed her to relax and induced thoughts of music and light conversation amidst the glitter of gowns and uniforms.

"Are you still in the bath, Mom? Mrs. Deacon is here."

Emily's voice cut through Ann's reverie. Glancing at her watch lying on the edge of the tub, she realized she had lingered far too long. She pulled the plug and stepped out of the bath then wrapped a towel around her body.

"Tell her I just need ten minutes."

Stockings, fresh underwear, black bra and silk slip were followed by the blue chiffon dress, high-heeled silver sandals, sparkling earrings, a chunky bracelet and an opal dinner ring that previously belonged to Edward's great-grandmother. After a quick spray of Fleur de Nuit, she stood in front of the mirror, turning one way then the other with a critical eye.

"I'm sorry I'm late, Louise. The bath was so soothing, I lost track of time."

"I'm sure that's exactly what you needed," the woman said as she started to brush Ann's hair, shaping it expertly into a chignon while leaving a few curls dangling to soften the look. She rummaged in a small basket of makeup, selecting blue eye shadow and light pink rouge. "You'll create more interest if you arrive late."

"Oh, you're just teasing me."

"No, I'm not. You don't realize how attractive you are." Louise stepped back to survey her handiwork. "Perhaps it's time to make Edward jealous?"

Ann laughed. "Edward as a jealous husband? I don't think that's a good idea."

* * *

With Edward away, she splurged on a taxi, and by the time the driver left her at the hotel, a crowd was mingling at the entrance. Ann waved at Edna Peters, whose husband was home on naval leave and looked handsome in dark blue with gold braid. His presence reminded her of the thirty-six downed merchant ships and she considered how Edna must feel with a husband at sea in wartime.

Enough of that, Ann thought. *Tonight is a party.*

In the lobby, conversation buzzed as people waited to greet Roy and Marge by the ballroom entrance. Roy had been Edward's best man, and over the years the women had become close friends.

"You look wonderful, Ann. Blue is my favourite colour on you."

Glittering with sequins, Marge's low-cut gown exposed more than an inch of cleavage, and for a moment Ann was reminded of the months when she first dated Edward and was jealous of Marge's sophistication.

"We're so glad you came. Where is that husband of yours? We hardly ever see him." Roy kissed her cheek.

"He's on one of his trips."

"Where did he go?"

"Montreal. He said to give you his apologies." Ann lied much more readily than she had when Edward first began taking his mysterious trips.

"Let's talk later, Ann," Marge said. "I've missed you. You'll find lots of people you know here."

With guests queuing behind her, Ann congratulated Marge on the décor then drifted into the room in search of friends. The ballroom at the King Edward Hotel could easily accommodate two hundred people. Twenty-foot ceilings capped with elaborate chandeliers glittered above the crowd. Multi-coloured gauze swooped across each wall like waterfalls lit with floodlights. One corner of the room featured a garden of tropical plants accented with red Chinese lanterns and stepping-stones to a jade Buddha atop a marble column. In another corner, a string quartet played light music as guests continued to arrive. *There's something about a man in uniform*, Ann thought, looking around at crisply attired men with polished buckles and flashing medals.

She approached Carl and Sheila Bradley, who were speaking with an army captain. Sheila volunteered at Signals Welfare and Edward knew Carl from the reserves. As Ann joined their circle, Carl gave her a hug.

"Ann, this is Richard Leary," Carl said.

"Lovely to meet you." She extended her hand and smiled into serious brown eyes.

"The pleasure is mine." Richard Leary looked her up and down with deliberate scrutiny.

Thinking him rather rude, she removed her hand. "Have you been in Toronto long, Captain Leary?"

"Richard. Please call me Richard. I've been here since the war began."

"And you're in the army. What do you do?"

"It's a training role."

"Machine guns, submachine guns, rocket launchers. You name it, Richard knows how to fire it." Carl joined the conversation. "Most people don't want to hear the details, that's why he doesn't say much."

"How did you learn all that?" Ann was interested, in spite of her earlier reaction.

"I grew up on a ranch and learned to shoot when I was ten.

In the first war I conducted rifle training."

"Did you serve overseas?"

"Yes, but I never saw any action."

"Looks like you might avoid going this time." Carl nudged Richard, as he made the comment.

"Carl, you shouldn't make jokes like that," said Sheila.

"You're right, dear. Sorry, Richard. I know you've requested overseas duty several times. Your work is critical. Without proper training, our boys can't possibly survive. Colonel Foster said so just the other day."

Richard's stony face eased and Carl soon had them laughing about an escapade that occurred when the army requisitioned a farmer's team of horses and Carl was the only one daring enough to drive the team and wagon. Chaos had ensued.

"I was sure the horses knew how to drive themselves," Carl said as he concluded the story.

A tall man wearing a tuxedo walked through the crowd playing a handheld xylophone to announce dinner.

"Ann, why don't you join our table since Edward isn't here? We'd love your company."

Ann smiled and followed Sheila to a table near the band, where two other couples and two naval officers were waiting. She was pleased that the awkwardness of coming alone had disappeared. Candlelight complemented the sparkle of crystal and silver cutlery, while soothing background music offered each guest a chance to step away from reality. Richard pulled out Ann's chair and waited for the other women to be seated before taking the spot next to her.

"Have you always lived in Toronto?"

"I was born here, but my husband and I lived in Montreal for a number of years. We came back in thirty-five."

"Which city do you prefer?"

She laughed. "That's a difficult question. Montreal feels so cosmopolitan compared with Toronto. But our families are here. What about you?"

Questions about their backgrounds gave way to a discussion about Richard's role leading a weapons training program. That topic sparked the interest of the man sitting on his left and soon conversation about the war took over. Ann leaned back and watched.

"Gentlemen. I think our ladies would prefer to talk about something else," Carl Bradley interrupted one of the naval officers who had been outlining losses in the Atlantic.

"Would you prefer us to talk about politics?" Richard asked.

"That's a dismal topic."

Sheila interjected with a question about Churchill's presence in Washington and soon the group was immersed in a discussion of America's involvement in the war.

After dinner the music shifted from soothing to lively and couples drifted to the dance floor. Richard extended his hand to Sheila and they got up to dance, leaving Carl and Ann at the table.

"Come on, Ann, I know you love to dance."

A little later, Roy Doney claimed a dance with Ann. "So tell me, how's the family?" he said.

"Emily is fine. Edward wants her to volunteer for that Ontario Farm Service program and she's resisting, but she needs something to do this summer, otherwise he'll badger her about it. Alex is studying for exams, which is a miracle in itself."

After another dance, Roy excused himself, but with men outnumbering women, Ann had no lack of partners and the time passed easily, her body relaxing as rhythms took over. When a Glenn Miller favourite ended, Richard tapped her shoulder.

"I've been looking for you. Will you dance with me before I leave?"

"Where are you going?" She spoke without thinking; his reason for leaving was none of her business, but the evening was still young.

"My lieutenant just told me there's a problem downtown. It seems that some of my soldiers are creating a ruckus. Unfortunately, they're my responsibility."

"Shouldn't you go immediately?"

"I should, but I'd like to dance with you first."

Ann raised an eyebrow. *Surely he's not flirting with me*, she thought. "I'd like that."

The music slowed and they waltzed together without speaking, Richard holding her firmly and just a little too close.

"Thank you," he said, leading her back to the table when the song ended. "I hope we'll meet again."

37 JUNE 1942

In Washington, meetings consumed both day and night. Each morning they began at seven with a briefing by Stephenson describing critical agreements reached the previous day and setting out analysis and further discussions required to implement them.

On the second day of the conference, Edward was in the main dining room for dinner when news of the fall of Tobruk arrived. After reading a message brought by an aide-de-camp, Churchill rose like an aging warhorse, face ashen, lines drawn deeper than ever into his famous scowl. He delivered the news without embellishment.

"As everyone in this room knows, Rommel has been waiting months to attack Tobruk and continue to Cairo, Alexandria and the Suez Canal. His intent is to present his Fuhrer with new supply routes while destroying ours in the process. Let me read from the dispatch I've just received." As Churchill continued, his voice boomed and scraped, the consummate orator.

". . . and our Armoured Corps and forces situated on the Gazala Line were forced to withdraw as Rommel's Afrika Corps overran two of our brigade boxes. Armoured brigades suffered badly during attempts to counterattack. Many men and tanks were lost. Amidst great confusion our troops fell back towards Tobruk. British and Free French forces fought fiercely, but in the end, Tobruk was captured. Rommel has taken more than thirty thousand prisoners . . ." Churchill lifted his head at the collective gasp of his audience, ". . . as well as vehicles, tanks and supplies. The Fourth Armoured Brigade and the Ninth Lancers have safely withdrawn to the Egyptian border. General Auchinleck has taken direct command of the Eighth Army from General Ritchie."

Silence descended. Losing their advantage in Africa was a terrible blow. Turning to face Churchill, Roosevelt was the first to speak.

"What can we do to help?"

With such a clear indication that the US was a full partner in the war, relief was palpable.

Although Edward was restricted from closed-door sessions, senior military and government officials were often quite forthright, even somewhat indiscreet, he thought, mingling in the bar on the second night. Conversation bounced amongst a group of mainly British officers.

"The most important question is whether the Soviets will hold out against the Germans."

"If they fail, Germany will shift more troops to the Western Front, and we all know what a disaster that will bring. But if they do hold on and the Americans successfully push for a cross-channel attack, we'll need a new command structure."

"A new command structure? The old man hates the thought of being controlled by the US. We fought more than two years without them, doesn't that give us some rights?"

"Not likely. Not when everything is so bloody political."

"What about North Africa? If we were to succeed there, we'd hold a vulnerable access point to Europe through Italy."

"The fall of Tobruk makes success in North Africa much more difficult. Admiral King said emphatically that we are already fighting on too many fronts, so Operation Gymnast must be shelved in favour of discussing Bolero."

"He's just annoyed that efforts in the Pacific have to make concessions."

"General Brooke said that if we are forced to pursue Bolero this year, it will be a sacrifice operation."

"I can't believe we would deliberately sacrifice so many men in the name of politics and ego."

"You're being naïve. How do you think tonight's news will change the landscape? Roosevelt implied that the US will help us. Mark my words, the next few days will be pivotal."

When the conference ended, Edward had a real sense of what Churchill and Roosevelt were planning, along with knowledge of the official agreements. The first agreement was for combined Allied command to give higher priority to a peripheral strategy, hitting Germany and its allies at various pressure points, rather than a cross-channel invasion. No one felt such an invasion would be successful. Secondly, plans were forming for a desert campaign in North Africa to be led by an American general. The third agreement was to share as equal partners in the research needed for development of an atomic bomb. Edward had been shocked to learn of the devastating power of this new technology.

While Britain led all Commonwealth efforts, Stephenson reassured them that Canada would continue to play a significant role as a centre for intelligence gathering and recruitment of field agents. Edward and his colleagues had much more work to do. During the closing dinner, energy and optimism filled the room. With full American support, Britain was no longer fighting Hitler alone.

* * *

Exhausted yet strangely elated, Edward arrived home Monday night just in time for dinner. After listening to Emily and Alex talk about their last week of school and upcoming exams, Ann suggested a walk.

"It's such a lovely night. We can go to the Jolly Miller and back."

The Jolly Miller was a tavern less than a mile from their house. During the winter, an ice rink was set up next to the tavern and in the past, the family had often skated together on weekends, Alex dashing here and there demonstrating his speed, Emily gathered with friends doing more talking than skating and Ann and Edward going sedately round and round.

When they reached the road, Edward took her hand and tucked it through his arm. "What did you do while I was gone?"

"Oh, the usual. We bundled Christmas packages at St. Margaret's and I spent quite a bit of time at Signals Welfare. Some of the women are in terrible circumstances. The government should be doing more for them."

"It's hard to prioritize the needs of families back here with funds required for our troops."

"I know. But so many women and children are suffering. I see their misery every time I go."

A boy passed by walking a large St. Bernard, the dog's lumbering steps an amusing contrast to the boy's bouncing gait. Darkness surrounded them, almost no lights visible from any house in the neighbourhood. Maple trees on the hill to their right hovered like an impenetrable mass.

"Did you go to the dance?"

"I did. Marge and Roy were asking for you. I sat with Sheila and Carl Bradley. And I had no shortage of partners on the dance floor." She glanced at him and squeezed his arm.

"You see. I said you'd have fun without me."

"I would have had more fun with you."

* * *

"I'm sorry I didn't call," he said later as they got ready for bed.

"You should be. I hate all these secrets. We used to share our concerns and now I rarely know what's going on or what you're thinking."

"You know I would tell you more if I could." Edward had a habit of tucking his chin in and looking down as if peering over a pair of reading glasses even though he did not wear glasses at all.

"Yes, I know."

He put his arm around her waist. "You're upset with me."

She leaned against him. "I am, but it will pass. I seem to be out of sorts these days. All I do is worry or try to help others who have bigger worries. And it never gets any better."

"There's some hope we're at a turning point," he said.

"Really? How can we be at a turning point when Tobruk has just fallen? I read every scrap of news and it sounds devastating. How will Britain regain what's been lost?"

"There's a plan in place." In response to Ann's encouraging look, he added one further piece of information. "An invasion strategy. And you know that's extremely confidential."

Secrets were his life. His inability to ease Ann's distress by telling her about the conference saddened him. Keeping secrets undermined their closeness and the mutual support of shared concerns. Like an eroding landscape, these foundations had slipped away as the demands of war took over. He wondered how they would recapture those times when they had talked at length about people they encountered or had fascinating conversations speculating about their future. *And when*, he thought sadly, *will we recapture the playful, loving language of bedtime?*

38 AUGUST 1942

By August, the optimism Edward felt at the end of the Washington conference had disappeared. Rommel continued the fight for North Africa striking hard at El Alamein, while in Russia the Germans trampled on Sevastopol then pushed towards Stalingrad. Two weeks of wet weather added to his gloom.

"Nothing we can do." Edward stood by the kitchen window looking out on rows of stunted vegetables whose normally perky leaves had flopped over into the mud.

"I know, but if we don't get some sunny weather soon, I won't be able to do much canning or pickling." Ann wiped a glass then put it away in the cupboard. "The farmers are complaining."

"Farmers always complain," said Edward.

"True. But we need to feed our troops." She dried another glass then reached for a handful of cutlery.

"Dad! Come and listen. Something big is going on." Alex

shouted.

Edward and Ann hurried into the living room where Alex sat on the floor in front of the radio. When initially purchased, the radio represented enjoyable evenings of music, comedy and drama. Now the fine piece of furniture merely represented bad news.

Emily and Ann took places on the sofa. Edward remained standing. *It must be Dieppe*, he thought, listening to the crackling sound of an overseas broadcast. For months he had known Dieppe was coming, although the actual date kept shifting. He hoped they were in better shape than the rumours he had heard.

"*. . . Armed Forces briefing. Let me read it to you. Some tanks have been lost during the action ashore and reports show that fighting has been very fierce and casualties are likely heavy on both sides. Full reports will not be available until our forces are back in England. In addition to the destruction of the six-gun battery and an ammunition dump, a radio location station and a flak battery were destroyed. Vital experience has been gained in the involvement of substantial numbers of troops in an assault and in the transport and use of heavy equipment during combined operations.*"

The reporter's voice grew more and more sombre and it became clear that thousands of Canadian troops were involved in an unsuccessful cross-channel raid. When the broadcast finished, Edward turned off the radio. *How many have we lost*, he wondered, shocked at the extent of the disaster. *What happened to our intelligence?*

"Ninety-five aircraft missing," Ann repeated the announcer's words.

He knew the direction of her thoughts. As a navigator, Ann's brother might have been in one of the missing aircraft.

"We don't know whether Alan was there," he said. "We don't even know if Canadian planes were involved."

"But they said aircraft of all operational commands. That includes us. I have to call Mother and Dad. They'll be dreadfully worried." She walked to the hallway where the telephone table and chair were located.

"Give them my love," said Edward.

"It doesn't sound good, does it, Dad?" Alex looked troubled.

Edward crouched beside his son. "I'm afraid you're right."

"Doesn't the army plan these things?" Alex voiced Edward's exact thought. His son looked worried.

"They do. Usually they plan for months. Maybe there'll be better news tomorrow."

"I read that we can't win this war unless we invade Europe," Alex said. "Since Russia is losing ground and Germany is still holding strong in Africa, France is the only choice. Maybe the generals felt they had to take a chance. What do you think made Dieppe so difficult, Dad?

This was an Alex Edward did not recognize. Informed, concerned, analytical. "Too steep, perhaps. Or maybe the Germans are dug in too well."

"I'm going to make cocoa. Does anybody want some?" Emily asked.

"How can you make cocoa after listening to that? I want to punch something."

"Shut up, Alex. Just let me be." Emily looked grim and far older than sixteen.

"Everyone deals with bad news his own way," Edward said, a hand resting on Alex's shoulder to prevent an argument as he watched his daughter get up from the sofa and head towards the kitchen. Keeping busy was Emily's way to cope while Alex tended to lash out at something or someone. *He certainly doesn't take after me*, he mused.

Alex's personality was mercurial while Edward's was calm and steady. His son seemed to dislike most of the activities Edward enjoyed like reading and learning, contemplative walks, the fatigue of vigorous physical work. As a little boy Alex hated being still, he whooped and hollered about the house, regularly got into trouble, came home filthy, invented endless games that were usually variations on hide and seek. The only activity he focused on was hockey and he would practice skating for hours.

In past summers they had fished together, still waters and the hush of misty dawn occasionally leading to more than everyday conversation, but since the war began, there had been no cottage vacations. *I wish we spent more time with one another.*

"If I was in the army, I'd show those bloody Germans a thing or two."

"Watch your language, Alex."

"Well, I would." Alex clenched his fists and punched an imaginary enemy.

Sweet son of mine, you have no idea what a fucking mess we're in.

Edward rarely swore in public and never in front of his children, but he often did in his thoughts. For some reason even thinking words like fuck, shit, asshole, bastard, bitch and a long list of phrases he had learned in the army released a tiny fraction of tension. He particularly liked 'cock-eyed cunt' a favourite of Sergeant Finnegan.

"Do you want to come outside with me? Your mother's still on the phone and I think I'll have a smoke."

"No thanks, Dad. I'm going upstairs."

Now why did I ruin that conversation, Edward thought, standing on the back porch. *He might have talked longer if I hadn't mentioned going outside.*

Raindrops dripped from the elm next to the house, a calming pitter-patter while a dense cloud of tree swallows chased about with acrobatic twists and turns. The heavy air was both sweet and earthy. Edward tamped a bit more tobacco into the bowl of his pipe then stuck it in his mouth. Often he forgot to light his pipe. Lit or unlit, it helped him think.

In April, two agents he had personally trained, Julian Shapiro and Louise Bedard, went to France with a mission to spread false information and confuse the Germans about location and timing of Allied landings at Dieppe. Edward had come to know them because he had taken over their wireless training when his chief instructor contracted a severe case of measles. Clearly, Louise and Julian had failed to convince the enemy.

Louise was a striking woman. Agents needed to be the kind of person no one noticed, so they could operate in the shadows, and on more than one occasion Edward had worried that her beauty would make her stand out in a crowd. But when the experts finished altering her appearance, he had failed to recognize her.

During the weeks Edward had worked with them, Louise learned another critical skill. She could send or receive Morse code faster than anyone he knew. He had tracked every one of her messages until twelve days ago, when they had abruptly stopped. And now it was clear that Dieppe was a disaster, just like Alex said. Worse news would no doubt emerge over the next few days. He needed to know whether Julian and Louise were safe. If not, they would activate other agents. Pipe clenched between his teeth, he walked to the edge of the stone patio and stared into the gloom.

* * *

The next evening, the whole family gathered to hear Brian Burgess, a war correspondent who had been on one of the tank-landing ships, give a firsthand account. As Burgess began speaking, Edward listened to the list of Canadian units involved, thinking of men he knew.

"... a lot of those men will never return to Canada. I believe more will return after the war if the German announcement of fifteen hundred prisoners is correct."

Hearing the number of prisoners, both Ann and Emily gasped.

"This was a combined operation, and playing an equal part with our troops were the air force, marines, commandos and the navy. At least nine aircraft fell to Canadian guns and

*many more were damaged. What a marvellous job they did in
the face of intense fire from accurate and powerful German
shore and Ak-Ak batteries."*

"Marvellous job," Edward snorted. "Sounds like the army is
trying to create something positive out of disaster."

"Shh, Dad," said Alex, grabbing a chunk of his light brown
hair. "Gerry said he thinks his brother was there."

*"Without this experience, a second front would have been
suicide. And now I'll read to you from notes I scribbled while
on the water . . .*

*"Our bombers are at work . . . more heavy flash of coastal
guns and bombs . . . our aircraft are flying in close to the water
. . . the ships are weaving in front . . . heavy thuds are shaking
us even this far out . . . destroyers are slinking along beside
us . . . there are fighter patrols like flocks of geese . . . fast
troop-carrying ships are passing us . . . the coast has suddenly
loomed up in front of us with its white hills . . . the destroyers
are laying a smokescreen to windward, turning broadside and
blasting the town with their guns . . . a Spitfire just crashed off
our starboard bow and into the sea like a stone, we can see the
pilot trying to get out but he can't . . ."*

Emily put her hand across her mouth, eyes wide with horror.

*". . . two Messerschmitts have tried to attack us . . . we're
shore-bound and in we go . . . we have to back off . . . I can see
casualties in the water . . . machine-gun bullets are winding
around us . . . the tank-landing craft ahead of us got its tanks
ashore but she's sinking now . . . the German shore batteries
are shooting at us, shells falling on all sides of us . . . we can't
get to the beach . . . three pilots are coming down by parachute
. . . the Germans on the cliffs are throwing hand grenades . .
. and now dive bombers are attacking us . . . some of our men
are wounded . . . our aircraft are suffering heavily . . . they're
fighting like fools on shore . . ."*

When the broadcast ended Edward and his family sat without moving, overwhelmed by what the reporter described. No

one spoke for a very long time.

* * *

"The Germans knew we were coming," Paul Hastings said after a briefing on plans to train agents for North Africa. "They hit our landing ships and escorts before we got to the beach. The main assault didn't have a hope. They slaughtered us with machine-gun fire."

"Why didn't we withdraw?" Edward paced up and down in front of Paul's desk, seething with anger. Though the door was closed, he heard the clatter of typewriters and ringing of telephones.

"We couldn't withdraw. The shoreline was far too clogged with boats delivering troops. Our men had nowhere to go."

"And our tanks were useless. Someone should have known what that kind of shingled stone would do to a tank."

Paul pinched the bridge of his nose. "Any word from Julian and Louise?"

"No. And now I'm even more worried."

"Four thousand casualties." Hastings snapped a pencil in half. "A fucking disaster."

* * *

That evening when he saw Ann's face, Edward feared the worst. "Is it Alan?" he asked.

"No, it's Michael Wilson. Bob called to say that he's missing. They don't know anything else.

"Oh, my God." Edward inhaled sharply.

"Bob and Hannah don't know whether he's a prisoner. They're in a state of shock. Bob said that Hannah can hardly function. He thinks it would help if I could spend a few days with her."

"Of course, you must go. The children and I will be fine."

Ann nodded. "That's what I said to Bob. Hannah's given me so much support, it's the least I can do." She leaned against him and he put his arms around her.

"Did you speak with Hannah?" He felt her nod. "How is

she?"

"She sounds fairly calm. I think she's numb from repeating the same story over and over. She wants me to come."

"The uncertainty will be dreadful. I'll give Bob a call."

"Will you? I'm sure he'd appreciate hearing from you. I've checked the train schedule and there's one leaving late tomorrow morning. I called Mother so she and Daddy will know where I am. Since they know Alan wasn't hurt, at least they aren't worrying so much about him right now. First thing tomorrow I'll make some phone calls for Signals Welfare and my committee work." Edward suspected from the furrow in her brow that his wife was forming a checklist in her head. "I'm sure I won't be away more than three or four days."

"How was it?" he asked when Ann returned four days later, fatigue and sadness evident in sagging shoulders and red-rimmed eyes. Since it was Saturday he had been able to meet her train and as soon as he found her, he took Ann's suitcase and put his other arm around her waist.

"They both looked dreadful," Ann said, "almost shrunken with grief. Bob looked as though he had already lost weight. The children were trying to help but I don't think they knew how to comfort their parents. At first I felt like an intruder, but eventually I realized that an outsider was exactly what they needed. The first thing I did was prepare a proper meal. Doing something ordinary seemed to help, especially the children, and during dinner while much of the conversation was about Michael or the raid at Dieppe, we did touch on other topics."

As they proceeded along the platform and into the station he shortened his stride to match hers and their hips brushed together in a familiar fashion.

"Yesterday, Bob went into the office for a little while so Hannah and I walked in Mount Royal Park. She told me that she keeps thinking of him landing on that beach, struggling to make it up the hill with artillery all around and no place to shelter. Or she imagines him imprisoned somewhere in filthy surroundings, possibly wounded. She never once mentioned that he might have died."

"What did you say?" They had left the station and crossed the road to wait on the streetcar platform.

"I told her that Michael is strong. That she and Bob have given him faith in himself and leadership qualities and that if he's a prisoner, he has the strength of character to survive and even look out for others. I know she feels helpless. All she can do is wait."

"I'm sure Hannah was pleased to have you there."

"She was. I told her to take it one day at a time. I'm going to call in a few days and see how she's doing."

39 OCTOBER 1942

War continued. With his job at the telephone company, the reserves and his secret activities, Edward's duties were endless. Since the Washington conference, the frequency of his travel had increased, and once again he was on his way to Camp X. A young reservist drove, while Edward worked in the back seat, no longer noticing the rolling countryside east of the city or the beauty of early morning quiet. Over the weeks, he had paid little attention to the change of seasons as June gave way to summer with its drifting haze of heat, the singing of hedge crickets, and green fields welcoming sun and rain, nor did he notice the glorious autumn colours in the aftermath of a surprisingly warm September.

While the miles unfolded, his mind went over and over the situation with Julian and Louise, dreading the possibilities of what might have happened and where they might be. Captured? Tortured? Killed? Betrayed? So many weeks of silence.

He looked up to see Thornton Road passing by. "You missed

the turn, Saunders."

"Yes, sir. Just following protocol. There's a pickup truck behind us."

Edward grunted. They were never to turn down Thornton Road if another car was in sight, but this rule always seemed rather extreme. "I don't want to be late."

"I'll turn off at the next intersection and double back. Shouldn't take long, sir."

He was out of the car almost before it stopped, crushed gravel scrunching as he crossed the road to a walkway where a group of women walked back to their barracks following night duty. To his left, he glimpsed a few officers gathered near the farmhouse. In the far distance, an instructor led a line of recruits on a cross-country trail, heads bobbing up and down over difficult terrain.

"Be ready to leave at four," he called over his shoulder to Saunders.

Camp X was like a separate world. Each time Edward arrived he felt the hush and observed the purposeful strides of men and women going about the business of espionage. Since the camp's opening, additional modest buildings, almost cottage-like in appearance, had been added, laid out on three parallel side streets with a view of Lake Ontario's windswept shores. The entire site occupied two hundred and seventy-five acres, plenty of space for their purposes.

One of the last buildings to be constructed was taller than the others, with narrow windows set high above the doorway. This building housed the Hydra facility, which enabled top-secret radio transmissions all around the world.

Edward spent most of the day assessing new recruits. Successful recruits were people of rare courage and dedication. During training, instructors constantly tested for endurance under stress, resourcefulness, discretion and good judgment. Though many agents were already behind enemy lines, operating escape routes and sabotaging networks, many more were needed.

Ray Leblanc and Michel Simard were two of Edward's recent recruits. For eight weeks the training team had prepared them to participate in an escape network for airmen shot down over France. Once Ray and Michel arrived in England, they would be equipped with the necessary tools of their trade as well as large amounts of francs and forged identity papers. Hydra staff would monitor their coded transmissions.

Mid-afternoon Edward briefed them one last time, repeating instructions they already knew. He did it for his own sake as much as theirs. Although Edward rarely conducted the training anymore—others had been hired for that purpose—he insisted on speaking to his recruits before they left Canada.

"You cannot operate solo. You'll need to collaborate with many local people. They will assist you with safe houses as well as food and clothing. And they will direct you to those capable of nursing wounded airmen back to health and producing false identity papers."

He walked to the window and watched a group of young men disembark from a large bus then huddle in small groups awaiting direction. From a distance they looked like ordinary citizens, some tall, some short, some dressed in the formal clothing of business while others looked like everyday working folk. *More recruits*, he thought as he turned back to Ray and Michel.

"Your initial contacts will start you off, but you'll need your wits and instincts to find others who can guide you to the rendezvous points once pickup is arranged." The men nodded, each face sombre.

"Michel will concentrate on logistics. Ray, you'll travel around the countryside looking for safe places from which to exchange coded messages. You'll have to relocate frequently to avoid being picked up by radio-detection equipment. German technology keeps getting better." He deliberately looked each man in the eye. "You both know that one small slip could be fatal." Again, they nodded.

"Beaulieu will give additional details when you land in England, however our instructions were to have you prepared to leave within two or three days of arrival." Edward closed his briefing book. "Any questions?"

After Ray and Michel left, Edward walked over to the farmhouse where he hoped to find Colonel Dupuis. An infrequent visitor to Camp X, Charles Dupuis spent most of his time liaising with BSC operations in New York from a nondescript Toronto office building. Paul Hastings had mentioned a meeting with Charles that afternoon; Edward hoped the colonel would have information about Julian and Louise.

The screen door shut with a sharp bang. Edward proceeded up the stairs and walked past several former bedrooms now functioning as offices. At the end of the hall, Hastings' adjutant stood in front of a closed door.

"Is he in?"

"Yes."

"May I join him?"

The man rapped on the door and poked his head inside. "Lieutenant Colonel Jamieson to see you." He gestured with a quick jerk of his head. "You can go in, sir."

After closing the door, Edward looked first at Paul and then Charles. "Any news?"

"Yes, finally. They're safe." Charles leaned back, hands clasped behind his head.

Edward did not realize he had been holding his breath until he let it out. "Thank God. What happened? It's been weeks."

"Louise picked up a tail. She and Julian tried to lose the man, but there must have been more than one. They figured their transmissions had been compromised and decided the only safe route was to disappear."

"Where are they now?"

"Back in England. Don't ask me how. They'll go to Scotland from there, either Morar or Arisaig. Command will probably split them up since they won't want to risk a repeat. Those two were lucky."

"More than lucky," Hastings added.

Charles looked at his watch. "It's only four o'clock, but I think a toast is in order. Do you have anything to drink in here, Paul?"

Later as Edward packed his papers, he pictured Julian and Louise leaving Camp so many months ago, exuding confidence with jaunty smiles and brisk strides, certain that their training would protect them. He squeezed his eyes shut. The feeling of doom increased with each group they trained and sent away. With the companionship of shared meals and evening laughter and the intensity of espionage training, these young men and women had become his second family. He knew the odds; soon someone would fail. Edward reassured himself that the training team had taught Ray and Michel as much as they could. He planned to say a final good-bye on his way out and a prayer on his way home.

* * *

Although the sanctuary of his home usually eased some of Edward's tension, today his worries about Julian and Louise were compounded with thoughts of Ray and Michel's departure. Intellectually, he knew not to get attached to his recruits, but these four had become closer than most, the men reminding him of soldiers he knew in the first war, while Louise looked so much like Emily, he had once called her by his daughter's name.

"Where's your mother?" Edward asked Alex, who sat at the kitchen table doing his homework.

"At one of her meetings, I think. I don't remember what she said."

His son preferred to work at the kitchen table. Alex hated homework, but he also hated being at the bottom of his class, so this year he had become more diligent. Grateful for this turn of events, Edward chose not to berate him for being unaware of his mother's whereabouts.

"Did she leave me anything for dinner?" It was almost nine

o'clock and Edward had eaten only an apple for lunch.

"There's something in the warming oven. Meatloaf again. Can't stand the stuff. Don't you wonder what Mother puts in it? I think it was pickles tonight. She knows I hate pickles."

Edward decided against a lecture on the sacrifices of wartime and their own good fortune of living in Canada rather than England. Alex was often grumpy when doing his homework but at least he was working which was better than last year. He had almost failed last year.

"Is Emily upstairs?" Best to let Alex get on with his studies.

"Yup. She's reading."

Edward left the kitchen to find his daughter. *Maybe she'll keep me company while I eat.*

"Hi sweetheart."

"Hi Daddy." Edward always felt pleased when she called him Daddy, an event that occurred much less frequently now she was older.

"Do you know where your mother is?"

Emily marked the page she was reading with a thick red ribbon and uncurled her feet and he was reminded of the days when he read Christopher Robin to her before bedtime. She loved the stories and giggled as Edward changed voices for Tigger, Eeyore, Pooh and the others.

"She's at Mary Henley's working on the Christmas bazaar. She said to tell you she'd be home around ten."

He rolled up his sleeves. "I suppose I can't expect your mother to be here when I'm always so unpredictable."

"How was your day?" Emily asked.

"Oh, you know, the usual. Meetings and phone calls primarily. I was at the Officer's club this evening." Lies came easily after so much practice.

"Mom left dinner for you in the oven. I'll come down and talk to you while you eat."

Five minutes later Edward found Emily waiting in the dining room, a plate set out at his usual place. She had poured him a scotch with a few chips of ice. The soda water dispenser was also on the table.

"What did you do today?" he enquired, adding a small amount of soda to his drink. As he took the first sip, he gave a silent toast to Ray and Michel. He dedicated his second sip to Julian and Louise. Purging the day's worries would likely require more than one scotch.

"I wrote a math test and was chosen to be in our production of the Mikado."

"The Mikado. Did you know that your grandfather worked for Gilbert and Sullivan before he came to Canada? Wouldn't he have been pleased to see you perform? I think The Mikado is also called The Town of Titipu or something like that. What part are you playing?"

"I'm one of the three little schoolgirls. Pitti-Sing. So, I'm in several scenes. What did Grandpa do for Gilbert and Sullivan?"

"He helped out with all the administrative matters of their work." Edward tried to remember what his father had told him. "He might have actually worked for D'Oyly Carte, the opera company that staged their plays."

"We start rehearsing next week but performances aren't until February."

"Lots of time then. What else went on today?"

"Miss Rother had us all down on our knees in the gymnasium." Emily looked rather indignant.

"What on earth for?"

"Well, apparently she caught a few upper form girls with skirts that were too short. We had to kneel for ages while several teachers went around checking that each skirt touched the floor. Can you believe that?"

Edward uttered sympathetic phrases that seemed to satisfy his daughter without directly criticizing the headmistress of St. Agatha's College. In addition to adherence to a strict set of rules, Miss Rother emphasized decorum and diligence. Edward thought she acted like a general commanding his troops but had never expressed that opinion to his daughter. Miss Rother was a frequent source of frustration. Edward felt that such frustration resulted from young women wanting to grow up faster than their parents—or the headmistress—deemed appropriate. He and Ann often chuckled over Emily's stories in private.

"Do you want to go to the Officer's Mess with me next Friday? Your mother can't attend because of the bazaar."

From time to time, Emily accompanied him to evening events when Ann had to be elsewhere. With office and military responsibilities, he was out one or two nights a week and had many weekend obligations. Ann's work with Signals Welfare as well as the Red Cross and church related events meant that she too had commitments. Conflicting schedules were inevitable.

"I'd love to go," she said. "Will I meet you there? Maybe I can borrow a dress from Joan. Do you think there'll be dancing?"

Edward smiled at his daughter's enthusiasm.

40 OCTOBER 1942

When Ann tiptoed into their bedroom, Edward was already asleep. In the bathroom she creamed her face and brushed her hair, two rituals adopted before her wedding when her mother said married women should always look their best before bed. She stared intently at her face for a moment or two, recalling the day's surprising events.

Ann had been heading to the streetcar stop following a Signals Welfare meeting. Late October storms had left puddles on the sidewalk making it difficult to negotiate without ruining her shoes. She had just stepped over yet another puddle and had been waiting to cross the street. Thick clouds darkened the sky. Without warning the wind had gusted and her umbrella had turned inside out.

"Let me help with that," said a voice from behind.

Ann turned and saw a familiar face. "Richard," she said.

"Ann, how lovely to see you. I'm always happy to rescue a damsel in distress, but now I'm even happier. Let's get out of this rain and find a place to talk."

Without waiting for a reply, he took her arm and held the umbrella so they would both be sheltered. Ann hurried to keep pace with his long strides, and soon they were inside a restaurant called The Shamrock. The space was long and narrow, a green Formica counter lined with bar stools situated in the middle of one wall. A dozen tables for four filled the room, only one of them occupied. On the counter were two cake stands, one with half a pumpkin pie, the other containing a single slice of chocolate cake.

"We'll sit here." He gestured at a table by the window. "Let me take your coat. How have you been?"

As Ann sat down, a waitress emerged from the kitchen and extracted paper and pen from the front pocket of her slightly grubby apron.

"Two teas, please," Richard said. "You look lovely, Ann. The wind has brought wonderful colour to your cheeks."

"Thank you," she said, putting a hand to her face. He spoke in such a matter-of-fact manner, she didn't know whether to be offended at the personal nature of his comment or put it down to natural exuberance. Exuberance, she decided.

"How have you been?" she asked.

Her inquiry brought a grin to Richard's square face. He was of medium height, his chest and upper arms as muscular as a boxer's might be, his appearance rugged rather than refined. When he smiled, the corners of his eyes crinkled and his upper lip almost disappeared. She imagined he had grown into his looks over time.

"I've been working day and night, just like everyone else in this bloody war. But I'm fine now that I'm talking to you."

"Are you flirting with me? I might have to leave if you keep saying things like that."

"You're smiling. That means you're not serious about leaving. But I'll behave. Tell me what you've been doing."

Relieved to take the conversation in a safer direction, Ann relaxed and told Richard about her activities at Signals Welfare, relating several amusing incidents that soon had him chuckling.

"Volunteer work has its challenges. Sounds like you know how to handle people."

"I've had lots of experience over the years. What about you? What have you been doing?"

"Training new recruits, as usual. Actually, I have a group of officers who put them through their paces. My job is mainly organizational."

"Do you like it?"

"That's a difficult question. I hate sending these fellows overseas, but the work is interesting. As long as senior officers don't get in the way."

"And do they?"

His smile disappeared into a scowl. "Today they did. Mainly they want us to train our soldiers quicker. I refuse to send them out before they're ready for combat, and that takes time. Can't have them unable to manage the basics, no matter what the generals say. Otherwise those bastards will just slaughter them." Ann's eyes widened in surprise. "Sorry, Ann. I shouldn't be so blunt."

"We're not doing very well, are we?" He shook his head. "Hannah's son—she's one of my dear friends—is missing at Dieppe. And another friend's son has just gone over to England. They've told me how they feel and I know they'd agree with you."

"It must be terrible to watch your child go to war."

"And much, much worse not to have them return. Do you have children?"

"No."

Hearing Richard's harsh tone, Ann decided not to probe. "My son is fifteen. Every day I pray this will be over before he's eighteen."

Ann caught a glimpse of the time in Richard's watch and knew she should leave. "I have to go," she said.

"You can't go until you tell me when you'll meet me again."

Richard put his hand on Ann's arm. "I promise I'll behave myself, if you'll agree to have tea with me again." He stared directly into her eyes. "Please."

Ann wondered why his eyes, which had sparked a response when they met in June, drew her in once more. It had been a long time since a man paid attention to her. *He's probably just lonely*, she thought, *and it's only a cup of tea.*

* * *

On Thursday afternoon, when Ann was finishing a meeting at Signals Welfare, the telephone rang. Angela poked her head around the corner.

"It's your husband calling."

Ann checked her watch then walked over to Angela's desk. "Hello, dear."

"Hi, sweetheart. How's my favourite wife?"

Edward had not teased her for a long time, so Ann continued the banter. "You have more than one? Isn't that illegal?"

He chuckled. "The reason I'm calling is I'm finishing early today, so I'm going to pick you up and drive you home. How's that for service?"

"You're finishing early." She looked at her watch again. Richard said he would meet her at four.

"Yup. I can be there by four or four thirty. Let's say four fifteen. Will you meet me out front?"

"Of course, dear. That would be lovely."

After putting the receiver back, Ann walked back to her desk, hands on hips and head down. She could not explain to Edward that she was supposed to meet a man for tea. Calling Sheila Bradley to ask for Richard's telephone number would set all sorts of tongues wagging, and she could hardly dash over to the restaurant and leave him a message. She consoled herself with the thought that it was probably for the best. His flirting was inappropriate.

On Monday morning, while Ann was tabulating expenses for Signals Welfare, the telephone rang.

"Hello." Ann held the phone in place by hunching her shoulder, so she could continue to sort through slips of paper.

"You stood me up." Richard sounded insulted.

"I didn't mean to. I didn't know how to reach you to tell you of a change of plans."

"All weekend I debated whether to call, thinking perhaps you never intended to meet me anyway. That you just said yes to get me to stop pressing you." He paused. "I couldn't let it go without finding out for sure. Did you?"

"No."

"Then why didn't you come?"

"I . . . my husband picked me up that day. He left the office early to surprise me. I couldn't tell him I had plans." The whole conversation felt awkward and she said nothing further.

"This Thursday." He made the words sound like both a statement and a question.

Ann wavered. "All right. Same place?"

"Yes."

"Bye." She put the phone down softly and wondered why Richard wanted to have tea with her.

* * *

Though Ann was busy, the days inched along, and when Thursday arrived, clocks seemed to tick from every corner of every room. That morning she had dressed with care in a brown tweed skirt that hugged her hips and flared around her knees, a long-sleeved silk blouse and fitted jacket. Tortoiseshell combs swept her hair back on each side.

At three forty she left the centre, pulling her coat tight against the blustery winds and damp chill. As she crossed Dundas Street, bits of paper gusted here and there along the road. She turned west, heading into the sun, which flickered in and out of dark, grey clouds. Her heels clicked as she walked past small stores and a corner smoke shop advertising Rothmans next to a sign for Coca-Cola. She arrived early and walked around the block twice before going in. Richard was waiting.

"Tea?" he asked.

Ann's mouth curved, enriching the smile in her eyes. "Tea, please," she said to the same waitress who had served them two weeks earlier.

Richard fiddled with the salt and pepper shakers, placing them close together then far apart. He cleared his throat. "I was at the armoury all day, running drills with a new group of recruits. They look so young to me. Sometimes I can't bear to imagine where they're going." He paused. "Were you at home?"

"No. I was at my usual Thursday meeting. I coordinate the volunteers on Thursdays."

To ease the awkwardness, Ann continued with a description of what Signals Welfare did and how she became involved at the beginning of the war.

"All sorts of women volunteer. I'm the current president, which comes with a lot of challenges, but it keeps me busy and at least I know I'm helping."

"I bet you're very good at it."

"Even though you barely know me?"

"I have psychic powers." Richard grinned. "But seriously, what sort of situations do you encounter?"

"More than half our clients have lost a husband or son. One woman I counselled the other day had lost both. The only thing that seemed to help was to hold her hands while she cried. She talked a little, but mainly she cried." Ann sighed and shook her head. "We also see a lot of young women who are recently married. They're often looking for housing or try-ing to cope with newborn babies. Happier problems."

"And I train those who go out and get killed or maimed. Sorry, that's much too gloomy. My CO constantly reminds me that my job is to train them enough that they don't get hurt."

Ann thought it inappropriate to ask whether he liked his work; none of the officers she knew spoke of their duties that way. Instead she listened closely as he told stories about the young men under his command. His voice was animated, his gestures emphatic.

"More tea?" the waitress asked.

Ann checked her watch. "No, thank you. Richard, I'm sorry but I have to go."

"Next Thursday?" he said as the woman moved off to another table.

"Don't you have better things to do than have tea with a married woman?"

"I spend all week locked away with sweaty men and mind-numbing paperwork. Thursday is changeover day. Graduates are heading out; newcomers haven't yet arrived. Things are quiet. For me, being in a woman's company is like finding an oasis in a desert."

Ann laughed. "I've never been called an oasis before."

Richard put a small piece of paper on the table. "Here's where you can reach me, if there's a problem."

She gazed out the window, watching a man unload boxes from a truck across the street. *It's only tea*, she thought, while a separate part of her mind asked what on earth she was doing. A moment later she turned her gaze on Richard and put the piece of paper in her pocket.

41 DECEMBER 1942

Snow spiralled across the front walk and pelted the windows like angry wasps. The city rarely had much snow before Christmas, but today was an exception, and Edward had been fortunate to arrive home before the streets became slippery and the hill to the valley treacherous.

"I'm home," he said.

"Hi, Dad." Alex was in the living room tossing a baseball from one hand to another.

"I thought your mother said no baseballs in the house." His son was athletic and played every sport he could, but Ann took exception to having a ball tossed around indoors, which was not surprising given the broken front window resulting from an attempt to bounce a ball off the top of a wingback chair.

"You're right." Alex lobbed the ball and Edward caught it with a grin.

"Edward, are you encouraging him?" Ann smiled.

"Sorry, Mom," Alex said.

Ann turned towards Edward. "You're home early, sweetheart." She wore an apron over a green plaid skirt and her hands were behind her back. "My hands are all gooey otherwise I'd give you a proper hug."

Edward stooped over to kiss her.

"Guess what?" She did not wait for an answer. "Hannah called. They've had a letter from the Red Cross confirming that Michael is in a prisoner of war camp. Somewhere in Germany, apparently. She and Bob are so happy. After such a long time, I think they had almost given up hope."

"Wonderful news. That deserves another kiss." Edward bent over again. "Will they be able to write to him?"

"Hannah said they could write via the Red Cross. I'm sure she already has one ready to go. Now why don't you relax with the newspaper while I finish dinner?"

* * *

"Ann, you have to hear this."

Edward strode into the kitchen, clutching the paper. A large pot filled with stewed tomatoes, chopped onions, carrots and potatoes simmered on the stove while pieces of beef sizzled in the frying pan.

"What, dear?" Using a slotted spoon, Ann began to transfer meat to the pot.

"I've just read Eden's report to the House of Commons. What he's saying about Hitler's plans for the Jews is so revolting, I can't fathom it. Listen to what he says."

"*. . . the German government, not content with denying to persons of the Jewish race . . . the most elementary human rights, are now carrying into effect Hitler's oft-repeated intention to exterminate the Jewish people in Europe . . . Jews are being transported in conditions of appalling horror and brutality to Eastern Europe . . . In Poland, Jewish ghettoes are being systematically emptied, except for the able-bodied who are slowly worked to death in labour camps. None of those taken*

*away are ever heard of again . . . those who are sick or injured
are left to die of exposure or starvation or killed in mass exe-
cutions . . . the number of victims of these bloody cruelties is
reckoned in many hundreds of thousands of entirely innocent
men, women and children."*

"Dear God," Ann said.

Edward threw the paper on to the table. "Hitler's planning
to exterminate the Jewish people."

"That cannot be. No one could be that evil." Ann's eyes
were wide with shock. She reached for the paper. "What does
Eden mean by 'immense geographical difficulties'?"

"Well, you would have to get Jewish people out of Europe
and transport them to places like Canada and the US. Not an
easy task, when we're at war."

Ann leaned over to read some of the article for herself.

"It says Canada has denied Jewish refugees access to our
country. How can we be so heartless?"

"I don't know. Mackenzie King says it's to protect employ-
ment opportunities, but I fear that it's really anti-Semitism.
Disgraceful. We have to stop Hitler," said Edward. "At all
cost. Otherwise life won't be worth living."

"Life already isn't worth living for millions of people. How
long can they survive? When will we start to win?"

Edward's grim face offered no reassurance.

* * *

She asked Richard the same questions when they met after
Christmas. Ann knew he would have no answers, but she needed to talk to someone, even if the conversation merely reflected
mutual rage.

After two months, Thursday tea had become almost a ritual although with Christmas and New Years, she had not seen
him for three weeks. Bundling a red scarf around her neck, she
walked in blustering snow from Signals Welfare to a restaurant
called Victory Café, a new favourite of Richard's.

Compared with The Shamrock, Victory Café felt cosier.

Shelves stood along one wall, filled with a collection of crockery and antique kitchenware. Seascapes and summer scenes occupied the remaining walls. Since it was close to the university, students came and went, their chatter creating a more leisurely mood.

Having only seen Richard in his army uniform, Ann thought his casual trousers and thick wool sweater made him look younger, almost boyish. Stamping snow off her boots, she waved and smiled, her cheeks bright pink.

"Where's your uniform?"

"I have a week off. So it's civvies for me."

"Why didn't you go away somewhere?"

"And miss our Thursday tea?"

"Be serious, Richard. Why not visit your family? Or friends?"

"You want a serious answer?"

Ann rested her chin on one hand. "I do."

"My only family is in Alberta and that's too far away for one week. I've seen several of my friends already. Sheila and Carl had me over for New Year's dinner. I even went skating one night. And now I'm seeing you. I like seeing you."

Ann considered how to respond to his last statement. Perhaps a light-hearted approach would be best. "I can't imagine why you want to spend time talking to a married woman with two children. Lots of single women would enjoy your company."

"I've met lots of single women. You're much more interesting."

"I hardly think hearing about Signals Welfare is interesting."

"Well, I do. Your stories help me understand more about the men I'm sending off to fight. And besides, we talk about lots more than that, and I enjoy hearing your perspective." He reached over and squeezed her hand.

Ann withdrew her hand. Instead of diverting Richard, her flippant comment had prompted the opposite. She sought a safer topic. "Did you play hockey when you were young?"

"A bit. I couldn't really skate fast enough. And most of
the farm boys were bigger than me. I remember this kid called
Hank. His proper name was Henry after his father, but everyone called him Hank. Anyway, he was a bruiser. Slammed me
into the corner one game then punched me with his fist. Broke
my nose. I bled all over the rink. And the referee didn't even
call a penalty." He laughed. "Can you see the bump?" Richard
turned his face in profile and pointed to a spot on his nose.

"A craggy nose adds character. That's what my father told
my brother Harry when he broke his nose. Alex plays hockey
for the school team. This year he's the goalie. He loves sports.
Much more than schoolwork."

"Most fifteen-year-old boys are like that. What about you?
Good Christmas?"

She related a few stories then changed topics again. "Did
you read Anthony Eden's speech to the House?" Richard nodded. "I can't fathom such evil. Why doesn't someone assassinate Hitler?"

"I feel the same way," he said. "I tell myself that every team
I train might be the one that makes a difference. If I didn't
think that way, I'm not sure I could keep doing what I do. As
it is, some nights I hardly sleep."

Ann folded her napkin into smaller and smaller squares.
"I've been there. To France and London. I can imagine the
streets of London and villages of France. And when Edward
and I . . ."

She stopped and glanced at him, a quick flick of the eyes.
She had a rule with herself not to mention Edward, as if she
could separate these afternoon conversations from her real life
as long as she did not speak her husband's name. And that
separation would somehow maintain the innocent nature of
meeting Richard every Thursday.

"When you and Edward . . ." he prompted.

"We went to Vimy for the dedication. In 1936. And visited
so many sites. I saw photos of what things looked like after
the first war, everything torn up and blown apart. Pictures of

little children with enormous, sad eyes, just standing there, watching. I'm sure it looks like that again. And the bombing in London. We've all seen pictures of those horrors." She let her chin drop.

For a moment or two Richard said nothing. He gulped the rest of his tea then set the mug down so hard she jumped. Frustration showed in the set of his mouth and clenched fists.

"I've put in to go overseas twice already. But each time I'm told my work here is more important. When I hear such sickening stories, I get so furious I want to smash something. I imagine taking one of those horrible people and killing them with my bare hands. Sometimes the rage boils over and I have to go outside to walk it off."

Richard's visible anger contrasted sharply with Edward's controlled demeanour. She knew Edward was angry and frustrated to be denied the chance to fight, but he seemed to channel his emotions into a sense of deliberate purpose. Ann marvelled that the two men reacted so differently.

They contrasted in other ways as well. Physically, Edward was tall and lanky while Richard's build was stocky, his chest and neck thicker, his hands blunt and strong, whereas her husband's fingers were long and slim. But the attributes that intrigued her were Richard's openness as well as his willingness to listen and confide. Unlike Edward, he did not keep feelings and thoughts hidden behind a mask of reserve.

Over the years, feelings of intimacy ebbed and flowed between Ann and Edward, and she was wise enough to know that every marriage went through such cycles. When times were calm, Edward disclosed more of himself. The early years of marriage had created many occasions when their love felt deeply profound. But with the Depression, his affair and now the war, they had fewer and fewer of those moments. Edward's secret life had begun to erode even the memories of better times. Despite Ann's efforts, she felt Edward slipping away.

Richard's gregarious nature drew her in. He offered compliments and paid close attention to her stories, probing for details and remarking on each situation she disclosed. No story seemed inconsequential, and she found herself noting events she could share with him as each Thursday approached. events she knew she should be sharing with Edward.

42 January 1943

The car chugged along Winchester Road, bucking and sputtering from time to time, while Saunders muttered encouragement as though a collection of metal and tires and glass could somehow hear his soothing words. With temperatures alternating between deep chill and just above freezing, the land was covered by frost, turning leafless trees into giant dandelion puffs. Edward barely noticed.

Disaster followed disaster. Whether day or night, communications came in at a relentless pace, necessitating more staff for the Hydra operation. At the same time, the war office demanded an increase in the output of new agents. In a rare moment of outward frustration, General Hastings had complained there were not enough hours in the day to meet everyone's demands.

As they approached the guardhouse, Saunders slowed the car and Mac McDonald, his grin barely noticeable behind a fur-lined hat, demanded the password then lifted the gate and waved them through. Edward looked up from his papers and glanced south of the apple orchard where a collection of giant poles topped with antennas marked the horizon. He wondered what news they would bring today.

Despite the cold, the streets of STS 103 bustled with people and he heard the hammer and bang of new huts going up. His breath froze as he hurried from the car.

"Colonel Jamieson." Betty MacLean called out as Edward approached. "The CO left this for you." She held out an envelope, which he scooped up with a quick word of thanks.

"Sorry, Betty. I can't stop to talk. I'm due at a meeting. When will General Hastings be joining us?"

"Not until late this morning. He's in some hush-hush meeting. Of course, most of them are hush-hush. I never know . . ."

Betty's voice grew faint as Edward opened the door. A blast of cold air greeted him and he jogged a few quick steps to the next building, which housed three large conference rooms. Camp X had grown from fifty personnel at its inception to more than three hundred. With so many agents to train and staff and officer meetings to conduct, the last round of renovations had included a series of small- and medium-sized rooms outfitted with blackboards, tables and chairs, maps, and in one case, a large projector for showing slides.

Edward shrugged off his coat and scarf and pulled a large stack of papers from his briefcase. He rubbed his hands together, hoping that his fingers would soon thaw. *Saunders needs to fix that damn heater*, he thought looking around. Eight men were in the Borealis Room, a rectangular space situated at one end of the officers' barracks and filled with plain wooden chairs and two tables. Hastings had asked Edward to start the briefing without him.

"Gentlemen, let's begin." Chairs scraped against the floor as the men sat down. "Britain and the US suspect Italy is the weak link in Axis defence. SOE, SIS and Camp X have been asked to assemble Italian-speaking agents to further that weakness. Some of you will have seen the memo, but if not,

I have additional copies." He passed them out. "We have to act quickly. Steve, I know you've studied the situation, what's your assessment?"

"We'll need agents to link up with major resistance outfits, particularly in the south," said Steve Shelley, a colleague recruited into the Camp X fold not long after Edward. "If the US is successful in Africa, we'll have a launching pad for invading Italy. Sicily is the obvious spot for an initial landing."

"Churchill calls it the underbelly of Europe," said one of the other men.

"Let's have a look at the map. I asked Steve to mark it with the latest information." Edward pushed back his chair.

Gathered around a map of Italy dotted with red pushpins to indicate resistance activity, the group became so engrossed with Steve's explanation, nothing else existed—not the glare of sunshine breaking through a previously grey sky, or the row of wire baskets full of paper, or the tickety-tick of a paper tape machine or the smell of disinfectant used by overnight cleaning staff. Resistance groups moved constantly in order to stay alive, so any map was almost immediately out of date. Nonetheless, everyone could see the concentration of activity around Taranto, Naples, Calabria and Messina.

"We'll need to train four teams, one for each of those areas. Who do we have?" Edward took charge again.

"Roberto Piannello is one possibility. He's a new recruit who's been training almost six weeks. Could be activated fairly quickly. Or what about Joe Debonis and Sal Bianco? Are they committed anywhere?"

"Good suggestions. Steve, can you work up as long a list as possible? If we can come up with more than twelve names, we won't have to recruit anyone and can get a team into the field more quickly. SOE wants to take advantage of the fact that support for the war in Italy is declining."

"But we'll have to recruit replacements."

Edward nodded to acknowledge John Foster's comment.

"Right, just not so urgently. Can you advise our recruiting

team? And I'd like someone to review what SOE has planned and pull together a briefing presentation for discussion first thing tomorrow. Any volunteers?"

At four o'clock, they wrapped up and Edward went to his small office. As he dumped a stack of papers onto the desk, the envelope Betty MacLean had given him that morning fell out. "Shit," he muttered, tearing open the envelope. He hoped the message had not been urgent.

GABRIEL TO JAMIESON
RE: EAGLE NEST STOP
FERRY RUNNING STOP

Edward ran from his office to inform General Hastings that Ray and Michel were back in business. Discussions with Hastings lasted until well after six. Back in his office once more, Edward called Ann.

"Hello." The sound of her voice always steadied him, reminding him what they were fighting for.

"Ann, it's me."

"Hello, dear. Are you on your way home?"

"No . . . a problem has come up, so I won't be home tonight. I'll call you first thing in the morning."

"Can you tell me where you are?" Edward heard her frustration.

"I'm at my usual location." He knew his answer would not satisfy. "How was your day?"

Ann inhaled then exhaled sharply. "I had lunch with your mother. She sends her love and says she's upset because she never sees you." He said nothing. "I was counting on having you home for dinner at least one night this week."

"I'm sorry, sweetheart. I know I keep disappointing you."

* * *

The following morning, the sun was nowhere in evidence when Edward left his cabin for the main building. The squeak of boots on snow and frozen breaths of air accompanied him. He had fifteen minutes for breakfast at the canteen before

taking a full mug of coffee with him to the Aurora room.
Though Camp X consisted mainly of simple, wooden buildings, someone had given each meeting room a name signify-
ing the beauty of time and space—Aurora, Borealis, Halley's
Comet, Galaxy, Copernicus. He no longer considered them
whimsical; whimsy did not belong in a place training men and
women for espionage.

Larry Paton conducted the briefing. Edward noted Larry's
red-rimmed eyes and wrinkled shirt, odd spikes of hair standing out from his head like a partially bald hedgehog. Clearly
the man had stayed up very late preparing—if he slept at all.

Making friends at Camp X was difficult. Officers joined the
effort then disappeared without warning for some urgent, nev-
er-disclosed assignment. New instructors arrived and stayed
for varying lengths of time. The nature of their work meant
that secrecy accompanied every event. A sign posted on the
Chief Instructor's door was an ever-present reminder: Know
Yourself. Know Your Weapon. Know Your Enemy.

Larry had been involved since the camp opened. Theirs
was an odd friendship born out of mutual dislike that over
time had turned to respect; respect had become friendship.
Edward was grateful to have someone who knew both his secret and public lives.

"Right." Larry cleared his throat and took a gulp of coffee.
"Allied intercept station at Asmara acquired raw intercepts
from a Japanese general based in Berlin. We have over three
hundred technicians manning Asmara, sending intercepts to
Arlington Hall for decoding. Once decoded, our people forward them to London for synthesis. We've learned a lot. The
Germans are worried about Mussolini, whose political colleagues are turning against him." Despite his obvious fatigue,
Larry delivered these facts quickly and precisely. "Influential
Italians are putting out feelers to our side. There are even
hints that King Victor Emmanuel is sympathetic to our cause.
Germany needs to hold the south to prevent us from getting
a toehold on Europe. They know we are amassing in Africa

and fear that a breakthrough there will be disastrous. Any questions so far?" Larry took another sip of coffee as he looked around the room.

"Germany is stepping up anti-resistance efforts. They're planning to reinforce manpower at Calabria and Naples. SOE wants a three-pronged campaign. The first is aimed at developing more sympathy amongst Italians in the south. The second is to disrupt German supply lines and the third is to help resistance leaders organize. We've been tasked with supply line disruption. SOE is mounting an information program and SIS will focus on resistance leaders. They need our plan by Saturday."

Everyone in the room knew there weren't enough hours to meet the deadline.

"Thanks, Larry."

As Edward took over the meeting, he knew he would have to tell Ann he would be away longer.

* * *

"Until at least Saturday," she said, twisting the telephone cord around her hand. "And what am I supposed to do with myself while you're away? Knit more bloody socks?"

"I'm sorry."

Ann knew she was being unfair but pressed on. "We can't keep going on like this. All we get are brief snatches of time. And it's always so unpredictable. It would be easier if you were overseas; at least then I could make my own plans."

His voice stiffened. "I didn't know you felt that way."

"I'm sorry. You know I don't mean it. I would hate to have you over there. It's just that I'm so frustrated. I can't even remember the last time we relaxed together."

"I know. I think next week should be fine. And maybe I'll be home Saturday night."

"All right. I'll give Marge a call and see if they'll take pity on me."

After the call ended, she untwisted the cord and hung up

the receiver then paced about the house, brooding over Edward's secret life. Emily was upstairs, but Ann knew she must not burden her daughter with the complaints of a lonely wife. *Resentful is a more accurate word*, she thought, and wondered how she could possibly resent a man who was only doing his duty. *Mother would say I'm acting like a spoiled child. She would tell me to stop thinking about my needs and think about Edward.*

* * *

For the rest of January and early February, Edward spent at least three days a week assembling and training the right team for Italy. Two rooms of the farmhouse had been made to reflect southern Italy, complete with magazines, posters, dishes and an old espresso machine. Edward was startled the first time he saw the setup; everything seemed so authentic. The supplies team had been relentless, gathering money, used tickets, old recordings, peasant clothing, handguns and wine to suit the mission's purpose. Even the telephone rang in the European manner.

General Hastings himself had conducted the initial briefing.

"The courses we take you through are extremely tough. You will be challenged both physically and mentally. Your instructors want the best possible outcome but will put no one at unnecessary risk. If they judge your skills inadequate, there will be no appeal. We prepare you to survive as secret agents and will teach you tactics you could never imagine. If at any time you find our expectations or the prospects of your future duties to be unacceptable, my door is open. No one will judge you inadequate should you choose not to proceed.

"Ladies and gentlemen, this mission will be pivotal to the war effort. I wish each and every one of you success. Now I'll turn the floor over to Major Jones who will take you around camp and then to your quarters."

* * *

Edward, Larry and seven men and women crowded around

a wireless transmitter in a corner of the Hydra facility. The massive receiver/transmitter whirred in the background, while nearby a row of punched-tape machines clicked and chattered, spewing rolls of tape on to the floor. Every fifteen or twenty minutes, a woman scooped the rolls into a basket and took them away.

"You have all passed your Morse code test and have been selected for advanced wireless training. What we need you to learn is how to assemble, dismantle and fix a transmitter in the field. You can't operate without being able to communicate and you can't communicate if your machine isn't working. Larry's the expert. He'll show you what to do. We have only two weeks left and I'll need four of you to know how to do this blindfolded. Larry, they're in your hands.

Ultimately the instructors chose nine men and three women who would soon depart for North Africa before making their way into Italy via various means. SOE had identified four resistance cells in southern Italy as their initial contact points.

As commanding officer of Camp X, General Hastings addressed them in the Galaxy Room, the only space that could hold everyone involved.

"We're proud of the work you've done preparing for this campaign and I am certain you will be successful. Those of us who remain here will do everything we can to support you over the coming months. American bombing raids are proving effective, and as you know, Germany surrendered at Stalingrad. I believe Italy will prove to be a turning point. A turning point enabled in part by the work you are about to do. May God bless you and keep you safe," he concluded gruffly.

The group broke into small clumps for conversation and Edward turned to Larry Paton.

"You did an excellent job coordinating the team. I've told General Hastings you deserve at least a week off."

"Thanks, Edward." Larry sounded tired and deflated, as though the adrenalin that kept them all going had suddenly

dissipated. "What are we sending them into? I hope it's worth
. . ."

"Don't torture yourself with questions like that. Ours is
a nasty business. You've done your best to get them ready.
Luck, skill and timing will do the rest." He said this in part
to reassure himself and put his hand on Larry's shoulder. "Go
home to your family."

Walking through six inches of wet snow, weariness marked
Edward's steps. The relentless pace of Camp X combined with
responsibilities to his job and to A Corps made for long days
and fitful sleep. Fortunately, Major Whitely had taken over
Saturdays at the armoury, but Dave Jenkins, while understanding, still made demands. With a driver waiting in the
small sitting room attached to the officers' barracks, Edward
packed his clothes then sorted through an accumulation of papers, designating some for filing and others to be destroyed. A
clock mounted above the door showed quarter to four. Edward
wondered if he would be home in time for dinner and whether
Ann would be there to greet him.

* * *

"You look exhausted." Ann took Edward's suitcase and
placed it at the foot of the stairs. "Alex can take that up for
you. We're having roast chicken. But you look like you should
go straight to bed."

"No, no. Just give me a few minutes. I want to have dinner
with you." He folded his arms around her and kissed the soft
nape of her neck. "You smell nice."

She rubbed her cheek against his. "Why don't you put your
feet up in the living room? I'll bring you a drink."

Hannah told her she should be thinking about Edward,
not herself, that whatever work he was involved in would be
important and Ann's way to support the war effort was to
support her husband as completely as possible. She had pon-
dered that conversation many times wondering how to be the
wife Edward needed when her own needs were so neglected.

She felt like a garden going weeks without water, her leaves withering and the soil hard and dry.

Edward's appearance was alarming. Considerably thinner than he had been in January, his skin was pasty, drained of its normal olive tone, and his eyes were bloodshot. As he walked away, she noticed a spot on the back of his head where he would soon be bald. Ann turned towards the kitchen, calling for Alex to carry his father's suitcase to the bedroom. Fortunately, she only had to call him once. When she returned to the living room with a glass of whiskey, her husband was fast asleep.

In bed that night, he held her and talked about the weariness of war and the impossible tasks asked of men and women who served. She knew it was his way of telling her as much as he could and she nestled against his body, offering her warmth and the kindness of asking him no questions.

"We'll have a quiet weekend," she said. "Just you and me. I saved some coupons so we can have something special on Saturday.

"I'd like that."

Moments later he was once again asleep.

43 February 1943

February was proving to be a nasty month with frequent snow and ice storms. The previous week, power outages had affected the streetcars. Ann had extracted Richard's telephone number from her jewellery box and called to let him know she was stuck at home.

"You look upset about something," Ann said the following week, pulling off her gloves, finger by finger before setting them on the table.

After four months of having tea on Thursdays, Ann knew when Richard's day had been difficult because his voice was clipped and he took more time to ease into laughter. Today, with his shoulders hunched forward, he looked like an angry bull. Other than Edward and her father, she had never observed a man closely enough to anticipate his moods or soothe the burdens that plagued him. After trying various strategies, she had learned that what Richard needed most was to talk.

"Bloody nonsense going on."

Having learned the art of silence from her father, she said nothing. Instead she extracted a pin from her hat then placed the hat upside down on the banquette with her gloves inside. She ran her fingers through her hair to loosen the curls and smiled.

"An accounting mess is preventing me from getting training supplies. Some bloody clerk who has no idea what he's doing, no doubt. Of course, my CO still wants the men trained in record time. How can I do that without enough weapons?"

"Did you say that to your CO?"

"I did. He just said that's what my captain's stripes are for and to use my ingenuity. Red tape and idiocy. Took me all day to make any headway."

"So your CO was right."

Richard narrowed his eyes and frowned. "What does that mean?"

"You used your ingenuity."

He laughed. "Well, I shouted a lot. Got my blood boiling. What about you? I mean your week. I'm not trying to imply that you shout at people."

"The usual sad cases at the drop-in centre. My friend Linda's making a wonderful contribution though. Did I tell you about Linda?" Richard nodded. "We can always rely on her even for the tough cases. I hadn't imagined she would be so good at it."

"Why's that?"

"She's always been a bit flighty. Mother used to say she was like a butterfly that couldn't decide where to land. Of course, she's older now."

"Aren't we all? And her son?"

"She thinks he's in Africa."

They sat in silence while the waitress served their tea. "We have apple pie," she said, balancing a tray of dirty dishes in one hand while mopping a spill of hot water from the table.

"We'll have two slices," Richard said.

Ann leaned forward after the waitress left. "That used to

annoy me."

"What do you mean?"

"The way you'd order without even asking me."

"Does it still annoy you?" She shook her head. "Do you want pie?"

"I'm sure I'll eat a few bites. Probably shouldn't." She smoothed the front of her tartan skirt. "What do you know about our troops in Africa?"

"Last year was a disaster until October. Now that the Americans are involved we have more tank power and more troops on the ground. And the Vichy French have switched allegiance. Took a while to sort out that mess. But Rommel continues to build his forces and their air strength is more easily deployed than ours. I think Tunis is the next target. But that's just a guess. Is Linda's son army or air force?"

"Army. But why is Africa so important?"

"Supply lines. And protection for Europe. If we get control of Africa, we can hop across the Mediterranean into Europe. Like a back door. The front door is through France. The back door is probably through Italy. There are rumours Italy wants to change sides."

"That would be a problem for Hitler."

"It's about time he had a few problems." Richard dug into his pie.

Compared to Edward's constant secrecy, Richard's openness was refreshing. The following Thursday, he told her about his childhood growing up on a small ranch in Alberta.

"The farm was my mother's inheritance," Richard said. "My father never wanted that life. He was more interested in his books, and once told me that he always wanted to be a writer. I think he regretted telling me that because he never mentioned it again." Richard folded his napkin and placed it beneath his plate. "He wasn't a happy man. When I was little, my mother helped with all the chores and they had one ranch hand to mend fences and herd the cattle to different grazing ground or round them up for slaughtering. It was hard work. I was in charge of the chickens from the time I was six."

Ann could tell from Richard's wistful tone that these memories saddened him. "What did that involve?"

"I fed the chickens twice every day, once in the morning and once after school. And I collected the eggs, so my mother could sell them. We had a rickety old truck for getting into town, which was more than an hour away."

"Do you have any brothers or sisters?"

"My sister Lily was born when I was nine. I found out later that my mother had four miscarriages after having me. She wasn't strong after Lily was born. My father used to say that daughters were of no use on a farm.

"I took over most of my mother's chores, working after school until late evening, milking the few cows we had and raking hay in the barns, brushing down the horses. Mum was never able to cope with physical labour again. Our nearest neighbour was a mile down the road, so the house was a lonely place. When I was older, I told them I wouldn't take over the farm. My father was furious. Fortunately, the war intervened and I was sent to Edmonton for training."

"Why was he furious?"

"I dunno. Probably wished he had the guts to stop farming."

"Did you go overseas?"

He nodded. "But the war ended a few months after I got to England. I took advantage of an education grant and didn't return to Alberta."

"Don't you miss your family?" The story of his childhood explained some of his aloofness.

"My mother died when I was twenty-five. Lily is married and lives near my father. I write to her quite often." He swivelled his teacup back and forth. "I never faced my father over the decisions I made. I just knew I didn't want to turn out as bitter as he is."

"Did he ever remarry?" She could not imagine her own father living alone for any length of time.

"No. Lily tells me that there have been a few women in his life. His drinking usually chases them away."

"Where did you live after the war?"

"I worked for an accounting firm in Ottawa. Steady work, but not very exciting. Better than farming, I suppose. After this war is over, I want to start my own business."

When the subject of marriage came up, he looked away for a moment or two before replying. "It didn't work out. Our wedding was the last time I saw my mother."

"And . . ." She prompted him to continue.

"Sally wanted children. We both wanted them. But after years of trying, the doctors told her that she would never conceive and our marriage came apart. Nothing I did or said made any difference. She began to drink. Once she threw a vase full of flowers at me. Eventually, I left her."

"I'm sorry. That's very sad."

"More than twelve years ago now. I don't usually tell people, but I find I can tell you almost anything. You're so . . ." Richard's voice trailed away.

The soft look in his eyes made her wonder what else he was going to say. "Thank you for saying that. I like hearing your stories. And I appreciate the way you talk to me about the war. Most men prefer to shelter women from what's going on."

"From the day we met I got the impression you were different. That's one of the reasons I like seeing you." He leaned forward, elbows on the table, chin propped against his knuckles. "One of them."

Ann considered Richard's words. Instead of sipping her tea or looking away, she fixed her eyes on his. For a long time, neither looked away.

"I have to go."

"I know," he said.

44 MARCH 1943

"Should only be three days this time." General Hastings' tone made it clear there was no option.

Edward hung up the phone and leaned back. Scattered on his desk were various piles of paper and a yellow notepad, the top page covered in his tight, slanted writing. The Defense Department had requested more equipment, but the telephone company's manufacturing department had insufficient materials to accommodate the military without adjusting supplies for internal needs. As a result, Dave Jenkins wanted revisions to the installation plan for the year and Edward's group of managers had been working solidly all last week to determine which changes to make. Jenkins wanted the final plans by Friday. Being called away to Camp X meant he would have to finish his review tonight.

God, he thought, *it never ends.*

Edward reached for the phone and told Barbara Nicholls to gather his managers together. Hanging up the phone, he rubbed a hand across his face and let out a long, slow sigh. Ann would be upset. After the long weeks preparing for Italy, she seemed to have stepped away from him in a fashion he could not quite understand. A bit remote, perhaps, as though she were analyzing something. Her voice just a little less warm, her body a little less welcoming.

Though he was busy and in the company of others almost all the time, he was lonely. Ann used to be the one who eased that loneliness. He sighed again and picked up his pen.

"Only three days," she said, when he told her. "But your estimates are never reliable. Alex, please pass the salt. At least salt isn't rationed. Our food would be tasteless if it was."

He found it easier to disclose his absences at dinnertime with Emily and Alex present. Ann was never sharp with him in front of their children, but talking about salt was definitely not a good sign. He knew she would say something later.

"Where are you going, Dad?" Alex said.

"Just out of town for a few days."

"I know. You said that. But where? You never tell us where."

Edward hesitated. He hated lying. "Montreal. Some meetings at head office. That's where I often go." *Two lies,* he thought, avoiding Ann's eyes. She had an uncanny ability of knowing when he was not telling the truth.

On many occasions he had considered revealing his role despite his oath of secrecy. Ann would not break his confidence, but he had not permitted himself the luxury of her understanding, and now he wondered again whether he should tell her just a bit, enough for her to know how he was serving his country.

Having survived the First World War, he often felt his life came at the expense of others. Thousands and thousands of others. Over time he had pushed his guilt aside as best he could. When war erupted again, guilt stirred like a nest of snakes emerging from hibernation. Camp X represented atonement, though he doubted his guilt would ever completely go away.

After two years of operation, they were having an impact. At first, sending an agent or two to France felt like filling a lake with a teaspoon. But now there were hundreds in the field and some of their results were astounding. He hoped the Italian mission would prove successful.

"How many shirts?" Ann set his suitcase on the bed with a thump.

"Come here," he said, opening his arms, and when she put her head on his shoulder he tried to find an explanation that would satisfy. "You know I don't go away because I want to." He felt her head nod against his chest. "You know I have work to do I can't disclose. I took an oath, you know."

"You did?" Her voice was muffled, but he felt her tension ease a fraction.

"Probably shouldn't even tell you that much." He let his hand rest at the base of her back where he could feel the pleasing curves of buttocks and hips.

"So that means you're involved in something secret."

"Yes. Does that make a difference?"

"I don't know. A bit maybe. I've been thinking about what makes it all so difficult. Partly it's your absence. I'm lonely, you know. But the secrets bother me. They make me feel like we're estranged in some way. It's almost as bad as . . ."

"As bad as what?"

"As bad as what happened after we went to Vimy."

He released his arms and stepped back. "But I told you before, it's nothing like that. I'm not involved with anyone. I love you. You know I do. And I'm lonely too."

"I'm sorry, dear. I shouldn't have said that. I know that whatever you're doing, it must be important."

"I think we're having an impact. With a little luck, we'll soon have more."

Edward moved to embrace her once again. Ann put her arms around him and held him close.

* * *

I'm always waving good-bye to him, Ann thought, watching Edward's car disappear down the street.

Shivering, she closed the front door and wondered where her husband was going this time. She had often speculated about his destination, reasoning that it could not be too far from Toronto given the frequency of his comings and goings. It was almost always the same driver who collected and returned him home, a youngish man with owl-like glasses and a pleasant face. Edward never mentioned the driver's name, which Ann thought was more than a little odd. He gave very few hints, merely an occasional sense of buoyancy or dismay in the way he carried his shoulders. She wondered what he meant by having a little impact and soon having more.

Returning to the kitchen, she found Emily making a bologna sandwich to take to school.

"Your father's off again."

Ann cleared four cereal bowls and poured another cup of coffee but added no milk, another show of sacrifice. First the sugar, then, as a New Year's resolution, she cut out milk as well.

"After this stupid war is over, I'm never going to eat another bologna sandwich. And don't lecture me about how fortunate we are. I hear that every day at school." Emily tore a strip of wax paper and began to wrap her sandwich. "When's Dad coming back?"

"He says three days."

"But you don't believe him, do you? I wouldn't."

Ann debated the wisdom of saying something critical of Edward. "He hasn't got a very good track record. Sometimes it makes me cross."

"I know. I can see it in your face."

"Sorry, sweetheart. I shouldn't burden you. He's your father. He has important work to do."

"Well, you're the one who does everything else. I'm sure you're lonely. I know I would be."

"I am, but it could . . ."

"It could be worse," Emily completed the sentence and they both laughed at a phrase that was repeated so often it had lost any meaning. "I'm going to miss the bus if I don't get going. I'll be home all weekend. Keith is off to Kingston. If Dad's still away we can do something."

"Thank you, sweetheart. You're such a lovely daughter. I don't know what I'd do without you."

Emily blew her a kiss as she rushed out of the kitchen. A few minutes later Ann heard the front door slam. She picked up the paper and took a sip of coffee. The headline read: US II CORPS REGROUPING. The article described General Patton's latest encounters with Rommel in Tunisia and the changes he was making to command structure, more flexible artillery, communications and air support. While generally positive, Ann wondered how much was propaganda and how much was truth.

She knew Linda would be worried about David. Although General Patton's II Corps had nothing to do with Canadian troops in North Africa, her friend agonized over every bit of information about that far-off continent.

"Please keep him safe," she muttered.

"You're talking to yourself, Mom." Alex poked his head around the door, dressed in his school uniform and an unbuttoned black wool coat.

While Emily looked a lot like her mother, Alex looked like neither of his parents. Instead of dark hair, his was sandy brown and his frame was stocky rather than lean and tall. Edward suggested he looked like his own brother Cyril, while Ann preferred to imagine that Alex looked like her paternal grandfather.

She had no idea her son was still at home.

"I was thinking about David Andrews. A little prayer to keep him safe. His mother is so worried."

"He didn't have to go, did he? He could've gone to university instead."

"That's right, dear."

"Why do you think he enlisted?"

"Why do you think he did?" Ann countered, wondering what her son would say.

"To serve his country. That's what I would do." Alex sucked in his breath and pulled his shoulders back. "I'm glad I went down to see him off. Mr. and Mrs. Andrews were pleased."

"So was I." She glanced at the kitchen clock. "Aren't you late for school?"

"We don't start until ten today because Mrs. Templeton just had a baby and there's no substitute available. I'm going now."

Ann followed him to the front door where Alex grabbed his hat and scarf. "What about your mitts?"

"Mother, I'm fifteen. I don't wear mitts." He slammed the door behind him.

When he called her Mother, Ann knew he was annoyed. She returned to the kitchen and sat down again, propping the paper against a bowl of apples. After reading a few headlines, she flipped through the pages but found nothing of interest except an advertisement for her mother's favourite hand cream. Ann cut out the coupon and put it in her purse. She would buy a jar and tuck it away for her mother's birthday.

Wednesday was never a scheduled day, not like Tuesdays and Thursdays when she went to Signals Welfare, or Mondays when she did most of the laundry and cleaning.

But today, she found it difficult to concentrate, her mind drifting time and again to Edward's oath of secrecy. The only task she could imagine was the use of secret codes for sending messages, which made sense given his experience in Signals. As in the past, she wondered where he went and why he disappeared so often.

45 MARCH 1943

Spidery shadows from a nearby tree marked the sidewalk in front of The Shamrock. Chimes above the door jangled and the waitress looked up from her post behind the counter, not the regular waitress, but a gaunt young woman with soulful eyes. Ann knew that look; she had seen it countless times on the women who came to Signals Welfare. The waitress sighed, pulled out her order pad and followed three teenage boys as they sauntered to a table at the back.

Ann's mouth twitched with amusement. Richard smiled in return. Afternoon tea had lingered longer than usual but still he made no move to depart. She wondered why.

He cleared his throat. "I have two tickets for a benefit concert. Would you like to come?"

Her face went still and flat. "Richard, you know we don't do that sort of thing. We just have tea. Remember?"

"They'll only go to waste. And it's too late to ask anyone else." He kept his eyes on hers.

"Why is it too late? When is this concert?"

"Tonight."

"You certainly know how to make a woman feel special." The moment she spoke, Ann wished she could take her words back; they were far too flirtatious.

"Now what's that supposed to mean? I'm just a guy with two tickets and a friend who might want to take one of them. You can have them both, if you'd like to ask someone to go with you."

Ann opened her purse and extracted a tissue. "Tonight." He nodded. "What time?"

Richard pulled the tickets from his breast pocket. "Eight o'clock."

"I would have to go home to change then come all the way downtown again. Can't you ask someone else?"

"You look fine. Why not just have dinner with me and we can go straight to the concert? I'll send you home with a driver."

"Richard." She made his name sound like three syllables.

"I've never asked you before."

"Well, if I come tonight, promise you'll never ask me again." A grin broke out on his face. "I'll have to telephone Emily so she doesn't worry." Ann tried to make her voice businesslike. She looked at her watch. "Where and when shall I meet you? I have a few errands to run." Ann wondered whether he knew she was lying.

"Meet me in front of the Elgin Theatre at six thirty. I know a restaurant nearby. We'll have enough time for a quick meal." He rose from his chair and helped her with her coat. "I'm glad you can come."

She permitted a small smile to form on her lips.

* * *

Except for the ambiance of white tablecloths and a black-jacketed waiter, dinner was not much different from meeting Richard for tea. But sitting next to him in the theatre, shoulders almost touching, his face close enough she could see the scrape of his beard, she felt awkward, almost shy, as if they were on a first date.

"I love the trumpet, don't you?" Richard leaned over. "Johnny Holmes is from Montreal. I once went to see him at Stanley Hall. He composes a lot of what they play."

Five other men were onstage playing piano, saxophone, drums, string bass and trombone, the saxophonist occasionally switching to oboe. The only woman in the group was a singer whose mellow, moody voice suited the music. During instrumentals her sequined skirt swayed as she shook the maracas and took small steps one way and then the other, in time with the tempo.

"Trumpets are wonderful but the singer's my favourite."

Richard peered at his program. "Her name's Lorraine McAllister. How can someone so young sing like she knows all the world's troubles?"

"Shh!" The woman next to Richard hissed.

"Sorry," he said, smiling at Ann before settling back to listen.

During intermission they wandered the lobby full of chattering voices, the crowd mainly middle-aged with a smattering of grey-haired couples and military men. Ann was on edge. What if she bumped into someone she knew? How would she explain being at a concert with someone other than her husband? Distracted she responded only vaguely to Richard's conversation and was relieved when they returned to their seats.

The band's second set was just as memorable, and after raucous applause, they played a few encore numbers to the crowd's delight. When Ann and Richard left the theatre, fat snowflakes were falling, and except for those attending the concert, the streets were empty.

"My driver's waiting around the corner." Richard put his arm through hers to guide them through the dispersing crowd. "Do you want me to come with you?"

"That's a lovely offer but I don't think it's necessary."

He opened the rear door and Ann slid in, revealing a glimpse of leg above the knee. "Thank you for taking me. I had a lovely time." A formal note marked her voice.

He leaned in, his face mere inches from hers, and brushed his lips against her cheek. "I did too." Richard closed the door and waited as the car drove off.

On the way home, she touched her cheek more than once, recalling his soft breath and the warmth that had filled her body afterwards. She did not know how to interpret his action or, for that matter, her own response. The husbands of some of her friends kissed her cheek in greeting, but Richard's kiss felt different. He had always behaved with impeccable courtesy, keeping a physical distance except when helping with her coat or holding her chair, and such courtesies were totally consistent with friendship. The kiss was not.

* * *

"Hi, Mom." Emily came into the hall just as Ann closed the front closet door. She wore a tartan dressing gown that Ann had patched more than a year ago because both elbows had worn out.

"You're still up," Ann said.

"I thought you might want to tell someone about what happened at Signals Welfare. Since Daddy's not home, I waited for you."

"Oh. That's nice, dear."

"I'll make us some tea."

Luckily, Emily pushed through the kitchen door before Ann had to respond. *I need to compose myself*, she thought. She had told Emily that an urgent situation at Signals Welfare required her to stay late. Now she would have to provide some details. Ann tried to think of something recent that had occurred, something serious enough to demand attention until after ten p.m.

"So, what happened?" Emily said, once they were settled with a cup of tea.

"A woman came in around four. A young woman, probably twenty-five or so. Ginny Marks was on reception and she came to find me right away because the woman was so agitated."

Ann sipped her tea. She had decided to embellish a situation that had occurred the previous week. Sticking to the facts as much as possible would allow her to tell the lie in a more convincing fashion.

"Her name was Vivian. Such a pretty thing. Anyway, Ginny and I both sat with Vivian, asking questions and trying to calm her down. After a while, she told us about receiving a telegram last week informing her of her husband's death—a ship torpedoed at sea. She had been all right for the first little while but as the days progressed she felt worse and worse and had no one to help her. According to Vivian, this morning she felt like her body and head were coming apart. She kept saying that she was outside her body and held her head with two hands as if to keep it attached."

"How terrible," Emily said. "What did you do?"

"Ginny sat with her in the sleeping room until Vivian fell asleep. When Ginny checked on her about an hour later, Vivian wasn't there. We found her in the kitchen holding a butcher's knife."

Emily's mouth dropped open. "Good grief," she said.

"I was glad I stayed. It took both of us to get her to put down the knife."

"Do you think she would have hurt herself?"

"Quite possibly." Ann gathered up the teacups. "Now, that's enough lurid details. You'll be having nightmares."

The following day when Edward came home, Ann disclosed nothing of the concert to him and he was too preoccupied to ask for an accounting of her day. *An omission*, she thought, *definitely not a lie.* But she hated the fact that she had lied to Emily.

On Wednesday she dug into her jewellery box for the small scrap of paper Richard had given her. Six days had passed and yet Ann remained unsettled by the concert, particularly Richard's kiss. She needed another week to pass, perhaps more, before seeing him again. If she saw him again.

Ann picked up the phone. No one answered the first time she called, but the second time a young man responded with brisk tones.

"May I speak with Captain Leary?"

She heard a muffled shout. "Woman on the phone for you, sir."

"Leary, here."

"Richard, it's Ann. Ann Jamieson."

"What other Ann would it be?" he said with a chuckle.

The warmth in his voice made her feel shy. "I'm just calling to say that I can't have tea this week."

"Oh. Why not? Is it because of the concert?" He sounded disappointed and slightly offended.

"No . . . I have to be somewhere else," Ann lied. "The following week should work."

"Are you sure you're fine? You sound tired."

"I've been busy. That's all. But everything's fine." She wrapped the phone cord around her fingers and said nothing further.

"All right then. I'll see you at the Victory next time."

46 MARCH 1943

Late March was warm with a tantalizing promise of spring, but Ann's smile faded when she saw Richard's agitation. She loosened her coat and sat down.

"What's wrong?"

He was in uniform, crisp and immaculate. "I can't do this anymore."

"Can't do what?" She searched his face.

He hunched over the table, leaning towards her. "I have to stop seeing you. It's driving me crazy."

Colour drained from her face. "We can't have this conversation here."

"Then let's go somewhere we can be more private." The chair scraped the floor as he rose.

Richard held Ann's coat and watched her fumble with the buttons. He put a few coins on the table and they walked out the door. Without saying a word, he took her arm and she hurried to keep up with his long strides, crossing Queen Street and Richmond Street then heading west along Adelaide Street until they reached the Victoria Hotel. A doorman opened the large wooden door and they stepped inside.

"There's a bar on this floor. There won't be many people in it."

Ann wondered whether he used such a cool, sharp tone with his men. He released her arm as soon as they entered the lobby and she trailed a step or two behind, passing the mahogany reception counter on the right, where a clerk held the phone in one hand and took notes with the other, and a tall buffet topped with a large spray of flowers on her left. Richard put his arm on the small of her back and ushered her into a dim space with cream-colored lampshades and plush but faded furniture.

"Over there," he said, indicating an alcove and two chairs grouped by a low, round table.

His brusqueness was disconcerting. Ann shed her coat and sat down. Something cold gripped her heart.

An aging barman with a long face and prominent ears approached. He pushed his glasses into place and stood ready for their order.

"Scotch?"

"Rye, please."

"One of each," he said, as if issuing an order to his troops. "I've come here with army friends a few times. Friday nights there's usually some music."

Ann said nothing. Being in a secluded corner of a dimly lit bar with a man who had just declared that he had to stop seeing her could in no way be construed as friendship. Leaving would be the sensible thing to do. *Go home, paste on your usual smile, feed your family, wait for Edward.* She remained exactly where she was.

When the barman returned, she sipped her drink and looked at Richard.

"I should go," she said.

He took her glass and placed it on the table then took her hands in his. "I'm falling in love with you. I can't help it and I can no longer see you every week knowing you go home to someone else."

The poignancy of his words stung like the unexpected slice of a knife. She looked at her hands captured in his strong, blunt fingers and felt the warmth of his touch. A deep pulse grew within her, suffusing her body with warmth.

"You've always known that."

"I know. I enjoyed your company. I thought it would be an innocent flirtation."

"It's no longer innocent, is it?"

"No. Each week I count the hours until our next time together. It's not a life, Ann. I don't want to hurt you and I'm afraid that's where we'll end. There's no future for us."

"I'm already involved. This," she spread her hands wide, "already hurts me."

Richard hung his head. "I'm sorry," he whispered.

"When did you . . ." Ann looked away, her eyes searching for something to focus on. Her lip quivered.

"After the concert. When you called last week to cancel. I couldn't . . ."

She waited for him to finish but he said nothing more, and for a moment or two she let the silence hang as she studied his face, each familiar contour, the crinkles beside each eye, the cleft of his chin and line of his neck. Beneath the guise of conversation and Thursday tea, this man had become something more than a friend. Concerns and hopes and speculation—the very things she used to share with Edward—had fused two ragged souls.

"Are you sure it's the right decision?" Ann asked.

"What do you mean?"

"You didn't ask how I feel." Ann hesitated as she spoke, acutely aware of her hands in his and the pulse throbbing at the base of her throat. *What am I doing? Leave now, leave before you do something you can't undo.* Her thoughts spun at the tipping edge of control. Nothing else existed except her and Richard and a pivotal few seconds. He ran a finger from her palm to her wrist and back again. She shivered.

"Are you cold?"

She shook her head. "No."

"So how do you feel?"

"I like seeing you." She echoed words he had spoken when they met after Christmas. "All week I look forward to Thursday." Ann knew she had tipped over the edge into something unknown and dangerous. Every part of her felt alive.

"I'd like to kiss you."

Her heart jumped. "Not here."

He stood. Keeping a tight grip on Ann's hand, he led her out of the bar and through the lobby, then up a wide set of stairs to the second floor. Richard looked at her, his face a curious blend of tension and anticipation. He found an open meeting room at the end of the hall and closed the door.

His kiss began softly then intensified until Ann thought her knees might buckle. He held her face as his tongue possessed her mouth. She reached for his shoulders to pull him close and felt the length of his body against her. Richard drew back for a moment, keeping his lower body touching hers but searching her eyes.

"I want to devour every part of you."

* * *

"Mom, what are we having for dinner?" Alex walked into the kitchen. "Are you okay? You look kind of funny."

"I've had a difficult day . . . with one of our welfare clients. It was very emotional. I can't seem to get her story out of my head." Ann tied an apron around her waist and turned away to wash her hands.

"Oh. What was her story?" He opened the breadbox and extracted a piece of bread. "Hungry," he said, folding it in half and taking a large bite.

She could not cope with Alex's chatter. "Can I tell you at

suppertime?"

His mouth full of bread, Alex nodded and wandered out of the kitchen. Alone again, she thought about Richard.

She had drawn away from him when the intensity of his passion threatened to push them down a maze of unknowable consequences. Ann had asked him to stop and he had, but not before trailing his hand down the line of her neck and kissing a spot just above the top of her blouse. He had gazed at her with such desire she had been forced to look away.

"We should go," Ann had said.

"I know."

"Otherwise . . ." Nothing more needed saying.

Walking from the hotel to Queen Street, they had exchanged fragile glances, but except for his hand beneath her elbow when crossing the street, they had not touched. From the streetcar window she had watched him standing at the corner until he had disappeared into the bustle of traffic and crowd of late-day pedestrians. Amidst the chatter of fellow passengers and the screech of grinding metals, she had recalled Richard's words, the look on his face, the feel of his mouth and his gentle hands.

Ann had little recollection of making dinner or listening to Alex and Emily talk. All she could do was nod her head from time to time, lift her eyebrows, smile vaguely. Afterwards, she picked up her knitting and turned on the radio, twisting the dial to music rather than news. Row after row, her needles clicked to an ancient, mindless rhythm as she drifted from memory to memory.

When did conversation become something else? Ann considered this question as she continued to knit. Perhaps she should have recognized her feelings earlier. Even when they first met, his comments and looks had been different from other men, sparking an emotional reaction that should have been a warning sign. She set her needles aside and counted on her fingers: October, November, December, January, February. Now that it was March, they had been meeting for more than five months. *What have I done?*

She was grateful for Edward's absence. The idea of being close to her husband after kissing Richard filled her with shame. *But he'll be home tomorrow night.* She tried to imagine acting as though nothing had occurred.

* * *

At half past noon the following day, the telephone rang. Ann was in the living room looking out at the front yard, the newspaper on her lap and a cup of lukewarm tea on the small table beside her. She thought about letting it ring, but instead got up to answer.

"Hello."

"It's me." Ann's heart buckled at the sound of Richard's voice. "I had to call."

"What if Edward had answered? Or my children?"

"I would have hung up. How are you?"

"I feel . . . Was yesterday a dream? I'm not that kind of woman."

"It was real. More real than I could have imagined. And wonderful. When can I see you again?"

"I don't know. The answer should be never."

"Are you regretting what we did?"

"No . . . Maybe." Her voice was husky and unsteady.

"Sounds like you are. I'm sorry."

"Richard, I can't talk to you right now. I don't know what to say and I need to think. You aren't married, but I am. I need to think." Words spilled almost of their own volition.

"I promise I won't pressure you. I'll wait as long as you need me to wait. I love you. It's as true today as it was yesterday."

"What have I done?"

"It wasn't you, it was me. It's my fault. If you want, I'll walk away right now. That's what I had planned to do."

"I just . . . I just . . ."

"You have my number. Call me anytime. Even at night they know how to reach me." His voice was gentle.

"All right. I'll call you."

She placed the phone in its cradle without waiting for his response.

* * *

Edward arrived just before six, letting a blast of cold air through the door. Ann had rouged her cheeks and lips to hide the pallor of her face. After Richard's call she had soaked in the bath then scrubbed her skin until it turned pink, all the while imagining topics to discuss over dinner.

"There you are," she said, offering her cheek in greeting. "You're cold. Let me take your briefcase." Ann walked towards the study. "We're having pork chops and I made your favourite scalloped potatoes." She leaned over the bannister. "Alex and Emily, you're father is home."

"Hi, Dad," Emily called from her bedroom.

Edward came into the kitchen holding a stack of mail. "God, the mail never ends. I'll look at it later. Dinner smells delicious." He leaned over and kissed the back of her neck. "You're shivering. Are you cold?"

"No, no. You just tickled my neck." Ann moved away to open the oven door and check the potatoes.

"What did you do while I was away?"

"Just the usual." She set out place mats and then cutlery, wondering if he could hear the guilt. Normal topics might steady her voice. "Yesterday I had a long day at Signals Welfare. Seven new women came in. It just keeps getting worse. I don't know how our existing volunteers will handle the load. Linda's a great addition, but really, we need at least four more because we lost Helen and Lucille. No one I've called has any time to spare."

"It must be nice having Linda there. I should catch up with Eric. I wonder what they're hearing from David?"

"She says they get letters almost every week." Ann stepped back to survey the table. "I think we're ready. Can you call Emily and Alex?"

Ann lingered in the kitchen long after Edward declared he was ready for bed, wiping the counters, straightening kitchen chairs, separating the mail into two neat piles, one for payment, the other for filing. She made hard-boiled eggs for tomorrow's sandwiches and washed apples for Alex and Emily's lunches.

All the while, like a swarm of butterflies, her thoughts refused to rest. The lure of Richard was so powerful, she felt as though she were under some kind of spell. Being close to him, touching him, kissing him had filled her with such intense desire she had been almost breathless. Even thinking about him made her pulse quicken again. *Lust*, she thought. *That's what this is. Lust.* Another voice intervened. *No*, it said. *More than lust. You love being with him. Admit it.*

The moon glimmered from behind the neighbour's house, pale and full. Nothing but the sighs of waving pines trees marked the passage of time. *I have a husband. I have two beautiful children. I'm a good woman. I promised myself to Edward. It's the war. We're just having a rough patch because of the war. But . . .*

Ann's thoughts bounced back and forth. By the time she went upstairs, Edward was asleep.

* * *

Richard kept his promise. Time inched along. During the day she kept a bracing schedule that allowed no pause for speculation, but at night she drowned in questions and rebuked herself for failing to keep her vows. Climbing the hill on Thursday, a fine drizzle chilled her to the bone. With each step she debated what to do. Disembarking at Dundas, she did not realize she had taken the wrong turn until walking more than a block heading east instead of west.

"Nasty out, isn't it?" Angela said when Ann opened the office door.

"Pardon?"

"Someone's lost in thought. I just commented on the nasty

weather."

"Drizzly."

"Yes. Are you all right?"

"Sorry, Angela. I'm fine. Just fine. Any messages for me?"

Within a short while, Ann was caught up in discussions with clients, one who had failed to receive her husband's salary for the fourth month in a row, a second woman with a sick baby and insufficient money to pay the doctor and a third whose husband had sent a letter requesting a divorce. Today, they were shorthanded and she was glad to be busy. Anything was better than the dilemma she carried inside her head.

After a late lunch, she stood by the front window watching a crowd gather on the sidewalk to listen to a man with one leg playing the cello. He sat on a stool with an Irish setter by his side and a basket for donations. When the music stopped, a young boy placed a coin in the basket and stroked the dog's head.

Ann turned away from the window. She went to her office and closed the door then dialled a number she now knew by heart.

* * *

Angela poked her head into Ann's office. "I'm going home now, Ann. Will you lock up?"

"I will."

"You're later than usual. It's almost four. Are you going out?"

"No. Just finishing a few things."

"I'll see you Tuesday."

Ann waved. Not long after hearing the front door close, she took her coat from the rack, locked the desk and made her own way out to meet Richard at the Victory Café.

* * *

"How are we doing?" Edward asked.

Larry Paton stuck another pin in the map of Italy. "Bonfire's here. Domino and Benedict are heading for Sorrento.

Marauder is up in the hills, so they're a bit more difficult to track." Each team of agents had been assigned code names.

"Good progress?"

"Yes. Did you see the report about a train carrying weapons and troops crossing the Volturno?" Edward nodded. "Domino blew the bridge. We've had varying reports of damage; around two thousand men is the best estimate. Looks like Jimmy's training was useful." Larry grinned.

"He knows more about explosives than anyone else. We're lucky to have him. What about Ray and Michel?"

"I know you're worried about them, Edward, but it's only been one week. Give it time. They're well trained."

"You're probably right. Sometimes my mind says one thing and my gut says another. At the moment they're at cross-purposes."

"There's little we can do from here."

"That doesn't make me feel any better. We've trained a lot of men and women, but for some reason those two got to me. When they left it was like watching my children go. I felt the same way about Louise and Julian."

"And they're safe now, aren't they?"

"I suppose. At least until their next mission." He rapped a knuckle on the table. "I have to go. Thanks for the update." As he headed out the door, Edward turned to look back at Larry. "And the encouragement."

Edward had told Ann he would be supervising a training retreat for A Corps from Thursday to Sunday, which was partially true. He would spend two days at Camp X then drive north of Toronto to join the Corps for two more days. *At least I'll be able to tell her about part of my time away,* he thought.

Ann had said nothing about this trip, nor had she expressed frustration in any way, and for some reason that added to his worries.

47 APRIL 1943

With each hour Ann had wavered, Richard pulling her forward, Edward holding her back. Like a tug of war, her decision wobbled back and forth. It was the man with the cello and the little boy stroking the dog that decided her.

All week she had thought of Richard's kisses, the warmth of his touch, his body pressed close and her own response, an inner fire like molten glass bending beneath gentle hands. The heat shot through her even in memory.

Intellect and morality fought with emotion. *What if it's love?* she thought. *You're bound to another. But he doesn't care and he's grown so distant. You'll get hurt. But maybe not. What if someone finds out? We'll be careful. What about Emily and Alex?* The last question had no answer.

Ann knew she should sever ties with Richard and never see him again. She knew the right course of action, the moral course, the course duty and faith would demand. She knew her commandments; thou shalt not commit adul-

tery came right after thou shalt not kill and right before thou
shalt not steal. She remembered Edward's affair and how long
their subsequent estrangement lasted. Yes, Ann knew what
she should do. She should slam the door tight before anything
further occurred.

But the man with the cello and the little boy shifted the
tug of war in Richard's favour, for he would understand how
that scene had affected her and would listen to the telling with
great care and empathy, while Edward would merely nod and
return to his newspaper.

Heading west, away from Signals Welfare, the promise of
spring sparkled with blue sky and trickles of melting snow and
a cardinal chirruping from a privet hedge, bright red darting from branch to branch. Lost in anticipation, a burst of
laughter from two passing women startled Ann, and glancing around, she was overcome by a sense of unfamiliarity, as
though the shops and street corners she had walked by so
many times had altered overnight. An inward smile unfolded,
suffusing her with warmth.

Ann turned the corner and there he was, waiting by the
café door. She slowed her pace, noting his uniform and soldier's posture, cap tucked beneath one arm, hand loose, sun
marking his face, eyes steady. A few more steps and she was
there.

"Hello," he said, lips curving slightly, his voice like a whispering wind, signalling everything.

"Richard . . ." Keeping her eyes on his, she said nothing
more.

"I want to hold you." Ann nodded. "Let's walk this way."
He gestured away from the café. "I . . . I have a place for us to
be alone." She nodded again.

At a nearby hotel, he stood by the door to a room marked
215 and asked, "Are you sure?"

"Yes, I'm sure."

He was infinitely gentle. As soon as they were beyond the
door, she put her arms around his neck and pulled him close,

submerged in the feeling of lips and tongues and an embrace that promised sanctuary. They swayed; his hands moved lower, pressing her body to his.

"All week I've thought of this," he said, warm breath against her cheek.

Ann trailed a finger along the line of his chin and then one ear, pausing to touch its soft lobe. Tracing the arc of one eyebrow and the tiny lines that deepened when he smiled, the clamour of her inner voice eased.

"So have I."

His eyes lost all hesitation. He undid the zipper of her dress and slid each sleeve from her shoulders. The dress fell. Clad in slip and stockings, Ann reached for his tie, loosening the knot and pulling one end through then unravelling the rest. With the tie undone, she slid his jacket off and ran her hands across his thick, wide shoulders and then his chest, taut from the daily drills of army life. Richard remained still, his eyes fixed on hers, his mouth slightly parted.

Ann unbuttoned his shirt and heard a sharp intake of breath when she touched his skin. Longing to feel his body against hers, she stepped back to shed her slip and stockings and then unfastened her bra.

"God, you're beautiful," Richard said. He held out his hand and she accepted the coming dance of intimacy and followed him to the bed.

Lying side by side, he caressed the curve of her shoulder, the length of her arm, the line from belly to hip. As he kissed the corner of her mouth, he cupped one breast, his thumb rubbing the nipple back and forth, causing muscles to clench deep within. When he dipped his head to suck her nipple, sensation rippled through her and she reached for his erection, feeling the hard softness that would soon be inside her.

"Slowly," he said. "I want this to last forever."

He ran a finger down between her breasts and over the

mound of her pubic hair and she restrained herself from pushing his hand lower. His mouth followed the same path. He nipped the skin at her hip while running his hands along the inside of her thighs. Ann's desire pooled into moisture.

Just when she was sure she could wait no longer, Richard entered her and the feeling of him deep within both stilled and heightened the intensity such that every nerve seemed ready to explode. He withdrew, but not completely, then thrust again. She moaned, her body quivering, her mind concentrating only on sensation. Another thrust and she lifted her hips to meet him, then again and again until orgasm took hold and they collapsed into one another.

For several moments, neither spoke. Ann's heart thudded so hard, she was sure Richard could hear it.

"That was wonderful," he said. "More than wonderful."

Ann smiled. He remained inside her, the weight of him making her feel safe and secure. "Wonderful," she echoed, keeping all other thoughts at bay.

On the streetcar, as the day's glow faded into evening, Ann relived the afternoon and the conversation that followed, which alternated between playfulness and the sharing of intimate thoughts. She had been surprised at her own lack of modesty when Richard wanted to look at her after making love, not just her face, but all of her, and he had continued to touch her as they talked.

Closer to home, thoughts edged towards self-reproach, but not regret, and her smile faded.

48 APRIL 1943

"When is Cousin Jack coming, Mother?"

Ann and Emily were in the kitchen following dinner. Her daughter used to consider drying the dishes annoying. But over the last two years, the chore had become a time when the two women talked about life and drew closer, beginning the transition from mother and daughter to a relationship where the bonds of womanhood bridged the generations.

"I think he arrives just after your birthday," Ann said. "His training begins in June, so he'll only have a few days with us before going out west."

"I can't wait. It will be so interesting to meet a cousin from as far away as New Zealand." Emily stopped drying and gazed out the window. "I wonder what it's like."

"The pictures I've seen make it look beautiful. Lush green in some parts, mountainous in others. They even have volcanoes. I'd love to go there. I had a letter from his mother last week. She said that she's comforted knowing Jack will be with us from time to time. I'm sure she's afraid for him, although she didn't use those exact words."

"Tell me again how we're related."

Family connections were an endless source of fascination. Ann smiled and began the story.

"Jack's mother is your grandmother's first cousin. Her name is Julia. Julia's father emigrated to New Zealand in 1870. His name was Henry Potts. That was about ten years after my grandmother left England to come to Canada. I've never met Julia, but Jack's aunt—Julia's sister—was a schoolteacher in New Zealand. She never married. Cousin Mary Potts, that's what we called her. I often thought her sense of adventure was too strong to let marriage tie her down. She visited us when you were little. Do you remember?" Emily nodded. "She said the most outrageous things."

Almost every year they received a postcard from some exotic location Cousin Mary Potts had visited—India, Singapore, China, Thailand. Ann's mother could be relied on to mention that it was unseemly of her cousin to travel to such uncivilized places on her own.

"So I'm Jack's second cousin."

"Actually, I'm his second cousin. You're his second cousin once removed."

"I can never get that straight. It's too confusing. It seems that we should be the second cousins, since we're closer in age." Emily paused while stooping to put the pots away. "I hope he doesn't treat me like a child. He's four years older than me."

"I'm sure he won't, dear. Keith is four years older and he doesn't treat you like a child."

Emily's boyfriend would soon finish university and join the army. Even now he was in an officers training program. Although Emily was more mature than many young women, Ann worried that Keith was so much older. She had her own experience to go by. Six years separated Ann and Edward, and there were times when she thought this gap caused some of their problems. She pulled the plug to let the water drain from the sink.

"I suppose we should clean the spare room so Jack has a comfortable place to sleep. Perhaps you can help me this weekend." Ann paused for a moment to wipe the counter. "Now, tell me what's happening between you and Keith."

Emily pushed her hair behind her ears. "I think he's becoming rather possessive. He seems jealous when I spend time with other people. We had a long conversation about it."

"How did he react to that?"

"He wasn't very pleased with me."

"You know, sweetie, he's an only child who has had every whim catered to by his mother. He's accustomed to having his own way." She hesitated. "Relationships between men and women should be fairly balanced. If one person is too dominant, it can cause difficulties."

"Well, isn't Dad the dominant one in your marriage?"

"Some of the time." Ann chuckled. "At other times, I just let him think he's in control."

Emily folded the tea towel and placed it on the rack. "Is that what all women do?"

"I'm not sure. I suppose everyone finds tactics that work for their situation. Men certainly aren't all the same but I think they share certain characteristics. For example, the need to be trusted and accepted for who they are; they need approval and admiration."

"And what about women? Don't they have needs too?"

"Absolutely. The trick is to fit them in without upsetting things."

"I don't know, Mom. It sounds very complicated to me."

"I didn't do it very well when your father and I were first married. We had quite a few arguments early on. Your grandmother once told me men alternate between needing intimacy and autonomy. I try to figure out which cycle your father is in before I act." Ann gave her daughter a quick hug. "But I shouldn't tell you all of my secrets. Don't you have any homework to do?"

After Emily went upstairs, Ann brought out her needlepoint. Knitting and sewing were for charity; needlepoint was
for pleasure. Right now she was working on a new cover for a
footstool positioned by the rocking chair in her bedroom. The
previous cover was threadbare from fifty years of use. Ann
had done the flowers first, the most difficult part, and was
now filling the background with soft green to match the chair.
It was slow work, but its regularity was soothing.

Ann was grateful for the opportunity to talk about relationships with Emily. If Keith went overseas, he might want to
marry, and she worried whether he was the right man. Pulling
the thread to flatten the stitch, she paused to recall a conversation her parents had after Edward proposed.

"Something in his eyes," her father had said. "Makes me
worry what the war did to him."

Ann had waited at the top of the stairs for her mother's
reply. "He's a kind man, John. Takes his responsibilities seriously."

"Yes, I agree with that. But when I took him fishing, I
asked what the war taught him and all he said was he learned
what it means to love his country enough to fight for it."

"What's wrong with that? Sounds like an honourable man."

"It's what he didn't say that bothers me. And the look on
his face and in his eyes."

Occasionally Ann had glimpsed that look, but Edward had
always refused to answer her questions. Until their marriage
almost fell apart. She continued to ponder, working the nee-
dle in and out, using a hesitation stitch to create a pattern of
small boxes across the tapestry.

Loneliness and secrets had opened a chink in their marriage, resulting in resentment, an insidious emotion that stifled desire. In their early years, desire had marked almost
every day. Edward's touch had filled her with longing and a
soft kiss could draw them into bed at any time of day. After
reconciling, intimacy had rekindled, but as war ground on, desire had slipped away, leaving behind feelings of courtesy and

tolerance and familiarity. Passion that had at one time left her
breathless now lay cold.

Is that why I'm drawn to Richard? she wondered.

Richard's love aroused Ann's passion like a spark in a bone-
dry forest. They had been intimate on three separate occasions. His desire for her stirred every inch of her body. His
touch triggered deep, sensual urges that left her panting. Afterwards, she ached with tenderness. Though infidelity taunt-
ed her with cold contempt, she could not stay away.

When Edward announced another three-day trip on Monday, Ann had immediately thought of Richard, a thought followed by such shame that she had turned her face so that her
husband saw nothing that might betray her feelings. Edward
had made love to her that night, afterwards holding her longer
than usual and whispering "I love you" before rolling away.
She had been able to do nothing more than stroke his arm in
response.

49 APRIL 1943

Spring came to Camp X, spawning fragrant smells of renewal and warm, moist air that brought energy and eagerness to those roaming the property. Edward arrived one morning just as sunshine broke through the clouds, creating a double rainbow from the farmhouse to the lake. For a moment he suspended logic and wondered if two rainbows were an omen of good fortune. News from Africa was good: the Allies had decimated Panzer Division formations and pushed the enemy out of Tunisia. Then, with enormous numbers landing on the coasts of Morocco and Algeria, they forced German and Italian troops to surrender, while Rommel fled to Germany to face Hitler's wrath. After three and a half years, the seesaw had tipped in favour of the Allies.

General Hastings was drinking coffee in the officers' lounge, a room where Edward began most days, its bare, almost tatty furnishings reminding him of sacrifice and the unique camaraderie of soldiers. Often six or eight men were present, providing an opportunity to catch up with events and feel the heartbeat of purpose once again. Many of his colleagues worked daily at the training school, while he was one of a minority who came and went. *Neither fish nor fowl,* he often thought.

"Did you hear about Operation Mincemeat?" said Hastings.

"No," said Edward. He had other concerns on his mind and hoped it wouldn't be a long story.

"We've managed to deceive Hitler about our Sicily operation."

"Really?" With so many agents in Italy, Edward became more attentive. Deceiving Hitler was a significant accomplishment. "What happened?"

"SOE floated a dead man's body in a life jacket off the coast of Spain. He was found along with his briefcase and fake documents identifying the man as Major William Martin. The documents also contained bogus war plans showing an invasion of Sardinia."

"How did it get to Hitler?"

"Apparently, local fishermen pulled the body out of the water and the Spanish authorities gave everything to Axis commanders in the area, who judged the papers to be real and sent the information along channels until it reached Hitler."

"How do we know all this?"

"Intercepts of Enigma messages. Since we've cracked their code, we have access to all sorts of information."

"And . . ." Edward could tell from the sparkle in Hastings' eyes there was more to the story.

"Hitler has demanded that Sardinia and the Peloponnese take precedence, and they are moving men and supplies out of Sicily."

"That's very good news, Paul." One positive piece of information was better than none. And this could help their Italian operation.

Edward went to his office, where Steve Shelley and John Foster were waiting for him. He was worried. Ever since October when Ray and Michel disappeared into France, he had received copies of their weekly communications. Though brief, these messages reassured him of their safety. Hints of danger surfaced amongst reports of pilots ready for transfer, French contacts established, location changes and sabotage activities. He kept each message in a file marked "Pirouette". Nothing had gone into the file in three weeks.

"Maybe we should send an outbound message," said Steve.

"I don't think we should do that yet," said John. "If Ray and Michel are in hiding, we could compromise their location. Besides, SOE is in charge of their mission. Not us."

Edward nodded. Increasingly sophisticated German equipment had already proven deadly to several agents. He'd seen a recent report about new enemy capabilities using detection equipment hidden inside delivery vans traversing the streets in seeming innocence, all the while detecting transmitters and receivers used by resistance groups. The Germans could now pinpoint locations to a dangerously small area.

"What does SOE advise?" Edward asked.

"They're nervous," said John, "but Gerald said this isn't the first time a team has gone silent." Gerald Butler was a Canadian stationed in England at Bletchley Park, a sprawling Victorian mansion housing MI6 code breakers. SOE and MI6 cooperated in some areas of espionage—a delicate arrangement involving demanding egos and separate chains of command. "We need to be positive. Remember when Julian and Louise went missing. Impatience is our enemy."

Edward remembered waiting weeks for Julian and Louise to communicate, weeks of worry and sleepless nights until they finally received a short transmission. He would probably never know the full story.

"Okay. Then we sit tight." Each face was grim as they turned to other matters.

50 JUNE 1943

Candles cast a circle of warmth on white damask. Silver, polished to a bright sparkle, defined each place setting. Though almost seven o'clock, sun streamed through the window, embracing the earth with promise. The rich aroma of roast beef filled the air. Eight etched-crystal glasses hovered in outstretched hands waiting for Edward to speak.

"I'd like to propose a toast." He cleared his throat. "We welcome Jack to his Canadian family and honour his wartime contribution. We welcome his friend Jim to our home. We give thanks for God's blessings. And we salute all those who struggle to overcome evil. Here's to Jack and Jim." His eyes glimmered, full of tears.

Echoes of "here's to Jack" and "here's to Jim" replied to his toast. Clinking glasses signalled the end of formality and conversation broke the emotion, enabling Edward to compose himself. Ann glanced at him, offering a quizzical look to bring him back from wherever he had gone those brief moments. He returned her gaze with a feeble smile.

Edward was grieving. In secret. Two days ago, they received word that Ray Leblanc had been captured, tortured,
and left hanging in public view in the town of Limoges,
France, as a lesson to other resistance fighters. Michel Simard was safe, for now.

It was a bitter blow, both personally and to Allied intelligence operations. He longed to tell Ann and feel the solace of
her soothing words, to seek her arms like a boy needing his
mother's comfort. He longed to bring them all back, all those
bright young men and women who offered such promise, such
dedication, so much life. He longed to put down the burden
he carried every moment of every day.

Edward looked at Jack: dark hair and high cheekbones,
shoulders broad from a boyhood of farm work, relaxed in
their company, treating them as he would his own family,
no sense of formality and yet respectful of Edward and Ann.
And here's another one we'll send off to dance with death.
There will be no reprieve, no sudden end to the war. It's all
such a mess, and we're still hopelessly mired in Europe, Asia
and Africa. I doubt he'll survive. Pilots have the worst odds.

He thought of the losses suffered in the Atlantic and the
horrifying news still emerging about the Warsaw ghetto,
where thousands of Jews perished from starvation and disease. And thousands more died battling with German SS
troops sent to clear the ghetto and crush all resistance. His
mind refused to release the image of those Jewish fighters
who remained in burning buildings until forced to jump or
else burn alive, who had then crawled, their bones broken,
into buildings not yet set on fire. He knew they stayed alive
until the last possible moment in the hope of killing just one
more German soldier.

Ann caught his eye again and he acknowledged her glance,
making an effort to bring himself out of the furious rage
that gripped him and into the bosom of his family. Jack
was charming Ann's parents, telling stories of his mother,

his aunt, Cousin Mary Potts, and the grandmother whom he remembered only a little. Ann's mother took to him immediately, exclaiming, "You look just like my Uncle George. What a strong family resemblance."

Jack had arrived on Friday, and since he had only a few days with them, Ann had invited her mother and father for Sunday dinner. To make it a special event, she had persuaded the butcher to give them a large pot roast using their rations as well as some of her parents'. Edward sliced the roast with care, making the most of this unexpected feast, ensuring the best pieces went to Jack and his friend Jim; a small token of gratitude he imagined they would not notice. Ann had set out the good china, spooning generous helpings of mashed potatoes, green beans and carrots onto each plate.

She creates such feelings of warmth and care, he thought. *It's one of her special talents.* Edward pulled his attention back to the conversation. Jack was regaling them with a story about learning to shear sheep when he was fifteen.

"Our neighbour up the road needed extra hands to shear all his sheep that year, so I volunteered to help. It was a chance to earn some pocket money. Most of the shearers were so experienced they could shear a whole fleece in less than a minute. They made it look as simple as peeling an orange or an apple, all in one piece.

"After watching for a while, I assumed I had it figured out. So I took a set of shears and grabbed one of the sheep. Imagine the lamb on her bottom, head braced between my left arm and thigh, one leg poking out between my legs as I bent over and shaved her stomach. Things were going fairly well. I was even keeping the sheep's skin taut, so I wouldn't nick her hide."

"And then what happened?" Emily leaned forward to look directly at Jack. She seemed enthralled by everything the young New Zealander said.

"Well, I sneezed. It turns out that I'm allergic to wool and after spending an hour with bits of wool flying about, my body couldn't handle it anymore. As soon as I sneezed, I lost my grip on the sheep and she scrambled to get on her feet. Then I sneezed again and lost my balance and my feet came out from under me. The poor sheep ran off bleating, dragging half of her fleece behind her. That was the end of my shearing career. One of the other hands had to finish her off."

Everyone laughed.

"It wasn't your best moment," said Jim, "but it sure was funny."

While conversation continued, Ann and Emily cleared the table. "Let's have coffee in the living room," Ann said, poking her head briefly into the dining room before returning to the kitchen. It was a Jamieson ritual to leave the table and relax after dinner with coffee. Edward often had a cigar and occasionally Emily played the piano.

As everyone settled into comfortable chairs, Ann distributed cups, saucers, small silver coffee spoons and milk.

"When does your training begin?" Edward asked.

"Jim and I have to leave on Wednesday to get there in time. It's a three-day trip and we report for duty on Sunday."

"We have a few weeks of initial training to learn the basics of military life," continued Jim, "then we go to elementary flying school. That's where they separate us into those who become pilots and those who do wireless, navigation, bombing or gunnery."

"We both want to be pilots," Jack added. "I've wanted to fly ever since my uncle took me up in a two-seater plane when I was twelve."

"My brother Alan trained in Alberta," said Ann, "not long after Canada set up the program. Men like you from all over the world come here to train."

"I heard they found instructors wherever they could—bush pilots, commercial pilots, WWI veterans," Jim said.

"We need more pilots if we're going to win this war," said Edward. "There are ninety-seven schools now. Three thousand new flyers a month."

"I'd love to learn to fly," Alex said. "Up in the air I'd feel as free as a bird. I wish I was older."

"Don't wish for that," Jack said. "My father was in the first war and he told me it was the most dreadful thing imaginable. Wouldn't you agree, Mr. Jamieson?"

"You're family, Jack. Please call me Edward. And yes, it was dreadful. I don't talk about it much but I remember watching scouting planes fly overhead, which always encouraged those of us in the trenches. Their size was inconsequential compared with the ones you boys will fly."

Edward recalled the buzz of airplane engines at first faint and then furious once directly overhead. He often wondered about that airborne world, the swoops and dives, the feeling of power mixed with vulnerability. He had met a few pilots who spoke of exhaustion and exhilaration and the fear of imminent death while embracing the beauty of life and the magic of flight.

"The airplane is certainly changing war strategy," Ann's father said.

"Why do you say that, Grandpa?" Alex asked, leaning forward to see his grandfather's face.

"Well, their ability to carry out bombing raids is one thing. Today's airplanes can travel farther and faster and carry much heavier loads than the first war. This means they have a real role in the fighting rather than being used for reconnaissance and communication."

"And they allow us to move soldiers to the places they're needed more easily," Jim added. "Even the navy has airplanes and their aircraft carriers can take them to places where we have no land bases."

"Maybe I should sign up for the air cadets this summer," Alex said. "Do you think that would give me a better chance of getting into the air force?"

For several minutes, Jack and Jim debated which cadet section Alex should try. Edward kept his opinions to himself, feeling that in his current state of grief he might ruin the con-

versation. In three years, Alex would be old enough to serve.
Edward could not imagine watching his son go off to war.

He glanced at Ann's parents. His father-in-law's wide shoulders seemed to have shrunk with each passing year and his
cheeks hugged the bones of his face like a mask, however, leaning forward on the edge of his chair, he was clearly enjoying
the evening. Listening to John Winston voice an opinion on
whether Germany or Britain had the more advanced air force,
Edward noted a sparkle in the older man's eyes for the first
time since Dieppe.

I wish Father was alive, he thought. Almost seven years and
he still caught himself storing away little things to tell his father. He longed for his advice and the quiet way they supported one another. None of Edward's brothers were close enough
for the kind of confidences he had shared with his father and
Simon, whom Edward had confided in from time to time, was
in some unknown location in the Pacific. *God, I hope he's safe.
And Cyril and Stan. Mother couldn't bear losing one of them.
I should see her tomorrow. She always says she doesn't see me
enough. What kind of son am I neglecting my mother so much.*
He sighed and looked around, wondering where the conversation had gone. Emily was asking something about volcanoes
in New Zealand.

Ann caught his eye and raised her brows to signal the end
of the evening. He gave a quick nod.

"Well, I for one have had enough talk of war to last a lifetime," his wife said.

"You're right. We should go, Ann. Your mother looks tired."
Ann's father rose to his feet and offered a hand to his wife.

* * *

"I've got everything tidied up," Ann said, joining Edward in
the study where he was chewing on the end of his pipe. "Emily
and Jack are still talking in the living room. He's such a nice
young man, isn't he? Alex has disappeared to the basement.
Last week he asked if he could take an old lamp downstairs. I
wonder how he stands the musty smell."

Edward waved his pipe. "He's at that age where he wants to be away from all of us. I used to disappear with Roy. And Simon took to spending time at the boxing ring. Mother hated that. I don't remember what Stan and Cyril did. At any rate, the smell is probably a small price to pay for privacy."

"Boys are definitely different from girls." She walked over to the window and stood for a moment without speaking. "Time for bed? You look exhausted."

"I am. Is it so obvious?"

"After twenty years, it is."

Edward set his pipe in a crystal ashtray given to him as a memento by his Montreal colleagues. He switched off the light and followed her upstairs.

"What was making you so upset this evening?"

He closed the curtains one by one. "Someone I know died overseas." He did not turn to look in her direction.

"Oh no." Ann joined him by the window and put her arms around him. "Can you tell me about it?"

Though he ached to share his sadness with Ann, Edward shook his head. "I wish I could," he said.

51 JUNE 1943

The Galaxy Room was crowded with men and a smattering of women gathered to hear General Hastings give an update on recent developments. Twelve tables, spaced in two even rows, were already full when Edward arrived, so he stood along the back wall next to an open window admitting fresh air and the sounds of chirping birds. He was surprised to see so many new faces.

News from various fronts usually came in dribbles, making it difficult to assess the overall war effort; the memo announcing today's meeting promised a broad perspective. Chatter rose and fell as more people gathered. Edward waved at Larry Paton, who made his way around the perimeter to stand beside him.

"Heard anything new?"

"Domino and Benedict are making progress." Larry referred to two of the four teams deployed in Italy. "But Bonfire and Marauder have had a few setbacks."

"Anything crucial?"

"Nope."

"Good. Guess it's out of our hands now. SOE knows what they're doing."

Larry bit his lower lip. "I hope so."

On the far side of the room, a door opened and General Hastings entered, along with two senior officers Edward did not recognize. Though in uniform, the General wore no tie or jacket, a concession to the less formal atmosphere of Camp X. Hastings thought an atmosphere of civilians mixing freely with military staff of all ranks prompted better ideas.

"Good morning, ladies and gentlemen. First let me introduce Lieutenant Colonel Fraser and Brigadier Wilson. Each will offer commentary during today's briefing. I scheduled this meeting to provide a summary of Allied progress, and while we cannot disclose confidential strategies, I believe today's discussion will help us all see where our efforts fit in. Please hold your questions until the end."

Two large maps, one of Europe and North Africa, the other of Asia, were mounted behind the general. For the next hour, Hastings reviewed circumstances on the Eastern Front and in North Africa, and bombing offensives combining US-led daytime raids with British night bombings of strategic German cities. As he spoke, he used a wooden pointer to show each area of conflict.

"As you know, with Europe occupied by either German or Italian forces for the past three years, we've used flanking strategies in order to prepare the ground for a European invasion. Teams you've sent throughout Europe will, and have already been, essential to this ultimate goal. Success in North Africa means we can soon invade Italy while Russia is now positioned favourably to invade German-held territory in Poland. Japan's hold over the Asian theatre is proving difficult to dislodge, although we are beginning to push back. German defeat remains our first objective."

General Hastings nodded as he scanned the audience, his

mouth pulled into a tight knot. "It's about time we inflicted serious damage, ladies and gentlemen, and we are beginning to do so. I'll turn the floor over to Lieutenant Colonel Fraser to review naval developments and then to Brigadier Wilson for an air force perspective." Hastings cleared his throat and handed the pointer to Fraser.

When the meeting was over, Edward and Larry walked back to barracks together.

"They're making it sound positive," Larry said.

"I'm beginning to think it is. From what Hastings said, Hitler underestimated the Russians. He didn't have enough manpower to take the oilfields and Stalingrad at the same time. And their supply routes weren't good enough to keep Rommel going in Africa."

"Supply routes were Napoleon's problem too. Sicily could prove to be a significant turning point. If it goes ahead."

"Rumour is Roosevelt and Churchill are using Sicily to divert German attention from Russia. Success in North Africa means we'll have men and materials available, but unless the generals stop bickering the whole plan might collapse."

"The good news is Hitler seems seduced by his own propaganda."

"I think you're right, Larry. I think you're right."

When Edward returned to his desk he found two reports: the first concerned combined British Commonwealth losses of dead, wounded and captured, noting that of six hundred and seventy thousand troops lost, over three hundred and fifteen thousand were known dead. He tried to imagine that many soldiers lying end to end. Would they reach around the world? Would the tears shed for them fill Lake Ontario or perhaps all the Great Lakes? How could his minuscule efforts make any difference?

The second report summarized activities of Camp X agents in the field. After reading the first few pages he went to find Larry, and together they worked with a world map, marking locations in different colours to signify successes and failures.

Neither man was happy with the picture that emerged.

* * *

"How was your day?" Ann said.

"Fine." Edward loosened the knot of his tie enough to slip it over his head.

Ann shrugged her shoulders and turned back to the sink, letting him know she doubted his word and he wavered, weighing the possibility of sharing his burdens.

"I listened to a presentation today, a summary of military status. We rarely see more than our small portion and I found it interesting to hear the big picture. General . . ." he paused, there could be no names. "The general said we're making progress. North African and Russian successes should let us get to Europe." He was not really telling her anything a person could not deduce from thorough analysis of news reports. And a little guess work.

"When do you imagine that happening?"

"No one knows."

"Let's hope and pray it will be soon."

"It's not hope or prayers that will make a difference, it's action."

Edward knew his tone was harsh and saw the look of hurt on Ann's face.

"Dinner will be about an hour," she said, turning away from him.

As they prepared for bed he apologized, but Ann was still upset.

"You disappear from me then reappear and expect that we are just the same. That I'll open my arms to you. But it's not that easy."

"I can't—"

"I know you can't. I'm just telling you how it makes me feel. The war is hard on everybody."

"You know I'm working hard."

"And what do you think I'm doing?" Ann slammed her

dresser drawer. "I'm going to sleep in the spare room." She scooped her housecoat up from the foot of the bed.

"Ann, don't go. I know you're upset." He reached the hall in time to hear a door click closed.

Frustration tangled him in patterns of avoidance and reticence, at times resenting Ann for her anger, at other times empathizing. He took his own frustrations about their circumstances with him to work and to Camp X, brusque irritability prompting startled looks and whispered conversations. Duty and sacrifice seemed to be battling against marriage. At the moment, marriage was losing.

52   JULY 1943

As June turned to July, Edward's absences were more frequent. Almost every week he disappeared for a day or two, continuing his pattern of secrecy, always taking a mix of civilian and military clothes. Ann had difficulty imagining a place where he needed both. She suspected he had already disclosed too much, and given her own dilemma, she pressed him no further. His mood alternated between gloom and faint optimism, brusqueness and silence, one following another like irregular heartbeats. She never knew what to expect when he walked through the door.

He's like a stranger, she thought, watching from the bottom of their drive as his car disappeared. Being alone was easier than being with him. Shouting at him had changed nothing so she stuffed her anger away and they went on as before.

With Alex away at cadet camp and Emily working at a homeless shelter, Ann had the house to herself. Feeling restless, she wandered from room to room. She knew she should write to Hannah and the bedroom curtains needed washing. A pile of ironing waited in the airing cupboard. She considered each task and rejected them; the weather was far too warm to be cooped up inside.

Dressed in faded shorts and brown sandals, she left the house with no particular destination in mind. At the end of the street she continued along the creek bed, following an uneven path fashioned by the footsteps of children playing by the river and others who chose the solitude of forest and stream. If she walked far enough, the path resurfaced on city streets, but for now, she could lose herself in calm. As she wandered, thoughts vibrated with intensity.

Ann stopped beside the creek where a log had fallen across the path and wedged her back against a large rock, in all likelihood washed to its current smooth shape a million years ago when the creek was part of a wide, surging river. On the far side two chipmunks dashed up a maple tree, the forest floor dappled with light and dark. A black butterfly with brilliant blue markings dipped and swooped amongst clumps of wildflowers, while close by two yellow-striped beetles sat on a wide, flat leaf. Pungent, earthy smells reminded her of the compost heap in their backyard. *I should be doing the gardening*, she thought, but made no move to get up, and musings took over again.

Ann was confused. Every day three or four voices inside her head clamoured for attention, voices that scolded and rebuked, voices that tempted, voices that said Edward was to blame. At times she was angry with herself, with Richard and with Edward. Angry with those who permitted war to continue, whoever they were. Angry with God, though she knew that was illogical.

Richard should never have pursued me. But he did, her inner voice replied. *He's a man with too many cares and no one to talk to. Right from the beginning the flirting should have warned me . . . I could have stopped it, though, couldn't I?*

But my head wasn't in charge. She snapped off a buttercup
and twirled it between thumb and forefinger. *Why do people
have affairs when they know it usually ends badly?*

She and Edward were at the same crossroads as before, where marriage was no longer the calm centre of life.
Shared tasks and meals and moments had disappeared, replaced by distance and estrangement. They no longer saw
one another clearly or treasured the small endearing traits
discovered over years of living together.

Whether it was the newness of their relationship or Richard's inherent personality, Ann felt that every moment with
him was one of discovery and delight. He seemed to cherish
her, both physically and mentally, such that every part of
her and every one of her senses felt alive in his company.
On the few occasions when he telephoned, the mere sound
of his voice filled her with happiness.

After the second time they made love, she had asked him
why he had been attracted to her.

"You're a handsome man," she had said. "Many women
would happily go out with you."

"I've dated other women. None of them were as interesting as you."

"But I'm an old married woman with two teenagers."

"Old married woman. Don't be ridiculous. I see a beautiful woman who's wonderful to be with and cares about
people. You're smart and intuitive. When I'm with you, I
feel like I can talk about anything. A man needs someone
who makes him come alive."

"Even if she's married?"

"Even if. I didn't set out to find a married woman. But
you came along and touched my soul the very first time we
met." With his fingertips, he had stroked the curve from her
waist to her hip. "And you're incredibly sexy."

He had kissed her then, a kiss that had lingered in her
memory. Even now, with the river burbling and crickets
chirping, the thought of that kiss made her shiver.

A group of dogs romped by, a dachshund racing beneath a golden lab and a terrier nipping the heels of a much larger mutt. Ann sighed deeply then threw a small stone at nothing in particular. Making sense of her predicament was like rowing against a powerful tide. Intellectually she knew there was no sense involved. The tide would win. She got to her feet and made her way home.

53 JULY 1943

Edward wondered where he belonged.

At Camp X he was one of a handful of specialists training spies; a tight knit group whose oath of secrecy meant they could only share that life with one another. As war unfolded, he spent more and more time amongst that crowd and the recruits they worked with day after day. The streets of camp, the officers' barracks, the canteen and meeting rooms and the surrounding fields were a home of sorts. There he knew what to expect, or at the very least, to expect the unexpected.

After meals he relaxed amongst colleagues with a glass of whiskey, listening to stories and enjoying the rough, often crude talk of men living under stressful circumstances. They all knew the same language of acronyms and military terminology, the sort of language that would make others feel they were in some foreign country. He had no need to pretend and no need to keep secrets.

At home his roles were a conflicting jumble of husband and father, businessman and leader of a reserves unit. Despite his best efforts, he never had enough time to do any of them well. Emily and Alex were growing up with little of his personal contribution, no longer children but young adults longing for independence and chafing under his infrequent bits of well-intentioned guidance. He was missing the pleasures of fatherhood and would never get a second chance.

At the office Dave Jenkins grumbled about needing more of Edward's time. While Jenkins had no official knowledge of Camp X, senior military officials had made it clear early on that Edward's expertise was essential to the war effort. By the beginning of 1943, Dave Jenkins had promoted a manager from another division to share Edward's role.

As a husband, Edward considered himself a failure. When he came home from his trips, he had no vitality left for Ann and his oath of secrecy meant that he could share almost nothing about his colleagues or his responsibilities with her. Lately Ann's behaviour had become erratic, jumping from calm acceptance to taut annoyance such that he never knew what to expect.

This morning he had been relieved to drive off to camp for another few days, pleased to be waved through the gate by the guard and then to get down to work with Larry Paton and a group of recruits destined for France.

At noon Betty MacLean knocked on the door. "General Hastings wants all officers in the parlour for a briefing."

"Now?" Larry held a sheaf of papers in one hand and a pen in the other.

"He said, and I quote, 'no one will want to miss this announcement'. I'm rounding up everyone as quickly as I can."

Larry and Edward exchanged glances. Edward shrugged. "We better go."

Paul Hastings stood near the fireplace waiting for the group to assemble, his sleeves rolled to the elbow and the slightest hint of a smile on his narrow face. Betty leaned through the doorway.

"I think everyone's here, sir."

"Why don't you stay, Betty? You deserve to hear this too." Hastings cleared his throat and rapped on the mantel. "Ladies and gentlemen, I've just had word that we've made a successful attack on Sicily." He waited while the group applauded amidst a buzz of excited chatter. "Let me tell you more." Paul Hastings read from a sheet of paper. "On the tenth, the Seventh Army established a beachhead fifty miles wide and captured more than four thousand prisoners. Axis counterattacks were fierce, backed up by Italian and German planes based in Italy. On the eleventh, Patton sent in more than two thousand paratroopers as reinforcements. And over the next two days, our American friends pushed beyond the beaches and into the hills. British Eighth Army coordinated their attacks with the Americans, concentrating on the eastern section of the island.

"My expectation is that the British will head for Messina while Patton digs in on the western side of the island. You know what this means. Once Sicily is in Allied hands, our Italian teams will be even more crucial to plans to invade Italy. They will also be at much greater risk. I want updates at any time of day or night to come to me personally.

"You've all seen maps of Sicily. The drive to Messina will be very difficult. The city is protected by rugged terrain and the Caronie Mountains. And we'll have to go around Mount Etna, of course. I don't know much more, but I'll reconvene this group in a day or two. Any questions?"

* * *

Two weeks later Larry and Edward were summoned to Paul Hastings' office. Dark eyes beneath thick dark brows usually made him look fierce, but today Paul smiled as they entered.

"Mussolini has fallen," he said as soon as Larry closed the door.

"What?"

He motioned them to sit. "They've just announced that King Victor Emmanuel has called Badoglio out of military retirement to head a new government. Mussolini has been arrested. Apparently, the Italians are celebrating by dismantling the statues and symbols of the Fascists."

"Will they join the Allies?" Edward had heard whispers of secret negotiations with prominent Italian businessmen and political figures.

"I imagine so, but it's too soon to know how much that will help. If I were the king, I'd be worried about a Fascist countercoup and German occupation of the country. Our teams are tracking German movements and it looks like they're increasing troops in central and northern Italy. Many Italians remain loyal to the Fascist cause. Hitler's smart. He'll want to maintain Italy as a defensive line. And for our part, having German forces committed to Italy overextends them."

"They're playing into our hands, in a way," said Larry.

"About time," Hastings added.

All three men nodded.

Edward sat back. He had been an observer of people ever since he was young. As the eldest of nine, much was expected of him, even as a child. Rather than engage with his younger siblings, he was called on to watch them and so he had, over time learning that the twitch in Cyril's right eye meant trouble and that Stan's clenched fists meant he was on the verge of tears. Through observation, he came to know all his siblings like a parent would, except Jimmy and Duncan, who were babies when he went off to war, and Elizabeth who had remained in England.

He carried this skill into adulthood. What others considered aloofness was nothing more than a keen desire to understand motivation and behaviour. Paul was pulling on his moustache, a sure sign that he was debating how much to disclose. Larry bounced his right foot up and down like a fiddler keeping time with a lively jig, which meant his friend was turning over possibilities.

"Do you gentlemen have time for a walk?" Hastings rose, stretching his shoulders and twisting his neck to work out the kinks.

Full disclosure, Edward concluded. *Otherwise we wouldn't be going out for a walk.*

The air was sultry, hardly a breeze stirring the trees. Earthy smells of morning rain lingered and small puddles lined the main camp road. Paul turned south towards the lake, taking a trampled path across what used to be a horse paddock. Neither Edward nor Larry spoke; protocol required them to wait for the general to choose the time and place.

Far off to the right, puffs of white smoke were visible from the firing range; splats of gunfire followed, sounding like popcorn. The newly formed French team was in their second day of training using French arms and later in the day would practice with French explosives. That night, Edward and Larry planned to conduct wireless training, beginning with the assembly and disassembly of wireless transmission sets. Recruits had to know how to work in daylight and darkness.

Angry clouds scurried eastward, taking the rain with them. On the lake's horizon, a freighter steamed along, its bulk and noise obscured by distance. The path was rougher now, its descent towards the lake steep, and Edward braced his knees, feeling sweat roll down his back and the sun on his face. With Mussolini's fall, the war felt somehow closer and more dangerous and he wondered why. As far as he knew, their teams in Italy were safe, but the mere fact of such unsettling change made him anxious.

Not far from the shoreline, but within the barbed-wire perimeter of camp, was a flat expanse of rock. General Hastings picked a piece of wild hay and twirled it back and forth between thumb and forefinger.

"Our information suggests Victor Emmanuel hopes the Germans will be expelled from Italy by our forces, with little military activity required from Italy. We are keen to broker an armistice and might go so far as to send a mission to defend Rome. The Italian government has a delegation in Lisbon discussing armistice terms. But plenty of Fascist supporters remain; some are hiding in the hills, others working directly with Germany.

"All background stuff, of course. Indications are we will soon take Sicily and the next step will be the mainland. After the armistice is signed and not before. Not sure if anyone really trusts them, but Sicily is our access point. And it means our teams will be more important than ever."

"But we don't control them. SOE does." Edward stated the obvious.

Paul nodded and stretched a smile across his lips. "They want someone to come over to England and work with them on tactics. I've recommended one of you."

Edward kept his face still. He could not imagine going to England without telling Ann, and yet he had taken an oath. With German subs active in the North Atlantic, there was also the possibility he might not survive, but assuming he travelled safely, he might be gone for weeks. She was already more than upset and they were increasingly at odds.

"What skills are they looking for?" he asked.

"The truthful answer is I'm not sure. They said they're looking for someone with a communications background who worked closely with the teams, so maybe the objective is to train more agents who will fit in with our crowd already on the ground."

"When?"

"You already know the answer to that. Immediate, as always."

"General, I'm prepared to volunteer," said Larry.

Hastings looked out across the water, his eyes following a small group of seagulls. "Thank you, Larry."

As they returned to barracks, Edward said, "Are you sure about this, Larry? Your children are young. I could go."

"I know you could. But you did enough in the last war."

Edward placed his hand on Larry's shoulder and said nothing more.

54 AUGUST 1943

Ann knew they had to stop. Each time she and Richard were together, the ties binding her to Edward grew more fragile and the risk of discovery more likely. Before she destroyed everything in her life, the affair had to end.

For three months they had been meeting at Richard's small apartment on Thursday afternoons. On some occasions they talked at length before making love, on others passion flared as soon as she walked through the door, and once, the desire for one another had been so urgent, they had not even removed their clothes.

Since the middle of July, she had rehearsed the words, imagining his reaction and the sadness that would follow. When the time came, her carefully chosen words vanished.

"I can't see you again."

Ann rolled away from Richard's warmth.

"I know."

"You know? How could you possibly know? I didn't know

myself until now."

He stroked her arm, but made no attempt to draw her back into his embrace. "You've been tense. Looking at me as though you're trying to solve a puzzle. I thought if I said nothing you might change your mind."

"I'm sorry, Richard. I just can't. You know I love you, but despite how I feel, I can't jeopardize everything else." She turned her head in time to see him close his eyes and nod. "I should go now. Don't you think that's the best way? I should just go."

Richard touched the tip of her ear then traced its curve and continued down the line of her chin. He drew her close and brushed his lips against hers. Ann felt the steady beat of his heart and began to weep. He held her tight and for a moment or two said nothing.

"I haven't been this happy for a very long time," he said, smoothing his hand down the back of her head. "I think I always knew we would only have a few months together."

"You did?" Ann's voice was muffled against his chest.

"Mm hmm. I wanted you from the very beginning. I should have left you alone but I couldn't. Seeing you each week for tea just made me want more."

Ann lifted her head and kissed him, a chaste, tender kiss.

"I know you've given me as much as you could," he said.

She kissed him deeply then wrapped her leg around his and eased him inside her one last time.

On the streetcar she mastered her tears by listening to bits of conversation and staring through the wide front window as cars and trucks manoeuvred the streets. Ann jumped when lightning split the sky and a crack of thunder followed seconds later.

"Geez, that was close," someone exclaimed.

Lightning forked again and a second burst of thunder rolled. Raindrops hit the windshield in fat splashes, drumming hard and furious. Wipers flapped back and forth. Ann smelled the rain and watched pedestrians race for shelter like scattering ants. The streetcar slowed to a crawl.

Without an umbrella, she was soaked through by the time she reached home, thankful in some curious way that her clothes hung like limp rags and dripped on the front hall carpet.

"Emily!" She waited for her daughter's answering shout. "Please bring me a towel. Quickly."

Footsteps hurried down the stairs and Emily appeared. Still wearing her dark blue school tunic, she handed her mother a towel. "You're so wet. Why didn't you wait at Smith's until the rain stopped?"

Ann wiped her face and hair. "I did wait for a bit, but the rain kept going." She squeezed the bottom of her skirt against the towel. "I'll run upstairs to change. Can you peel some potatoes?"

"Will Dad be home?"

"He said he'd be late."

In bed well before Edward arrived home, Ann feigned sleep as he pottered about their room removing cufflinks that clinked against the glass-topped dresser, and shoes, which he placed beside the chair, one by one. Her husband was a creature of habit. Cufflinks and shoes were followed by the snap of a releasing belt buckle, the slide of his zipper and the rustle of each pant leg. She pictured him padding across the hall wearing underpants and white shirt. His pyjamas were on a hook in the bathroom and she knew he would toss his dirty clothes into the wicker basket next to the bathtub.

Edward returned a few minutes later, turned off the bedside lamp and eased into bed. He stroked her shoulder and whispered, "Good night, dear."

* * *

"You look dreadful," he said when she got out of bed the following morning.

"I have a terrible headache."

"Maybe you're coming down with something. Why don't

you go back to bed and sleep it off?"

Ann needed no further encouragement. When Edward looked in again at the end of the day, she continued the pretence.

"I'm sorry dear, I'm still feeling miserable. Perhaps you should sleep in the guest room for now. You don't want to catch whatever I have."

"Can I get you anything? A bit of toast or some tea?"

She shook her head. "Emily brought me some soup when she came home from school. I really don't feel like eating."

Pretending to be sick allowed Ann to grieve without the burden of obligation or having to cope with Edward. From the bedroom she heard him shushing Alex as he clumped down the stairs, his feet too big for his body. She heard the banister creak, the forlorn plea of one piano key as Emily passed by, the clink of a spoon on a coffee cup, the clatter of pots. Then all was quiet. She must have dozed, for the ringing of the telephone woke her, jarring in its intensity. Edward's hello was followed by silence then the low rumble of his voice, words indistinguishable. Ann listened for clues to the caller's identity but none emerged.

Numbing days followed. When her thoughts weren't preoccupied with Richard, she agonized over how to restore her feelings for Edward. One morning she struggled out of bed feeling weak and dizzy. She looked in the mirror and shuddered at the drawn, haggard face with bags under her eyes and unkempt hair. Her body felt fragile, her stance that of someone buffeted by a hurricane, bent almost to the snapping point.

"Should you be out of bed?" Edward appeared at the doorway. "You still look ill."

Clad in blue pyjamas, he entered their room, making his way to the tall mahogany bureau to select clothes for the day. On previous mornings he had tiptoed around in the darkness to avoid disturbing her, unaware she was only pretending to sleep.

"Perhaps I should call Dr. Felton and ask him to visit the

house?"

Alarmed at the suggestion, Ann gathered her strength to make as normal a reply as possible. "I'm feeling a little better. I think I'll get out of bed today. No need to call him." Her body sagged. "I'm going to run a bath."

"Can I do anything? I can't remember the last time you were so ill. You look like a ghost."

"No, I'll manage. A soak will do me good."

Ann went into their bathroom to turn on the taps, letting the water run until it reached the right temperature then putting the plug in place. She added a few bath salts before returning to the bedroom.

"Are you home for dinner tonight?"

"I'm supposed to be at a Signals meeting, but I could cancel if you'd like me to."

"No, that's not necessary. I won't be much company tonight. Perhaps tomorrow?"

By this time, Edward was fully dressed and putting the finishing touches on his tie. "I'm worried about you, sweetheart. If you aren't better in a few more days, I'll call Dr. Felton, even if you do protest."

"I'm sure I'll be fine. Is today Thursday?"

"Yes it is."

* * *

At three thirty the telephone rang. Ann went into the hall and picked up the phone.

"Hello," she said, her voice husky from disuse.

"It's me." Her heart thudded at the sound of Richard's voice.

"You can't call me. We agreed to end things. You and I both know it's the right decision."

"I had to hear your voice."

Ann said nothing. If she spoke she would cry.

"You're right. I'm sorry. I won't . . . I won't call again. Good-bye, Ann," he whispered.

Richard kept his promise. Emptiness surrounded her. She moved on legs that did not feel like hers. Full of dull pain, her head refused to concentrate longer than a moment or two. Days marched by with so little definition she had difficulty tracking time. Loneliness left her breathless.

Walking the hill to catch the streetcar was the only place she permitted herself to weep for what she had lost. *Into each life some rain must fall*, she thought as she made the long climb one day, repeating one of her mother's favourite phrases. *But this isn't rain, it's a hurricane.*

Ann buried herself in volunteer activities, absorbing extra duties so that she was exhausted by nightfall, avoiding corners of the city where she might encounter Richard. At home music took the place of tears, and when she was alone she chose slow-moving piano concertos or sombre choral works as her companions. Time was an anaesthetic.

With daily news of atrocities, deprivation and cities bombed beyond recognition, no one questioned her sadness. Deceiving Edward was easier than she had imagined, as he too was preoccupied with the never-ending demands of war. Her heart felt like a corpse frozen in ice. Making love was a pantomime she endured, moving her body in all the familiar ways until it was over.

Ann hated herself. Believing she had to be dressed up both outwardly and inwardly to greet God, she stopped going to church because her inward self was full of shame and anger. Edward had been surprised the first Sunday she refused to go.

"I can't go. I'm too upset that God has permitted such evil in this world. Our prayers aren't answered. More and more people are dying."

"But Ann, we've always attended church together. It's a great comfort to me. The music and prayers are so soothing. Please come."

Despite his pleas, Ann would not yield, for she knew that church could be her undoing, the pivot point between light and darkness.

55 SEPTEMBER 1943

A whole team wiped out. Edward had known the news was dreadful as soon as he had seen Paul Hastings' face, which looked like the half-dead men on the battlefields of the First World War.

"This was forwarded overnight from SOE." General Hastings handed it over without a word.

Marauder extinct. Details to follow.

"Shit."

"There's more."

Edward braced himself, but said nothing.

"Larry's ship went down. Torpedoed by one of their fucking subs."

"Larry?" Paul nodded in a dazed sort of way. "Damn it to hell. Jesus, Paul, he was like my younger brother."

"He was on his way home. They said he did a great job."

Edward put a fist to his mouth and closed his eyes. He breathed in and out until he thought he could keep his voice steady. "I offered to go in his place. You know what he said? He said I did enough in the last war. Well, I didn't bloody well die in the last war, did I?"

"It's not your fault."

Anger churned like bubbling acid. "Four years, Paul. And where are we? We train them, send them overseas into God knows what, like lambs to slaughter. And what do we do to protect them? Precious little. I don't know how many more I can send."

"I know. At times like this I feel the same way." He stood up and looked out the window of what was once a bedroom. "Someone needs to tell his wife."

Imagining that conversation, Edward's head slumped. "I knew him best. I'll do it."

"You can tell her it was a secret mission."

"Right. A secret mission."

* * *

Saunders drove Edward straight home. Lights glowing through the bay window offered small beacons of comfort. Walking through the front door, the warm smell of stew greeted him along with Ann's footsteps descending the stairs. Although her flu had cleared up, she was thinner than before, especially her face, and her eyes retained a somewhat dull sheen. He put his briefcase on the floor and shrugged off his jacket.

"What's wrong?"

"Someone died." Fear washed over her face. "No one you know."

"But you do." Ann put her arms around him. "Tell me about it, Edward. You need to share these burdens. You can't keep piling them one on top of another."

"Are Emily and Alex home?" She shook her head. "I'll pour us a drink."

Instead of his usual wingback, he sat next to her on the sofa, a drink in one hand, his other resting on her thigh, feeling the comfort of warm skin through her skirt. He swirled the amber liquid then took a large gulp.

"I know you've wondered what I'm doing. The truth is I'm training people for special duties overseas. That's why I go away. I can't say what they do. But it's very dangerous work. In February we sent several people to Europe. Today I learned that three have been killed. Two men and a woman."

"Oh, no." Ann put her glass down and held his hand in both of hers.

"They were young, Ann. All under thirty. I trained them, but not well enough."

"Surely, you can't blame yourself. The casualties of war are so random, like a cancer that attacks some and not others. No one's safe, regardless of how well they train. I think that's what drives those of us left behind crazy."

"I can't help it. I feel responsible. It's almost as though I sent my own sons and daughter into danger. And there's more. One of my colleagues was killed on a ship returning from England. He was my friend and he has a wife and two small children. I had even offered to go in his place." He saw her look of shock, but pressed on. "Yes, I did. I felt I had to. But he said it was his turn. That I did enough in the last war. How do I live with that? What will I say to his wife?"

Edward slumped forward, staring at the far wall, his glass empty. Ann turned and put her hands on his cheeks and made him look at her.

"You are a very good man, Edward Jamieson. You have served your country to your utmost ability. I know you would not do it any other way. We will visit his wife together. Having a woman there will help."

"I can't ask you to do that. It's my responsibility."

"You're not asking. I'm offering. Let me do this for you."

* * *

Larry Paton's house was a tidy, yellow brick bungalow, the front door flanked by cedars, curtains drawn across what Edward assumed to be the living room. He wore his uniform, service cap tucked beneath one arm. Ann was at his side dressed in navy blue. A dog barked.

"Hunter! Be quiet. Bobby, watch your sister while I answer the door."

Edward heard a woman's voice and the sound of footsteps approaching. He tightened his shoulders and took a deep breath.

"Mrs. Paton?" he said to the red-haired woman dressed in a plain black skirt and yellow sweater. She was tall and wiry, a woman who likely excelled at tennis or swimming before the demands of motherhood and war got in the way.

"Yes." He watched her smile fade into uncertainty.

"I'm Lieutenant Colonel Jamieson. This is my wife, Ann. May we come in?"

"I'm not . . . What do . . . Why are you here?" Her eyes flicked back and forth and she raised a hand to cover her mouth.

"May we come in, Mrs. Paton?" Ann's voice was soft and warm. "Edward and I need to speak with you."

As Mrs. Paton stepped aside to allow them to enter, her eyes clouded, face sagging with the pain of anticipation. She gestured towards the kitchen. "The children."

"What are their names?" said Ann.

"Bobby and Sarah."

"May I meet them?"

A brief flash of upturned lips appeared on Mrs. Paton's face. Edward watched the two women disappear into the kitchen then heard the clanging of something like a spoon on metal and the giggle of a little boy. *How will they cope without a father?* He tried to imagine Alex and Emily carrying on without him, the pain of marking milestones with only memories of who he had been.

In the living room a piano stood along one wall with an open book propped against the music rack. Wooden blocks marked with letters of the alphabet were organized into small towers on a coffee table smudged with fingerprints. A pot of yellow chrysanthemums was on the window ledge and a knitted blanket draped one corner of the couch. Edward noticed two tiny socks beneath the rocking chair next to the fireplace.

Larry's wife reappeared. "I know why you're here," she said. "I can guess anyway. It's Larry, isn't it?"

Edward nodded. "We've worked together for three years. I imagine he didn't talk much about what we do but he was on a secret mission, a very important one, when . . ."

"When he died." She said the words as a statement rather than a question.

"When he died," Edward echoed, the words slamming into him with unexpected force. "Mrs. Paton, I'm so very sorry."

"Moira," she said. "My name is Moira."

"Moira, your husband was my friend. He would have wanted you to know that the work he did is making a difference to the war."

Moira's cheeks flattened, as the life seemed to disappear from her face. "Was he overseas?"

Would the truth help? Edward wondered. Hastings had suggested nothing beyond the notion of a secret mission. "Yes. How did you know?"

"Larry told me nothing except that he would be away for a month or two. But the night he was packing he had a phone call and while he was out of the room, I saw some British pounds tucked into his toiletry case. I wasn't snooping, I was putting a letter into his bag for him to . . ."

Moira began to sob, her shoulders heaved and she shook her head back and forth. The babble of children's voices emanating from the kitchen stopped.

"Mommy! Mommy!"

Edward heard Bobby calling followed by Ann's calm, soothing tones, the same tones she had used when Emily and Alex were younger. Shoes slapped the kitchen floor and Bobby burst into the living room and flung himself at his mother. Ann soon followed holding a small child against one hip.

"Bobby," she said. "Your mother needs your help. Can you

be a big boy and be quiet for her?" Ann propped Sarah into the corner of the couch then sat beside Moira. She put her arms around the young woman and drew her close.

Ann said nothing distinguishable, merely soft shushing sounds and the occasional murmured phrase. "There, there." "I know how hard this is." "Bobby and Sarah are right here." "We won't leave you alone." Moira's sobs gradually eased.

"Edward, can you find Moira's address book so we can call someone. It's probably next to the kitchen telephone. Moira, dear, what's your maiden name?"

An hour later, after Moira's parents had arrived and Edward had gone through some official documents with her father, they were able to leave for home.

As they drove away, Edward placed a hand on his wife's knee. "You were wonderful. I don't know how I would have handled Moira's tears and Larry's children without you."

Ann covered his hand with hers. "You may not realize it, but that was the kind of conversation I often have at Signals Welfare."

"You do? I've been so wrapped up in what I'm doing. I didn't stop to appreciate your contribution. How do you do it week after week?"

She shrugged her shoulders. "It's my way of helping, I suppose. I'm not the kind of person who can stand by and do nothing."

"You didn't stand by during the Depression either. What you did with Hannah at the women's shelter made me so proud of you." He put his arms around her. "Does it make you sad?"

"Sometimes. But it's been four years now. You can get used to almost anything, you know."

56 OCTOBER 1943

In October, Jack finished his training and returned to Toronto for two days before going overseas. He arrived mid-afternoon on a Saturday and now stood in the kitchen with his arm around Emily's waist.

"Why don't you two go out for a walk," Ann said. "I'm sure Jack needs to stretch his legs after being on the train so long."

"I'll come too," said Alex.

"I think your sister needs a little time alone with Jack. You've been monopolizing him ever since he arrived."

"Have I?" Alex grinned. "I guess I have. Emily, he's all yours. See you at dinner."

During dinner that night and the next, Ann seated Jack next to Emily and pretended not to notice when Jack's hand rested on her daughter's knee. Emily's bright eyes followed Jack's every move and from time to time Ann caught a look between the young couple that made her want to weep.

On the day of departure, Ann and Emily saw him off, walking through the great hall of Union Station, heels clicking on the flecked marble floor. Jack was in uniform, a duffel bag over his right shoulder and a smaller bag in his left hand. Emily's arm was linked with his. Once in England Jack would begin flying for real; in all likelihood, he would soon be dropping bombs on enemy targets.

The station echoed with footsteps and conversation. Loudspeakers proclaimed the departures of each train with a swoop of place names—North Bay, Sault Ste. Marie, Fort William, Port Arthur, Brandon, Winnipeg—conjuring images of stations large and small, where anguished parents met polished caskets and women waved lovers good-bye, where bewildered children in starched clothes watched fathers in unfamiliar garb climb narrow, iron steps then lean from windows with mouths stretched in grotesque smiles.

The hall was crowded. Ann remained with Jack's bags as he and Emily searched for information about his train to Halifax. She knew they were fond of one another; writing frequently while Jack was at flight school and spending hours together whenever he visited Toronto. She imagined they would find a quiet spot for a last embrace before joining her again.

"Cousin Ann, thank you for looking after me. I've told mother that your place has become a second home for me. It's meant a lot to have family here."

While officers walked up and down the platform urging men to board, a sharp whistle sounded again and again. Jack hugged them both.

"Don't worry about me, Em," he said, squeezing Emily's hand one last time before disappearing into the train. "I'll write as soon as I can."

Emily tried to keep her lips steady as the train pulled out of Union Station, watching until she could no longer see anything of Jack or the handkerchief he waved from the window. Ann put her arm around her daughter's shoulder and gently pulled her away from the platform.

As they walked through the gates back into the main hall, someone bumped into Ann and stopped to apologize.

"I'm sorry . . . Ann, I can't believe it's you." Richard looked from Ann to Emily. "This must be your daughter. She looks just like you."

He was thinner than the last time they had been together; his eyes were rimmed with fatigue but his voice was full of warmth. Being near him threatened her composure.

"Hello, Richard. Emily, this is Captain Leary. How have you been?"

"Not great," he said. "And you?"

She avoided his question. "We've been seeing off a young pilot from New Zealand. He's a distant cousin who stayed with us on leave while training." Another pause. "I'm sorry, Richard. We need to go."

"I'm going overseas myself next month. I'd enjoy seeing you before I leave."

"I doubt I'll have time for that." Ann kept her tone brusque.

"I'll call you. Nice to meet you, Emily."

Observing this interchange, Emily looked puzzled, and while they walked towards the exit she asked who he was.

"I met him at a party last year. He's a friend of Sheila and Carl Bradley."

"You don't seem to like him very much."

"I found him . . . arrogant or something."

"Oh." Emily gave her mother a funny look. "Well, he seems to like you."

"Does he? I doubt that."

While starting their car and backing it out from a spot beside a concrete pillar, Ann remained silent. She had learned to drive the year after marrying Edward. In a curious way, driving symbolized independence, a distinctive skill that set her apart from her friends who depended on husbands to take them around. She normally felt decisive and in control behind the wheel, but with gas rationing, she rarely used the car anymore. Negotiating traffic kept her mind off Richard.

"I'm going to write to Jack as soon as we get home. I promised I would. He doesn't leave Halifax until Sunday. Do you
think a letter would get there before his ship goes?"

"That's a good idea."

"Mother, you're not even listening."

"Sorry, dear. Just a few worries. Dad's home for dinner
tonight. That will be nice, won't it? You'll have to tell him all
about Jack's situation."

Richard called the next day. "You looked thin," he said
when Ann answered the phone. Though she considered letting
it ring, she knew he would keep trying. It was easier to speak
with him when she was alone.

"I can't see you."

"Please, Ann. I'm leaving in two weeks. I need to see you
before I go."

Emotions tossed her one way and then another. "Richard,
you promised me."

"I know, but I'm lost without you." He waited for her response but Ann remained silent. "I'll be at The Shamrock on
Thursday." He didn't need to say what time.

* * *

As the hours inched closer and closer to Thursday afternoon, Ann's nerves stretched with indecision. Whenever
Edward looked at her, she was certain he knew. She drifted through the house without remembering what task had
prompted her to be in the living room or kitchen or bedroom.
Every hour she told herself not to go, and every hour she
asked the question again.

On Thursday morning, she looked in her closet. A navy
suit hung next to one in soft grey, which was next to a black
dress with gold frog fasteners and a high neck—an outfit Edward called her Chinese look. Ann paused a moment to run
her hand along each item then took a simple black skirt and
red sweater from her closet. Once dressed, she added a gold
chain and pearl earrings.

By three o'clock she had conducted two meetings at Signals Welfare, met with one of their suppliers and written a report to be presented at an upcoming board meeting. The hallway was quiet except for the clatter of Angela Houston's typing and the zip-ding each time she pushed the carriage return. Ann stacked her papers, slid a three-ring binder into her briefcase and reached for her coat.

The bell jingled as she opened the door to The Shamrock.

"You came," Richard said. A huge grin filled his face and he stood, ready to help with her coat.

"When a man is going off to war, it's hard to refuse him," she bantered to keep emotion from her voice.

"I've missed you. Every day I've had to restrain myself from calling you."

She decided not to respond to his comment. "Are we having tea?"

"I'd rather be alone with you."

She smelled his aftershave. "That wouldn't be a good idea."

"It's hard to refuse a man who is going off to war." He held out his hand.

Ann knew she should say no. She had one more instant to make the right decision, but instead she took his hand, the desire to touch him again stronger than her ability to resist.

Ten minutes later, in the confining space of the apartment elevator, his nearness took her breath away. Examining his familiar face, she touched his lips. He captured her fingers and held them to his cheek.

"I know there's no future for us," he said.

"There's now."

Before opening the door, he whispered, "Are you sure?"

She nodded one more time.

His words filled her heart. Swaying slowly, feathered fingers writing poems on her skin, belt buckle dropping, nipples hard, sweat gathering in intimate pools, tongue tasting tongue, welcome weight of arms and legs, scent of fresh sheets, raindrops glimmering on the window as day faded. Guests of one another's senses. Two hours. Impossibly brief.

Richard watched her dress. Stockings encased her legs: a slip covered her breasts and belly. She bent to pick up her red sweater and black skirt and put them on without any hint of sensuality, then stepped into one shoe and the other, and ran her hands quickly through her hair. The clothing closed her in.

He got out of bed to embrace her, holding her so close she could feel his heart beat. Once, twice, three times. She touched his cheek then pulled away from his arms.

"Be safe," she said, turning to walk across the room, hearing the click, click, click of her heels, the squeak of the floor, and the soft sigh of the door as she left him behind.

When Richard departed for England, Ann did not see him off. They had said their good-byes that afternoon after the tenderness and passion of making love. Fierce kisses lingered on her lips, possessive, poignant. Images, touch, sound and smell were all that remained of that afternoon. She had nothing to remember him by, no letters, no pictures, no clothing, no favourite books or theatre tickets, nothing except a scrap of paper and a phone number.

57 NOVEMBER 1943

Ann pushed the sofa up against the window then moved the chairs, lamps and small tables one by one into the dining room. With the room almost empty of furniture, she rolled the Persian rug into a large coil and dragged it into the hall. Waxing wood floors was one of her least favourite chores, but they needed to be done and the living room was the last of seven rooms. Her hair was pinned back and she wore an old pair of Alex's pants. Though waxing floors often made her grumpy, the task allowed time to think.

Richard would be in England by now, closer to danger. Even before making love with him again, she had accepted the fact that they had no future together. Setting aside her feelings for him and deciding what path to follow occupied her thoughts.

As soon as she opened the bright yellow tin of wax, its tangy cedar smell filled her nostrils. She knelt on a folded towel and with a clean cloth cut from an old undershirt, began in the corner nearest the fireplace. Smooth swirls of wax created patterns on the floor, obscuring the grain of wood underneath as well as the nicks and scratches and rough patches.

Nicks and scratches like my marriage, she thought. *Maybe I can polish that too.*

The years had taught her that marriage grew quiet over time, leaving a hum of comfort and familiarity mixed with bouts of frustration and disinterest. Edward's secrets and disappearances had fostered anger. Anger had obscured her path. With war grinding on and on, she had stopped believing in the sacredness of their lifelong commitment and allowed her moral code to fail. Ann knew she had to stop blaming her husband. One thing was clear: Edward needed her. Perhaps more than she needed him.

She stood up to stretch her back then retrieved the polisher from the hallway and began the same rhythmic strokes her mother used to polish the wax. Back and forth, back and forth, the heavy stone clunking each time she changed direction.

Edward had become a mystery to her. She thought she knew him, but now understood that whatever he had been, he no longer was. They were no longer intimate, not sexual intimacy, although that too had been badly damaged, but the intimacy fostered by conversation and shared experience and an open heart. Like a prayer mumbled so many times the words were indistinct, their relationship had lost its enticing harmony and become unfathomable.

Do I love him? Ann asked herself the ultimate question, the same question she considered many years ago at Bea's house. *Perhaps, I no longer see the real Edward, only the one I've invented. And if that's the case, who is the man I live with?*

* * *

We might as well be on different planets, Edward thought. Ann was so preoccupied she rarely heard what he said. And even when she replied, he had the distinct impression she was responding to someone else. Thinking back, he realized she had been distracted for a long time.

Of course, he had been equally distracted, if not more so. Edward tried to determine when their relationship had begun to change. In June she had been rather morose, but he put that down to Jack's visit and her worries about a pilot's longevity. In July she had complained when he was away three weeks in a row. During August and September she was cool towards him, but he imagined her coolness was because he forgot their twentieth wedding anniversary. These days she was either prickly or remote. Edward concluded Ann's changed behaviour had been gradual, not precipitated by a particular event at all.

He glanced her way. His wife's nose was buried in a book, not a surprising event because she was an avid reader, but she had stopped tucking her toes beneath his thigh or lounging against him when she read. And she no longer exclaimed about interesting scenes or stopped to read him a particularly memorable passage. He wondered what this change signified and was ashamed he had not thought to ask.

We aren't newlyweds, he thought. *But we're comfortable together. God, that sounds like I'm comparing Ann to an old shoe.*

"What are you reading?" he asked.

Ann looked up. "A book about Elizabeth the First."

"Fiction, then?"

"No, nonfiction."

"You like nonfiction?"

"I do. I like the history."

"Oh. I see." *When did she begin to enjoy nonfiction,* he thought.

"It's well written. I never liked history at school, but this is fascinating."

She picked up her book again and he wondered when their conversation had become so stilted. Buried in the attic of his mind were memories of carefree times, love readily exchanged, lighter burdens. Such memories were like forgotten trinkets waiting for spring-cleaning, when they would either be reclaimed as treasures or discarded from misuse. Until he stopped living in the shadows, telling lies to hide what he was doing, their marriage would be in danger.

* * *

Edward's boss, Dave Jenkins, told him about Tayma Jewellers, a small second-floor shop in an old building on Kensington Avenue. Sam Tayma specialized in antique jewellery, collecting items from estate sales and pawnshops east and west of the city. According to Dave, Sam had the best sources, like Jerome's, which specialized in European styles and Wittington's, an auction house favoured by upper-class families. After so many years Tayma Jewellers had a large, loyal clientele.

"Can I help you, sir?"

"Maybe." Edward bent over to examine a display case of brooches, some large, some small, some sparkling, some understated.

"A brooch is it, sir?"

"Perhaps." He moved along to a display of dinner rings.

"Is it for your wife?"

"Yes. For Christmas." Edward pulled on his lower lip. "I have no idea what I'm looking for."

"You've come to the right place then, sir. Tell me about the jewellery your wife already has."

Edward opened his mouth then closed it. Other than her engagement ring and a brooch shaped like a butterfly and a single strand of pearls, he had no idea what Ann wore. "This and that," he said.

"I see, sir."

Sam Tayma moved around the room, opening cases and placing various items, each handled like a delicate treasure, on a blue velvet tray. By the time he showed the collection to Edward, the tray contained three rings, two brooches, a hatpin, two bracelets and a necklace. Each choice looked perfect.

"How did you do that?"

Mr. Tayma smiled. "I've been in the business over forty years. Sometimes, I just sense what a person needs."

When Edward left less than twenty minutes later, he had a black box containing a gold bracelet studded with sapphires. The purchase was worth every penny.

58 DECEMBER 1943

The morning's innocent dusting of snow had given way to a raging winter storm. The wind moaned through leafless trees. Drifts accumulated like waves on an angry ocean, spilling over rooftops and laneways. Ann wondered, as she did every year, at the whim of nature to create such havoc.

The storm contrasted sharply with her cosy surroundings. A Christmas tree shimmered with an array of ornaments collected over the years, carefully unwrapped each season, stories retold about when and where acquired and just as carefully put away after New Year's Day. Alex had built a fire, which now tossed flickers of light across the room and crackled cheerfully. Emily had turned the lamps off while carols played on the radio. Ann felt a stirring of contentment.

Even when they were little, Emily and Alex had helped with the tree, creating a clutter of decorations along the bottom boughs, which had always made Edward chuckle. As a family, they had driven to Mr. Butterworth's farm

north of the city, tramping through fields where tufts of grass
poked above the snow like errant whiskers until they found
that year's treasure. Sometimes Edward would hoist Alex on
his shoulders or throw snowballs, which sent their children
scurrying to a spot suitable for counterattack. Giggles and
shouts would follow as Edward allowed his son and daughter
to be victorious, often staging a dramatic snowball defeat by
tumbling to the ground. In all their years of marriage, those
outings had been the only times Ann could picture her husband as a young boy.

During a recent telephone call with Hannah, Ann had debated telling her friend about Richard.

"And what have you heard from Michael?" Ann had asked
not long after Hannah answered the phone.

"We haven't had one for three weeks. And so every day
feels like an eternity as I wait to hear from him. Did I tell you
that the Red Cross put me in touch with another family whose
son is in the same camp? We share our letters and she had one
last week. Her son always includes a mention of Michael. So
I'm trying not to worry too much."

"Oh, Hannah. How awful for you. I'm sure he's writing as
much as he can."

"I know. I'm sure he is too."

"Are you all right?"

"I'm OK. What did you tell me? One day at a time."

"One day at a time. That's what I tell myself these days.
Can I ask your advice about something?"

"Absolutely."

"It's about Edward. You won't mention anything to Bob?"

"Of course not."

"I suppose it's really about our marriage. I've told you
about all the travel he does but these days he's gone more and
more. He says he can't tell me anything about it. Extremely
confidential is the way he put it. And I feel so . . . so lonely
and unloved. I feel like he doesn't see me anymore. We're like
distant friends occupying the same house. It's as though our

love has faded away."

Distance fostered candour between the two women. Ann went on to talk of listening without hearing, of finding fault with Edward, of deliberately picking fights in order to spark emotion and test his endurance. As the conversation continued, they had spoken about living under stressful circumstances and how the incessant pounding of everyday responsibilities eroded love.

Ultimately, she had resisted mentioning Richard, not because Hannah would condemn her actions but because Ann feared disclosure would forever tarnish the memory.

Hannah's right, Ann thought as the radio played Silent Night and the wind continued to buffet the house. *Marriage is complicated, binding two selves together in some intricate drama of acts and scenes and imagined happiness.*

Ann wanted her family back, not just their presence, but also the intensity of intermingled lives and knowledge of everyday thoughts and challenges. She looked at Alex, who sat on the floor with his back against the sofa, shuffling a deck of cards from one hand into the other. Then she glanced at Emily, who was reading a book, using the latest letter from Jack as a placeholder. They were drawing away from her, leaving childhood behind, and she could not halt the process. But, as Hannah had pointed out, she could restore her relationship with Edward to ensure that Alex and Emily always had a safe haven and an example of what marriage could be when both parties work to keep it strong.

"What are you thinking about, Alex?" Ann asked.

"Nothing much, really." He continued shuffling the cards. "Actually, I'm thinking about David. What do you think his Christmas will be like? There won't be a tree or anything, will there? Do you think he's scared?"

"Well, we don't know where he is exactly. If he's in England, I'm sure there will be some sort of Christmas. He's no longer in Africa but he may have been posted somewhere else. Do you think he would be scared?"

Alex shrugged his shoulders. "I don't know. He always seemed fearless to me but now I think that's because he's always been the oldest. The stuff I read makes me realize that every soldier is probably scared some of the time."

"Your father told me he was afraid during the first war."

"He did?"

"Mm hmm." Alex was not normally a worrier and Ann wondered whether that piece of information would help him feel better about David. "The weather's getting worse. I hope he's home soon."

Anxious words brought their peaceful mood to an end. She got up to look outside and could hardly see across the street. Crossing to the radio, she adjusted the dial to listen for news of the storm, pacing back and forth while the announcer talked about road closures.

Emily, who usually read more than one book at a time, set aside the one she was reading. "I think I'll go upstairs to write to Jack."

"Have you heard from him recently?"

"I had a letter yesterday." Emily blushed and turned away to hide her feelings.

"Did you, sweetie. How's he doing?" Ann knew letters travelled across the Atlantic several times a week.

"He sounds very cheerful."

"Is he flying already?" Alex said. He admired Jack and read as much as he could about warplanes and RAF successes.

"He's started flying Mosquitoes across the channel. Some of the details are censored, but his spirits are good. His friend Jim is in the same unit."

"That's nice," said Ann. "You go ahead upstairs, love." *Dear God*, she thought, *don't let him die.* "Alex, do you think we should clear the driveway? You know your father will appreciate it. I'll be out as soon as I hear the weather."

She was grateful Alex didn't make his usual protest. Five minutes later, after hearing that the storm was tapering off, she put on her winter coat, heavy boots and mitts—her fingers numbed too quickly in gloves—and went outside. Feeling the brisk, cold wind and watching snow swirl about the house was strangely exhilarating. A long, spindly icicle fell from the gutter and smashed to pieces.

Since Alex was at the end of the drive, Ann began with the walkway. The wind made conversation difficult, and after a few attempts she was left to ruminate.

Her time with Richard had been an escape. The fantasy was over, reality resurfacing. She had to build a bridge back into her marriage and find the love that had sheltered their little family, enabling each of them to grow beyond what they were individually. After long, melancholy months, she understood how Edward must have struggled with his feelings for Helene. But in this case, she knew Edward must never know about Richard. He would not recover from a wound so great.

"Mom! Why aren't you shovelling?" Alex seemed indignant.

"Just thinking about something, dear. Let's finish this quickly and then we'll make hot chocolate."

Lift, toss. Lift, toss. An easy rhythm, crisp, cold invigorating, straining muscles unaccustomed to winter work. By the time they were almost done, the storm had eased, snow falling like drifting feathers. Car lights glowed faintly on the road as Alex and Ann stamped their boots by the back door.

"That must be Dad," he said, heading into the house.

"You go on in. I think I'll wait for him outside."

59 December 1943

On Christmas morning when Ann came down to start the coffee and prepare breakfast, she entered the living room first and turned on the Christmas lights, dispelling the gloom of low-hanging clouds and light snow. Of course, there were only a few modest gifts beneath the tree, but one in particular stood out, a small rectangular parcel carefully wrapped in shiny red and encircled with silver ribbon. Edward had placed it there the previous night.

"No peeking," he had said with an unexpected twinkle in his eyes as she fit oranges into the toes of Alex and Emily's stockings, followed by other small treats, including Hershey bars her father had provided, admonishing her not to ask how he had acquired them.

"Something special?" she had asked.

"Never you mind," Edward had said. "You'll see tomorrow."

When they had climbed the stairs afterwards, he had held her hand and she had wondered whether he planned to make love to her. Instead he had kissed her then turned away to settle into sleep.

Noting again the small red package that sparkled in the glow of Christmas lights, Ann smiled and made her way to the kitchen.

* * *

"How beautiful, Edward. Where did you find something so perfect?"

Ann extracted the bracelet from its box and held out her arm, admiring the glint of sapphires set in a series of gold links as he fastened the clasp. *Jewellery*, she thought. *it's been a very long time since he bought me jewellery.*

"A small store called Tayma Jewellers. The man who owns the place gave me several items to choose from and I chose this."

"Mom, that's gorgeous," Emily said, kneeling in front of her mother so she could see the gift. "I didn't know you had such good taste, Dad."

"I thought your mother deserved something special this year."

Ann kissed him on the cheek. "Thank you, sweetheart."

Throughout the day, every time she moved her arm the bracelet's light touch felt like a caress. Edward's gifts were usually much more modest and she wondered what such an expensive gift signified. He had surprised her. That he had chosen something so special made her feel hopeful.

The last time he had given her jewellery had been their fifteenth wedding anniversary, two years after the trip to France. They had been deeply in love again, not like newlyweds but something more profound because they had known what they had almost lost. Edward had chosen an opal ring surrounded by tiny diamonds and when he had put it on her finger, he had told her he would always love her and no one else.

Yes, the bracelet made her feel hopeful.

* * *

Edward had been pleased that Ann chose to wear the bracelet all day. Their tradition was to have lunch with the Jamieson clan, hosted, as always, by his mother, even though the gathering was now more than forty, and then dinner with Ann's family. On seeing the bracelet, his mother-in-law had been particularly effusive, saying she had never seen such a beautiful design.

"Do you really like it?" Edward had his shirt undone and was in the midst of removing his cufflinks.

"It's truly lovely, dear. You didn't need to be so extravagant."

"I wanted to. Here, let me help with that. The jeweller said it was made in 1851. Apparently you can tell by the hallmarks." Edward released the clasp then showed her a series of marks located on the bracelet's underside. He had studied them under a magnifying glass one night when Ann was out.

"Remember when you said I wasn't good at telling you my thoughts?"

Ann stopped studying the hallmarks and looked at him. A brief smile was followed by a wrinkled brow, as if she was trying to guess what he might be about to say. She stood less than an arm's length away, dressed in a nightgown of blue silk.

"I know I'm in that same pattern again. Not from choice this time, but still, I can see the effect it's had on you. I'm sorry, darling. Hopefully, this bloody war will be over soon and we can get back to normal."

"Normal," she said. "Will things ever be normal again?"

He drew her into his arms. "God, I hope so."

"Come to bed," she said, her voice inviting and warm.

Their crisp white sheets were cold and he spooned against her, front to back, until she stopped shivering. They had lost the comfort of making love and he wondered whether tonight he might rekindle some measure of it. He kissed the nape of her neck and pulled her closer. His erection stirred.

"Shall I take off my nightgown?"

He let his fingers linger on her curving hip. "There's no

hurry," he said.

"No hurry at all," Ann replied.

Edward pulled the edge of her nightgown up far enough to feel skin instead of fabric. His wife really did have the most wonderful figure, hips wide enough to entice as she walked, breasts full enough to encourage more than a passing glance, and a pleasingly slender waist. He pulled up her gown just a little more and slid his hand across her belly then to the spot where leg and torso met, a spot that always made her shiver.

Ann shifted onto her back. "Kiss me," she said.

With his hand reaching lower, he kissed her lips, and when she parted them, their tongues touched. Edward was gentle, wanting nothing to disturb the slow passion of lovemaking. Slow was much better than fast. He licked her bottom lip and then the top and kissed her again. Ann's soft moan told him everything he needed to know.

His fingers found her moist center and he explored with infinite care. Ann lifted her hips to press against him. His erection hardened even more.

"Now?" he whispered.

"Yes, now."

60 JANUARY 1944

On the third Wednesday of January Edward was off to Camp X again. Ever since he had disclosed the bare bones of his reasons for travel, he felt less tension leaving the house for a few days' absence. When he kissed Ann good-bye, he thought her smile was genuine, and as the car drew away, he recalled her eyes glittering with emotion after opening his Christmas gift and the lovemaking that night, which had sparked feelings of true tenderness rather than routine.

Saunders drove with his usual steady hand, offering only a crisp "good morning, sir" as they set out. Other than the buzz of tires on pavement and the whine of changing gears, the two men rode in silence. Edward glanced at his briefcase. He knew he should check a report stamped SECRET in large red letters, but he was tired. He leaned back and closed his eyes, allowing the car's jostling to lull him to sleep.

At Glenrath all indicators were business as usual: guard detail just as strict, the Hydra building just as secretive, staff striding about with serious purpose. As soon as he arrived, Edward left his suitcase at the barracks and walked along to Building F where Jim Ferguson was waiting. Jim, a barrel-chested redhead from Scotland, was an experienced SOE man who had transferred to Camp X within weeks of Larry's death. At first Edward resented him, but now the two men worked seamlessly together.

After Marauder's demise, SOE sent additional teams to Italy to augment those already in place. Allied leaders had expected September landings in Calabria to lead to the capture of Rome by Christmas, an ambitious but flawed expectation. German troops were too well entrenched and, even though Italy had joined the Allies, Italian army command had collapsed. Just before Christmas, General Hastings said every inch of Italy would have to be fought over, necessitating significant and ongoing espionage. Jim and Edward were organizing yet another team for departure mid-February.

Looking back at the last months of 1943, there had been hints of progress. In October Italy finally declared war on Germany, then in November the Russians captured Kiev and British air raids pummelled Berlin. In early January Russia advanced towards Poland while Allied attacks against German positions in Italy began to have an effect. These were small sparks of hope that he knew could just as easily die as catch fire.

"Do you think this will be the year we start to win?" Edward asked Jim as they settled into work.

He had been preoccupied with this question ever since New Year's Day, when the family had raised their glasses for a toast. He wondered if their lives might ease a little, the strain and worries lessen. More importantly, he wondered if they would all return, those he sent out from Camp X and those dear to them who had enlisted to serve.

"I dinnae ken."

At first, Jim's accent had baffled him, but gradually its lilt and rhythm became familiar. When Jim was angry, unknown words tumbled out.

"There's too much blether aboot the future. You and I must get doon to business, else those galoots will continue to win."

Edward smiled. Jim was right; they would not win by speculating.

* * *

When he arrived home three days later, his family seemed relaxed and the house oddly tranquil. Dinner was a calm affair, Alex relaying a story about his geography teacher while Emily disclosed that she had joined the school newspaper. With a soft smile on her face, Ann nodded at their children and murmured encouraging words. As he enjoyed an after dinner coffee, Edward mused that 1944 was already looking promising.

"I'll get the door," he called out from the living room.

A skinny man, little more than a boy, stood on the front porch dressed in a plain blue uniform. Edward knew at once the purpose of his visit, before the man said good evening, before the man reached into his faded grey pouch and well before the man handed over the envelope. He wondered what horrible news the telegram brought and how they would cope.

Edward took the envelope, surprised at how thin and insubstantial it was. He had the irrational thought that terrible news should come in large, weighty packages. When he saw the New Zealand stamp, he knew.

"I'm sorry, sir."

"Thank you," he said, watching the man pull his collar tight and hunch his shoulders against the wind. Edward closed the door.

Ann appeared, wiping her hands on a blue apron embroidered with pink and white flowers by his mother. A Christmas gift. "Who was it, dear?"

"A telegram," he said, "from New Zealand."

"Oh, dear God." Ann's hand flew to her mouth, eyes closed tight. Air hissed through clenched teeth.

He opened the envelope.

RECEIVED WORD FEB 13 JACK'S PLANE DOWNED RETURNING TO COAST OF ENGLAND STOP NO SURVIVORS STOP BURIAL IN ENGLAND STOP THE WHOLE FAMILY IS DEVASTATED STOP WE KNOW HOW TERRIBLE THIS WILL BE FOR EMILY STOP PLEASE GIVE HER OUR LOVE STOP LETTER WILL FOLLOW VERY SOON JULIA

Edward passed the telegram to Ann. *Another nightmare,* he thought.

When the war began, he had never imagined his children being affected; at twelve and thirteen, they were too young to serve and the prevailing opinion at that time was that war, though difficult, would be over in a year or two. That was four and a half years ago. Well before Jack appeared for training and David Andrews and Michael Wilson enlisted.

"Where is she?" He stroked Ann's cheek, wiping a tear away.

"In her bedroom. I think she's writing him a letter."

On the way upstairs, he held Ann's hand, their footsteps soft and slow. When they approached Emily's door, Ann took a ragged breath and braced her shoulders. Emily must have heard them, for she had closed her book before they came through the door. Her forehead furrowed as she looked from one face to the other.

"Sweetheart, we have something to tell you." Edward crouched down in front of his daughter. "Jack was killed in a plane crash on his way back to England."

Ann sat on the bed and put an arm around their daughter as shock and disbelief flooded Emily's face. Edward found it almost unbearable to watch.

"That can't be," she shook her head back and forth. "I received a letter from him today. Tell me it's not true. Mom? Daddy? It can't be true."

"I'm sorry, sweetheart. Your mother and I are so upset to have to bring you this news." Edward handed her the telegram. "His mother sent word. They heard just yesterday."

"But you said he was on his way back. Pilots don't die on their way back." Emily still had not read the telegram; she held it away from her, as if by refusing to read it she could deny what had occurred. Her voice was little more than a whimper.

"You have to be brave, darling. This is terrible, terrible news." Ann hugged her close, rocking back and forth.

"He's gone?"

Edward could hardly bear the pain in his daughter's voice.

"Yes, sweetheart. He's gone."

Emily dissolved then into sobs that shook her whole body.

Alex poked his head into the room, his eyes flitting from his sister to his mother and father. "Is it Jack?"

Edward nodded, too distraught to speak.

"Plane crash?"

Edward nodded again.

"Damn those bloody Germans. Damn them to hell."

All night they took turns sitting with Emily, whispering words of comfort. Alex insisted on sharing this duty and when Edward came in around four a.m., he found Alex with his arms wrapped around his sister. Both of them were asleep.

* * *

"She's hardly eating anything," Edward said as he and Ann watched departing troops parade down University Avenue.

Normally, Edward would participate in such a ceremony, but today he had chosen to be with his wife. Wailing bagpipes and swirling kilts and the sound of hundreds of boots marching in unison brought emotions to the surface. She wiped her eyes and tightened her grip on his arm, hunching close to shelter from gusting winds.

"I know. I don't know what to do."

"Is she talking to you?"

"Not much." Across the street, a small child waved the British flag.

"What about her friends?"

"Joan's been around and Barbara. Yesterday Keith appeared on his motorcycle. He hasn't seen her in months. She talked to him for a little while. Mainly, she goes to school, comes home and sits in her room."

"Would she talk to me?"

"She might. It's worth a try."

When they did talk, on a quiet Sunday afternoon, pale sun casting thin shadows, Emily was reticent, responding to his questions in monosyllables until he disclosed some of his own sorrows, telling stories of friends who died in France when he was only a few years older than his daughter.

"The last one was my friend, Bill Simpson. What made his death so painful was that he died from one of our own rifles." Emily's eyes grew round. "They call it friendly fire. Can you imagine such a term? There's nothing friendly about being shot by one of your own. I was furious at the time. I wanted to find the man responsible and beat him up. I even imagined what it would feel like to shove my fist into his face."

"Did you find him?"

"No. My sergeant persuaded me to cool down. He said we needed to keep our strength for fighting the enemy." Edward remembered the sergeant's angry face and blistering words— words he could not possibly repeat to Emily.

"Why do you think Jack's plane went down on the way back to England?" Her voice was like a seeping wound.

"I don't know, sweetheart. Planes are complicated machines. They might have taken a hit that he thought wasn't significant enough for him to parachute out. We'll never know. But he would want you to get on with your life. You know that, don't you?"

Emily nodded. A tear dripped onto her skirt.

"He meant a lot to me, Daddy," she whispered.

"I know. I know. He was a very fine young man. You will always remember him."

She nodded again and leaned against his shoulder.

61 FEBRUARY 1944

"I have to go."

Ann looked at him as though he had grown another head. "You can't. I won't allow it."

"Someone has to go and I've been selected. I can't tell you much, except there's a major battle planned and people are needed to lay the groundwork."

"Train them here like you always do." Ann's hands were on her hips, mouth pursed so hard her lips were white. She shook her head. "You can't go. Think of what happened to Larry."

Larry had been Edward's first thought when Paul made the request that afternoon.

"They're short of communications experts," Paul had said. "With the invasion coming, SOE wants to send a series of teams to strategic locations and they need men like you. The teams will be deployed faster if you're in England. Steve Shelley and John Foster are also going."

Edward had not asked whether Jim Ferguson would be a

better choice. This time he refused to let a younger man take
the risk, and Jim was only thirty.

"I'm to leave on Friday, which means I have two days to
get ready." Edward bridged the distance between them and
put his arms around Ann. "I'll be careful."

Her body remained stiff. "You can't be careful if some German submarine targets your ship. Or a destroyer."

"That's why I'm flying." Drawing back from him, Ann
frowned. "I'll fly from Toronto to Gander then Gander to
England. It's done all the time now."

"Who's to say that's any safer? And what about when
you're there? German planes are still raiding England."

"Ann, please don't make it any more difficult than it already is. I have to go. I'll tell Emily and Alex over dinner. You
can help them by being calm."

She stared at him. "That's what you want from me? Calm
acceptance." He nodded. "All right, I'll do my best. Maybe
getting the dinner ready will calm me down." Ann turned
away from him and left the room.

Edward sighed. Thumping footsteps and banging cupboards made his wife's anger clear. Anger went hand in hand
with fear and he had seen the look of panic in her eyes when
she had challenged his decision. After he had enlisted in the
first war, his mother's face had looked the same.

* * *

"I'll be gone six to eight weeks," he concluded, stabbing a
mouthful of turnip with his fork.

"You can't go, Daddy. Think of what happened to Jack. If
you die . . ."

Emily burst into tears and he reached for her hand to offer
a squeeze of comfort. Ann rose and stood behind their daughter, smoothing her hand gently from Emily's forehead to the
back of her neck.

"Your father will be fine, sweetheart. I know he will. Planes
from Gander fly north to avoid German detection. It's done

all the time."

Alex looked puzzled. "I thought you were too old to go overseas. That's what you told us."

"It's a special duty. I'm forbidden to talk about it."

"Forbidden? Wow, Dad. That sounds important."

"It is. But you mustn't tell any of your friends. Do you promise?"

Alex nodded. "I promise."

"I'm going to my room." Emily pushed her chair away from the table, ignoring the restraining tug of her mother's hand.

"Emily, please don't leave," Edward said.

His daughter gave him a look and ran from the room.

Later that evening after an unsuccessful attempt to speak to Emily, Edward knocked on Alex's bedroom door.

"Can I come in?"

"Sure, Dad." Alex put down his pencil and tipped his chair back.

His room was a mess. Books and clothes strewn everywhere. At least three sweaters hung on the bedpost while Alex's hockey stick and goalie gloves occupied the corner nearest the window. An apple core, wrinkled and brown, lay on top of the bedside table. Edward said nothing. There were more important matters than the tidiness of his son's room.

"While I'm gone, I need you to help your mother." Alex nodded slowly. "And your sister." Alex nodded again. "They're both very upset with me."

"Mom didn't look upset."

"She just didn't want you to know. She wants to protect you two. I'm sure you'll find out one day that women are complicated." *Now why on earth did I say that*, Edward wondered. *This is my sixteen-year-old son.* But nothing was normal anymore.

"I see." Alex said.

"Perhaps you could think of your job as helping them to stay calm. Anticipating what your mother might want without her having to ask you."

"You mean things like putting out the garbage and shovelling the snow?"

"Exactly that sort of thing. And doing your homework without nagging or coming home before she has to call around to find out where you are. You could even ask whether she needs your help when you get home from school."

"Dad?"

Edward had been examining a split fingernail, the one that always split no matter how many raw almonds or primrose oil pills he took. Alex's questioning tone made him look up.

"Yes," he said.

"Will you really be safe over there?"

Did his son's question call for an honest answer? Was Alex old enough for the truth? Edward would be in constant danger as soon as he stepped on the plane in Gander.

"You've been reading the papers so you know England is a risky place to be." Alex nodded. "The Germans aren't bombing like they were during the blitz but there's still a lot of night action. From what I know they concentrate on major cities and I'll be in a much smaller town. So I should be fine. Does that help?"

"I think so." His son's voice was subdued. "Be careful, Dad."

* * *

On Thursday afternoon Ann helped him pack. When they went to bed Thursday night, she removed his clothes piece by piece and they made love, tender at first and then with rising fever, until he called out her name and shuddered in climax.

Early Friday morning, Ann, Emily and Alex hovered by the front door as Edward checked his list one last time. A sedan waited in the driveway, the driver standing by the passenger side, stamping his feet. Wisps of glittering snow blew across the road.

"Do you have everything?" Ann said.

"I think so. I suppose if I need something I can get it over there."

"Their rationing is worse than ours."

He nodded. "You're right."

Edward knew banal bits of conversation were typical when families parted, trivialities masking unspoken concerns. Ann had wept after their lovemaking, resisting his attempts to comfort her, and this morning her eyes were puffy, though she made an effort to smile during breakfast and touched his cheek with one hand while pouring his coffee. He looked at his family and for one terrible moment imagined never seeing them again.

"I think I'm ready." He wrapped an arm around Ann and the other around Emily. Alex closed the circle and Edward grabbed his son's hand. "I'll send a telegram when I land. Ann, you know how to reach me."

As the car backed down the drive, Ann pulled their children close. They waited on the front step while the black car drove away, Edward watching from the window until they were no longer in sight.

62 FEBRUARY 1944

The flight across the Atlantic was uneventful compared with the flight to Gander. Leaving Toronto, the pilot had assured Edward they would not take off if conditions were the least bit dangerous, but landing in Gander a crosswind caught the starboard wing and the plane had careened towards the edge of the runway on only one wheel, the engines screaming as the pilot struggled to steady the plane, finally setting it down close to a large barn used for maintenance. During one awful moment, Edward had been sure the plane would flip over and had braced for impact.

After calming his nerves with a scalding cup of coffee, he had looked around Gander. The airport handled hundreds of planes every day, and beyond the control tower were hangars, a hospital and bakery, warehouses, barracks and mess halls. Men and women, bundled in coats and gloves and boots, strode from one building to another. A collection of communications equipment marked the top of the main tower.

Six hours later Edward stood on the tarmac, waiting to take off in the black of night. For security reasons, General Hastings had arranged for his communications specialists to travel separately, so Edward's fellow passengers were strangers. He noticed a few American uniforms amongst the group of civilians and uniformed men.

"The DC-3 will fly to Scotland to avoid Jerry," said the base commander, a thin man wearing a flamboyant yellow scarf around his neck. "You can travel by train from there."

"Where do we land?"

"Prestwick. You'll be met and driven to the train station. The flight is more than twelve hours, but we have a tailwind tonight and fine weather predicted for Prestwick. Should be good flying."

"You have an impressive operation here, Commander," Edward said.

The man chuckled. "You wouldn't believe what it looked like when I first arrived. Gander was quite a sleepy little place then. The Brits finally woke up to our potential."

Within fifteen minutes, the plane was airborne. Once they had reached cruising altitude, Edward rolled his coat into a bundle and propped it beneath his head as he leaned against the window. He had a thermos of tea and a salmon sandwich to eat when he woke. After landing, he would go straight to Beaulieu and a briefing with those in command. He expected the pace to be punishing.

* * *

During the first week of Edward's absence, Ann's days had little definition, each one followed by sleepless nights. Every sharp noise startled her. With every knock on the door or ring of the telephone, fear bubbled in her throat. Edward sent the promised telegram, but she remained tense, worry causing such distraction that her usual efficiency disappeared.

"Damn," she said, watching blood bubble from a spot on her finger. "Emily, can you bring the first aid kit? I've cut my finger."

"That's the third time this week, Mom," Emily said, bringing a black metal tin into the kitchen. She lifted the lid and extracted a roll of gauze and some white tape. Emily giggled. "Soon you won't have any fingers left. Why don't you let me finish dinner?"

"I do look rather silly." Ann chuckled. "Angela said I've become more of a hindrance than a help. I was insulted, but I suppose she's right. My head just isn't working. Anyway, I'm glad to hear you laugh."

"It's Dad, isn't it?" Emily cut a piece of tape and handed it to her mother.

"You're right. Except for Jack, our little family hasn't lost anyone close, and I can't help worrying that our luck will run out."

Ann glanced at the calendar. Edward would be buried in his work. He had warned her that the pace would be frantic, so she had no expectation of letters, and overseas telephone calls were almost impossible to arrange.

"I crossed off day eight this morning," she said. "If he remains six weeks we have thirty-four more days, and if it it's eight weeks then forty-eight more days. One day at a time. That's what I told Hannah when they learned that Michael was missing. I suppose I should follow my own advice."

"What's for dinner, Mom?" Alex entered the kitchen. "Good grief. Have you cut another finger?"

Emily and Ann burst into laughter.

* * *

"God, what I would do for more than a few hours sleep." Steve Shelley yawned and rubbed his eyes. "I feel like shit."

Edward and Steve had worked together since arriving in Beaulieu. The head communications instructor felt they would be more effective that way. John Foster had joined the weapons group. When they were briefed, Colonel Sherman told them that the teams they sent to Europe were part of a strategy to convince the Germans that invasion landings would occur elsewhere.

"We don't want Jerry increasing troop presence in Normandy now, do we? So we're creating the impression that our attack will be in Pas-de-Calais. A separate group is working a parallel diversionary tactic for Norway. We've got to keep the enemy guessing and we have to be convincing enough that German reserves will remain in place instead of shifting to Normandy after our attack commences. Hitler and his generals have to think that Normandy is merely a diversion in advance of either Pas-de-Calais or Norway."

Colonel Sherman had addressed more than twenty men and women tasked with preparing agents to operate in France, Germany, Norway and Holland. These agents would augment existing teams in advance of June.

"We have only a few weeks to finish training which is why each of you has been handpicked for duty. You are considered the best."

After his introductory remarks, Sherman had turned the briefing over to his second-in-command, Major Robertson, a man of average build whose pink cheeks and round face made him look more like a university student than an experienced officer. In comparison, Edward felt old.

The days blurred. From early morning to late night they taught wireless skills, encryption techniques, the use of invisible inks, Morse code, ciphers. Each team had a dedicated wireless operator who also had to know how to repair their equipment, keep it secure, assemble and disassemble the wireless, adapt enemy equipment and cannibalize other electronics if necessary. They trained and tested their trainees and then trained them again. During trial missions, they tried to make them fail.

Steve Shelley's yawn was contagious. Edward stretched his arms above his head. "I'm worried we'll make a mistake, if we don't get some time off soon."

"That could be deadly."

"More than deadly."

From the window, remnants of Beaulieu Abbey dominated the view. Though Henry VIII had destroyed much of the abbey, gothic arches still defined the cloister where monks from as early as the thirteenth century read, walked or sat in contemplation. In late February the cloister and abbey church looked bleak, grey stone matching low hanging clouds, a ragged patch of grass the only colour.

"Looks like rain," Edward said.

"That's all it seems to do here. Never thought I would say this, but I think snow is preferable."

The two men leaned against opposite ends of the window frame. Steve yawned again.

In his room that night, Edward took out a sheet of thin, blue paper and composed a letter to his family. He said nothing about the work he was doing or the bombs dropped on a nearby airfield and instead filled the space with details of the countryside, a few people he had met and the atrocious English food. Just before turning out the light, he touched the picture of his family taken at Christmas, tracing their faces one by one.

* * *

Ann extracted the blue envelope marked with Edward's narrow script from the letterbox and held it for a long moment while the wind blew cold, damp air into the house. She checked the postmark and calculated that the letter had taken three weeks to cross the Atlantic. Almost five weeks had passed since his departure, the calendar documenting each day with another red X. Gradually she had grown accustomed to his absence and returned to the busy pace of volunteer work that had previously occupied her time. Weekends had been filled with family visits, evenings spent primarily with Emily. Shivering, she closed the door.

Dearest Ann, Emily and Alex,

I'm sorry it has taken me so long to write. I've been working day and night and time has passed very quickly. My trip was very smooth, a small plane from Toronto then a larger plane crossing the Atlantic and a train to my final destination. Alex, you would have been interested in the flying techniques employed to cross the ocean. Did you know that pilots still navigate by the stars if necessary?

I can't tell you my exact location, however, I am surrounded by gently rolling countryside and many fine old homes, some built as long ago as the Tudor period, although often these are in ruins. I suspect it looks beautiful in summer, but right now everything is quite gloomy and we've had rain most days. The villages are quaint, full of white-washed houses and small churches and a pub or two, often topped with thatched roofs. I've had no time for the pubs, although I hope to visit one that's nearby, as I understand that the music is lively.

My work has brought me into contact with men and women from all over Europe. One fellow is a terrible curmudgeon whose temper flares at the least provocation, so I try to stay out of his way. Another man walks with his head down and always seems to be muttering to himself. He is said to be one of the smartest men in England. There are many women here—some not much older than you, Emily—and they work just as hard as the men and often in very important roles. Unfortunately, there is little time for small talk.

You can't imagine the food. Gruesome is the only word. Yesterday, the gravy covering my meat was grey and tasted like paste. The peas were equally grey. The only palatable item was rice pudding, although nowhere as delicious as yours, Ann. The coffee is ersatz, so I confine myself to tea.

The days rush by and I still hope to be finished in the six to eight weeks I promised. I wish I could see you sooner.

My love to you all,
Edward/Daddy

Ann read the letter a second time imagining her husband sitting at a desk in front of a window, with a view of fields divided by stone fences and a few sheep grazing in the distance. No doubt he would pull on his lower lip occasionally as he thought about what to write. Perhaps his pipe would be smouldering in a nearby ashtray. The image brought him close. *At least he's in the countryside rather than London*, she thought. *London's such a target for German planes. Please keep him safe. Please.*

63 MARCH 1944

Edward perused the equipment room, a long rectangular space with three rows of shelving, each shelf mounted on rollers for easier access. Beaulieu had an enormous collection of weapons, devices and radios, including a number of German pieces taken from enemy agents. He had never seen so many ingenious items assembled in one spot. He picked up a woman's shoe with a concealed heel blade and wondered at the circumstances and presence of mind required to activate such a device. Returning the shoe to its shelf, he continued his search.

Tomorrow they planned to test agents on the Type A Mark III suitcase radio and the S-Phone, a high frequency radio telephone used for coded conversation between London and agents in the field. Edward wanted a variety of radios to use for comparison purposes.

With three teams scheduled to depart in ten days, they were running out of time. Edward found what he was looking for and piled six radios on the cart, which squeaked as he rolled it towards the checkout desk, where a woman in the khaki uniform of Lance-Corporal in the British Auxiliary Service, bent over a leather-bound ledger.

"You're here again, Lieutenant Colonel Jamieson."

"We'll be out of your hair soon, Miss Godfrey. I don't expect too many more requisitions."

The woman smiled and flipped to a new page in the ledger where she wrote the details of each piece of equipment, then turned it around so Edward could affix his signature.

"And when do you expect to return them?"

"Probably Wednesday."

He rolled the cart along a tiled corridor. Before going outside, he covered the radios with a large piece of canvas then hurried across an open courtyard, weaving a path between two jeeps and a battered but polished, silver Bentley. After a long spell of wet weather, the sun offered a hint of spring and crocuses lined the path to the building where Steve waited. Edward whistled. After five weeks, the three men finally had a night off and they planned to visit the local pub.

* * *

The Fiddler's Roost stood at the corner of King and High Streets. Protruding more than a foot beyond the first floor, an upper storey was marked with crisscrossed beams of dark wood interspersed with grubby white stucco. Edward, Steve and John ducked their heads to enter through a rough wooden door that looked as though it had seen centuries of use. They passed by a small dining area and into a second room full of noise and tobacco smoke. Near the fireplace, an old man tuned his fiddle.

"Looks like a bit of a character," said Steve, as they settled around a table.

"I wonder if he gets his beard caught in the strings." John chuckled. "What's your preference, lads? I'll get this round."

John ambled towards the bar, where a line of stools clustered at one end and a barmaid pulled one of four taps to fill a glass with dark amber liquid. While he waited to pay for their drinks, a woman and a boy of no more than fourteen joined the man with the fiddle, and following a brief huddle punctuated by nodding heads, the group began to play a soft lament. Conversation paused while the woman's poignant voice carried through the room and beyond, singing a tale of forbidden love and treachery.

When the last note faded away, applause erupted and someone shouted, "Give us another one, our Jenny." The singer nodded then tossed her long, dark curls. The fiddler's foot bounced and the boy spread his accordion, fingers chasing a lively jig that soon had patrons clapping and joining in for the chorus.

Edward bought the second round during a lull in the music. The three men said little, in part due to fatigue, but mostly because their work was so highly confidential, they could have been accused of treason had anyone overheard them. Edward undid his top button and loosened his tie.

"Hot, isn't it?" he said.

"You're right. And rather thick in here." Steve gestured at the singer with a tilt of his glass. "She's a pretty little thing."

"Not as pretty as my Betty," said John.

By the time they finished their second drinks, the crowd had thinned a bit. "Time for one more?" asked John.

"I'm rather tired. Maybe we should head back," said Edward.

"So am I, but who knows when we'll have another night off." John lifted his shoulders to emphasize the point.

Steve checked his wallet. "My turn to buy."

Edward watched his friend approach the bar and lounge against one of the stools. Steve leaned close to get the barmaid's attention. Edward saw her wide red smile. The fiddler struck another tune.

Wondering at a faint sound he could hear above the noise of music and clapping, Edward cocked his head. Beyond the pub a whining gathered, spiralling, swirling, gaining in intensity. He cupped his ear and tried to separate the sound outside from the lively tune inside. The whine became a scream and suddenly he knew.

"Get down," he shouted. "Get down!"

Edward threw himself to the ground just as a corner of the pub blew apart and a deafening roar shook the ground. tossing tables and chairs about as though they were nothing more than toothpicks. Cries of terror echoed all around him then the windows exploded, launching thousands of glass projectiles across what was left of the room.

64 MARCH 1944

From Emily's bedroom where she was hanging freshly cleaned curtains, Ann heard the sound of knocking. She sighed. Leaving half the curtain dangling, she climbed down the short, rickety ladder and proceeded along the hall. More knocking.

"I'm coming," she shouted, shoes slapping each stair.

A man with wide shoulders and a brown briefcase stood on the front step. Though dressed in civilian clothes, Ann knew from the precisely trimmed hair and perfect knot of his tie that he was military.

"Mrs. Jamieson?"

"Yes."

"I'm Paul Hastings, a friend of Edward's. May I come in?"

Paul Hastings. General Hastings. Ann made the link to Edward's secret work. The appearance of such a senior officer could only mean one thing. The very thing every soldier's wife feared, every hour of the day.

Ann's face crumbled. "No, no, no," she said, clutching the

doorknob as if it were a lifeline.

He held up a hand. "It's not that, Mrs. Jamieson. May I come in?"

She covered her mouth and closed her eyes before taking a deep breath. Without a word she gestured towards the living room. All she could think of was the visit she and Edward made to tell Mrs. Paton of Larry's death. Paul Hastings closed the door and followed her. She sat on the sofa then stood again.

"Can I offer you something . . . something to drink?"

"No, thank you. I'm fine. Are your children home?" Ann shook her head. "Won't you sit down again?"

She sank down. "Please tell me what's happened, Mr. Hastings."

"There was an accident during a German bombing raid. A few planes dropped their loads before reaching London. Edward and two others were in a local pub when it happened. One of them was killed." Hastings cleared his throat. "Edward and the third colleague were injured and taken immediately to a military hospital. They're getting the best of care. I've spoken to one of the doctors who assured me Edward will recover. One leg is damaged and he sustained a severe concussion. For now, that's all I know."

Ann found it difficult to take a full breath. "Can he come home?"

"Not yet. The doctors won't release him until they're sure he's in the clear."

"But you said the doctors told you he'll recover."

"I'm sure they're just being cautious."

"Can I go over there to be with him?"

"I'm afraid not, Mrs. Jamieson. He'll be getting the best of care."

"You're General Hastings, aren't you?" The man nodded. "Did he finish the work you sent him over to do?"

The general raised his eyebrows. "Almost. Others are stepping in. He's a splendid man, one of our best." Hastings opened his briefcase. "He dictated a letter for you. I have a transcript with me." He handed her a folded piece of paper secured with a piece of tape and a business card. "My assistant knows how to reach me. But I will call you when I hear more. I'm sure you realize that no one must know where he is. Will you be all right, Mrs. Jamieson? I could wait until one of your children comes home."

Ann tried to steady her face. "No, Mr. Hastings. Thank you for coming."

Tears pricked her eyes. She rose to her feet with the hope that he would leave quickly. As soon as the door closed, she stifled a sob and tore the letter open.

*March 28*th

My dearest Ann,

I don't know exactly how this letter will reach you, but if you're reading it you will know that I'm in hospital. The doctors say that my leg will recover. For the moment it is suspended by an elaborate pulley and completely bandaged. I can wiggle two toes, which they tell me is a good sign. Other than a few deep cuts and a concussion, I am all right. One of my friends died in the blast, the other is here in the same hospital, although no one will tell me the extent of his injuries. I know there were other casualties.

We were in a pub. The first night we had off since my arrival. A lively spot with small tables and a huge fireplace. We were having a last drink before heading home. I wanted to leave earlier and now I curse myself for not insisting on it. XXXXX might still be alive if I had. I heard a faint buzzing, but the music was loud and no one paid any attention until it was too late.

I would like nothing better than to come home and see your beautiful face and Emily and Alex, however, the doctors won't let me leave until they are satisfied with my leg. I fear that might take weeks. Keep strong until I do come home and know that I love you.

Edward

A notecard had been clipped to the letter.

Dear Mrs. Jamieson, we are taking good care of your husband. The doctor is quite certain that he can save the leg. Yours sincerely, Nurse Juliette Cummings

Ann pressed the letter to her lips and began to cry.

* * *

The front door opened with a squeak. Sitting in the gloom of a late winter afternoon, Ann did not move from the sofa. She had been in the same spot ever since General Hastings had departed. Edward's letter, which she had reread several times, lay on the cushion beside her.

"Are you home, Mom?" Emily called out. A moment later she appeared in the living room. "Why are you sitting in the dark?" She stepped a little closer. "Are you okay?"

Ann shook her head. "Not really."

Emily sat down beside Ann. "You've been crying."

Ann nodded. Her throat felt constricted, as though full of dust, and words would not come. Her eyes stung.

Emily put her hand to her mouth. "Is something wrong with Daddy?"

Ann nodded again. She wanted to tell Emily about the general's visit but the phrases she had rehearsed had disappeared as soon as Emily walked through the door. Instead, she held out Edward's letter.

As Emily read, her eyebrows flicked and her eyes darkened. At one point Ann heard her gasp. "Oh no, Mom. I'm so sorry Alex and I weren't here. Daddy sounds all right though, doesn't he?"

Ann forced a word through her lips. "Maybe."

Emily took one of her mother's hands. "You're freezing. You need a whiskey. I'll just be a moment."

When she returned, Emily draped a shawl over Ann's shoulders and handed her a generous serving of rye whiskey. "Maybe you'll feel like talking when Alex gets home. I'm sure he'll be here soon."

"Dad told me England was dangerous," Alex said, after he had listened to Emily describe the situation and had read the letter for himself. "He thought the danger was in the big cities though, not the countryside. Are you going to be all right, Mom? Your cheeks are pale."

Emily and Alex's concern boosted Ann's spirits. She knew she had to pull herself together. Edward would expect her to. She cleared her throat.

"I'll tell you what happened." Ann relayed Hastings' afternoon visit, pausing now and again when she felt overwhelmed. "He said your father is getting the best care possible and that the doctors have assured him he'll recover. I'm sorry I was so upset."

"You were probably in shock, Mom," Emily said.

"I think you're right."

65 APRIL 1944

Paul Hastings telephoned two weeks later. After identifying himself, he wasted no time on pleasantries.

"I've had word that Edward's leg is healing and he's taken his first few steps. He's still convalescing, but they've moved him into a different wing of the hospital where the emphasis is on rehabilitation."

"That sounds encouraging. Will he . . . will he come home soon?"

"I knew you would want to know, so I asked the doctor, but he prefers to wait two more weeks before setting a date. If the leg continues to heal, Edward might be able to manage the travel by then. How are you bearing up?"

"I'm all right. My children have been keeping an eye on me. They're worried, of course, but I didn't show them what the nurse wrote."

"I wondered about that. Almost told my secretary not to include that note, but I knew that if I were in hospital, my wife would have wanted to know everything."

"I must be like your wife, then. Is there a way for me to reach him?"

"If you'd like to write a letter, I'll have it picked up tomorrow. I can get a message through, although someone will have to transcribe your words."

* * *

Knowing some stranger would see her letter, Ann wondered what to write. Every day since hearing the news, she had thanked God for Edward's life. The first night she had even sunk to her knees beside the bed to pray, just as she had when she was a child, just as she had taught Emily and Alex, the sight of their small fingers clasped together often bringing a lump to her throat. As she gave thanks for his life, she prayed for him to heal and come home safely and felt the hard bud of neglected love begin to unfurl.

Dearest Edward,

Every day I thank God you're alive. When Paul Hastings arrived at the house, you can imagine that I feared the worst. Of course, he hastened to reassure me otherwise; still, news of the explosion was a terrible shock. I shudder at the thought that you might not have been one of the lucky ones.

Although the general calls every few days with an update on your condition, I wish I could be there and see with my own eyes that you are truly all right. And I hate the thought of you being alone in hospital.

Today Hastings said that you have taken a few steps. What wonderful progress! I know how impatient you are and how frustrated you will be if there are any setbacks, but don't push yourself too hard. Give your body time to heal properly.

Ann added several stories about Emily and Alex as well as news about Edward's family.

My darling, I am so very, very happy to know that you are safe.

Come home to me.

Much love, Ann

When she finished writing, Ann folded the pages in thirds and placed them in an envelope, ready for Alex and Emily to add brief notes. The following morning a young corporal picked up the letter. As she handed it over, she imagined Edward reading her slightly stilted words and hoped he would understand.

News of Edward's improving condition buoyed her spirits and she arrived at Signals Welfare in a flattering shade of blue, a touch of rouge on her cheeks. With several new women helping out, the monthly volunteer schedule needed revision, and after making tea, Ann sat down at her desk and began to work. She had developed a system, colour coding her regulars in green, occasional volunteers in blue and newcomers in red so she could be certain to have at least one regular on hand to help new volunteers. With the colours, she could see gaps at a glance. When Angela tapped on the door, she was still moving small squares of paper around.

"You startled me."

"Sorry, Ann. There's someone here to see you."

"Who is it?"

Angela leaned close. "I don't know, but it's a man. And he's in uniform."

For an instant Ann wondered how Paul Hastings would know where to find her, but quickly discarded that thought as preposterous. She pushed her chair back and went out to the front entrance. Though the man had his back to her, there was no mistaking the line of his shoulders or his thick, tufted hair. Her breath caught in her throat.

Ann breathed a sigh of relief. Both of the men she loved were still alive. Perhaps she would not be punished after all.

"Richard. What are you doing here? I thought you were in England."

"I've only got a few days. I called your house but there was no answer and I thought you might be downtown." Richard gripped his peaked cap and turned it around and around. "Can you meet me for lunch?"

Although Angela pretended to be occupied with filing various papers in a narrow three-drawer cabinet, Ann knew she could hear every word, and to avoid prompting gossip, she agreed to meet Richard at the Victory Café.

Back in her office, Ann's hands shook as she resumed the task of moving coloured squares around the schedule. She had not expected to see Richard again. They had agreed. *Damn,* she thought.

Memories she had tucked away burst like a geyser, hot and dangerous. The way he looked at her, touched her, made love to her. Their easy companionship. His eyes bright with laughter. The passion he had for fighting tyranny. The care and affection for those he trained. The concert they attended. His sadness as she had turned away from him that very last time.

She could have refused him, but he would just come to the office again. Better to get it over with.

"Damn, damn, damn," she muttered under her breath so Angela could not hear.

* * *

"I know I promised," he said, even before she took her coat off. "But the last six months have been hell without you."

Richard had chosen a corner table positioned at the back of the room and flanked by a column on one side and a large potted plant on the other. The nearest table was a discreet distance away, occupied by two old men, one talking loudly in between slurps of soup, the other cupping his ear to listen.

Ann was angry; angry that she had been coerced into seeing him, angry that Richard had appeared without warning. Angry to feel desire stir.

"We agreed," she said stabbing a pin through her hat to secure it once more. The pin pricked her head and she winced. "We ended things. You can't just show up whenever you want."

"I'm sorry. I know I promised. And I didn't write you, did

I? All that time I wanted to, but I didn't." He looked sad and hopeful at the same time.

"Richard, we have to move on. I have to move on. I can't save my marriage if you're lingering in the wings. I just can't. You aren't being fair."

A blue-eyed waitress appeared, slapping menus down in front of them. Pouring two glasses of water, she seemed oblivious to the emotions billowing across the table.

"There's nothing fair in the way I feel about you," he whispered as the waitress walked away. "Don't you think I've tried to forget? I thought being far away would help, but it didn't. You're in my head. Every day."

"Why are you back in Canada?" Ann sought a safe topic.

"To learn about a new weapon for our troops. I've spent two days with the manufacturer to make sure I know everything about it. We're going to be using them . . ." He stopped. "I can't tell you why exactly."

"When is this mess going to end? I need something to hang onto. We all do. The news is confusing, although it looks like Hitler's having trouble in a few spots. I hoped Italy would turn things, but we seem to be bogged down there."

"We are." He covered her hand with his. "Please don't pull away. Please, Ann."

As always, his touch was soft and warm and she left her hand where it was while he told her about Italy and Russia, successes in Crimea, India and New Guinea.

"These may seem like small inroads, but Germany is also reeling from the bombing of their cities and factories. They've bombed London in recent months and the rumour is they're running out of planes and have little capacity to build more. Japan remains a problem. If the Americans could divert manpower and ships from the Pacific, that would make a big difference."

Ann had closed her eyes when Richard spoke of the bombing of London. She knew firsthand about those bombs. After Edward was injured she had read everything she could find.

"But they can't. Even though Pearl Harbor happened more than two years ago."

Richard nodded. Ann withdrew her hand and stared at a bowl of mushroom soup. Her appetite had vanished, but she forced herself to take a few mouthfuls while Richard ate his sandwich.

"Do you have time for tea?" he said when the waitress re-appeared.

She checked her watch. "I have a little more time." She owed him that, at least.

Leaving the restaurant, reflected light dazzled in the chrome of nearby cars. Richard glanced towards her and then away. Alongside the street, apple trees waved tiny buds in the breeze. Ann knew he was oblivious to the hints of pink that promised renewal and hope.

They moved aside to make room for a woman pushing a baby carriage. As they approached the corner, Richard tugged her arm so she would stop and face him. For a long time he said nothing. His gaze flicked up and down before returning to her face.

"Thank you," he said, close enough for her to feel his breath.

Ann's eyes filled with tears. She touched his cheek and walked away.

66 MAY 1944

"What time will Dad be home?" Alex said, glancing down the street at an approaching car.

"Not until five or so. Mr. Hastings is picking him up."

Ann had argued with Paul Hastings, saying that she had a right to meet Edward's plane, but her request had been denied and she imagined the reason had something to do with Edward's secret role. Although he made an attempt to be affable, Hastings seemed like a tough man, accustomed to command. No doubt he would demand a briefing from Edward, as soon as they left the airport.

Alex had just cut the lawn. Emily was inside preparing vegetables while Ann dug the front garden, loosening the soil around the hostas, hydrangeas, irises and rose bushes and snipping tulips to place in a vase on the dining room table. Roast pork was in the oven. Tomorrow night they would visit Edward's family, but tonight she wanted just the four of them to be together.

Edward had been gone almost three months. His latest letter said that he was walking on his own with a limp. It said nothing about other wounds and she presumed that these would be well healed. He would hate to be coddled in any fashion and Ann tried to imagine treating him as though surviving a bomb blast was a trivial event.

All week she had put the house in order, tidying Edward's clothes, ironing a fresh pair of pyjamas, plumping pillows, shaking out curtains, filing paperwork. She had even cleaned Edward's study and purchased a fresh package of pipe tobacco. After working in the garden, she took a bath, sprinkling scented salts in the water and allowing the heat to soothe her muscles.

How would he act after so long away? Would they be the same with one another or different? She had no idea.

After lunch with Richard, she had pushed aside thoughts of him and instead concentrated on her feelings for Edward. Each evening she brought out old albums and remembered the life they had built. Wedding photos, baby pictures, cottage trips, birthdays, Montreal, Christmas—all were organized with care, their edges tucked into small black corners that Ann had painstakingly glued into place year after year. Every night she touched the bracelet he had given her for Christmas.

A few minutes before five she was downstairs, dressed in a light brown skirt and patterned blouse. The skirt flattered her legs and rustled in a pleasing way and the blouse with its soft, floppy bow made her feel feminine. She wore a necklace and Edward's bracelet.

The crunch of gravel signalled his arrival. As he got out of the car, Edward held the driver's arm, a smile pasted on his face. He used a cane and grimaced as his left leg touched the ground. Knowing he would hate her to fuss or hover, she hurried down the walk and greeted him with a long hug and brief kiss.

"I'm so happy you're home."

Edward's reply was lost in the clamour of Alex's boisterous

greeting and Emily's chattering. Alex took his father's suitcase and Emily his arm, and step by step they progressed into the house.

"Sit here, Dad. I'll get you a drink. Would you like scotch?" Emily said. When he nodded, Emily headed for the kitchen. "What about you, Mom?"

"Yes please, dear." Ann called out to Emily's disappearing back. "Let me help," she said, slipping Edward's jacket off his shoulders, noting the fatigue evident in his pale lips and slumping posture.

He gave her a wry smile. "Some things are still difficult."

"You're tired. I have a roast planned, but there's no rush if you would like to rest for a while."

"I feel like the stuffing has been knocked out of me. The doctor warned me that two long flights would be exhausting. I'd been lying around for so long, I thought I would have lots of energy."

Ann moved closer and took his hand, examining the long tapered fingers. "You have a scar." She pointed to a spot on his wrist.

"I have a number of scars. And a leg that doesn't work."

Edward's tight jaw and flared nostrils warned her not to offer soothing platitudes. "Your mother is happy to have you home. I think she's invited the entire family for dinner tomorrow."

"What did you tell her?"

"That you had an unfortunate automobile accident while away on military business."

He nodded. "Good."

Edward withdrew his hand as Emily returned with their drinks and Alex thumped down the stairs.

"I put away what seemed to be clean, plus your uniforms and shoes. I've left the rest for Mom to sort out." Alex seemed pleased with his resourcefulness. "Dad, you have to tell us all about England. Were there soldiers everywhere? And Americans?"

Edward's tight mouth relaxed and he looked fondly at his son. "Let me start with the flights over."

Edward indulged Alex with a lengthy discussion of the two planes he had taken, weather conditions during each flight, the scene at Gander airport, the DC-3 instrument panel all the while answering a host of eager questions. Then he described the military presence in every town and city he had visited.

"Did you meet a lot of local people?" Emily asked.

"Some. In the village stores and pubs and, of course, the nurses and doctors."

"How are they bearing up?" Emily said. "I can't imagine what it must be like living under threat day by day."

Ann remained quiet, content to watch her children and husband and listen to their chatter. After so many weeks on edge, she could finally let go. Edward answered several more of Emily's questions before turning back to Alex.

"How did it feel when the bomb exploded?" Alex said.

"Alex, that's an inappropriate question." Neither Emily, nor I, nor your father, I suspect, want to pursue that gruesome topic."

"It's all right, Ann. The answer is that I have no idea. One moment I was listening to music and the next moment I was in a hospital bed, bandaged up and aching all over. The doctor was shining a light in my eye. It reminded me of . . ."

Ann knew he was thinking of being wounded in the first war. "That's enough you two. Your father is tired. You can grill him with more questions tomorrow."

Edward chuckled. "They're rather like the Spanish inquisition, aren't they? I wouldn't want to be a spy caught by Alex and Emily."

What an odd thing for him to say, Ann thought.

* * *

Edward sank gratefully onto the bed and looked around. After such a long absence their bedroom felt unfamiliar, feminine touches and soft colours and hints of lilac so different from the way he had lived in Beaulieu and later at the hospital. Ann's lacquered jewellery box glowed in the lamplight next to bright silver brushes and a perfume atomizer with a small blue bulb and tassel. His own dresser top was precisely organized, just the way he preferred. A box of cufflinks and his father's watch were on the left, a book he had been reading on the right next to an ivory shoehorn. He wondered whether Ann had tidied it in advance of his return or whether she had not touched his things while he was gone.

He removed one shoe and then the other, pushing them aside with the toes of his good foot. He stood, weight mainly on his right leg, to unbuckle his belt, undo his zipper and let his pants fall. If he got into bed quickly, Ann would not see the ugly red scar travelling from hip to knee or the others marking his torso like weeping craters. The doctor had explained that stitching deep, irregular wounds required speed, not delicacy, in order to halt the bleeding.

With no physical scars from the first war, it surprised Edward to know how damaged these made him feel. Psychological scars did not make people stare or engender the kind of clucking sympathy that made him feel diminished. Except for Eric, Ann and his mother, no one knew of the nightmares that had plagued him for years. Everyone would see him differently now.

"Do you need help, dear?" Ann's voice called up the stairs.

"No, I'm fine."

She would respect his desire to manage on his own, nonetheless, he hurried to remove the rest of his clothes then put on the fresh pyjamas she had laid out for him. He limped to the bathroom and a few minutes later slipped beneath the covers and propped himself against two pillows so he could read.

Sentences blurred as he remembered Steve Shelley and John Foster and The Fiddler's Roost. The story given to the press was that a German pilot had gone astray and dropped a bomb intended for London. But occasionally Edward wondered whether Hitler's generals had figured out that Beaulieu was more than a sleepy English village. Steve was dead and John would never see again.

Edward let the book fall against his chest. He remembered Steve insisting it was his turn to pay. So it was Steve who had been standing at the bar next to a rack of beer pulls, talking to the barmaid with plump red cheeks while two elderly gentlemen perched on stools nearby. All four were dead.

Every day Edward cursed the decision to have one more drink. He had the senior rank and if he had insisted, they would have departed before the blast. Steve would be alive, John would not be blind and Edward would not be scarred forever. Beyond this feeling of guilt was the fear that Ann would consider him damaged.

Guilt and fear had to be stifled. Work would help; it always had in the past. Travelling home from the airport, Paul had told him that all agents were in place and Operation Fortitude was already having success.

"The Germans have always believed that Pas-de-Calais is the most likely place to mount a cross channel attack, because it's the shortest route from England and makes sense for our supply lines and air support. They're taking the bait hook, line and sinker."

Paul also said they were eager to have him back at Camp X, particularly Jim Ferguson. "With Shelley and Foster gone, we need you quite urgently, Edward," he had said. "But you be the judge of your stamina. If you need more time, we'll understand. Lovely wife you have, by the way. I admire the way she's handled things."

Hastings was right. Ann had handled things beautifully. The house was immaculate, Alex content, Emily's sadness clearly easing. Paperwork tidied away, bills paid. Lawn and garden blossoming. All the comforts ready.

Perhaps she no longer needed him. Three months was a long time to be absent from one another, particularly in a marriage frayed from tension. They had only eased that tension a fraction before he went away, and now he was damaged goods, a scarred, limping man who would never walk properly again. He knew he should talk to Ann and explain how he felt. *Soon.* he thought, *I'll be able to tell her soon.*

67 MAY 1944

When Edward told Ann he would be away for one night, she looked at him as though he had lost his mind. He broke the news while sipping coffee in the living room where Ann had helped him ease into his chair after dinner.

"But sweetheart, you've only been back a few days. You're tired. Your leg is clearly painful. Why can't you wait a bit longer?"

"General Hastings . . ." Edward stopped. There was no point in explaining that Paul Hastings expressly asked him to come to the Camp as soon as possible. "I'm needed. My leg will be fine."

"And what about Dave Jenkins? Doesn't he need you here?"

"I've spoken to Dave."

"I see. Well, I suppose you have to do what you have to do." Ann took a sip of coffee.

"You're upset with me."

"I'm worried about you. Not upset with you. And I've only had you back for a few days. But let's talk about something else. Tell me how the English are coping with everything."

Ann put a bright look on her face as he told her about some of the villagers he had encountered, their faces calm and their attitude resigned in the face of so much turbulence. Later, while he lay in bed with his book unopened on the bedside table, she packed a small suitcase, moving briskly to fold and store each item in its usual location.

"I'll ask Alex to bring it down in the morning," she said, snapping the lid closed.

Ann was already downstairs when he woke. Porridge was waiting in the kitchen along with coffee strong enough to keep him alert for hours, just the way he preferred. She kissed him good-bye, a light brushing of her lips against his.

"I'll be back tomorrow night." Ann looked at him through questioning eyes and he knew she doubted his word. "I will, I promise."

"Good to have you back, sir." Saunders stood beside the passenger door.

"Thank you, Saunders. Just give me a hand for a moment, will you? I'm still adjusting to this bum leg."

Ann waved as Saunders backed down the drive.

Bright skies and vivid greens accompanied the car along country roads devoid of traffic. Except for an occasional tractor, the peacefulness contrasted sharply with England, where roads bristled with army vehicles beneath the gloom of low-hanging clouds. In London and the towns near Beaulieu, people went about their business with determined cheerfulness, accustomed to sandbags shielding monuments, the absence of road signs, half-destroyed buildings paying tribute to British stamina, tidy piles of rubble, the Home Guard patrolling streets and byways, women dressed for heavy work, and shops with barely stocked shelves. Edward admired their willingness to look fear in the eye and barely flinch.

Turning into Camp X felt like a second homecoming. The

apple orchard was blossoming and Mac greeted him like a
long-lost friend even while demanding his identification and
the daily password. Men jogged single file along the hill in
front of a web of Hydra antennae. The air smelled of freshly
mown hay.

Saunders drew to a stop beyond a line of chestnut trees
near the farmhouse and opened Edward's door. "I'll take your
bag to barracks, sir."

Edward considered protesting, but Dr. Lewis said he would
have to allow for some adjustments if he wanted his leg to heal
properly.

"Don't be a fool," the doctor, an ascetic looking man who
the nurses called The Monk, had added. "Major trauma requires rest and proper rehabilitation. Have your doctor send
you to a specialist as soon as you return."

Edward was certain Dr. Lewis' definition of soon would
differ from his own. In the meantime, he would let Saunders
carry his bag.

Once inside the farmhouse, the familiar embraced him: tartan curtains, the clatter of typewriters, lingering hints of pipe
tobacco, dog-eared magazines and the squeak of wooden floor-
boards. Edward looked around and smiled.

"There you are, sir. Saunders said you were already here.
The general is waiting for you and I believe Jimmy is with
him. You'd better go on up." Betty MacLean gestured towards
the stairs. "Can you manage?"

"Definitely."

Dr. Lewis had not specifically forbidden Edward to climb
stairs. Taking the steps one at a time by placing his right foot
first then swinging his left up to join it, he felt like a baby
learning to walk. At the landing, he waited a few moments
to catch his breath and allow the throbbing pain to subside
before proceeding to Paul's office. Bent over a thick document,
the general waved him in. Jim Ferguson acknowledged Edward with a wide smile and both men waited for the general
to speak.

"D-Day is two weeks from today. I don't have to tell you what that means. Agents in the field continue to perform well, although progress in Italy is much slower than we had hoped. If the landing is successful, we'll begin the push across Europe, which means further activities required in places like Poland and Romania, as well as France. I asked Jim to prepare a game plan. Stuart, who is one of our new boys, will join us as soon as he's available. But Edward, it's crucial for you to admit what you can and cannot handle. And if you want out at this point, I won't stand in your way."

After two months of inaction, the familiar surge of purpose rose.

"I'm in. Nothing will keep me out of it now."

* * *

Though Jim Ferguson needed him to stay longer, Edward kept his promise to Ann and returned the following evening. Dusk lingered in crimson streaks and burnt clouds, but he was too preoccupied with the outline of a training program to notice. Espionage was more and more deadly; radio operators rarely lasted longer than six months. Demand was inexhaustible.

The team agreed that securing additional trainers was one task Edward could handle better than the others, a task he planned to begin as soon as he had the opportunity to speak with Dave Jenkins about a leave of absence. Paul Hastings had assured him that Jenkins would be agreeable. Edward wondered whether he could avoid telling Ann.

"You're home." A small smile crossed her face when he came through the door. "I kept dinner waiting for you. Are you hungry?"

"I am."

He forced heartiness into his voice. What he desired most was sleep, but Ann deserved better. Being in hospital had provided ample opportunity to think, and Edward had returned time and again to the subject of his wife and their marriage.

He missed Ann, not merely her presence but her lively company and sense of humour. He missed their banter and the unspoken understanding developed over the years, at times knowing the other better than their own selves. He missed the way she challenged his opinions and her optimistic outlook on life. Before the war Ann saw their lives as full of possibilities; now her view seemed increasingly dour and he was aware that his actions had changed her; secrets and absence had created small fissures that had grown into deep crevices.

"Emily and Alex have already eaten."

"Just us then."

While occupying several minutes with inconsequential conversation, Ann seemed to be studying him and he had the sense that she would soon change the topic.

"Can you tell me what it was like?"

Edward put down his fork. He knew exactly what she meant, but pretended otherwise to give himself a few seconds to think. "It?" he said.

"Edward Jamieson, you know what I mean. The explosion. I want to hear about it. In the last war you bottled everything away and we know where that led. Tell me, darling, please."

It might have been the word "darling" that prompted him to tell the truth or the fact that honesty might be the only way to restore what they once had. Edward steadied himself with a deep breath.

"It was dreadful. Steve and John and I had gone to the local pub for drinks. We'd been working nonstop for weeks and we all needed a break. Other men had told us about the music at that pub, so we went for a few drinks after dinner.

"We'd had two rounds but Steve insisted it was his turn to buy. He was leaning against the bar when the music started again. I remember watching him talk to a barmaid wearing bright red lipstick. I still remember the lipstick. I heard a noise. Nothing significant at first, and with the music so loud, by the time I realized what it was, it was too late. I shouted and threw myself to the floor just like we did in the first war.

Maybe that was what saved me.

"As the bomb hit, I heard shouts and screams and the sound of shattering glass. Then nothing else. I must have been unconscious after that."

Her expression grim, Ann held his hand. "Did you wake up in the hospital?"

"I did. Apparently, I was out for more than twenty-four hours."

"Did that include the operation?"

He nodded. "The doctor told me it was a difficult operation."

"I know. One of the nurses added a postscript to your first letter saying that they hoped . . . they hoped to save your leg. It made me weep to know how badly wounded you were and I could do nothing for you. Nothing." Her voice trailed away as tears filled her eyes.

Edward squeezed her hand. "I didn't want you to know how bad it was."

* * *

For the first week, Edward was always in bed before her with pyjamas on and the sheet pulled up to his chin. Some nights he was already asleep and on the nights when he was awake, he did not turn to embrace her, nor did he offer more than a brief kiss as she slid into bed. Ann was so pleased to have him home she said nothing about his behaviour, but when the second week passed in the same manner, she began to worry.

"Have you heard from Hannah?" Edward stifled a yawn as they sat in the living room after dinner.

"Yesterday. We try to talk every two or three weeks. They've had another letter from Michael, so she told me all about that. He said conditions have deteriorated but the details were censored. She sounded more worried than usual."

"Hmmph. I can imagine they're keeping as much food as possible for their own troops. I don't know anything about

POW camps, but I could ask a few questions."

"Could you? I'm sure Bob and Hannah would be glad to have any information you can find. Bob doesn't have the contacts you do. Everyone else in the family is fine. Bob has plans to be in Toronto next week."

"I'll give him a call. Did you tell them about my accident?" Ann nodded and Edward grunted in acknowledgement. "What about David?"

"Linda says he's back in England. She and Eric are pleased. I imagine they think he's much safer there. Do you?"

"Do I what?"

"Think he's safer there."

Her husband paused before answering. Concern flashed across his face. "Could be. Unfortunately there's always another action planned."

"Sounds like you know something."

Edward's look was cool. "You know the answer to that." He set aside his book. "I think I'll go up to bed."

"I'll come with you."

"It's early for you, isn't it?"

Ann merely smiled and said nothing. She proceeded upstairs ahead of him and down the corridor to peek into Emily's room. "Will you turn out the lights, dear? Your father and I are going to bed early."

When she got to their room, Edward was staring out the window. Ann closed the door.

"It's not pretty," he said.

"What's not pretty? The view out the window?"

"No. The scars on my body."

"Is that why you've been avoiding me?"

"Yes." He turned away from the window and faced her.

"I thought you didn't want to be with me and I was driving myself crazy wondering why." Ann wrapped her arms around him. "I'm just so happy to have you back. Don't you know that? Every day I worried. Every single day. And when Paul Hastings came to our door, for a moment I imagined the worst had happened. Edward . . ." She tilted her head. His dark, sombre eyes seemed larger than normal; his cheeks drooped as though carrying the weight of the world. "It doesn't matter to me. You matter."

Ann knew not to push. He would show her in his own time. Too much coddling and he would back away. Patience was the only avenue open to her. Edward had to deal with difficulties his way, not hers. He leaned his cheek against her head and held her for a moment.

"I'll undress in the bathroom."

68 JUNE 1944

As they did virtually every night, Ann, Emily and Alex sat in the living room after dinner with the radio on. First the announcer gave the official time signal and then listed a few matters of national significance. All three leaned forward when the announcer reported that Germany's Caesar line in Italy had finally collapsed and Kesselring was in retreat.

"That's very good news, isn't it, Mom? They should be able to take Rome soon."

Ann nodded. "That's what the paper said this morning. Let's listen to the news from London."

A thin crackling sound emanated from the radio. *"This is Graham Follett, speaking to you from London. We heard and saw our portents in the sky today as we did yesterday and the day before, the solid booming of many engines as clouds of bombers passed overhead. We've wakened to that sound on many mornings now and we know what it means. It's the rising prelude to the coming operations in Europe, and sometimes it sets the sky in such a mind-filling roar that we're apt to wonder "has it started?" There's no denying the acute sense of imminence that manifests itself in spite of all the traditional British nonchalance. There seems to be some sort of mass telepathy among people conscious that they are living on the extreme edge of tremendous events, and this weekend found everybody progressively, and a little more perceptively, keyed up to the big preoccupation, the question of when it's going to happen."*

Alex turned towards his mother. "The invasion has to come soon. With all that bombing, do you think Hitler knows when it's going to happen?"

"I don't know, dear. I hope our armies use diversionary tactics to keep them guessing."

Suddenly she knew Edward's trip to England must have had something to do with the invasion. He had sworn an oath. He trained people for dangerous assignments. Two men and a woman had died overseas. Espionage? Was that too far-fetched? Wireless operators who worked behind enemy lines? After all, his specialty was communications.

During the past few days, Edward had been wound up so tight, she thought he might burst. *Perhaps he knows what's coming*, she thought. *Something has to happen soon.*

* * *

On the evening of June sixth, Edward and his family remained glued to the radio as news of the D-Day landings came through. Winston Churchill spoke, his growling voice riveting.

"During the night and the early hours of this morning, the first of the series of landings in force upon the European Continent has taken place. An immense armada of upwards of four thousand ships, together with several thousand smaller craft, crossed the Channel."

Like a sail filled with buoyant breezes, every word Churchill spoke lifted Edward's spirits. *We'll do it*, he thought. *The end is finally in sight.*

As Churchill continued Edward recalled the fall of To-bruk when the British Prime Minister had spoken. The man's gravelly voice with its slow steady beat combined with evoc-ative images and simple words still had the power to inspire. "*Massed airborne landings . . . vast operation . . . formidable danger and difficulty . . . tactical surprise . . .*"

Edward had played a part in that element of surprise. He had a limp and scars all over his body to prove it.

When Churchill finished, Alex was the first to speak. "What does it mean, Dad?"

"It's the invasion of Europe we've all been waiting for. Churchill and Roosevelt must believe that the time is ripe. I saw evidence of troop buildup while I was in England, but the scale of our attack is incredible. And it looks like the Germans were caught napping."

"That's fantastic news, isn't it?" Alex's tone was part ques-tion, part assertion.

"Definitely."

"Why is this different from Dieppe?" Alex, who sat in his usual spot on the floor, turned around to look at his father.

"Well, one difference is the single command structure under General Eisenhower. Churchill mentioned that in his speech, didn't he? It helps eliminate confusion and rivalry between the countries and allows clearer communication of successes and failures as our troops attack. Imagine playing football without a quarterback."

"That wouldn't work very well," Alex said.

"You're right. Same thing on a massive scale in war. Be-yond Eisenhower, there's the combined strength of American and British forces and all the bombing we did leading up to today. And the element of surprise. "

"It's amazing to think that Hitler didn't know where we were going to attack," said Emily.

"You're right, sweetheart. It's amazing."

* * *

Broadcast the following day, firsthand accounts transported Edward to the heat of battle. He heard the shells bursting up and down the beach and felt the confusion of hundreds and hundreds of landing craft jockeying close enough for troops to disembark; he pushed through chest-high water, muscles straining to make the beach and passed the wounded and dead because to stop would have been suicide. He was the one who tramped across the pebbled beach to claw his way up sloping hills while snipers' bullets zinged left and right and planes droned overhead releasing bombs from gaping underbellies. He imagined reaching the top to watch parachutes mass like a swarm of welcome clouds, dropping soldier after soldier onto nearby fields as dawn emerged from gloom to pearl grey and then to golden rose.

Edward saw and felt and heard it all.

"What will our armies do next?" Ann laid her hand on Edward's arm.

"They'll begin to liberate Europe from that monster," he said.

Edward knew what was required. British and American troops had to push south and east from the landing zones. Progress would depend on the success of German counterattacks. Hitler would throw everything he could at them.

69 JUNE 1944

Four nights after the Normandy landings, the telephone rang. Edward peered over the newspaper and watched Ann's face shrink into sadness.

"Oh, no! Yes . . . yes . . . Eric, I can't believe it . . . yes . . . yes, we can . . . Edward and I will be right over."

"What is it?" He set the newspaper aside.

Her hand resting on the telephone, Ann did not move. "David was killed in the D-Day landings. They don't know anything else. I said . . . I said we would come right over."

"Oh. God." Each word was a sigh.

"We should tell the children," Ann said.

Edward closed his eyes for a moment. "You're right. But . . ." The news would crack open Emily's barely healed wound. She had only recently begun to smile again, to lose the ghostly pallor caused by Jack's death, to emerge from the grey cocoon of her bedroom.

Ann called to them. "Alex and Emily, can you come downstairs? Your father and I are in the living room."

Edward heard muffled sounds and brief chatter as Emily and Alex emerged from their bedrooms then soft footsteps mingled with large clumping ones.

"What's wrong?" Emily said.

"Sit down, dear." Emily sat upright at the very edge of the chair by the fireplace, her favourite chair for reading, a place where she could curl her feet beneath her and sit for hours.

"Eric Andrews just called. They've had very bed news. David was with the landing force on Juno beach. He died in action. Your mother and I are going straight over to their house but we knew you would want to know."

"David? No, no, no, not David," Alex said.

"I'm afraid so," Edward said.

Emily seemed to shut down, her shoulders hunched and hands lying limply in her lap. "Why," she said.

"There's no answer to that, sweetheart." Ann perched on the armrest of Emily's chair and put an arm around her. "There's no answer to any of this."

"He was like my older brother," Alex said. His nose had reddened and he rubbed the tears from his eyes. "Sarah and Robert must be feeling terrible."

"Would you like to come with us?"

Alex looked at Emily. "I think I'll stay here with Emily. Is that all right with you, Em?"

Emily said nothing.

* * *

As the Buick rolled into the Andrews' driveway, Eric opened the front door. In the fading light, he appeared shrunken and old, his tie loosely askew, arms hanging without purpose. Ann rushed up the path and hugged him hard.

"Where's Linda?" she said.

"Living room." Eric made no move.

With someone else Edward might have shaken hands, a warm, firm grasp meant to indicate deep sympathy, but this was Eric, the man who had endured war with him, who would have died to keep him safe and who ultimately helped him recover. Edward put his arm around him and led him inside like a lost child.

* * *

At the memorial service during a moving solo of *The Lord is My Shepherd*, a few tears rolled down Edward's face. When the music finished, the minister nodded and Edward limped towards the lectern. He had the honour of doing the eulogy for the son of his best friend, a young man Edward had known since birth. When Eric had asked him, he had said he could think of no one else who meant more to their family. Edward cleared his throat and glanced at those assembled.

"We have much to be thankful for in David's short life," he began.

Edward spoke of childhood antics where David was the ringleader, other children following him wherever he went, doing exactly as instructed. He recalled episodes of innocent mischief, including the time David organized a group to collect apples in cover of darkness from a farmer's orchard. He spoke of David's teenage years as he captained the high school hockey team to its first victory in three years. He spoke of his academic success, his kindness, his dedication to family and his willingness to serve his country.

As he spoke, he saw Ann sitting behind Linda and Eric, holding Emily's hand, occasionally dabbing a handkerchief beneath her eyes, but otherwise stoic. Next to Emily, Alex sat upright, looking neither left nor right, his suit immaculate, his black tie knotted tight, hair slicked back. David was the older brother Alex never had.

* * *

While light glowed in neighbouring houses, night gathered its cloak of protection. Sitting on the back porch, he held Ann's hand and took momentary comfort from the soft scent of roses and the low chirp of a bullfrog.

"Will they ever heal?" Ann's voice croaked with grief.

"I don't imagine you ever recover from losing a child."

Ann's sigh was jagged, edged with sorrow. "You spoke very well. Perhaps it will have helped."

"Perhaps."

"I'll visit tomorrow."

He rubbed his thumb across her hand. "That's a good idea."

Edward knew the hole in their friends' lives would last a lifetime, threatening to swallow them up at the sound of a voice like David's, his favourite song, the sight of a similar profile, the touch and scent of his clothes that would, no doubt, be kept for years with the ridiculous hope that he might walk through the door one day.

70 JULY 1944

The sound of weeping woke him, muffled sobs from some other part of the house. Edward reached out a hand. The space beside him was wrinkled but cool to the touch. He raised himself onto one arm, squeezed his eyes closed and opened them again. Another sob, this time followed by a hiccup and a sharply drawn breath. He threw off the sheet then padded to the doorway and looked along the hall, where soft light spilled beneath the guest room door.

"What's wrong, sweetheart?"

Ann's back faced him and she did not turn. "I don't know. Everything, I suppose. I couldn't sleep so I left the bed, but I couldn't sleep here either. I've tried to read. Nothing makes sense anymore. Nothing."

Edward sat on the edge of the bed and touched her shoulder. "Is it David?"

Ann nodded. "And Linda. And Michael. And Jack, and Hannah. And all the sad, sad women I've met. And you. And this whole bloody mess. I can't stand it. Really. Edward. I can't bear any more of it."

He lifted the covers and lay down beside her then pulled her into his arms. She leaned against him, stifling another sob. Crickets chirped and the birch outside the window made a shushing sound. The curtain billowed like a slow moving ghost. He kissed her neck.

"We're making progress. Paris is ours now. Soon we'll be pushing into Belgium and then into the Netherlands. Russia is squeezing Hitler's Eastern Front. Germany is retreating north in Italy. Troops are landing in the south of France. I was looking at a map this week. It's slow but steady." He kept his tone gentle.

"What if someone else dies? Like Alan. I don't think I can do it anymore. Be cheerful and soothing and try to solve everyone's problems. I'm so tired."

"I know. You're exhausted. I see it in your face every day. I'm sorry, sweetheart. Sorry that I've been away so often. I should have helped you more."

Since D-Day he had known it was only a matter of time, further deaths a necessary prerequisite in the march towards peace. Accustomed to a world of secrecy, he had failed to share his views with Ann. Why had he allowed his military role to take precedence over his role as a husband? Surely he could have made more effort to calm Ann's fears and ease the day-to-day stress. She deserved better. His behaviour had driven her away. He knew that now. He could have lost her. Or perhaps he already had. Would she ever be the same? Would *they* ever be the same? He knew he had to try.

Edward stroked her arm. "Would you like to come back to bed now?"

"Will you hold me so I can get back to sleep?"

"Of course I will."

* * *

A few nights later, she nestled into his arms again. "Linda came to the centre today. She didn't stay very long, but I think it's a good sign, don't you?"

"A very good sign."

"Healing is a long process."

"You're right."

Ann turned so she could see his face. "And are you healing?"

"A bit. My leg has more strength. Not as painful as it was."

"Will you show me now?"

He stiffened. He knew exactly what she meant. For almost three months he had kept his wounds hidden. All that time they had not made love, for he was afraid of her pity and the sorrow she would be unable to hide. The room was dark, nothing but vague shadows cast along the wall. She was his wife. Who else could he show? Maybe showing Ann the damage was part of repairing their love.

He sat up and unbuttoned his pyjama top. She slipped it off his shoulders, tracing her hands across his chest, his shoulders and arms. She knelt beside him and kissed the scar beneath his collarbone, then the one that had come close to puncturing his good lung. He closed his eyes as she moved to his back, which was peppered with small bumps where shards of window glass had penetrated his skin. The doctors had had to dig each piece of glass out one by one, and sometimes when he moved in a particular fashion, he thought they had missed a few. Her hands and lips were everywhere.

She undid the drawstring of his pants.

"No," he said.

Ann ignored him, undoing both buttons and wiggling the pants off. She touched the scar that ran from his hip to his knee, feeling the raised ridge and jagged line. She bent her head and kissed every inch then knelt in front of him again, her mouth close to his.

"Will you make love to me?"

71 SEPTEMBER 1944

In September Edward took a week's vacation, his first time off in more than two years. He and Ann went to a cottage on Sparrow Lake, just the two of them.

Both the lake and the air remained warm, and they spent quiet days reading, fishing, sitting on the dock, occasionally swimming to a raft anchored twenty feet from shore where they lay in the sun. For a few days they talked of family and friends and the war's progress towards victory. It was clear Hitler was on the road to defeat.

While taking long walks along narrow dirt roads, Ann picked wildflowers, assembling little bunches of white, blue and yellow to place on various window ledges and on the kitchen table. They watched the birds heading south, exclaimed over vivid autumn colours, savoured the occasional wild berry, noted squirrels gathering nuts for the winter and listened to the cry of the loon. It was enough just to be.

Edward led them down various footpaths, often ending at

someone's vacant cottage, where they sat on warm, flat rocks jutting out into the water, or paddle their feet along the shore. Occasionally they encountered another wanderer, but kept their comments brisk in order to protect their sanctuary.

"Shall we take our coffee to the dock?" he said on the fifth morning.

Ann smiled and reached for her book then padded barefoot along the path and selected one of two large chairs. Edward sat in the other, his feet propped on a metal cooler they used for picnics. Sun peeked above the island east of where they sat, casting beams through the morning mist while tiny insects skittered across the water's surface. Maple trees released their leaves like chicks from the nest, wavering one way then another in the soft breeze, as if reluctant to reach the ground.

When he caught her profile looking off into the distance, it was as if twenty years had disappeared and once again they were on their honeymoon and his desire for her filled each moment and everything seemed possible. Sadness tightened his throat as he wondered whether they would ever be that way again.

"What will we do when the war is over?" he said, more to himself than to Ann.

"We'll rebuild our lives."

"Yes. They will need rebuilding." He captured her hand in his and kissed the tips of her fingers. "Even for people like us, it's been a dreadful struggle."

"People like us?"

"You didn't have to watch me or Alex go off to war."

"Oh . . . but we've been surrounded by tragedy. And your wounds. You've dealt with it more than me. I know you can't tell me, but I can see it in your face."

"Am I that transparent?"

"To me, you are." She touched his cheek.

"Someday . . ."

"Someday what?"

"Someday I'll tell you. But right now I want to talk about

us."

"Us?"

"I don't know how to say this."

"Edward," fear washed over her face, "don't do this to me again."

"No, no! It's not that. It's something else . . . more difficult to describe. We've been solitary and remote for a long time. We've each been so preoccupied. And I've been away far too much. I haven't been a husband, really." He held her eyes. "Do you know what I mean?"

Ann looked away. "I think so. We've coexisted, almost like two friends, rather than husband and wife. I didn't want to admit it."

"What should we do?" Holding his breath, he dared to hope.

After years of marriage he knew something had happened to Ann. There were months when she seemed like a ghost drifting alongside him. Although he touched her, he could never really hold on to her; she slipped through his fingers like a doe through the forest. She would look at him without seeing him, staring into the distance, as if the weight of the world rested on her shoulders. And then he would dive deep into his work again, forgetting for a while what his instincts had revealed.

Ann saw hopefulness and uncertainty on his face, a face she woke to every morning; a man whose comfort she sought, a man who knew her strengths and flaws, knew every part of her. It was a face worn with worry and responsibility, a face that had seen little pleasure for so many years, only duty. The face of the man she loved.

A memory of Richard's probing eyes and lean body came to her unbidden and she thrust it away. War had exacted a heavy price. Edward's had been sorrow and wounds that would never heal. He had almost paid the ultimate price. Hers had been loneliness and great stress, as well as the loss of Richard. She had almost paid a heavier price, the loss of her marriage.

As husband and wife, their journey together had times of joy and comfort, pain and sadness—a seesaw life of ups and downs, estrangement and togetherness. *What is marriage but discovery?* she thought. *Of self, of man and woman, of another being whose strengths and imperfections are exposed to a microscope of proximity.* Edward was the one she wanted—his calm intelligence, unwavering integrity, devotion to family and children, steadfast capabilities and his deep love for her.

Ann held out her hand. Edward pulled her up and enclosed her in his arms.

"I love you," he said. "I haven't said it often enough. I love you completely. I want you, no one else. I want us to be like we were before."

Ann looked into his hopeful brown eyes. "We used to cherish one another and find joy in each other. We used to share our thoughts and worries. When I think back, our early years were like that, and we found the magic again after Vimy. But it's been missing for a long time. Ever since you began going away, I think."

"Do you want what I want?"

She did not hesitate. "Yes. More than you can imagine."

A feeling of peacefulness filled her. Protected by the warm comfort of his body, she lifted her lips to his.

AFTERWORD

Throughout my school days, I was never a student of history and so I was startled to find researching WWI and WWII such a fascinating exercise. Fascination was followed by anger, sorrow and bewilderment—anger at the incredible ineptitude of military and political leaders and sorrow for what soldiers and everyday citizens had to endure. My bewilderment centered on questions of humanity. Why did soldiers put up with unspeakable conditions for so long? How could leaders use such appalling measures as poison gas? How could parents bear the loss of more than one son? How could citizens endure nightly bombing raids knowing that at any moment their turn might come? How could officers send their men 'over the top' time after time when they knew death would greet so many? I shake my head even now.

Life inspires fiction. Because of my grandfather's experience, Edward Jamieson is a signaller who fights at Vimy Ridge and returns in 1936 for the Vimy memorial dedication ceremony. Family myth has my grandfather involved with William Stephenson and hence Camp X, Canada's spy training centre, plays a major part in the story. My grandmother's involvement with Signals Welfare—a real WWII organization—prompts Ann Jamieson's role in the same volunteer group. I tried to translate my grandmother's steady, yet zesty approach to life into Ann's character. Jack—the man from New Zealand—is real. He trained to fly bombers and was stationed in England. He and my mother fell in love and Jack died on one of his flights. Apart from these bare bones, the rest of the story is entirely a product of my imagination.

Beyond my grandparents' personal mementos and my mother's stories, I found excellent information in books, museums and websites. *Vimy* by Pierre Berton traces the build-up to that famous battle as well as the battle itself. *Letters of Agar Adamson* edited by Norm Christie offers a day-by-day look at WWI through the eyes of a 48-year-old Canadian

Army Captain. Novelists Anne Perry, Pat Barker, Ben Elton, Joseph Boyden and Frances Itani illuminate life on the front lines. Canada's digitized war diaries, available from Collections Canada offer a military accounting of individual unit activities. Websites such as www.firstworldwar.com contain a wealth of information, maps, photos, and memoirs.

For WWII, I listened to CBC radio broadcasts for events like Dieppe and D-Day and consulted with a BBC site called WW2 People's War, a source full of maps, timelines, battle descriptions and photos. I read *Inside Camp X* by Lynn Philip Hodgson, *Camp X The Final Battle* by Lynn Philip Hodgson and Alan Paul Longfield, and *Unlikely Soldiers* by Jonathan Vance for a detailed look at Canada's secret agent training program. Other works inspired me including *Charlotte Gray* by Sebastian Faulkes and *In the Garden of Beasts: Love, Terror, and an American Family in Hitler's Berlin* by Erik Larson. I also consulted frequently with Canada At War (www.canadaatwar.ca) for details about WWII campaigns involving Canadians.

Researching was almost as much fun as creating the story. Authors writing about WWI and WWII are blessed with an abundance of documentation. Battles and campaigns mentioned in *Unravelled* are as accurately reflected as I could make them. Any errors are solely my responsibility.

ACKNOWLEDGEMENTS

Unravelled began on the thirty-second floor of a Hong Kong apartment building overlooking Victoria harbour. My husband had taken a three-year assignment to Asia and I was the trailing spouse. What was at first a way to keep busy has transformed my life.

Writing is a solitary pursuit but I have been blessed with the steady support of family and friends. Many have read earlier versions of *Unravelled*, offering critique and suggestions as well as much needed encouragement. The story is so much stronger because of them. I have also encountered a wonderful group of writers through the Historical Novel Society as well as Facebook and writing workshops. These individuals have given feedback on everything from back cover copy to opening paragraphs.

I am grateful for the excellent editorial support provided by Jenny Toney Quinlan and to beta readers, Rachel Bodner and Debbie Robson, who spent many hours helping me finalize the manuscript. My children, Lesley and Brian, have also helped get *Unravelled* off the ground by lending their expertise in marketing and digital media.

And finally, I could not have produced this novel without my husband Ian – also known as the production department. From the very beginning he had given his unstinting encouragement and love.

About M.K. Tod

I have enjoyed a passion for historical novels that began in my early teenage years immersed in the stories of Rosemary Sutcliff, Jean Plaidy and Georgette Heyer. During my twenties, armed with Mathematics and Computer Science degrees, I embarked on a career in technology and consulting continuing to read historical fiction in the tiny snippets of time available to working women with children to raise.

In 2004, I moved to Hong Kong with my husband and no job. To keep busy I decided to research my grandfather's part in the Great War. What began as an effort to understand my grandparents' lives blossomed into a fulltime occupation as a writer. Beyond my debut novel *Unravelled*, I have written two other novels with WWI settings. I have an active blog— www.awriterofhistory.com—on all aspects of historical fiction including interviews with a variety of authors and others involved in this genre. Additionally, I am a book reviewer for the Historical Novel Society. I live in Toronto and I'm happily married with two adult children.

I am delighted to hear from readers. Please contact me at mktod@bell.net.